Art on Fire

Hilary Sloin

Ann Arbor
2012

Bywater Books

Bywater Books First Edition: October 2012

Printed in the United States of America
on acid-free paper.

Cover designer: Bonnie Liss (Phoenix Graphics)
Cover photo: Barbara Hadden

Bywater Books
PO Box 3671
Ann Arbor MI 48106-3671
www.bywaterbooks.com

ISBN: 978-1-61294-031-1

This novel is a work of fiction. Although parts of the plot
were inspired by actual events, all characters and events
described by the author are fictitious. No resemblance
to real persons, dead or alive, is intended.

I dedicate this story about love and art and death to my canine companion in all those endeavors for fifteen years, Zen. She was the most beautiful soul I have ever encountered, and I am fairly certain she will never be rivaled. She was with me all through the writing of this book. She died on July 21, 2011, at the age of 15. Not a day goes by that I don't feel her absence and thank whatever force it was that brought us together.

There's no place like home,
and many a man is glad of it.

F. M. Knowles, *A Cheerful Year Book*

On March 12, 1989, at 3:12 a.m., a greedy fire erupted in an otherwise placid neighborhood, decimating the modest house at 312 Riverview Street,[1] along with its residents: Alfonse and Vivian DeSilva, Isabella DeSilva, and Francesca deSilva,[2] foremother of pseudo-realism and arguably one of the greatest American painters.

Approximately nineteen of deSilva's paintings were destroyed in the fire. Their monetary worth is undetermined; their artistic value, immeasurable.

The perspicacious reader will visit the Francesca deSilva Memorial Museum in Truro, Massachusetts, where the thirteen paintings discussed in this volume hang side by side, to devastating effect. This is how the work was meant to be experienced, and this encounter, more than any words you will read in any pages, provides the truest testimony to deSilva's genius.

1. Because of the odd coincidence that the numbers 3 and 12 were so disproportionately represented in the particulars of the fire, police suspected arson. An investigation ensued. No cause or culprit was determined.
2. deSilva claimed aesthetic preference and a quest for autonomy led her to spell her surname with the lower case "d," thus distinguishing herself from her family of origin.

A Cry from the Attic

New Haven, 1974–1981

Chapter One

Unlike her sister Isabella, whose genius was of a flamboyant variety, Francesca deSilva exhibited no early signs of excellence. At best, she displayed a vague propensity for mechanical repair: tinkering with broken radios and jammed doorknobs, devoting entire afternoons to the assembly of a new purchase—a fan, a chair, a light. A sturdy, somber girl of few words and a solitary nature, she spent her ample free time playing along the river that ran across the street from her home. It was a wide, brisk river that rolled around bends and over hills, splashed into smooth, open pools, some of which were deep enough to float in. She passed many hours on its sandy shores, lying flat with her eyes closed and listening to the inside of the world.

Each day after school, upon stepping off the bus, Francesca waited—tying and untying her shoe or searching for a stick of gum—until the other children had dispersed. When she was certain of her solitude, she swung her book bag across her back and spilled down the embankment, twisted around prickers, and hopped rock to rock over the gelatin swamp, until she arrived at her destination: a slice of river beach, far from her house, smoother than the shores of the Long Island Sound. There, she stood at the shore and let water lick the rubber tips of her sneakers.

She longed to be Sam Gribley, the boy in *My Side of the Mountain*:[3] to run away from home and survive on instinct, live alone with a wild

3. George, Jean. *My Side of the Mountain.* New York: Scholastic Book Services, 1959. A child's book that tells the story of Sam Gribley, a discontented boy who runs away from his Manhattan home to live in the wilderness. (It is actually wooded property in the Catskills, owned by his well-off family; this is the detail that escapes children who, striving to emulate the protagonist, set out for the nearest unmarked woods with a Swiss army knife and a worn copy of the novel). deSilva's earmarked copy of the book was found after the lethal fire, wrapped in a Grand Union bag and tucked high on a shelf in the family garage.

animal she'd tame. Bathe in the river, stew berries. Instead of living inside a hollowed-out tree as Sam had, Francesca would furnish a hut. She'd drawn up specs and pilfered a sheet of chamois from her father's collection to make a door. But being a pragmatic child, and having long been accustomed to delayed gratification, she'd resolved to start construction on the perfect day, when the sky was clear and the air crisp, when she could be certain several hours preceded nightfall. When at last this day arrived, Francesca scoured the woods like a rabbit, piling fallen branches on her outstretched arm. She sought out the evergreens, whose green needles clung like curtains long after the sap had dried up. With these branches she would form the walls of the hut; for the base, she needed thicker, sturdier boughs of oak or maple. She worked without pause, running up the embankment and back down, wiping her forehead with the back of her soiled hand, growing her two piles—evergreen, miscellaneous hardwood—higher and higher, until they were as tall as Francesca herself.

The day grew dark suddenly, the way it does in September in New England, as if winter had been hovering the whole time, picking its moment. Without warning, she could see nothing. The river was just a rushing sound to her right; the woods were black and filled with sudden slapping sounds. She scrambled back through the marsh, swatting at prickers, twisting her ankles into soft spots. Exhausted, she scaled the embankment on hands and knees.

A blaring porch light announced her house on the other side of the street. She plodded across the road and onto the lawn, ignoring the walkway her father had carved in the center of the tidy, square lot. Blinking against the sudden brightness, she pressed the doorbell, then held onto the threshold and emptied pebbles from each shoe onto the freshly swept porch. Twigs perforated her dusty hair. She cupped her hands and peered into the picture window. Through her own reflection she saw bowls of chips and candy set out on the lucite coffee table. The sheets had been removed from the furniture.

Vivian DeSilva opened the door, erect as a sailor in her navy blue dress, a gold chain-link belt tight around her narrow waist. Her burgundy hair was piled on her head, twisted and tucked in a complicated design. Thick, orange paint made her lips glow in the dusk.

"You look nice, Mom," said Francesca.

Vivian dragged her gaze down until it found Francesca's face. "Oh, Francesca!" She covered her mouth and clasped the girl's small shoulders, pulled her into the house. "Alfonse! Alfonse!" (louder the second time). "Honey, don't touch anything," she said, her face collapsed with worry. She held Francesca's dirty hands in the air.

Alfonse, also gritty after a long day planting perennials around a new shopping center, trotted down the stairs and arrived in the foyer. "You rang, Madame." He roughed up Francesca's dusty hair.

"Honey, go get your toothbrush," she told Francesca. "Papa will bring you to Grandma's."

"I don't need a toothbrush. Grandma lets me use hers," said Francesca, boasting.

Vivian looked at Alfonse. She popped her eyes wide and opened her palms. "Well? What are you waiting for? I have eleven dinner guests coming in an hour. Could you lend me a hand here?" Alfonse rubbed her back and kissed her spuriously on the cheek, then rested his heavy hands on Francesca's small shoulders. "Let's go, Tiger." He guided her through the kitchen and out the back door.

In an effort to give a leg up to the lagging social development of her older daughter, Vivian had located the families of four other child geniuses in Connecticut and invited them for dinner. But now that the event was imminent, she was stricken with a pervasive sense of doom. She trotted to the top of the stairs, then knocked cheerfully on Isabella's door. "Bella!"

Slowly Isabella pulled back the door. She stood solemn and erect, in an old brown sweater and black wool skirt. Vivian half-recognized the outfit as the one she'd worn to her father's funeral eleven years before. The skirt hung to Isabella's ankles, punctuated by white knee socks and misshapen black shoes. "What are you wearing?" she demanded.

"My outfit."

"I see that! But we have people coming over." She pressed two fingers of each hand to either temple, holding the sides of her head together as if they might come apart.

"This is what I'm wearing to the party. I'm dressed as someone important. A great hero of this century."

7

Vivian forced a chuckle despite the fever of panic beginning to rise inside her. She couldn't stand how much she loved this child. "Okay, Miss Smarty Pants. Who? Who are you dressed as?" She crossed her arms and tapped the floor with her foot.

"Guess."

"Oh, I don't know . . . Annie Sullivan."

"Wrong."

Vivian searched her watery memory for dowdy female heroines. "Virginia Woolf?" she asked, hoping she wasn't entirely misinformed. It wasn't easy, being less intelligent than your eleven-year-old daughter; she shook her head, enjoying every moment of it. Brains like these had to come from somewhere, and certainly Alfonse's family hadn't cultivated them in the pizza kitchen in Wooster Square.

"I'll give you one hint," said Bella. "I live in an attic."

Vivian hesitated, twisting her face in concentration. "Not your sister . . ." she said, blanching with dread.

"What? Are you nuts?"

"Oh! Oh!" Vivian snapped her fingers, thinking fast. "Emily Dickinson!"

"She didn't live in an attic," Isabella sighed, then brightened. "Okay, really, really, the last hint. Put on your thinking cap." Vivian gestured as if she had. "I have a boyfriend named Peter," certain this was the give-away.

Vivian was distracted by thoughts of the lasagna sizzling in the oven, whether Alfonse would return in time to shower, how to get Isabella out of this ridiculous outfit and into her party dress. "I'm sorry, pumpkin. You're much smarter than your old Mom." She guided Isabella into the bedroom.

"Duh. Anne Frank. I'm Anne Frank."

"Of course you are! Anne Frank! We should show your grandmother. Did you know she was once in a play about Anne Frank?"

Isabella shrugged, unimpressed. "I've written a play about Anne Frank." She lifted her arms and waited for Vivian to pull the sweater over her head.

❏   ❏   ❏

Francesca rode with her body pressed against the car door, the handle digging at her hip. She breathed on the window, made circles with her finger. Already she could smell the ladies' itchy perfume, hear the cracking of mahjong tiles and gum. She imagined her entrance: The game would be underway, so that anything she did would garner a sigh of feigned exasperation. She'd call out Hi! and run down the hallway to her grandmother's bedroom, throw herself onto the bed, and bury her nose in stinky fake furs. Then she'd hole up in the dark TV room, eyes fastened to the Friday night lineup. During the commercials she'd wander out to the kitchen and stand around coyly, stab melon balls with toothpicks, bite into the Russell Stover chocolates in search of caramels. "Gross," she'd say when confronted with a dribble of strawberry cream or rum. (One of the ladies would finish the confection so it wouldn't go to waste.) She'd wear her grandmother's bifocals with the rhinestones in each corner, walk around the card table with her hands extended in Frankenstein position, the cool chain tickling her neck.

She did anything for the ladies' attention, doled as it was in scraps between hands. She fetched their pocketbooks and refilled their glasses with Tab, emptied ashtrays, and closed the window if it grew too chilly. They teased her about being a tomboy, pinched and kissed her, made her feel loved and abused at the same time.

"Francesca, what you do in the woods?" Alfonse inquired.

"Nothing."

The houses in her grandmother's neighborhood were separated by faded ribbons of grass the color of limes, just big enough for a lawn chair, a kettle grill, maybe a dog. Alfonse turned onto the street without signaling. The driver behind him held down the horn, swerved around the left side, waved his middle finger in the air. "Idiot," Alfonse muttered, imagining Italy where, he imagined, people were civilized, where a little blinking light would not be necessary to inspire common sense. He glanced at Francesca. Her face was turned away from him. He snuck a look at her thick, dark hair, like his, a pointy chin, again like his, and a take-charge body, sturdy and tall, capped off by thick hands and grounded legs.

"Do you play with the frogs?" He glanced at her. "Are you a friend to animals?"

Francesca turned and looked at her father. She felt ashamed, as if he had guessed something simple about her, something obvious. "I like animals," she said nonchalantly.

"I, too, have always loved animals. When I was a boy, I used to feed the squirrels, which you can imagine went over big with my mother." He rolled his eyes. "They're rodents, you know." He stopped at Evelyn's driveway. "Do you play in the river?"

"Mostly."

"Alone? Or with friends?"

"Alone."

"How about I come sometime? We could play in the river together."

"Okay, sure," said Francesca, looking up at her grandmother's picture window. The light was on over the kitchen table. She could see it through the threshold. "It's really kind of boring." There was nothing in life less boring, she knew, nothing so full of possibility, with such a strong pulse. To bring her father there would interrupt the gentle ecosystem. He could not see the hut or he might start to suspect her larger plan. No matter; she knew from past conversations of this nature that he would forget all about this one.

"Hey, I know." He pounced on the brake. "How about we go for an ice cream?"

"No thanks, Papa." Francesca hopped out and slammed the door. She could hardly wait to be inside the small, warm house and see what treats her grandmother would produce—always magically—from some obscure cabinet or cubby beneath the oven door.

Stiff as a stick of stale gum in her velvet jumper and white bow tie, Isabella sat at the kitchen table and watched Vivian tuck her head inside the oven to check on the lasagna.

"Sylvia Plath committed suicide that way," she said.

"That's certainly not what I'm doing." Vivian backed out at once and wiped her forehead with the silver oven mitt.

Isabella sighed. She pilfered a Hershey's kiss from a tulip-shaped bowl that was filled to the brim, unwrapped the candy, and tried to stand it upside down. No luck. She bit off some of the point to flatten it, then tried again. Some days, this being one of them, she hated to talk. She hated the sound of her voice, the scratchiness at the back of her throat, the feeling of her teeth slamming down on each other. Other days, there seemed to be a dearth of words in the world. On these days, she'd read entire books aloud, just to hear her voice dip and climb, reveling in her perfect articulation. Then there were the confusing, disorienting days, the ones that started one way, then switched to the other, leaving her breathless, confounded as to how to slow the busyness in her brain.

"Tell me about Anne Frank," her mother said.

"You know about Anne Frank," she whined and pulled on her collar. She took two more chocolate kisses, plugged each into a nostril, then an ear, then held them up to her nipples.

"So tell me again," Vivian turned. "Bella! Stop that. Those are for the company!"

Alfonse opened the back door and wiped his sneakered feet thoroughly over the spiked welcome mat. He greeted them with swollen eyes, giddy from having had a little cry after he'd dropped Francesca off. He'd succumbed to his ever-lingering, rarely conscious feeling of failure as a parent. He was more willing to acknowledge his shortcomings as a husband, largely because he felt he wasn't to blame for the bitter marriage. On the other hand, his inefficacy as a father was only partly Vivian's fault; he knew he was culpable, and couldn't bear it.

"Oh good," said Vivian. "Isabella's about to tell us the story of Anne Frank."

"Holy cow. That's terrific!" He patted Isabella's head and ran upstairs to shower before the company arrived.

They filed in at 6:30, children first. Chips and dip, M&Ms, and chocolate kisses were set out on the coffee table for the kids, pinkish port wine cheese in a plastic tub and Triscuits for the adults. The frightened children scattered, fists clenched at their sides, eyes averted—especially from each other—checking every instant for their parents' faces to make sure they hadn't been left behind.

11

Isabella was most perturbed by Robert Michaels.[4] The others, it was apparent, were no match for her. But something about this boy: the way he took root with his thick arms and tree-stump legs, a mess of red hair atop his elongated head, his squinted eyes and freckled face. Sadistic, she thought. The kind of kid you hate just from looking at him.

"I'm going to high school next year," he announced in a voice like onions hitting hot oil. "Are you?" He poked Lisa Sinsong, a small Chinese-American girl dressed in ill-fitting black pants and a white turtleneck. She shook her head and glanced at her father.

"Me neither," said Isabella who had the loudest voice and took up more space in every way. She put her hands on her hips and stared him down. "You're uglier, Sluggo," she said.

"Isabella!" scolded Vivian.

"Oh please." Mrs. Michaels pressed Vivian's knee. "He's a handful. Besides, if we were responsible for everything these little ones said, well . . ." She stopped, the rest being obvious.

After dinner, fortified by two pieces of lasagna and a generous scoop of chocolate ice cream, Isabella waited until the mothers had finished clearing the table and spread out beside the fathers on the sectional sofa. She dragged a small end table into the center of the room, put her Panasonic tape recorder on the floor beside her, took a deep breath, and climbed onto the table, waiting for everyone's full attention. Vivian stood behind Alfonse, squeezing his shoulders.

"I," Isabella spoke at a slight downward angle to reach the microphone, "am Anne Frank. I was born in Germany, but my family migrated to Amsterdam during the Nazi regime. After a small, brief period of living like a girl, i.e., being an exceptionally bright student and having

---

4. Michaels went on to write *The Final Diet* in 1981, a weight-loss plan based on a distortion of Buddhist practices. One could eat as desired, mixing balls of "special cotton" in with each meal. Once in the stomach, the cotton allegedly expanded, thus suppressing the appetite. Many dieters wound up in the emergency room, constipated to the point of obstruction, and Michaels was left penniless following a 1983 class action suit.

boys fall in love with me everywhere I went, my family was forced to live in the small annex of a factory building. An attic, really. For those of you who don't know your German Fascist history, I'll make it simple: the Nazis were scary blond-haired, blue-eyed men who busted down the doors of people they felt were inferior, which was basically everyone who wasn't German—particularly Jews and homosexuals—poked guns in the chests of terrified individuals just going about their daily business, and said—" (here she shoved her index finger hard at Robert Michaels) "COME VID US OR DIE."

The performance continued, a tossed salad of fact and fiction, until Isabella reached the arrival of "Mr. Dussel," with whom Anne was forced to share a small room. "All night long, like a train in my head, I heard this terrible, nasty man breathing as if through a kazoo, in and out, the snoring loud enough to knock me out of my bed.

"Then, of course, there were the other times, when I would be awakened by some odd groaning and I'd turn to see him, covers rolled down, wearing just his underclothes, pleasuring himself."

"Isabella!" Vivian shouted.

Quickly, Isabella continued. "But the most devastating consequence of being trapped in the attic was the isolation. Being a small girl, an adolescent girl who is not even allowed to step out into the world, to have normal adolescent girl experiences, who day after day, month after month, is trapped in a tiny little room while before her the world changes and people fall in love and die and do their laundry and cook dinner together and go to amusement parks and take the golden retriever out for a walk and listen to the Beatles sing 'I Want to Hold Your Hand' and rake their leaves before the first snowfall . . ."

Alfonse had stopped paying attention. This is the fascination with Anne Frank, he thought. She is trying to tell us that she is unhappy. That she wants to be normal.

". . . and try out for cheerleading and smoke cigarettes and kiss boys—well she did kiss Peter, and actually did more than that! But it wasn't as if she got to choose whom she kissed; for chrissakes, he was the only boy she'd ever meet for the rest of her life!"

Vivian clapped urgently; the others followed suit. Isabella glared at her mother, bowed once, and hopped down from the table.

I have failed both my daughters, Alfonse thought.

"Very impressive," said Robert Michaels' father.

Robert Michaels was tired of everything about Isabella. He leaned over toward Lisa Sinsong. "Your mother killed herself," he whispered.

"So," said Lisa.

Isabella overheard and stepped closer to where they stood by the breakfront. "What did he say?" she asked Lisa.

Lisa gazed at Isabella with shiny brown eyes. "My mother killed herself. Big deal."

Isabella tucked a strand of hair behind Lisa's ear and whispered "Come up to my room." She turned to her parents. "We're going upstairs for a few minutes. I'm going to show Lisa my room."

"What about the others?" Vivian pursed her lips and opened her eyes wide, demonstrating her disapproval. "That's not nice." She mouthed the words so only Isabella could see them.

"I'll show them later," Isabella flashed a phony smile to the other guests and ran up the stairs. Lisa followed behind, glancing back at her father as he faded behind the wedged wall of the staircase.

Lisa stepped into the center of Isabella's room and rotated slowly, taking in the white bed, white walls, white curtains. Every single thing in the room was white. Even the stuffed animals, yellowing from age, had once been white. "How come there are no colors?" she asked.

"Nice, right?"

"I guess. It's clean," she said politely.

"Exactly. Nothing interferes," Isabella pointed to her head. "Sit down, take a load off." She plopped heavily onto the mattress, the springs rocking and creaking beneath her. Lisa perched at the foot of the bed and dangled her thin legs over the edge.

"How did she do it?" Isabella asked, shifting closer and mimicking Lisa's delicate movements.

"Jumped off a building." Lisa stared at the white wall, her face stripped of expression.

Isabella pictured it: a small Chinese woman falling from a building. Lisa Sinsong, only larger. With glasses. A pocketbook. Wearing a ladies' coat. Camel color, the skirts of it flying up over her head as she cut through the air, buttons popping off, panels busting open. Flapping her coat like wings, soaring over the tops of buildings until, without warning, she began to drop, down, down, down, then crashed into a parking lot.

"How come she did that?" Isabella blinked from having seen it all. So vivid.

"She was depressed," replied Lisa for the ten-thousandth time. She hopped off the bed and walked out of the room, closing the door behind her. Isabella sat calmly, waiting for Lisa to return. Instead, she heard a brisk knock and the voice of her mother, ordering her back to the party.

Woman and Stool, 1988

In what is perhaps Francesca deSilva's most revered painting, *Woman and Stool,* the artist depicts her mother, Vivian DeSilva, a formidable, unflappable figure, seated precariously on a spindly barstool, clad in a high-collared, pressed, navy-blue dress, with a thick belt around her small waist. Her form is pressed so far to the back of the canvas as to be quite small in relation to the slick, orange floor upon which the stool rests. The subject squints against an intense brightness, as if outside a meteor had moments ago exploded or a mushroom bomb made contact with the earth's floor. Such strange, unearthly incandescence is a signature of deSilva's work: "Her subjects seem, collectively, to struggle against an unidentified, intrusive light."[5]

The painting is four feet tall by three feet wide, vast and stark. Excepting the shiny, papaya-colored floor and the chalky yellow walls, there are only five disparate images: the woman; the stool; a prominent white door in the left hand corner of the room; a child's book, *My Side of the Mountain,* strewn on the immaculate floor (so incongruous is this object, it appears to be an oversight, as if, having forgotten to put the book away before beginning to paint, the

5. DeVaine, Paul. "QuikPiks." *New York Nights,* April 1989. Esteemed critic Paul DeVaine urged readers to attend deSilva's groundbreaking show at Gallery 19, Soho, calling her use of light ". . . revelatory, transcendent. Through the intrusion of light, she creates a world outside the world she is painting, one that taps at the borders of the painting, begging entry like an animal or a small child. This world is as interesting as the subjects themselves. It is as though the subjects were simply the jumping-off point, an excuse to paint the artist's true concerns."

artist simply decided to leave it in); and a small, framed photograph of a young girl with cascading brown curls, thought to represent Francesca's older sister, Isabella, to whom the mother was deeply, some have said psychotically, devoted.

Lucinda Dialo, in her book *Women Paint!*, describes deSilva's portraits as deeply psychological in their "depictions of individuals trapped inside distorted realities."[6] Dialo says of *Woman and Stool,* "deSilva has undertaken and succeeded at the ultimate task of the disenfranchised artist: to forgive the source of her suffering—in this case, the mother— by immortalizing her, infusing her portrait with compassion and objectivity."[7]

6. Dialo, Lucinda. *Women Paint!* New York: Little, Brown, 1991, page 149.
7. Ibid.

Chapter Two

Lacking specifics, Isabella fashioned her own history of Mrs. Sinsong and how she came to take her life: Before plummeting through the air at 90 mph and crashing into a construction scaffolding, Mrs. Sinsong had been employed by the Little Maiden Bra Company, a sweatshop on 34th Street that sprawled over three levels of a factory building with warped floors and windows that could not be opened. The monotonous job of sewing hooks on the backs of bras had left her brain stiff as dried-up putty. She'd resorted to reciting old recipes to hone her mnemonic skills. The rare highlight of her ten-hour work-day was when, instead of the usual box of nude bras with lace around the edges, an unexpected carton of black or, best of all, hot pink ones squeaked past her station.

For her lunch breaks Mrs. Sinsong walked up 7th Avenue to 36th Street, bought a falafel and a Sprite from the Arab on the corner, and sat on the steps of a vocational high school to eat. Each day at 12:28 she returned to the dark factory building with its green linoleum floors, and popped a mint into her mouth. She stepped inside the elevator car and gazed at the metal doors, then pressed the number three. Her body disappeared as the car ascended the narrow canal at the building's core.

It was an intervention of fate perhaps, or some unconscious act of will, that caused her finger to slip one rainy April day and land on the number 13, the only button on the panel that still lit up. At once the doors crashed shut, the cage hopped in the air, rushing by the first 12 floors as if there were not a moment to spare, then landed quiet as a spaceship, bounced a moment, and came to rest.

Mrs. Sinsong stepped out. Cool air roused her skin. Below her the city was a speedy, gritty haze. Below her, freedom rushed and honked and picked the pockets of disoriented foreigners. She walked to the tarred ledge of the roof and peered down into the busy office of a publishing company on the other side of the street, then farther down at tiny people busy with lunch hour destinations. Everyone is so busy, thought Mrs. Sinsong. But where is there to go?

Then she threw herself from the building. The End.[8]

Still, Isabella longed to ask many questions. Prurient, inappropriate questions that she knew to keep locked inside her mouth. She was infinitely intrigued by Lisa's vast, impossible tragedy, her quiet, perfected indifference. She neglected Anne Frank, instead pored over Vivian's shelves of shiny paperbacks on raising a gifted child, finding particular solace in a chapter entitled "Is There No One Like Me in the World?"[9] Here, the author suggested that any difficulty a genius child might have in finding suitable companionship—no matter how enduring— was appropriate. She shared this passage with her parents, pointing emphatically as she read aloud: *When the intense, passionate genius child finally makes a friend, the parents must not interfere.*

"In other words," she said, gleefully, "Butt out!"

Vivian could not understand what it was about this small, plain child that so captivated Isabella. It occurred to her that it might have something to do with the mother's unfortunate demise, but she couldn't bear the idea that Isabella's preoccupation with dead women would go so far as that. "Why that girl? Why not the little Cohen girl?" she asked Isabella. "She seemed like a lot of fun."

She felt, for the first time, unnecessary. It was one thing for Isabella to be obsessed by Anne Frank, who was rendered harmless by extinction, but quite another to see Isabella so enraptured by a live person. Isabella seemed less interested in sharing the riches of her genius with her old

8. Actually, Mrs. Sinsong jumped from her apartment window while Lisa was at school. The apartment, a one-room, bathroom-in-the-hall situation that straddled Little Italy and Chinatown, sat above a thriving new Chinese restaurant called Buddha's Belly. The restaurant closed soon after the tragedy, and the two remaining Sinsongs migrated to New Haven, where Mr. Sinsong obtained a job in a candle factory.

9. Sventhrup, Brad. *Mommy, Daddy, Can I Have a Sliderule for Christmas?* Chicago: Random House, 1972. Considered the definitive text on the subject. Sventhrup, renowned for his 1984 *Avocado Diet*, a textbook/workbook designed to increase mental aptitude through strict dietary regimen, devoted his scientific career to the study of genius—its causes, and characteristics.

mom. She came downstairs only to grab a Hostess snowball or Ring Ding and to exchange one volume of psychobabble for another. Vivian walked around all the time feeling as though she might cry, that the least little complication—a flaccid head of lettuce in the refrigerator, a knocking noise in the car's engine—could reduce her to a blubbering mass.

❑ ❑ ❑

Lisa Sinsong was scheduled to visit on a Saturday afternoon. That morning, Isabella sprung from bed while it was still dark outside. She ran her hand along everything she passed—countertops, banister, coats—her fingertips tingling for no good reason.

Vivian prepared magic tunafish for lunch. Isabella divided her surveillance between her mother and the sluggish minute hand on the kitchen clock. "Come on already . . ." she muttered, snatching a celery stick. She took a bite and put it back. Finally, the doorbell rang! She smoothed the front of her white sweater and skated in socked feet to the foyer, her happiness so huge, she wished she could scream or bite down very hard on something. She threw open the large door and pulled Lisa inside, helped shake off her small, pink peacoat.

"Come on." Breathless, she pulled Lisa up the stairs.

Isabella had melted the bottoms of several birthday candles and stuck them to a plate. She lit them now in a solemn ceremony. She produced a thick bar of white chocolate from her nightstand and undressed it slowly, peeling off the wrapper as if she were changing a baby, then snapping off a triangular slab with the tips of her teeth. She offered the piece to Lisa, then sucked avidly on a larger shard, studying Lisa's metal black hair, powdery cheeks, widely spaced eyes, her delicate, stick figure frame, the slivers of bones threatening to tear through the light cloak of skin.

"I thought Americans don't stare," Lisa said.

"Who told you that?"

"My father," Lisa replied, suspecting he'd once again given her bad information.

21

"It's not true. But, anyhow, I wasn't staring. I was looking at you. Because you're pretty."

"Oh. Thanks." She forced a smile.

They sat facing the same wall, legs swinging. The digital clock flipped its number once, then again. The chocolate was gone. Isabella swallowed loud as a drain sucking down the last of the bathwater. She could think of nothing to say, no acceptable questions to ask; she wasn't in her usual, inferior company, so she knew better than to brag. And she'd promised herself that Lisa's mother was off-limits.

"What's that?" Lisa tilted her head toward the ceiling, listening.

"What? That?" The tiny, muted rhythm of Francesca's record player ticked through the plaster ceiling. "That's my sister." Isabella rolled her eyes. "She lives in the attic."

"Why?" Lisa looked up.

"Because she likes it. She could have had this room—I wouldn't have minded living up there, though in the end I'm glad to be here. It would have been hard to make that room white."

"I've never been in an attic before." Lisa cocked her head, angled her chin upward.

"You want to go up *there?*" Isabella considered it. She was running out of polite things to say. And after spending a few minutes with her sister, Lisa would surely be anxious to return to the white room. "Okay, sure. If you want. But I'm warning you, she's a real weirdo." She led them out into the hallway, dragging her hand along the bumpy flowered wallpaper, then knocked politely on the attic door.

"I knew it was the Beatles!" Lisa leaned closer to the door. She examined the yellow lucite *Francesca* in cursive writing, tacked to the wide-planks with two fat-headed nails.

Isabella pounded. "Helloooooo!"

Finally, Francesca opened the door. Behind her a smoky light, thick with the aura of afternoon rain, shrouded the pointed room, darkening the edges of her tall form. She hovered at the top of the three steps, arms folded across her chest. Her bell-bottoms fanned out over her dirty, bare feet. She looked past her sister into Lisa's dark eyes.

"What," she said.

"This is Lisa. She wanted to see the attic," Isabella said.

Lisa waved tentatively. She peered over Francesca's shoulder into the attic, smelled the dark, damp wood, noted the sloped ceilings and exposed beams covered with tiny, glow-in-the-dark stars arranged in perfect imitation of the solar system.

"Can we come in?" Isabella asked sweetly.

Francesca shrugged and stepped out of the way.

"Lisa's mother committed suicide," Isabella whispered as they entered, as if this somehow explained their arrival.

"Just now?" Francesca asked.

"Four months ago," said Lisa. Her eyes dusted the hodgepodge of objects: the soiled, yellow beanbag chair; frayed curtains with little puffballs hanging from strands of white yarn along the hem; the sunken double bed on a gray metal frame; a yellow nightstand, its surface captured beneath the ceramic base of a huge lamp. A folded metal chair was pushed into a metal desk and tucked into a corner. There was a pile of wire-rimmed sketchpads on the desk, several pencils, and one of those gummy erasers Francesca had molded into a dog. At least, Lisa thought it was a dog.

Lisa scanned the worn books that were piled willy-nilly in the small black bookcase: *The Phantom Tollbooth, My Darling My Hamburger, The Pigman*, the entire Nancy Drew series. An incomplete set of the World Book Encyclopedia from 1962 lined the bottom shelf. *My Side of the Mountain* was placed, reverently, on top of the bookcase.

"Is the anatomy page still in there?" Lisa jutted her chin toward the encyclopedia.

"Yup," Francesca said. "That's my favorite page."

"Mine, too!" Lisa cried out unexpectedly.

"Mine, too," Isabella blurted, though she'd never seen the anatomy page.

Francesca knew much of the encyclopedia by heart. Every paragraph of information had been reviewed, until she'd carpeted her head with facts, just to have them there, to fill the space. She loved knowing things, even things of no consequence. She'd committed to memory, for example, all the lyrics to "I am the Walrus," even the goo goos, and how many there were before the joo joos came in. She knew that "Lucy in the Sky with Diamonds" was about LSD and that LSD stood for lysergic acid diethylamide and that it could alter the entire world and make it seem, suddenly, interesting. And she knew entire paragraphs from *My Side of the Mountain, Squanto: Friend to the Pilgrims,* and *Miracle Worker.* Anything that moved her, she attempted to memorize.

"I've read almost all of these books," Lisa smiled at her, revealing a dimple in the center of her chin. Francesca noticed immediately that Lisa's smile was the opposite of her sad, tense face, everything pointed up instead of down, emphasizing her finely etched eyes, the arc of her eyebrows, her long pale lips. "Which is your favorite?" Lisa asked.

"*My Side of the Mountain,*" Francesca said at once.

"Mine is *The Phantom Tollbooth,*" Lisa offered. "After I read it, I tried to drive through the bedroom wall in my wagon!"

"You what?" shouted Isabella, appalled.

Lisa sat beside Francesca on the bed. She measured the length of her own dangling legs against Francesca's longer, thicker ones. "How come *your* room isn't one color?" she asked Francesca, looking hard into her eyes.

"Why, is yours?"

"*Mine?* I don't even have a room. I sleep in the living room." She pointed to Isabella. "But *she* has a white room. Don't you want a white room?"

"Are you nuts?" whined Isabella, "She has no aesthetic sense. Let's go." Isabella hopped down the steps on one foot and out into the hallway. "Lee-sa," she demanded.

"I'd want a purple room," Francesca said suddenly, imagining the whole oddly shaped room coated an inky purple; thick, porous paint on the rough walls and beams.

"Me too!" Lisa bounced up and down on the bed. "How come Francesca doesn't get a purple room?"

"Because I'm a genius," Isabella shouted.

"Oh." Lisa nodded, as if that explained it. She spanned the breadth of stars and orbs on the ceiling. "Is that the solar system?" she asked.

Francesca nodded.

"Do they glow?"

"You have to hold a flashlight on them for a while before you go to sleep."

"Lee-sa. Mother made magic tuna fish," whined Isabella.

"I hate tuna fish," Lisa whispered. She looked down at her feet in white, narrow tennis shoes and compared them to Francesca's bare ones, ashen dirt darkening the creases. "Do you know how to play chess?" she asked.

Francesca shook her head.

"Too bad. I'm the national champion. Which means I've never been defeated. By a girl," she added with obvious bitterness.

Isabella climbed the steps and leaned into the room. "My mother slaved all morning over this tuna fish. This is not like a can of Bumblebee in a bowl with mayonnaise. It's a secret family recipe."

"She'll be right there," Francesca said firmly.

Lisa stood up and took a final whiff of the dusty room. She walked to the edge, where the floor dropped off into three steep steps. "Maybe I could teach you how to play chess," she said.

"Okay," Francesca shrugged, as if it made no difference one way or the other.

After the girls had eaten, Vivian scrubbed the insides of the kitchen drawers with Fantastik and a sponge. The silverware and utensils were laid out on the surface. Francesca entered, silent as a panther, took a sandwich from a plate on the counter, and sat down.

"Mom," she said. "Can I paint my room?"

"Jesus!" Vivian dropped the plastic bottle, put her hand over her heart. "Francesca! You scared the hell out of me!" Her fingers were sweating inside flannel-lined rubber gloves. She turned and leaned her back against the counter, tossed her head to throw a strip of hair off her left eye. "Now what is it?"

"I want to paint my room purple," said Francesca, pressing the thin rubber flap of a spatula against her palm.

"You do, do you? And I'd like to paint mine ..." Vivian looked in the air and rolled her eyes extravagantly, "Oh, I don't know ... polka dots."

"Okay." Francesca smiled.

"Stop it, please. I'm busy. Why don't you girls ever play outside?" She returned to her task, shaking her head.

"I have an aesthetic sense too," said Francesca, rather forcefully.

"You have a *what?*"

"At least, I'd like a purple bedspread. Isabella has a white bedspread."

"Listen, Sarah Heartburn, I let you put up that poster. And those little stars—"

"The solar system," said Francesca. "It's a re-creation of the solar system. Done precisely to scale."

"And that's very impressive. You did a good job with that. But I don't want you to paint the room purple. It would ruin the wood. The thing—" Vivian scrubbed harder, the friction making a tiny, high-pitched sound, "—about painting raw wood, is that you can never go back."

"But I wouldn't want to go back," said Francesca.

"Francesca, I appreciate your creativity. I really do. But some girls have nothing, you know. Look at that poor little Chinese girl," she whispered, shooting her eyes toward the ceiling. "You could be her."

"Well, what about blue? Could I paint it blue?"

"What sort of blue?"

"Light blue. Cloud blue."

Vivian stopped cleaning for a moment. She recognized the opportunity for a compromise. She stared ahead, as if picturing it. "Oh," she said. "I really need to think about it. I don't like the idea of painting that room. What if we need to sell the house? What if all your father's work dries up and we need to move into a tiny apartment in downtown New Haven? A mother worries about these things. It's not your job to worry about them, but someone has to. I don't think so, honey. Sorry." She tipped her head and shrugged, then tore a fresh sheet of towel paper from the roll and spritzed some Fantastik into the potholder drawer.

Francesca put the spatula down. She let her hands fall hard onto the table. "Forget it," she said. She stood up and walked through the side door, slamming it behind her, out into the gray afternoon.

Under the rhododendron bush she found a green tennis ball. She tossed it in the air, each time higher and higher, gazing up at Isabella's window. When she tired of this, she began throwing it against the house, but no one noticed. Finally she threw the ball at her sister's window and ran away, across the street and down the hill to her hut.

❏   ❏   ❏

After Vivian deposited the Chinese girl at her decrepit apartment building, she drove to Loehmann's, where a sale on linens was in progress. She'd decided that purchasing a lavender bedspread for Francesca would satisfy both of them: Vivian could not stand unadulterated purple. But lavender—a more feminine, subtler hue—was still in the purple family, and so ought to mollify Francesca. After all, Vivian decided, this was less about color than it was about sibling rivalry. By procuring the bedspread, Vivian would acknowledge Francesca's rightful place in the family and encourage her importance as a separate, autonomous being. Anyhow, this nonconformity was something she admired in each of her daughters—even if Francesca seemed to possess more oddness than talent.

The bedspread would be a present, a gesture of affection, and it would honor what was, after all, a fair request. Isabella asked for and received multifarious white items as well as writing utensils and rare manuscripts about Anne Frank and other dead heroines. And Francesca asked for pretty much nothing. Plus, Vivian wanted to be a kind mother, to love both her daughters with the same force, even if that didn't always come easy. She loved them, of course, and she told herself that she loved them equally. For example, she often imagined running into a burning building for Isabella (easy!) and for Francesca (of course!), knowing that, as their mother, her instinct to rescue them would prevail over any consideration of her self-preservation. But she knew whom she would rescue first. She could not escape the feeling that Isabella's life was just the tiniest bit more valuable than Francesca's, what with the certain contribution Isabella would make to scholarship, her quick wit, her worldly grace at such a tender age.

She loved her daughters differently, rather the way a man loves his wife versus how he loves his mistress. Francesca received the wifely love—dutiful, steadfast, a bit stolid; but Isabella occupied Vivian's thoughts with the force of a paramour, like Léon obsessed Emma in *Madame Bovary*.

She parked the Valiant in a space designated for the handicapped, crossed the lot, and stepped onto the rubber mats, forcing open the automatic glass doors. She'd worked in this store as a dressing-room clerk during high school, just after it became Loehmann's and not whatever it had been before, something sprawling that sold lawn furniture and cheap housewares. Working at Loehmann's had been her least favorite job. Worse than working without pay in her father's auto parts store. Each time she'd enter the brightly lit, low-ceilinged dressing room, trying not to look at the women cramming their bodies into designer clothes, their skin reddened by triple-hook bras, high-waisted underwear and girdles, she'd feel sick with dread, as if she were witnessing her future. The cruel fluorescent lights accentuated every scar and wrinkle and birthmark, every roll of flesh and riverbed of stretchmarks. And the lack of privacy created an atmosphere of frenzy, the women hurrying to get the clothes off and on before anyone could take note of their imperfections.

Vivian chose two clingy blouses to try on, both of them a happy and youthful size eight. She could not refrain from prancing back and forth across the wide room in her underpants and blouse, frowning in the wall-to-wall mirrors and tugging to no avail at a threadbare blanket of flesh across her middle.

The dressing room clerk wore a Danskin top that accentuated—rather cheaply, Vivian thought—her eager, young nipples.

"Nothing today," Vivian handed her the blouses, then zigzagged through the busy aisles to Linens. She flipped through crunchy, plastic packages marked for clearance and squeezed into the formica bins until she—finally!—stumbled on an affordable lavender bedspread onto which were printed swollen heads of wisteria connected by leafless brown branches.

On her way to the register she was distracted by a soft terrycloth robe, virgin white, wrapped around a mannequin. She pulled the price tag out from inside the sleeve and gasped, incredulous. The point, she rebuked herself, was to buy for Francesca. Isabella had not asked for a bathrobe.

❑　❑　❑

Vivian stopped the car just shy of the garage, beeped twice, then held down the horn until Francesca appeared in the doorway. "C'mere!" she called.

Francesca skipped down the stoop, then hesitated when she reached bottom. She walked toward her mother slowly, then stopped and fingered her initials in the dirty hood.

Vivian held out a shopping bag.

"What is it?" Francesca asked, passing the parcel from hand to hand. She lifted it to her ear, then wrapped it into a tight package.

"Surprise," Vivian shrugged. "Go inside and open it. But wash your hands first."

After Francesca had gone, Vivian removed the other bag from the front seat and carried it by its sophisticated wire handles. She followed at a distance into the antiseptic kitchen, then put the second package on a kitchen chair and tucked the chair into the table. She took a new pack of Larks from the potholder drawer, slapped the top several times on the counter, expertly unraveled the plastic belt, opened the foil corner, and shook a cigarette from its tight space among the others in the dark, red pack.

Francesca returned from the bathroom with moist hands. She never bothered drying them, something Vivian found crass and, inexplicably, unhygienic. But she wasn't going to carp at Francesca now, when the point was to make her happy.

Francesca unfolded the heavy bag, splitting her gaze between its contents and the handles of the other package, which peeked over the tabletop. She reached inside the bag and felt stiff plastic wrapped around a rectangular shape.

"Jesus, Francesca, it's not going to bite you," said Vivian.

Francesca pulled the bedspread out from its sleeve and looked at it. "But it's not purple."

29

"It's lavender," said Vivian, prepared for Francesca's lack of enthusiasm. "Unfold it."

Francesca shook open the big square of fabric, gritty as sugar. "I asked for a purple bedspread."

"Purple is not a suitable color for a bedspread, Francesca. Why don't you give it a chance? Try it out on your bed and see how it looks. I think it'll be lovely at night with all your glowing stars." Vivian smiled eagerly.

Francesca attempted to refold the bedspread into its original, impossible dimensions. She gave up and stuffed it into the bag. "What's in that one?"

"Never mind," said Vivian. She rested her cigarette in the cradle of the ashtray and pulled a head of iceberg lettuce from the fridge. She tore off the cellophane. When next she looked up, Francesca was in the hall, clutching the wire handles of the fancy package. For a quick moment, their eyes met.

"Francesca," Vivian said. "I'm warning you. Put that down."

Two at a time, Francesca ran up the stairs, her ears hot as tiny burners. The door to the attic closed behind her, the latch clicked securely.

Vivian followed. "I'll count to three. One . . . Two . . ." She ran up the stairs and rapped on the attic door, then jiggled the latch up and down, kicking at the bottom panel of the door with the hard tip of her shoe. "Goddammit. Francesca, open the door."

Francesca held the gleaming robe high in front of her. It smelled clean, felt cool as fresh snow. This is how it would feel to be Isabella, she thought, imagining her mother spotting the robe, after she'd already purchased the bedspread on sale. The beautiful white robe off to the left, lit a clean blue by the filtered afternoon sun, draped over a stately mannequin.

She pulled off her Captain Kangaroo sweatshirt and the blue T-shirt she wore underneath, dropped her rust-colored corduroys to the ground, yanking each leg free with the opposite foot, then removed her socks in the same fashion. She stood naked but for her white, cotton underpants dotted with generic pink flowers. Slowly, she pushed her right arm through the heavy, terrycloth sleeve, felt the soft fabric on her skin. She lifted the heavy collar to cover her neck, rolled the sleeves up an inch or so, and pulled the girth tight around her, wrapping the long belt twice, and double knotting it so no one could slip it off when she wasn't looking. She felt like a movie star, like Rock Hudson or Gary Cooper.

Splayed diagonally across the bed, her belly pressed into the bumpy blue blanket, a twinge shot through her groin. She pressed her hips into the mattress and felt the swells of her breasts against the padded springs. Her hands found the warmest spot between her thighs and settled there. "I'm a genius. I'm a genius," she snickered.

Chapter Three

Lisa Sinsong visited Isabella again the following Saturday. The day was drizzling and chilly and, confined to the white room, a friendly game of chess between the two girls morphed into a marathon. Each time Lisa won, Isabella cleared the board and insisted on a rematch. "It doesn't count," she'd say, claiming her game had been compromised by a headache, the need to pee, or the rhythm of Francesca's record player tapping at the ceiling.

"Checkmate," Lisa yawned after the fourth game, too bored to gloat.

Isabella's eyelids twitched above the desolate board. "I'm hungry," she whined. She gathered all the tiny wooden men, dumped them into the storage compartment, and clapped the two sides of the board together. "How 'bout some Yodels and lemonade?"

"Sure."

"Be right back." Isabella lifted the chessboard by its wooden handle, slipped out of the room, and stampeded down the steps.

Lisa lay back on the white bed, her stomach growling, and stared up at a brown water stain on the ceiling, the only imperfection in the white paint. She could hear Francesca's record player, like rain on a tin roof.

Quiet as mist, she stepped out of the room and walked down the hallway. She hooked her pinky around the "F" on the nameplate and pressed her ear to the door, inhaling the dusty insides.

"Hello?" Lisa asked. The music stopped. "Hello?"

Francesca opened the door. She towered over Lisa from the second step, fingering her puka shell choker.

"Hi," Lisa waved.

"Hi." Francesca peered into the hallway, expecting her sister to jump out from a corner or behind a door.

"Can I come in?" Lisa took a small, suggestive step forward.

Francesca shrugged and climbed the steps backward, then moved aside and watched as Lisa's white party socks came into view. "Aren't you having a good time with my sister?"

"Mostly we play chess." Lisa shrugged and sat on the bed. "Over and over and over. It drives her crazy because she can't beat me. Not to brag, but I am the National Champion. Anyhow, I'm exhausted." She said this like an old lady, followed it with a grand yawn—her eyes filling with tears—then shook her head hard to finish it off. "What have you been doing?"

"Reading a book."

Lisa nodded. "The encyclopedia?"

"No. It's about fish."

"Oh."

"I'm going to ask for a fish tank for Christmas."

"That would look good up here."

"I want to put it right there, in the corner." She pointed to an empty space, between her bookcase and the small window that faced the backyard.

"I used to have a goldfish," Lisa said. "But it died. Then I got another one. But it died, too. So I gave up."

"They always die."

"I know," Lisa said. "I like your name."

"Thanks." Francesca stood against the desk, her feet crossed at the ankles. This was the moment she dreaded, the one where she could think of nothing to say. What did one do with a friend? "I built a hut," she said suddenly.

"A hut? You mean like what Indians lived in?"

Francesca nodded. "It isn't a specific kind of hut, just something I made out of branches and mud."

"Can I see it?" asked Lisa, trying to seem equally intrepid: A girl so tall, with such dirty feet, who lives alone in an attic, surely is afraid of nothing.

When Isabella returned, holding two glasses of lemonade, two yodels stuffed in her pockets, and a magnetized chess set under her arm (she hoped this one would bring her better luck), the white room was empty.

☐ ☐ ☐

Immediately, upon stepping off the reliable pavement and onto the bumpy ground, Lisa regretted her feigned insouciance, her cavalier "Can I see it?" when Francesca mentioned a hut. She imagined savages, bears, gorillas. Her father had said of the woods, in that spooky tone he used to shake her: "You go in, you never come out."

She positioned her feet sideways and moved down the embankment in baby steps, searching for grooves and ledges. Francesca moved nimbly ahead, the distance between them increasing. The incline stiffened and Lisa felt her body hurtling forward even as she tried to slow down. She grabbed for a branch or a vine, something to steady her, but her fingers clutched a switch of prickers instead. She screamed and tumbled the rest of the way down the embankment, landing in a crusty mattress of leaves at the bottom. Tall trees blocked the lightness of the sky. Sharp rocks popped out like broken bones. The screaming of black birds cut through trees. She tried not to think of how much trouble she'd be in—defying her father, soiling her new sneakers. She turned and searched for the DeSilva house but could see only the treetops swaying like giant, wagging fingers.

There had been days of rain and what was normally just dirt had become a bit of a swamp to wade through. Francesca, who was used to navigating the woods in all sorts of conditions, had already made it through the murky puddles.

"Are you alright?" She squatted down and lifted Lisa's wounded hand.

"Look," she whispered and pointed to a nervous chipmunk at Lisa's left, a bright yellow stripe down its back.

Even Lisa could see the beauty in that. Nothing threatening in that. "Cute," she tried to smile. She followed Francesca, who now maintained a mindful distance as they stepped into the swampy terrain. Cold, pasty water crawled inside Lisa's sneakers. She resisted screaming as things stringlike and slippery tickled her ankles and focused instead on the back of Francesca's head, the thick helmet of hair, the dipping, rising shoulders, hands flapping at her sides for balance, like a penguin.

34

Finally, they made it to the other side. Lisa wiped damp hair off her forehead.

"Tada . . ." Francesca imitated a game show girl, pointing to a drunken structure camouflaged into the woods, its walls covered in evergreen switches, its base built from stones fitted together and shored up with dry mud. An occasional burlap scrap plugged up a stubborn hole. PRIVATE was painted in black on a plywood post stuck into the sandy ground, the "E" squashed to fit.

"You built this?" Lisa circled the hut.

"Actually, this is just a rough version of what the final thing will look like." Francesca put her hands in her pockets and sloped her shoulders, masking her pride. "You can go in." She bent down and pulled back the chamois door. Lisa peered in cautiously, then crawled through the threshold. Her navy cardigan sweater hiked up her back, exposing knobs of white spine.

"Wow!" she called from inside, inhaling the damp smell of the woods. She moved to the back wall to make room for Francesca and patted the floor, fingering the many bottle caps fastidiously pounded into the dirt. "Tiles," she said.

The air was moist and syrupy, like being under covers: the heaviness, the closeness of breath. The girls filled every inch of the interior. Lisa grinned, so pleased to have escaped Isabella and to find herself here, with this girl instead. She felt safe. Her breaths spread into wide aisles of air. She giggled, which she never did, and found the widest part of the hut. There she sprawled on her back, pressed her feet to one end, her head to the other.

"Lie down," she said, folding her hands behind her head and exposing her pearly stomach.

"I'm too tall."

"So bend your knees." With black eyes, Lisa stared far into Francesca's face, pulling her down without moving: a magician extracting a rabbit from his hat.

Everything in Francesca's life seemed to have changed. She landed so close to Lisa, she could feel the steady rhythm of breathing, see the pulse in Lisa's neck. Her feet extended under the chamois door, out into the cool air. Water beat the river rocks; a car passed on Riverview

Street; the wind whispered and tugged on the frail autumn leaves.

"Don't you want to ask about my mother?" Lisa turned onto her side and faced Francesca. "Everybody wants to know something: how she did it or who found her. Why she did it or how high the building was."

Francesca stared at the ceiling and felt that, like always, she was failing some essential test. But these were not the sort of things she wanted to know from Lisa. There were other things she wanted to ask. Under her bed, for instance, were finger paintings she'd made on huge pieces of shiny paper. She wanted Lisa to look at them and guess what they were.

"Do you think my sister's smart?" she asked.

"My father says she's crazy."

"He does?" This was not a bad answer. "What about me?"

"He's never met you," said Lisa. "But he hates Americans."

"I'm not American. I'm half-Italian, half-Jewish."

"He hates Jews. He hates everyone but Chinese. That's why we live in the ghetto. With other Chinese." Lisa swallowed hard. "My guidance counselor says I'm wrong, but I know my mother did it because I lost the big chess game. It was my first defeat. You might have heard about it; it was in the papers and magazines. There were even pictures."

Francesca nodded, though she hadn't.

"She lived for my chess matches. If it hadn't been for her, I would never have learned to play."

"Do you like chess?" Francesca asked.

"I love it," Lisa said. "I love all the pieces."

Again, Francesca nodded. She, too, had always admired the intricate, distinctive figures.

"My feeling is that each one has (1) motivation, (2) moral character, and (3) a purpose in relation to the queen," Lisa said, bending back one small finger on each of the three attributes, for emphasis. When she saw that Francesca would not interrupt, that she seemed to listen ardently, Lisa continued, espousing her philosophy of the game, how it functioned as a replica of the world, a miniature society, complete with cruelty, loyalty, and class struggles. "The pawns are poor

Chinese people," she spoke with great authority, "the under class. The Queen is Chinese, beautiful and mean, with huge boobs, always wearing velvet against her white skin. I call her Jacqueline, because I love and hate the name. And the King is American. He's stupid, with a red face and blue eyes and gray hair. No one takes him seriously, especially Jacqueline. She makes all the rules. She invented the game; that's why she gets to do whatever she wants. She hired the horsemen, twins named Billy and Willy. The rooks were just pieces of the castle until she brought them to life. And then are the pawns: sycophants." Lisa made a disgusted face. "But you can only trust the Bishops. They're noble and good. And they can cross the board in one long stroke. So they're very effective." Lisa flipped onto her back, her legs spread flat like a corpse. She lay like that for a moment.

"You can kiss me," she said.

Reflexively, Francesca leaned back. She'd wanted to kiss Lisa since they'd sat in her room, but she felt sure it was a perverse thing to want. She'd wanted to touch Lisa's hands, even though Lisa was a girl. She'd wanted something she could not define since that first meeting in the hallway.

"Don't you want to?" asked Lisa.

No, no, no, thought Francesca. She nodded.

"So?" Lisa puckered up and waited.

Francesca leaned over slow as a bending branch, inching her face closer and closer until she could feel Lisa's breath across her lips. She pressed her mouth down onto Lisa's and held it there, perfectly still. How complicated it was, the dry moist soft cool sending her body orbiting into space, then thrusting into deep, wet earth. Her head was dizzy. She leaned her weight on her hand so as not to collapse like a building onto the girl's small frame. Her mouth slackened, lips parted, making room for Lisa's tongue. And then it came, the tongue, feeling in her mouth nothing like her own tongue, making the world open like a door into hot sunlight. She felt herself bleed inside. Lisa hooked her feet around Francesca's legs and pressed hard at every possible intersection, until they were moving and rolling, bearing no resemblance to the two awkward, introverted girls they'd been all their lives.

□ □ □

"They're back, Mom!" Isabella bellowed, her arms folded across her chest. She pulled the door open and let Lisa and Francesca into the foyer, trying not to stare at Lisa's underwear showing through her wet, pink pants.

The smell of butter, chocolate, and grease followed Vivian out of the kitchen, where she'd been making tollhouse cookies. She wiped her hands on a dish towel.

"She'd never seen the river," Francesca said.

"Is that right?" Vivian's voice was sweet and sharp. "Isabella, why don't you run upstairs and get Lisa another pair of pants and we'll put these sopping wet ones in the dryer?"

Lisa dripped on the floor. Her thumbs moved in circles at her sides. Vivian knew it had been only months since the mother's suicide, that the girl must be fragile as a soufflé. "Go on honey," she said gently. "Take those off." She squatted down and skinned the heavy fabric from Lisa's body.

Isabella returned, carrying a pair of white pants.

"How 'bout a towel, Bella?" asked Vivian.

Still winded from her last trip upstairs, Isabella ran up again, pulled a white towel from the rack in the bathroom, panting exaggeratedly, her shoulders rising and sinking on each breath. Vivian dried off the bright red legs, cold and skinny as hoses. Lisa stood in her clinging undershirt, looking at Francesca's darkened, muddy sneakers. Cautiously, she placed one hand on each of Vivian's shoulders and stepped into the pants, several sizes too large, that Vivian held open before her. The thick, soft material bunched at the belly; the hems hung well below her ankles. Vivian rolled bulky cuffs, patted Lisa's hips. "There. No one died, right?" Isabella shot her a horrified look. Vivian immediately regretted her choice of platitude, but, oh well, nothing to do about it now. She smiled. "Run upstairs and I'll bring your pants when they're dry."

Francesca began to follow Lisa upstairs.

"You," Vivian reached out and grabbed Francesca's belt loop, stopping her at the third step from the bottom. "Where do you think

38

you're going?" she whispered. "You'll help me in the kitchen and leave your sister's friends alone. What's the matter with you? Trying to steal your sister's best friend."

"Hah!" Francesca said, then crashed her mouth closed.

Vivian let go of Francesca. She bent down and mopped up the water with Lisa's pants. "Your sister is special, Francesca. She may not be the easiest person to get along with, but we have to make concessions for her. We have to nurture her so she can develop some social skills."

"What are social skills?"

"A successful way of interacting with people in the world. I can't explain this now." She opened the front door and wrung out Lisa's pants on the front stoop, standing back to stay dry.

"Can I have a cookie?" Francesca asked.

"You can lick the bowl. The cookies are in the oven. And then I want you to stay in your room until dinner."

"Fine with me," Francesca muttered, thinking how she'd been kissed. Nothing else mattered.

Rake, 1986

Rake is a haunting portrait of an ordinary household tool stuck, upside down, into the soft soil of a suburban yard, the green tines fanning prophetically toward the nighttime sky. The sky is an eerie backdrop, lit from behind, a sheer shroud of cheesecloth or gauze over the not-quite-right neighborhood. Behind the rake is a house in which a teenage girl, probably a babysitter, sits in an armchair. She stares ahead into a puff of gray light—the unseen television, its picture bloating out into the room. We watch her through a large picture window with no curtain, privy to only her profile, dark hair, and reclined posture. She lounges lazily, perhaps loafing on the job.[10] The door to the house is halfway open; only a screen door separates the young girl from the predatory world.

In a 1994 article in *Caleidoscope,* Lucinda Dialo unveiled her theory that *Rake* is a metaphor for Rape. The demonic within the mundane, the threat lurking in the "whitest, most placid neighborhoods, the neighborhoods where we're assured we are safe."[11] Others have elaborated on this interpretation, pointing to the open door as evidence that in this painting, the real story is about to happen.

Phillip Hamil, columnist for *Illustrated Gent,* dismisses Dialo's interpretation as ". . . feminist paranoia.

10. Paul DeVaine points out that, as with so many of deSilva's works, *Rake* presents a secondary subject within the painting, one that takes the viewer inside the work, forcing us to participate in the events that are about to occur or are already in process. *Metaphor and Madness.* Chicago: ARTBooks, 1994, page 115.
11. Dialo, Lucinda. "Counterstrokes of Violence: How Society Informs Women's Art."*Caleidoscope, A Journal of Feminist Art,* Winter, 1994.

deSilva would have been offended by this distortion of her meanings, the idea that nothing in her work—not even a gardening tool—is exempt from the onerous duty of representing misogyny or sexual perversion . . . There is no evidence of deSilva's hatred of men. She was, in many ways, one of the boys, and was revered by the men who had the good fortune to know her."[12]

Of the use of light in *Rake*, Hamil writes, "deSilva's knack for setting and mood is unrivaled. The light in this painting—the gray/purple/blue/white/yellow hue which, to my knowledge, has never before been achieved, not even in the most spectacular L.A. sunset, not even in Van Gogh's sunflowers—looms over the painting like the impending apocalypse. *Rake*, as deSilva herself told me in one of our many discussions about her work, is about Godlessness, all that is cold and soulless. The garden tool is man—not the gender, but the species—evil, defiant, its broad shoulders clawing avidly in every direction. deSilva emphasizes her loss of faith in humanity by reducing the female subject to a set piece and featuring the rake front and center, as the protagonist."[13]

Other interpretations abound. Cynthia Bell, in *Lesbians in Oil*, theorizes that *Rake* is less a metaphor

---

12. Hamil, Phillip. "Men Think She's Hot; Women Thinks She's, Well, Hot." *Illustrated Gent,* April 1994. Photographs by Frannie Lieber. The column was to run as part of the "Women We Love" feature, but editors felt deSilva's sudden death made its inclusion inappropriate. Instead, Hamil turned the article into a post-mortem tribute.
Author's Note: Hamil, who claims to be the only man deSilva ever dated, proposed marriage to her repeatedly. Though deSilva repeatedly refused, the two maintained a friendship, the intensity of which varies according to the source. Many have dismissed Hamil's prolific writings on deSilva as obsequious and fawning.
13. Ibid.

for Rape, than Race, and that beyond race, it is a meditation on homosexuality, specifically lesbianism. The painting is concerned with "otherness," according to Bell, the rake representing the alienated other, forced to remain out on the lawn like a second class citizen, well into the nighttime hours. The rake, she says, "is deSilva keeping her polite distance from the object of her desire, in this case the babysitter, who it may be postulated, represents Lisa Sinsong."[14]

Michael Wright, in his examination of the link between art and mental wellness, *Art That Heals,* asserts that the rake represents Alfonse DeSilva, whom he claims Francesca hated and feared. "The rake, a tool Alfonse wielded throughout the day, is presumably an innocuous object, set against a garage wall and there expected to remain all through the night, beside fertilizer and shears and shovels. But deSilva shows us the rake as she'd have us see her father: prowling the neighborhood, stalking his prey, when he ought to have been in bed with his wife."[15]

14. Bell, Cynthia. *Lesbians in Oil.* Atlanta: Amazon Press, 1991, page 69. *Author's note:* There is nothing in the painting to support any connection between Lisa Sinsong and the babysitter. Though the babysitter has black hair, we cannot discern her features or determine her race. She could be Chinese in as much as she could be Inuit. It could as easily and with as much credence be claimed that the rake represented the insane Mr. Sinsong or Isabella, who later in life took to roaming the neighborhood in the dark, frightening children and setting dogs howling for hours.
15. Wright, Michael. *Art That Heals.* Minneapolis: night-night press, 1992, page 112. *Author's note:* Wright bolsters his argument by pointing out the encore appearance of the rake in *Wash-O-Mat.* In *Wash-O-Mat,* which Wright describes as "Hopperesque in its spartan and somber silence," the gardening tool is propped against the back wall of a late night laundromat, beside an old woman drinking coffee. A young girl, thin and tall, is seated at the front of the dusty gray room, wearing a sweatshirt, muddy sneakers and jeans, and fervently biting her thumbnail. Wright insists that here again, the rake represents the stalking father figure, and the young girl is, who else?, the artist. *Wash-O-Mat* perished in the 1989 fire.

Chapter Four

Francesca fell asleep while it was still light outside, then awoke to a dark and silent world. She could smell Lisa's baby powder and sugar breath. She licked her lips, remembering the long white stretch of Lisa's neck. Hot tears loitered behind her eyes. A crooked bolt of sensation traveled down her spine and sent a shock to her groin. She pressed her fists against the zipper of her jeans and rolled left and right. The thin murmur of Isabella talking in her sleep drifted up through the floorboards as the previous day returned to her like fragments of a dream: Mr. Sinsong clenching Lisa's thin arm, dragging her down the porch steps and over the slate path, Lisa's feet barely touching the ground.

"Good riddance to bad rubbish," Vivian had said.

"It's your fault," Isabella had whispered to Francesca, giving her the evil eye.

And Lisa had become tinier and tinier, like a strand of hair, a blade of grass, finally a blurry profile trapped inside the prison door of the Buick.

She pulled her knapsack down from its hook on the back of the door and packed her Captain Kangaroo sweatshirt, then double-knotted her shoelaces and tiptoed downstairs into the dark kitchen. She cracked the refrigerator door for light, then removed the telephone book from the potholder drawer and quietly flipped pages. There were so many S's. Her finger glided up one column, down the next, landing upon two Sinsongs, but only one in New Haven. 496 Temple. She memorized the address and put the thick book back in the potholder drawer, positioned the remaining half of an Entenmanns chocolate cake at the top of her pack, then adjusted the pack so it sat comfortably on her shoulders. This, too, she'd learned from Sam Gribley: Never be hampered by awkward apparatus.

The night air smelled sweet and earthy. Francesca edged along the driveway to avoid the clamor of gravel, and crossed the street. The sky was spotted with marble stars, a nearly full moon. She rolled down the embankment, only half on the path, recognizing enough of the girthy pines and spindly birches to know she was in the vicinity. Still, the milky darkness infused everything with danger. She plowed into prickers, splashed across the thick black swamp—a mystery of underlife and cling—repeatedly reminding herself that these were her favorite woods, and that although she never wanted to see her parents again, they were, dependably, just across the street.

The hut appeared at the center of a round blue clearing, lit up by the night sky and surrounded by darkness. She pulled back the door and scrambled inside, slid her body all the way to the back wall, and extended her legs straight out in front of her. A car passed on the street above—nearing, nearing, then fading like something that changed its mind. She removed her flashlight from the shelf overhead and aimed its beam all around the small room to remind herself where she was, how many afternoons she'd spent by this river, never attacked, never eaten by animals. What was the worst thing that could happen: Bobcat? Rabid dog? Pack of hungry wolves? Grizzly bear? Sadistic teenage boy? Hadn't they caught the legendary Hillbilly Hermit after he strangled a young girl with strings from his banjo? Even so, there were always more murderers, ones who sought girls like Francesca: ugly girls, girls overgrown and devoid of form, who kiss other girls and build huts at the riverside.

She pulled her bag toward her and removed the cake, opened the box, let the sweet muddy smell of chocolate drift toward her face. She scooped out a clawful, stuffed it into her mouth, the crumbs falling down the front of her sweatshirt. In minutes, it was gone. Francesca sat dumbfounded and stuffed, her eyelids sinking closer and closer together. She pulled the wool blanket down from the shelf overhead and curled up beneath it, fell into a deep, sugarcoated sleep.

Hours later she awoke to a stiff neck and aching bladder. She pulled back the door and blinked against the earliest morning light, unfolded into the misty air. Her stomach growled, more from sickness than hunger, and her head ached as though she'd been spinning around and around. The sticky smell of chocolate lingered on her fingers and around her mouth. She stepped away from the hut and squatted to pee. The structure no longer looked impressive. It seemed childish and pathetic, like a good wind could send it into the river. Her eyes filled with tears. She hated it. She would never come back here. Ever. Thus it was decided: She would fetch Lisa and leave New Haven, never see any of them again. Except maybe her grandmother. But it would all have to be hush-hush, their whereabouts kept secret from Mr. Sinsong, from Vivian and Isabella and Alfonse.

"Meet me across the street," she would tell Lisa from a pay phone. "Pack a bag." She'd borrow her grandmother's Chevy, speed down Fountain Street, past the decrepit synagogue, past the library, past Kentucky Fried Chicken with its rotating portrait of the colonel. Past the duck pond where Evelyn had brought her as a child, covered now with green scum. Lisa would be waiting, denim jacket over her pajamas, eyes still sticky with sleep, hair in a zigzag part. Francesca would toss the suitcase into the trunk, open the passenger door, close it after Lisa got in, then tap on the window and mouth "Lock up" with authority. She'd saunter around the front of the car, climb behind the large brown wheel, and grab a confident hold. Then she'd lean over and kiss Lisa kind of rough, kind of tender. The way a man does when he's got a woman to himself. They'd follow the low orange moon, speed through red lights, floating like a whisper over highway pavement. Stop at Denny's for breakfast, just as the light was thin and smoky like milk around an empty glass. Have coffees, why not, big omelets with bacon. Then crash their tall, plastic juice glasses together in a toast.

She fastened the door to the hut and headed back along the path, through the swamp, the prickered eaves, until she reached the bottom of the embankment. There, her legs aching, she exhausted her reserves scaling the steep incline. In front of her sleeping house the only evidence of life was a tall rake with green shoulders. The post was plunged into a newly dug flowerbed alongside the house. The sky was light but still sunless; the only sounds were faraway trucks, a barking dog. No cars moved along the street. She knew it was very early. Her sister was asleep. Her parents were facing opposing sides in their double bed, the beige comforter pulled up to their chins, the black and white TV hot from running all night.

Alfonse would soon awaken, load his tools into the station wagon, yank the rake out from the dew-soaked ground. Sundays he worked at the high school, his biggest account. Often Francesca would tag along, pull weeds drowsily, play in the dirt. There was an intimacy to those outings, nearly silent but for Alfonse's whistled renditions of Italian opera. Even without words, Francesca could tell it was Italian music. His jaunty fingers bounced on the steering wheel, his knee danced. He'd look over at Francesca and wink. He seemed to be somewhere else, somewhere happy. Then, on the way home, they'd eat butterscotch sundaes at Farm Shop. Alfonse would finagle the waitress's pen, and they'd play tic-tac-toe on sandpaper napkins. Stuffed and silly, as they waited at the cash register to pay, he'd tickle Francesca until she promised to eat all her dinner, even the vegetables, so Vivian wouldn't know they'd been bad.

Francesca moved farther and farther away from the house, toward the main road. This is the last time I'll ever see this place, she thought, turning back once more for a good, long look. Nothing, I feel nothing. She shrugged. Her body seemed light, as if she'd shed weight or thrown off a heavy garment she'd never needed.

By the time she arrived at her grandmother's house, the sun was up. Evelyn, hair still in curlers, adjusted the waistband of her powder blue nylon pajamas and pulled Francesca inside. She sat her down at the kitchen table, poured a steaming cup of coffee, and pushed the jar of Cremora across the table. Francesca dumped three heaping teaspoons onto her coffee, then exploded the hills of sticky, sweet dust with her finger and watched the beverage turn a caramel color. Magically, a tupperware of rugelach appeared on the table. Evelyn sat kitty-corner and pulled the airtight lid off of the container. The sweet, buttery smell made Francesca salivate.

"Here," said Evelyn.

Francesca took a pastry. She bit far into it, found it was not apricot, but prune. "Are they all prune?" She tried not to sound disappointed.

"Oh, they're delicious. Prunes are good for you." Evelyn reached for one, as if to set an example, took a bite, and wiped some fallen crumbs from the yellow, vinyl placemat in front of her onto the floor. She untangled the clips from her hair, letting the brassy toboggans unfurl and bounce toward her shoulders. Carefully she deposited the clips into a plastic box that said Evelyn's Things in white writing on the lid.

"Gramm?" Francesca said sweetly.

"What is it, Bunny?" Evelyn put her hand over Francesca's. "So cold. Where have you been?" She took Francesca's hand in between her two veiny ones, rubbed it firmly, her wedding band bumping Francesca's knuckles.

"Can you take me somewhere?" Francesca asked.

"Of course I can. Where do you want to go? Florida? Hawaii? Where should we go? Like a couple of gangsters," Evelyn winked.

"I need to visit my friend."

"Well, that's easy. Where is she?" Evelyn closed up the plastic box of curlers and pushed it to the side.

"She lives downtown in the Chinese neighborhood."

"Wha—?" Evelyn squinted up her face, pushed her fingers through her hair to loosen the curls.

"The Chinese neighborhood," Francesca said loudly. Sometimes Evelyn was hard of hearing.

"There's no Chinese neighborhood," Evelyn waved her hand and made a face. She took another pastry and bit into it, chewed with her mouth open, the crumbs clinging to the corners.

"There is so," Francesca insisted. "She lives there."

"Who is she?"

"Lisa."

"Lisa? What's Lisa doing in a Chinese neighborhood?"

"She's Chinese!" Francesca stood up.

"Alright. Calm down. I just never heard of that neighborhood. Where is it?"

"Temple Street."

"Temple Street? No—" Evelyn made a big, dismissive gesture.

Francesca walked to the sink. She stood facing the backyard, her arms folded across her chest. "Forget it. I knew you wouldn't help me."

"Alright. Alright. So, you have a Chinese friend. Does your mother know?"

Francesca nodded.

"Alright, so?" Evelyn stood up. "Let me call your mother so she knows where you are and we'll go. Okay? Everything better now?" She reached out, grabbed hold of Francesca's chin, gave it a squeeze. Years before, she'd vowed not to disappoint her granddaughter. But this promise she'd made in her fifties, when energy still rippled through her body, before it became evident how miserably her own daughter would fail at motherhood, how much would be left to do.

"Thank you," Francesca said quietly, after Evelyn had left the room.

Chapter Five

Evelyn's tobacco-colored Chevy Impala was littered with gum wrappers, broken cigarettes, discarded tissues, grocery lists scrawled on the backs of envelopes, receipts in faded blue ink. The air conditioner button was jammed, so it ran all the time, filling the car with a sick, fruity smell. They rode in silence through the center of New Haven, past the large, brown shopping mall propped several feet off the ground on cement stumps.

"It's so ugly," said Francesca.

"Everything's ugly," Evelyn answered, dismissing the world with a flash of her hand.

They crossed a river on which wrappers and cans floated like tiny ships. The street grew narrow, filled up with dark-skinned people. Cars were double-parked, sometimes with the doors hanging open, making it nearly impossible to pass. Baby strollers and bicycles popped out from between buildings, everything crisscrossing and sudden. No longer did anyone seem to follow a pattern, to move at a rhythmic, ordered pace. Evelyn blinked her eyes to burn a line of vision through the commotion. She felt an ineffable shame, unwelcome, as if she were trespassing in another world.

"Whew!" she said, when they'd finally paused at a red light. She wiped her forehead with the back of her hand. The light switched to green, and a man wearing sweatpants with one pant leg long, one cut short darted directly out in front of the car.

Evelyn held down her horn, then looked away when the man gave her the finger. "What kind of outfit is that?" she wrinkled her face at Francesca. "Lock your door."

Music played through open windows, people greeted one another ebulliently in Spanish. Stores had signs painted on plywood: Rosalee's

Bodega, Allen's Discount Warehouse. In the window of Miguel's TV and Appliances, carpeted steps displayed a dusty turntable, two televisions, an iron. Evelyn pulled off of Chapel and onto Temple. Immediately, the world quieted.

"I've never seen no Chinese people here," Evelyn said.

Temple Street ran eerily through a section of low-to-the-ground warehouses—no apartments, no people—until it metamorphosed into a residential neighborhood. A series of short apartment buildings sprang up.

"Here it is!" Francesca sat up straight, pointed to a putty-colored building. "496."

A Chinese family emerged as if on cue. Evelyn stared, shaking her head, incredulous. "This is no neighborhood," she scowled, irritated at the city for changing surreptitiously, making her feel extinct. She pulled the car alongside a dumpster.

"I'll keep the car running."

Graffiti covered the outside walls as high and wide as a person could reach hanging from the railing. Most of it was in Chinese, but there were the usual American imperatives: Suck my cock, Eat Shit, etc. Inside was dark even though it was still morning. Francesca ran her hand along the bumpy walls, guided herself past the mailboxes, all in various stages of disrepair—doors pried open, hinges hanging, locks broken and popping out like eyes. She climbed a staircase, two steps at a time, her heart pounding. The air smelled of burnt toast and old smoke. She heard water running through the pipes, silverware being shuffled, people speaking in Chinese. A piece of Scotch tape pressed to the center of a door said "Sinsong" in thick, black marker. Cigarette butts had been swept from all sides of the hallway and left in a pile in the corner.

She knocked quietly.

"Yes?" a man bellowed.

"Is Lisa home?"

"Lisa? Who there?"

A latch opened, then two bolts, then the door peeled back. Mr. Sinsong stood in a stained undershirt and belted pants. His black socks had holes at the big toes. His hair was greasy and very black, slicked to the back of his age-spotted forehead.

51

"Yes," he said loudly. "How are you? What you want?"

"Is Lisa home?"

He looked beyond Francesca, wondering how she'd come to be here, standing alone in the hallway. "Lisa—" he bent backward. "Someone here for you. Yes, come in." He stepped out of the way.

The room smelled thickly of bacon, as though it had been cooked there every single day, without the windows having once been opened. There was a damp, wet-carpet smell as well. Lisa stepped out of the bathroom wearing a worn blue bathrobe over Scooby Doo pajamas with feet. Her hair was bent in different directions, frizzy strands everywhere. "I knew it was you," she said.

"Meet me at the Wash-O-Mat." Francesca pointed toward the window. "I have a plan." She was a character in a book now. Everything would come together.

Lisa shook her head.

"But my grandmother's waiting. She'll take us to the bus station."

"I can't." Lisa took a step back, glanced toward the kitchen.

"The Wash-O-Mat. Across the street."

"I know where it is!" Lisa said, pushing Francesca toward the door.

"I'll be at the Wash-O-Mat. Waiting."

"I'm not coming," whispered Lisa, pressing closed the door.

Francesca galloped down the stairs, out into the blinding day. She perched on the edge of Evelyn's passenger's seat, one foot firmly rooted on the pavement. "Gram," she said, as Evelyn shifted into drive. "We have to wait here. Lisa's coming."

"What do you mean, she's coming?"

"She's coming with us."

"Close the door," said Evelyn.

"You don't understand—" Francesca's voice was desperate and high. "Lisa needs our help." She held onto the door latch.

Evelyn turned and glanced at the building as if it were Chinese. "I told your mother I'd have you back by noon. You said you needed to see your friend. Now you've seen her. Now we're going."

"No." Francesca got out of the car and slammed the door behind her. Without turning back, she crossed the narrow street, onto the sidewalk, glancing up once at the beaten-up WASH-O-MAT sign, its edges rusted and bent, before boldly pulling back the glass door. Inside felt like another country: humid, tumbling, filled with the muted sounds of machines and jingling coins. She did not look back at her grandmother. Instead she walked to the back of the room and glanced up at a bulletin board perforated by a smattering of pushpins. There were two index cards posted, written in Chinese by the same hand, with the same phone number at the bottom. In the middle of the wide, empty board was a poster for an MS walkathon with a pocket stuffed with postage-paid reply cards. And in the far corner a red sign announced a spaghetti supper and bake sale at a nearby church. Someone had written FUCK FAGS in ballpoint pen and DUKE AND LISA FOREVER inside a heart, with an arrow through both sides, disappearing in the middle. Francesca knew it was her Lisa in question. "Stupid boy," she shook her head.

She turned toward the street. Evelyn's car was gone. "Okay," she told herself, holding her hands in front of her and pressing her palms toward the ground. Her pulse was everywhere, making it hard to stand still. She felt her pockets, took out the twelve dollars she'd put there earlier, and counted them. "Okay," she said again. A woman passed her, carrying pillowcases overstuffed with laundry. Francesca stepped outside. Still, the car was nowhere in sight. The sunlight hit her face, making it difficult to determine which window was Lisa's. She made a visor with her hand and saw someone watching her. Frantically, she gestured.

The Impala reappeared in front of the laundromat. Evelyn leaned toward the passenger's side and rolled down the window. "Get in," she said.

Francesca shook her head, newly emboldened by Evelyn's return.

"I mean it. That's enough. We can call your friend later."

Francesca folded her arms and pretended not to hear a word Evelyn was saying. She whistled and looked left to right, willing Lisa to emerge from the flesh-colored building.

"I will not leave you in this neighborhood. It's a bad neighborhood," Evelyn said in a desperate whisper, so as not to anger lurking hoodlums.

Francesca re-entered the laundromat and feigned interest in a Chinese newspaper sprawled on the folding table. She heard Evelyn pull away again and would not allow herself to look. The door to the laundromat opened, thrusting cold air inside, marked against the heat of dryers and the humidity of washing machines. Lisa had changed into pants, a turtleneck, and her white tennis shoes, still soiled from the day before.

"Where's your grandmother?" she asked, worried lines darkening her forehead.

"Gone." Francesca shrugged.

"Gone?" Lisa looked out the window. "What do you mean? Where did she go?"

Francesca shrugged.

"What will you do?"

"I told you, I'm running away." She patted her pocket.

An old woman entered the laundromat. She wore a pink cotton housedress under a yellow apron with bulky pouches weighted down from coins. Her hair was mostly gray, with a few sharp black strands like cracks in a moonlit sky. She smiled at Lisa, looked suspiciously at Francesca.

Francesca sat in a plastic chair that was attached to a line of others pressed against the wall. She gathered up the Chinese newspaper and opened it in front of her face. "I'm not leaving without you," she said into its folds.

"Okay," said Lisa. "But I'm going home." She waited.

The Impala reappeared. This time Evelyn parked and got out. She entered the laundromat, pulling her coat closed around her substantial girth, doing her best not to look at anything around her. "Is this the friend?" She nodded toward Lisa. "She looks alright to me."

Lisa backed away, toward the door.

"No!" said Francesca, standing up. "Don't go—"

"She has to go," said Evelyn. "Go on now," she smiled at Lisa. "Go on home. Franny will call you tonight and you girls can make a date to see each other. I'll even pick you up."

Lisa waited one more moment, then turned and passed through the door, out onto the narrow street.

"See?" said Evelyn. "She went home like a good girl." She pulled on Francesca's sleeve and led her out to the car, this time meeting little resistance. Francesca was relieved by the familiar smell of the broken air conditioning. She hadn't chosen this. She'd tried to save Lisa, but Lisa wouldn't come. She peered through the back windshield, thought she saw Lisa's shiny black head, but as the car moved several feet forward, she saw that it was only the darkened window, venetian blinds pulled closed against the day.

❑   ❑   ❑

For dinner that night, Alfonse took Francesca to Pepe's pizza on Wooster Street, his old neighborhood. He pointed out, as he'd done many times before, the small brownstone where he had been reared by his aunt and uncle. (His parents were killed when he was only three, victims of an airplane crash on their way home from a holiday in Italy. It was because of this tragedy that he'd never been there.) Alfonse once again showed Francesca the old storefront, now a Subway shop, in which his uncle had run a pizzeria. It was there Alfonse had been employed all through his adolescence until the business could no longer hold its own against Pepe's and Sally's, and had finally surrendered. Alfonse had gone to work for Luciani's landscapers, and had soon moved out of the old neighborhood into downtown New Haven.

No one at Pepe's remembered Alfonse, and though he claimed to remember the pizza maker, he did not try to say hello. They chose a table up front by the window and ordered a small pepperoni and a pitcher of ginger ale. Alfonse told Francesca he was sorry "about all that had happened with your little friend—"

"Lisa," interrupted Francesca, almost violently.

"Lisa. I'm sorry, baby." He hesitated before bringing up the topic in which he was most interested—his own intruded-upon love, a young, perfect (more perfect with each passing year) love, scribed on a face that remained fresh as white sheets on the line in the backyard of his mind. Still, almost thirty years later. He shook his head. "Your sadness reminds me of a girl I loved."

"What girl?" asked Francesca.

"A girl I knew before your Mama, long, long ago, way back in medieval times," he joked in that adult way, simultaneously relishing and resenting his ripened age. Outside, a man was walking two strange dogs with rat ears and skinny, nervous bodies. One sprayed against a lamppost, the other, at the same moment, began compulsively rolling on the ground. Alfonse stared with a blank expression; Francesca considered laughing, but decided against it.

"You know, baby, each thing that doesn't work out means something else will."

"I don't care about anything else," said Francesca.

The pizza arrived, and Alfonse began pulling the slices apart, loosening them, making the cheese bleed onto the metal plate. Francesca quickly pulled a slice away and dropped it onto her plate, blowing on it. Her stomach was empty; she hadn't eaten anything since the rugelach at her grandmother's that morning.

"You know," Alfonse said with his mouth full, then stopped to chew, having secured his position as speaker. He swallowed. "You can talk to me about anything." Francesca thought he sounded like a faker, like he was recycling lines he'd seen in a movie scene between a father and daughter. "Anything at all. That's why I'm your Papa. To help you."

"Okay."

They ate for several moments. Alfonse took a sobering sip of ginger ale, swallowed. He looked up toward the kitchen, where one could watch the pizza maker throw the ball of dough into the air, catch it on his hardened fist so that it immediately spread out and dripped down the length of his wrist. In quick, fleeting thoughts, he remembered the old restaurant, all his dead relatives.

"Grandma says you were very upset."

"Not really."

Alfonse was an ambiguous father, a quixotic, kind presence who lurked about in the children's lives, surprising them with stuffed animals and tickling. But it was clear Francesca needed someone here, and Vivian had been too repulsed by the day's events to lend a hand. So the task had fallen upon Alfonse, and he was flailing about in the dark, trying to prove to himself that his parental love was unbiased and blind and that it mattered not to him that Francesca appeared to be taking her tomboy-ness to a pathological level.

"Is your friend in some kind of trouble?" He stopped eating and folded his hands under his chin, resting his elbows on the table. An isosceles triangle, thought Francesca.

"No." She threw her crust back onto the pizza plate.

"Well, then why did you tell Grandma it was an emergency? Why did you have her bring you to such a bad neighborhood?"

"It's not a bad neighborhood." To Francesca, it was a perfect neighborhood. Its residents, and all the Chinese people of the world, were supremely fortunate and imbued with a magical quality: All of them were related to Lisa Sinsong.

"Mama said it was a terrible neighborhood." Alfonse collapsed his hands and picked up his half-eaten slice of pizza. A group of four college students spilled into the restaurant. It was immediately discernible they were from Yale—not Southern or Quinnipiac or the University of New Haven. They were paler, with powdery fine skin. The girls wore long, lightweight scarves even though it was still balmy outside; the boys were quieter than regular boys. Was it breeding, Alfonse wondered, that made them so distinctive? He decided it was. They possessed an inherent superiority that could not be learned; it was sewn into their fabric by a long, uninterrupted thread.

"Papa," Francesca said suddenly, wresting him from his reverie. "Why do I love another girl?" She tried to stop herself, but—there—it jumped out of her mouth.

He stared at her because, of course, he and Vivian and Evelyn had all wondered this. And then, with the force of a benign dictator making a ruling of what was and wasn't permissible, he spoke: "You think—you might think you love a girl. You probably do love this girl, the same way you might love a very best friend." He made a distinct separation from this normal, best friend love, and the other sort of love which he was deeming nonexistent, as if separating them from an embrace. "You spend too much time alone, Francesca. You need other friends. This girl just came along and she made you realize you were lonely. For a friend."

"But I do love her," Francesca said, her voice tiny, resigned.

He shook his head. "You cannot tell your mother about this. It's more than she can bear. She's got her hands full with Isabella. You are a good girl, Francesca. You always have been." It was less an observation than a command.

Francesca felt sick. The college students had finished their first pitcher of beer. They were arguing about a movie they'd just seen, something that had a love story which the boys found implausible; the girls, romantic. It was a conversation that was being overheard in that moment in pizza restaurants across the country.

"Can we go home?" she asked. "I don't feel good."

"You feel sick? Was it the pizza?" He turned to find the waiter. He was relieved that the conversation was over and he wouldn't have to listen to Francesca confess any more of her strange secrets. It was one thing to be a father, to provide money, to play catch, to bring Francesca with him on his jobs sometimes and help her with her homework. But if this newest incident were really an indication of some sort of perversion in her development, he'd rather pretend not to notice it and hope it would work itself out.

They were quiet on the car ride home, so Alfonse put on the game. The Dolphins vs. the Redskins. Francesca never paid attention to the specifics of football, but she enjoyed the sounds of the game over the radio—the announcer's enthusiasm, excited but muffled, the warm shifting of the crowd's roar, like someone turning over in bed. It made her sleepy. In this moment, it soothed her. It reminded her not to rely on anyone, least of all her parents.

Chapter Six

When Isabella was 14, her manuscript, *A Cry from the Attic,* was published by Random House. Comprised of thirty-six sonnets written in the fictionalized voice of Anne Frank, the volume was hailed as "an unprecedented genre . . . historical poetry—unwieldy as it is thorough,"[16] "a visionary deconstruction of reality, dappled with piercing insights,"[17] and, cryptically, "the author glimpses the fourth dimension."[18]

Isabella's literary agent, Mrs. Val Noonan, suggested a party to celebrate. Invitations went out to major players in the industry: newspaper and magazine publishers, critics, Anne Frank scholars, and Elie Weisel. Vivian prepared magic tuna fish. She peppered the pink flesh with paprika, cumin seed, and chopped celery; pulverized it with a fork; then set three scoops on a large plate, in the design of a face. All of this she framed in a halo of cocktail rye breads. She created myriad hors d'oeuvres, all of them inexplicably childlike: pigs in blankets, Swedish meatballs, tiny salami and American cheese sandwiches on miniature buns with yellow mustard. Arrangements were made in advance for Francesca to stay at Evelyn's.

Cars from New York parked side by side in the DeSilva driveway. A case of champagne chilled in the refrigerator. Isabella stood pressed into the corner, largely avoided by the guests. Alfonse, too, evaded the commotion, hiding in the kitchen and replenishing hors d'oeuvres, impressing the female guests with his exotic nonaversion to housework. On one foray out of the kitchen, tray of pigs in blankets extended as

16. *The New York Times Book Review,* August 18, 1976.
17. *New England Poetry,* August 21, 1976.
18. Gensler, Allen. "An American in Deutschland." *Village Beat,* September 1976.
Author's Note: A Cry from the Attic became a major text in junior high schools, was translated into Italian, French, Spanish, and, after some consternation, German, and brought unexpected chaos to the DeSilva home.

a shield, he was accosted by an erudite American to expound on Sonnet #19 in Isabella's collection. Alfonse nodded and smiled, trying to place the man's remarkably unpleasant accent (was it New York or Boston?) and conceal the fact that he had not read beyond the first two poems in his daughter's volume. (He kept his autographed copy—*To Papa, Love I.*—its cover shiny with infancy, binder arthritic from unuse, on its own shelf in his nightstand, where each night he passed it over for his well-worn copy of Italo Calvino's *Italian Fairy Tales,* a wonderfully dreamy and slumberous collection that reminded him of what he considered his home, even if he'd never been there.)

Mrs. Val Noonan suggested that Isabella be allowed a sip of champagne. "After all," she told Vivian, "The party is in her honor. And at 14, she's a young lady herself." She chucked Isabella's chin.

"She's right, you know, you're a perfect young lady," Vivian gripped Isabella's arm and held on, as if it might float away.

Isabella watched carefully as Mrs. Val Noonan poured the champagne. Bracelets jingling, teased red hair spraying the air with the choking scent of roses, the agent brought the plastic cup to Isabella's lips, tilted it just enough so the bubbles scratched at the inside of her mouth and made a clear, hot stream to her stomach. Isabella snatched the cup from the veiny, jeweled hands and cemented it to her lips. A long smooth swallow sent the liquid through her body, calming her bones, slowing her hyper brain, making her eyes sink like pillows into her head. She seemed to have been dropped, feet first, into the living room. She looked down at her body, her knees, her fingers, felt her throat, and emitted a large sigh.

"Mmmm." She smiled at Mrs. Val Noonan, unglued herself from the corner, and thrust her body into the crowd like a volleyball. Most remarkable to her was the utter absence of fear; in its place pulsed a golden warmth toward all humankind, particularly the thirty-two guests who edged about the living room—dipping things, bumbling through mundane conversation in four-syllable words, drinks in hand, cigarettes burning, glasses and suits and stale, day-long breath. She looked into each pair of eyes and smiled, welcoming them, one at a time.

"Excuse me, sir," she pressed her small fingers into the back of a young man with a thin, sand-colored beard; he smiled and stepped aside. She spun through the crowd like a ballerina, entered the kitchen, opened the refrigerator, and counted nine bottles of champagne waiting for her. She gripped one about the neck and flew up the stairs to her bedroom, pressed the door closed, leaving sweaty prints on the white, semigloss paint. "Ouch, ouch, ouch," she said, kicking off her pinching penny loafers. She flopped down onto the bed.

She stared, rapt, at the dark, chubby bottle. Her fingers traced the crinkled gold foil, separating it carefully from the narrow neck. With bitten-down nails, she pulled at the wire basket, loosened it and threw it to the floor, then went at the large swell of cork with her teeth. Biting, pulling, until finally, like a shot, the cork slammed the wall of her teeth, the champagne forging a passage down her throat, taking with it, like driftwood, her left canine. Greasy blood pooled in her stomach, the champagne making it all seem to be only half happening as she poked her tongue at the new hole in the side of her mouth.

Hugging the cold bottle with her bare thighs, heart racing, skin hot, Isabella began to laugh. It was a low and spooky laugh, fermented from having been bottled up too long. Her head felt soft as a stick of butter left out overnight. She fell back on the bed and poured the champagne onto her face from above, swallowing what she could. The rest of it landed in a sweet yellow puddle around her.

Vivian exhausted her remaining crumbs of patience watching Alfonse drive up and down each row of the hospital parking lot. "This is the worst time to go to an emergency room," she snapped. "Saturday after midnight. All the crackpots come out. Jesus, Al. Just pull up to the door and drop us off."

"Ow," said Isabella.

"I know, baby," Vivian petted Isabella's head absentmindedly, breathing through her mouth to evade the putrid smell emanating from her daughter's pores. Alfonse waited at the entrance while the two women extracted Isabella from the backseat.

"If only we'd been able to save the tooth," said Mrs. Val Noonan, taking one side of Isabella. Vivian took the other. Together they dragged her through the automatic doors.

The waiting room smelled of booze; Isabella made her own contribution, as did Mrs. Val Noonan and Vivian. They sat her in one of the pear-shaped plastic chairs, left an empty seat to her right for Alfonse. Mrs. Val Noonan paced pathologically, smoking and frowning compassionately at Isabella, hoping this show of concern would deter a lawsuit. She wasn't sure what she'd done for which she was liable, but she knew there was something. Perhaps she shouldn't have treated a fourteen-year-old girl—no matter what her IQ—as an adult. Perhaps it was the suggestion of the party in the first place or offering that first sip of champagne. Though Vivian had been there, had gone along with it.

The glass doors swung open and Alfonse entered, smoothing his hair to the side nervously and diffidently peering about the queer room. Evelyn bounded in behind him, wearing a housedress with her faux beaver coat over it, her hair clips protruding like badly installed hardware. Her face was so compressed from irritation it looked as if she'd bit a lemon. Francesca lagged behind, wearing her grandmother's nylon pajamas under a denim jacket, her hair still sound asleep. Vivian saw them approaching and turned away to roll her eyes, appalled by their appearance. She pulled Isabella closer.

"Look who I found," Alfonse held out his arm, too exhausted to muster his usual good cheer.

"What happened? What's the matter with her? She looks drunk!" Evelyn shouted. She glared down at Isabella. Francesca glanced at her sister, then lost interest and disappeared into the haze of cigarette smoke.

Vivian explained calmly, as though she was giving directions, how Isabella had swallowed her canine.

"Jesus Christ Almighty," Evelyn wrinkled up her face in sympathetic pain and stared down at the girl's bloodied mouth.

"It was an accident," said Vivian.

"Of course it was an accident. No one swallows her tooth on purpose." Evelyn leaned in closer. "Open up. Let Grandma see."

Isabella, no longer drunk and beginning to feel irritable and sore, glared spitefully at her grandmother. The throbbing was now constant as waves in the back of her head, and there was a second, more dissonant thud beginning where her tooth had escaped.

"What's the matter, you swallowed your ear? Open your mouth!"

Isabella obeyed, and Evelyn was practically knocked down by the rancid odor of vomit, blood, and liquor. "My God!" she said, examining, from farther away, the black hole in the right side of the girl's mouth.

Isabella slammed her mouth shut.

Francesca found a dark corner near the pay phone. She slid down onto the floor, her legs extended out in front of her. "Paul, listen, Ursula had an accident," said a sweaty man between drags of his cigarette. "Yeah. St. Raphael's. We're waiting to see the doctor." It was a candy store of drama, people camped out for hours, covered in flannel blankets. There were broken bones; drugged teenagers hanging their feet over the backs of chairs; sweaty, beet-colored faces attached to shivering bodies. The floor was littered with gum wrappers and empty potato chip bags, abandoned bottles of soda and cups of coffee, cigarette butts and balled-up Band-Aids. The walls were scuffed eggshell, the windows covered in old, bent blinds with the lights of Main Street bleeding between. It looked messy, like one of her finger paintings. In the distance she saw her own family bunched together. She studied her mother's face. Her sister's head was toppled, as if she'd finally abandoned the battle to keep it upright.

Nothing in the world made any sense. Everything seemed unreal and not to be happening, as though they were all characters in a movie and when the projector was shut off, they would, all of them, herself included, cease to exist. A glowing object in the corner near the entrance to the bathroom caught her attention. It seemed to have a tiny red jewel at the center. She leaned forward on hands and knees to investigate, but it turned out to be an old gumdrop flattened by a shoe.

Evelyn turned, having suddenly realized that Francesca was no longer beside her. She scanned the waiting room. "Where's Franny?" she shouted.

"Francesca!" Alfonse popped out of his seat.

"Oh great. That's terrific," said Vivian, throwing her arms in the air.

"I'll find her," Mrs. Val Noonan offered, pleased to do something.

Evelyn watched her walk away. "Who the hell is that?" she scoffed.

"It's the agent, okay, Mother?" said Vivian, rummaging through her bag for a cigarette.

Mrs. Val Noonan was curious about Francesca, having watched her enter. Perhaps, she considered, Francesca might also be a genius, and a less self-destructive one at that. She spied the younger sister squatting in the corner of the room, staring at the floor.

"Francesca?" Mrs. Val Noonan extended her hand, "I'm Mrs. Noonan, your sister's literary agent." She pulled a Tootsie Pop from her purse. "Hungry?" she asked.

Francesca stared at the candy, then gazed into the woman's face. How old does she think I am? she wondered, taking the lollipop. She stood up and glanced in the direction of her family. "Thank you," she said.

"You're most welcome. How about we go for a walk? I have an inkling we'll be here awhile." She gestured for Francesca to follow. They stepped out into the quiet, damp night, now cooler than it had been only half an hour ago. Mrs. Val Noonan's pointy shoes clicked along the pavement. She dropped her cigarette on the ground and demolished it with her shoe, then lit another.

"I was born in New York City. Have you ever been to New York City?" she asked.

Francesca shook her head and unwrapped the lollipop.

"My family was quite well off. We lived on the Upper East Side. That may not mean anything to you, but we had an apartment on Central Park, which is quite exclusive." She took a loud drag on her cigarette. "I had an older sister, June. She was a gifted pianist. Not a genius like your Isabella, of course. But from the moment June touched that keyboard, it was spectacular! Miraculous! Even when she didn't know the notes, long before she could read music, she could pick out complicated melodies—Mozart, Chopin, Bach. It seemed she could play anything. Absolutely anything."

Francesca listened closely with vague recognition and stared down at shiny puddles and soggy yellow cheeseburger wrappers, the streetlights distorted on the wet, black pavement. They walked the perimeter of the well-lit area, not venturing anywhere dark since it was after

1:00 and the hospital was located in what Mrs. Val Noonan called a bad neighborhood.

"I was also talented."

Francesca unplucked the lollipop. Her cheeks slackened. "What did you do?" she asked.

"I played the flute."

"Oh," she said, unimpressed.

"One night," Mrs. Val Noonan sighed heavily, "June was practicing the piano. She was doing scales over and over. Da da da da da da da . . . Up. Da da da da da da da . . . Down. Over and over and over, the metronome clicking and clicking and clicking in the background." Mrs. Val Noonan rolled her eyes. "My sister," she paused, the whole thing coming back in a flood, "could practice those scales all night long." She reached in her small pocketbook for another cigarette as an ambulance pulled up. Francesca turned toward the screaming siren. The hospital doors flew open.

"I was upstairs practicing the flute," continued Mrs. Val Noonan, entranced. "My parents had gone away overnight to a wedding in the Hamptons. On my bookshelf was a giant rock I'd brought home from a trip to the Peabody Museum one summer. It was a fossil rock, said to contain a fragment from a footprint of an actual Tyrannosaurus Rex. Just a toe, really. Could have been anything."

"Supposedly, a Tyrannosaurus Rex would be the size of a football field. That's larger than this parking lot," exclaimed Francesca.

"That's interesting," Mrs. Val Noonan said absently, lingering at this last hopeful point in the story. "I still don't know what came over me. I picked up that rock and, God help me, I walked down the stairs. I heard June practicing those goddamn scales and before I knew what I was doing I slammed that rock down onto the keys, just the bass notes, where June's fingers weren't playing, of course. And in one, impulsive gesture, I destroyed the priceless baby grand Steinway that had been in my father's family for generations."

Breathless and energized, Mrs. Val Noonan shook her head and closed her eyes, the whole thing happening again behind her eyelids. She chucked her spent cigarette and stepped onto the rubber mat, forcing apart the glass doors. They re-entered the busy room.

Francesca quickly found Evelyn and sat close to her, feeling disoriented from the lateness of the night and the creepy story. She unclasped Evelyn's pocketbook and removed a stick of peppermint gum to lift the Tootsie Roll from the crevices of her teeth. Evelyn reached over and squeezed Francesca's nylon-covered knee, then looked suspiciously at Mrs. Val Noonan. The agent paced the bright room, wishing she'd thought of more appropriate conversation with the younger daughter, hoping she hadn't worsened her own standing by unearthing her dark tale.

❑   ❑   ❑

The doctor said it was likely Isabella would expel her tooth within the next couple of days. He advised poking around in the vomit, the carpet, and bedspread, to see if it might have already passed. If the tooth were found within forty-eight hours, it would be possible to reattach it. "Failing that, you'll need to see a dentist." He shrugged, smiled, and left the room, stopping in the hallway to note something on his clipboard.

Later, Vivian and Alfonse took turns checking on Isabella. Mrs. Val Noonan, having consumed a fair share of the champagne supply on her own, was beached on the largest piece of the sectional, chain-smoking Tareytons, staring off into space and chastising herself for her poor judgement. "I should have known," she said aloud. "It's a genius thing. At the very least, it's a writer thing." She tried to reunite a run in her stockings.

"How could you know?" asked Alfonse. He gathered small, pink paper plates containing soggy toothpicks and balled-up napkins.

"Look at the odds." She sat up with some effort, stubbed out her cigarette, and rearranged her legs on the coffee table to examine her ankles. She adjusted the straps on her shoes, not missing the opportunity—Vivian was upstairs checking on Isabella—to examine Alfonse's behind, which made her feel a little weak in her middle, the walnut-shaped tussy, tight and small, grabbing her attention, no matter how well it was hidden under baggy trousers.

"Hemingway, Joyce, Faulkner, O'Neill. My God, I could go on

66

forever," she watched him bend down and pick up some fallen Triscuits. "And that's saying nothing of what becomes of the women."

Alfonse looked up with knitted eyebrows. These, too, she found adorable—the little wiry hairs running in different directions.

"What about the women?" he asked, straightening up with a small groan.

"You don't want to know." She turned her attention to the staircase where Vivian was descending with a bucket, a look of deep despair revealing lines in her face that hadn't been there hours ago.

Vivian collapsed on the couch, kicked off her navy-blue pumps, and undid the sailor's bow on her perfectly matched dress. She stared at the floor.

"Cheer up baby," said Alfonse.

"Kids are naturally curious," added Mrs. Val Noonan.

"I did this sort of thing myself," said Alfonse.

"I did as well!" chimed Mrs. Val Noonan, experiencing, in that very moment, a deepening bond between her and Alfonse.

Vivian looked up slowly, dragging her scowl over each of them. Her pancake was slick as silly putty. Her bloodshot eyes were pushed far into their sockets, sketchy mascara dripping down in spider's legs. "She drank a whole bottle," she said slowly. Hatefully. Still waiting for someone to explain how this could have happened to her, when only hours ago her life had seemed blessed by some infinitely generous force.

"Well, no. No, she didn't." Alfonse had already thought this through. "Because she spilled a lot of it."

Vivian spoke slowly. "What made her do it? What made her run to the refrigerator, steal the bottle, and drink it? Open it with her teeth! She opened it with her teeth!" She looked at Alfonse as if this last part were the worst of it.

"I insist on paying the hospital bill," said Mrs. Val Noonan.

No one protested.

Emergency Room, 1986

It is a paradox that the lackluster parenting of Alfonse and Vivian DeSilva prepared Francesca for her initiation into the fraternity called American Art. Often faulted by the academy for being lazy, uneducated, and intellectually vacant, she was also said to have a minuscule vision, be overly concerned with matters sexual, and to possess "a generous, audacious talent dwarfed by an uncurious mind."[19]

The painting most often cited in discussions about deSilva's narrow scope of vision is the 1986 canvas *Emergency Room.* First exhibited in *Primal Scream,*[20] a short-lived international exhibit in 1987, *Emergency Room* depicts a late-night, inner-city trauma unit. The clean, beige check-in desk is illuminated by a stray light from an unknown source above the counter (quintessential deSilva), the overflow spilling across a scuffed linoleum floor. At the far left of the canvas, draped in darkness like a bit player waiting to make a stage entrance, is a bucket with a mop standing idly inside it.[21] Nearby, a young girl, dressed in powder-blue nylon pajamas and a denim jacket is crouched

19. Richardson, Warren. "Who's Hot (and Who's Not) on the Soho Scene." *ArtSpeak: A Monthly Guide.* New York City: Pier Publications, 1987.
20. This show represented a wide cross-section of female artists: Diane Podolske, a Polish-American who painted portraits of her eastern European ancestors; Jacqui Cane, an African-American who combined oils and collage in her depictions of inner city families; Lili Cooke, the Oscar-winning movie actress/painter; Nina Maria Pinto, a half-Indian, half-European American, whose live installment parodied the "men's movement" so popular in the late '80s and early '90s, in which men on vision quests banged drums and mimicked Native American rituals; and Francesca deSilva (half-Jew, lesbian).
21. The parallels between the mop and pail in *Emergency Room* and the erect tool in *Rake* have not gone unexplored, especially since deSilva, who often worked on two pieces at a time, created these simultaneously. See

beneath the seats, one palm extended, apparently searching for treasures on the floor.

Hurriedly sketched patrons slouch in the colorful plastic seats, their faces drawn by flashes of a thin brush, each one down-leaning and sleepy. The central focus of the painting is the bright counter where the late-night nurse is engrossed in a romance novel. The cover of the paperback is one of two focal points of the painting—a burly male embracing, rather violently, a bare-shouldered redhead whose neck is bent unreasonably, its images in stark contrast to the general wash that softens most of the canvas. Hanging above the counter, several feet to the left, beside a deconstruction of the Heimlich maneuver, is the second focal point of the painting, the public service poster picturing a racial melange of benevolent children holding hands and smiling. The words "Imagine . . . These Youngsters on Heroin," written in 1960s Fillmore East-style writing, float psychedelically above their heads."[22]

"The poster is so authentically executed, deSilva seems to have taken it down from the wall, shrunk it, and glued it to the canvas," says Dialo in *Women Paint!* "Clearly, this advertisement and the book cover beneath it superseded, in deSilva's mind, the usual horrors of an emergency room. Of course, this

Metaphor and Madness (DeVaine) and *Art That Heals* (Wright) for examinations of the symmetry in the two works.

Author's note: It is perhaps no surprise that the use of phallic imagery in de-Silva's work—specifically in these two paintings—is discussed at length by both writers.

22. deSilva was a tremendous Lennon fan. She contacted Yoko Ono for permission to use Lennon's lyrics in the piece. Ono, it turned out, was an admirer of deSilva's work and the two women became fast friends. In the two years before deSilva's death, they were several times spotted together strolling through Central Park. Ono later purchased *Virgin.*

is the beauty of the work, the element of unexpectedness, the focus on insipid reading material amid the most urgent undulations of life and death—the very hub of it all. Here, as always in a deSilva canvas, the artist's inimitable subconscious drips onto the page."[23]

One area of polemics has been whether or not the poster and book cover ever existed. Anna Leighton, a Marlboro College Art History major, class of 1995, launched a thorough investigation into both artifacts, found nothing conclusive about the poster, but did unearth a pulp novel from 1958, *The Longest Kiss*. The salacious tale recounts a man who wrenches a lesbian from her plethora of admirers by a kiss that, literally, narcotizes her for many years. It is eventually learned that he is a vampire. The woman, rendered hopelessly heterosexual, is forced by the puritanical townspeople (as recompense for her immoral deeds, many of which involved local wives and daughters) to stab a cross through the vampire's heart. (And then, of course, to kill herself in the village square, thereby restoring morality to the town.)[24]

Art aficionados, historians, and critics alike have wrestled virulently with deSilva's choice to illuminate two icons of pop culture amid what is arguably one of the most dramatic arenas of human activity: a late-night, inner-city trauma unit. Why, they try to understand, is she concerned with a public service announcement and the cover of a pulp-fiction paperback at the expense of human life?

23. Dialo, Lucinda. *Women Paint!* New York: Little, Brown, 1991, page 169.
24. Anna Leighton, "Pseudo-Realism and Lesbianism in the Work of Francesca deSilva," 1995. Paper on file in Marlboro College Library.
25. Wright, Michael. *Telling My Truth*. Minneapolis: night-night press, 1995, Introduction.

Says Michael Wright in *Telling My Truth*, "*Emergency Room* is about alienation. The explicit focus on these inanimate objects amid a roomful of people illustrates deSilva's persistent sense of isolation. The selected objects present two areas where the artist remains eternally unfulfilled: childhood happiness and hetero-sexual love."[25] He goes on to say that the poster might express the flagrant neglect of deSilva's child-hood. Obviously her parents did not know where their child was.

Lucinda Dialo offers another interpretation. "This work, more than any other by Francesca deSilva, has been ambushed by friendly fire. Scholars are so enamored of attacking one another's shoddy brainwork, that they fail to examine the significant depiction of a young girl, dressed so very closely in the style of the artist herself, scrounging about on the linoleum floor. Is there no intention, no artistic meaning to be found in the girl's positioning—far away from the other humans, far away from the central metaphors? Isn't it possible that deSilva's intent was to contrast reality (the life or death cadence of an emergency room; the lonely, unsupervised girl on the floor) with the absurd depiction of life presented in these artifacts?"

25. Dialo, Lucinda. "Counterstrokes of Violence: How Society Informs Women's Art." *Caleidoscope, A Journal of Feminist Art*, 1994.

Chapter Seven

The next three years took much from Isabella and passed it, some might say judiciously, on to her sister. Francesca was chiseled from the rough, boasting two spectacular cheekbones; an olive complexion and dark, wavy hair; a lean, strong body with thick hands and wide feet; and a smooth, watery way of walking—swishing left, pause, right, pause, always stopping a moment in the doorway to investigate before entering a situation, always taking her time. Her voice was deep and rich, particularly for a 16-year-old, escaping from a wide, crooked mouth that, while it appeared to be perpetually on the verge of smiling, rarely did. Her stance was that of a sturdy, young boy: one foot pointing sideways, one hip forward, one hand in her pocket. And in her eyes was a rare intelligence, a gaze that made people uncomfortable, impelled them to check between their teeth, look down at their zippers. Even her teachers had begun to notice her; her gym teacher saw in Francesca shadows of her younger self and took extra time to teach her the basics of meditation, in which Francesca expressed a particular interest.

In tenth grade, she won a state-wide art competition for her series of abstract finger paintings,[27] most of them concerning rodents, moss, and other relics of the outdoors. Her art teacher recommended she attend a school for the gifted, a program fully funded by the state.

---

27. Francesca persisted in this medium until the second semester of her senior year, when she discovered oil painting. Her finger paintings were strikingly complicated, often relying upon a thick application of the shiny paint, applied by the entire, flattened hand in a "sweeping stroke, almost a swash," recalls her art teacher, Molly Blume. Blume remembers that others of deSilva's paintings stood out because they "captured vital moments in nature—an ant carrying the corpse of a queen on its back, a mouse trembling in a bush, small things which, through Francesca's gaze, seemed to tell of some larger, almost epic, struggle."

Only seven students were admitted from her high school, and Francesca was to be one of them. Vivian was skeptical, but Alfonse thrilled at his daughter's talent: It alleviated his guilt (which was beginning to age him unkindly), but also, this particular talent made him feel that Francesca resembled him in some small way. His great-grandfather had been a portraitist, the sort that did harried drawings for small change. Alfonse, too, felt that had he not been strong-armed into working in the family pizzeria instead of going to college, he might have become an artist. Isabella had inherited her intellectual whatever it was from the Jewish side of the family, but Francesca's gift for art and her appreciation of natural beauty had surely sprung from his lively genes.

She was separated from the high school masses each day by a small van that took her and six other students to an after-school program downtown. There, she sat on the floor with other would-be artists and peered up at female models in bathing suits positioned high above them on a desk. In thick charcoal pencils, they sketched as the models moved in and out of unnatural poses.

Isabella, who had long since refused home-schooling, spent her afternoons reading the distraught poetry of dead females and writing articles for an underground publication, *Born to Die*. Inviting profound dread were Thursdays, the day that the DeSilva family, en masse, traveled ten minutes to Evelyn Horowitz's house, where they subjected each other to an emotionally—if not gastronomically—harrowing meal. Isabella made sure to get drunkest on Thursday afternoons; the mere thought of the weekly dinner—her family stiff as insects pinned to cardboard—impelled her down the carpeted staircase to the liquor cabinet, over and over again.

One particular Thursday, after phoning sporting goods stores and pawnshops to inquire about purchasing a gun (without a permit no one would help her), she glued the bottle to her lips and ingested large, thankful swallows, then shook her head left to right like a dog with fresh kill. She awoke to Vivian hollering: "Pumpkin! Time to go!"

Through a thick blanket of sedation she waded, propelling each foot forward from its spot in the rear. Inside her head, something seemed to have cracked. Air poured in, air that wasn't supposed to be

74

there, freezing the back of her eyeballs, the canals of her nose, the nerves at the edges of her gums. She managed to negotiate the living room and traverse the kitchen. There, hazy through the side door screen, she saw her sister—unless she was hallucinating—seated on the stoop with her legs crossed and eyes closed, her palms facing the heavens, looking like some kind of hippie.

She squinted for a closer look, then pushed the door open and tossed herself outside into the cool air. "*What* are you doing?"

"Shh," Francesca said. "I'm meditating."

Vivian appeared on the other side of the screen, wearing a stubborn, artificial smile. She, too, dreaded these family dinners and always outfitted herself with a hardened, I-dare-you-to-crack-this smile, behind which she was made of powdery sand, dispersible by a whistle of air. She carried her fake snakeskin bag by its chain link strap and smelled of Jean Nate. "Okey dokey," she pressed her face to the screen, cracking her gum compulsively. "You okay, pumpkin?" she asked Isabella.

They floated along cushioned suburban streets that separated the DeSilvas' unremarkable neighborhood from Evelyn's arguably less remarkable one. Cars passed in clusters, followed by the sound of a barking dog came on and faded, followed, maybe, by a distant siren. A sprinkler system hissed. Otherworldly, monotonous music escaped though an open window, preceding the six o'clock news. A phone rang while they waited at a stop sign. Isabella blinked, half awake. She muttered something, smacked her lips, and turned her face toward the cool air.

Alfonse helped himself to some Russell Stovers from the cabinet where Evelyn kept her mahjong supplies.

"Mama," Alfonse called to Evelyn, who was at that very moment removing the heavy Pyrex pan containing a steaming, thick, and sweet-smelling brisket from the oven. "Did you know that Francesca did a paper on Anne Frank and got an A+?"

He raised his eyebrows at Francesca.

Evelyn put the pan down on two wicker mats in the shape of palm leaves, placed next to each other on the dining-room table. She walked toward the living room, her hands huge inside yellow oven mittens. "Anne Frank? Wha—?"

"They gave me Anne Frank as a topic," Francesca stated quickly.

Isabella watched her sister with newfound envy. They seemed to have traded places. Francesca was writing papers on Anne Frank (as if she couldn't in three sentences explain what that was about) and flitting along the edges of the living room, while she, Isabella, exhausted her mental reserves just trying to stop the room from spinning.

Vivian returned from the bathroom, her smile again cemented on her face. "Okay," she said. "What did I miss?"

"We were just discussing Francesca's paper." Alfonse sat on one of the couches that was covered in thick, crunchy plastic and located in the back of the living room. Evelyn kept her long living room divided into two sections. The front housed the TV and an older, gold couch covered in a threadbare white sheet, with an olive-colored afghan she'd knitted herself always tossed over one of the cushions. Two ladderback chairs were pushed against the wall. The window was covered in a drab shutter through which the light slid in at interesting angles. Francesca liked to sit in its path and study the contrast of lines on her pant legs and hands.

"What, specifically, was your paper about?" Isabella asked menacingly.

"The relationship between Anne Frank and her sister," Francesca said, knowing how bad it sounded. She scooted up close to the TV and pulled out the little power button, then studied the tiny dot exploding from the center of the concave glass. She turned it off, waited a few moments, turned it on again. Again, she watched the light grow.

"Do you think the teacher knew about me? And that was why she picked that topic?" Isabella postulated.

"Probably," said Francesca.

"Definitely," said Vivian, protective of her poor, sodden daughter, too exceptional to function in the pedestrian world.

Francesca removed a ballpoint pen from her back pocket and absentmindedly began to darken a doodle on her knee. Alfonse came up behind her.

"Look at that," he cocked his head and chewed a caramel, examining the inky sprawl on Francesca's knee, his mouth full of candy. "Is that a good idea? Drawing on your pants?"

Francesca drew one line after another, on a slant, coloring a Navajo pattern along the bottom of a teepee. She'd been drawing Navajo designs ever since learning about the various Indian tribes of the West in history class.

"What does it mean?" asked Alfonse.

Francesca ignored him.

"What did you write about Anne's relationship to her sister?" Isabella demanded.

"Well," Francesca cleared her throat. "I theorized . . ."

"Oooh, big word—" Alfonse mussed Francesca's hair and laughed.

". . . that part of what caused Anne to act like a brat was that no one saw her for herself. She was always seen in comparison to her older sister."

"Her sister was the brat!" Isabella sat up.

"That's your opinion."

"What are you, nuts? Anne Frank was a genius!"

"Like one can't be both." Francesca tilted her head in perfect concentration.

"Where are you getting your information?" demanded Isabella.

"Bella, everyone is entitled to an opinion," said Alfonse.

"There's room for both sisters to be geniuses," said Vivian, feeling ridiculous. She knew full well Francesca was no genius, but to not go along with these ridiculous conversations was to favor one child over the other and she had vowed not to do this. She patted Isabella's sweaty head, looking down at the ruins of a beautiful fortress, a felled forest. Isabella's failure was her failure, too. She didn't know why this was so, but it was. They were both desperate to return to how things had been before that night when all was lost with one celebratory sip of champagne.

"Supper!" Evelyn called.

A basket of challah was set in the middle of the table. A brick of margarine softened in the butter tray next to a bowl of steaming kasha varnishkas. In another bowl were roasted potatoes smothered in margarine. At the opposite end of the table a plate was piled with asparagus that had been cooked so thoroughly it could be sucked with a straw. At center, in a rectangular Pyrex dish, a brisket luxuriated in dark, orange fluid, translucent pearl onions floating alongside.

"Bravo, Mama!" pronounced Alfonse upon tasting the brisket.

"What's the matter with her?" Evelyn jutted her chin toward Isabella, whose head was dipping dangerously close to her plate.

Isabella lifted her head and forced open her eyes. She surveyed herself. "What," she said.

"Nothing, sweetie. We were remarking how pretty you are," Vivian winked.

"Yeah, right," said Bella, looking down at the baggy Yale sweatshirt given to her by Vivian long ago when the prestigious school had seemed her destiny. The treads of her brown corduroys were worn to the dull, flat fabric. Her hair was greasy, her skin pale and yellow.

"You're a very pretty girl." Vivian cut a piece of tender brisket with the side of her fork.

"And so is Francesca," added Alfonse.

Francesca looked at him like he was psychotic.

"It's true!" he cried. "Isn't it?"

"Francesca's got her own style," Evelyn winked at her grand-daughter.

"You people are crazy!" Isabella ranted. "Look at us. We're ugly. A couple of ugly chicks. A couple of ugly white chicks sitting around—"

"That's enough!" interrupted Vivian.

Isabella looked down at her plate of food, smelled the sweet and sour tang of brisket. She pushed it away. "I feel sick," she said.

"Oh Jesus. Not again. I just had the carpet cleaned—" Evelyn threw her hands in the air.

"I need to lie down." Isabella held onto the table to steady herself. She waddled across the bumpy carpet to the sofa and collapsed onto her side, the springs creaking beneath her weight.

"That girl smells like a distillery," said Evelyn. "She got that from your people, Alfonse."

"My people? We don't drink. Just a little wine with dinner."

"Well, our people don't drink. Everyone knows that," said Evelyn, dipping a piece of challah in the greasy sauce.

"Francesca, go sit with your sister," Vivian said. "Now."

Francesca shoved her chair back, sighed audibly, and threw her napkin roughly onto the table, just missing the brisket pan. Capitalizing on the opportunity to appear put-upon and mistreated, she escaped happily into the stillness of the living room, and snapped on the television.

Vivian tore the cellophane sheath from a new pack of Larks, unfolded the foil corner, and slammed the pack on the edge of the table until a stick broke free.

"How can you smoke those?" Evelyn lit a True Blue. "What happened to the low tars?"

"Research shows it's all the same." She turned her body away and pulled the ashtray inches closer.

Evelyn spotted a stain on Isabella's unused knife, snatched it up, and breathed on it several times. She rubbed it furiously with her linen napkin. "What's she doing? Messing up my furniture?" She strained her head but could see nothing beyond the threshold connecting the two rooms.

"She's not *messing up your furniture*. She's not a dog."

"Thank God I left the sheet on." Evelyn took a long drag from her cigarette. "Didn't I warn you this would happen?"

"Yes, you did, Ma," said Vivian. "Every single week for three years you've reminded me that I'm a lousy mother. Just in case I forget for a minute." She stood and pushed her chair back, crashing it against the wall.

"I never said that! Don't be so sensitive." Evelyn waved the comment away. Alfonse stood up, plate in hand. "I said I was joking. Sit down!" She glared at him.

"Don't order him around like he's Daddy," Vivian snapped. She put her hand to her head, overwhelmed by a sharp pain. Slowly, she moved into the living room and sat at the foot of the couch, lifting Isabella's leaden legs to slip her lap beneath them. She patted the limp ankles, then rested her fingers over them. Her eyes met Francesca's and she winked. She heard Evelyn sigh and felt—

immediately, profoundly—guilty. What have I done to feel guilty about? she asked herself. But the answer didn't matter. She didn't need to do anything. She was guilty. Some things just were so.

Chapter Eight

At age 18, Isabella's raison d'être was suicide. Sylvia Plath and Anne Sexton had upstaged Anne Frank in her gallery of suffering. She cackled inwardly at the dark sarcasm of their words, their penetrating portrayals of human existence as a series of cleverly gift-wrapped torture devices—motherhood, marriage, life. These women understood. They understood that it was only a matter of time until the female genius ended it all: Life was not a viable option.

Still, she knew that to thrust herself from the second-story window in her bedroom onto the soft grass would be foolish, might leave her crippled, her brain furiously intact. Pills and vodka were a possibility, but the idea of choking on her own vomit was . . . unappealing. Head in the oven was impractical since the stove was electric and she did not want to burn. Her grandmother had a gas stove, but she never visited her grandmother and this seemed a rude reason to call. She thought of provoking Francesca into murdering her (she detected aggression under her sister's resigned surface), but though they weren't close, she didn't want her sister, for whom things were finally looking up, to spend the rest of her life in jail.

Some people overdosed on aspirin, by all accounts a gruesome death—cerebral hemorrhaging that lasted up to twelve hours before, bloodied and convulsive, you expire. Hanging was out of the question; she could not bear the sound of her neck snapping. (Just the thought of it made her knees cave in.) She could not imagine where she'd find a needle to pump air into her veins, and, even if she did, how horrible, inflating herself like a leaky tire. Her only option seemed to be the old car-running-in-the-garage routine. For this she'd have to wait until both her parents were out for a prolonged period. Perhaps while her mother was at the grocery store, her father at work. Fortunately, the blue Mustang still convalesced in the garage. Sometimes on Sundays her father did things to it: wiped it down, revved the motor, changed the oil, occasionally filled the tank with gas, but it never actually moved.

She liked the carbon monoxide scenario. It was romantic, metaphorical: running car with nowhere to go, symbolizing her inability to escape the boundless agony of her life. Her backup plan was the sleeping pills/vodka/plastic bag over the head method, though people had been known to wake in the night and claw themselves free, ruled by some inverted instinct that left them half-witted and at the mercy of the very people they'd hoped to avoid.

She eagerly awaited her monthly copy of *Born to Die*, "a newsletter by and for those who know death is their destiny," which arrived in a brown paper envelope with no return address. The publication featured excerpts from a forthcoming book by iconoclastic California psychiatrist Dr. Earl Mervins, a self-proclaimed expert in the holistic treatment of depressive disorders. Dr. Mervins claimed that some of his patients, having failed every attempt to chase off depression the old-fashioned way, had induced their own deaths through guided meditation. Isabella returned again and again to the story of Graham Wilson (excerpted below), used to illustrate Mervins' cutting-edge approach.

Today I met "Graham," a young man who lives at home with his two parents and older sister. At age 22, he is handsome in a plain, willowy way, with fair skin and light hair, an un-shaved face. He wears ragtag clothes and tries very hard to smile, though that pathetic simper seems only to make him appear sadder. He sleeps in his boyhood room with its NY Mets and Barbarella posters, lava light, matted black animal rug with a fake panther's head.

Graham has tried it all: slit wrists, pills, carbon monoxide, hanging from a light fixture (the ceiling gave way, sending plaster and Graham crashing to the ground). Each time, no matter how carefully he timed the suicide, something interfered, usually one of his well-meaning family members. He claims he no longer feels alive, that his spirit "long ago evacuated the premises." And who can blame it?

> Graham spends all day, every day sitting silently at the kitchen table, eating only when he cannot stand the hunger anymore. He speaks to no one. His parents and sister treat him like a piece of furniture, which, he says, furthers his despair. He recounted one incident in which his sister was talking on the telephone. Long accustomed to his lifeless ubiquity, she told the other party to hold on while she found a cigarette, then draped the receiver over Graham's shoulder to free up her hands so she could search the pockets of her coat![28]

Isabella made the page soggy with tears. She looked away from the newsletter, out across the backyard, rocked back and forth in her chair, picturing the boy's sister—long red nails, red lipstick, a low-cut shirt, smoking slim cigarettes, leaning on poor Graham as if he were a counter. She wiped her dripping nose and continued reading.

> When I arrived today, Graham explained how he had given away all of his possessions. Materialism, he said, kept him bound to the unholy world. I sat with his family for a long time, explaining Graham's decision, and how it was, in a sense, the only treatment for his "allergy to life."[29] Thus we began Step One: letting go.
>
> After 29 days, Graham finally drifted like a cloud into the next world, eyes closed, serenity softening his face. His parents told me they'd never seen him look so happy.[30]

Isabella folded the newsletter and stared out at the green lawn. Sappho, the neighbors' golden retriever, barked at a child walking by. Vivian knocked on the door. She shoved the newsletter under her mattress and tried to erase any sort of intent from her face, replacing it with a vacuous gaze.

28. Mervins, Earl. *Now I Lay Me Down to Sleep: 12 Cases of Passive Suicide.* New York: New Books, 1982, page 31.
29. Ibid., page 45. "Allergy to Life" was Mervins' terminology for his patients' affliction. He proposed treating the chronic condition the way we would any other allergy, through managed care.
30. Ibid., page 32.

"Pumpkin," Vivian called, "Mrs. Noonan is on the phone."

The agent called weekly, hoping for news of a burgeoning project.

"I have nothing," said Isabella.

Later, Vivian knocked again.

"Honey? Lunch."

Isabella heard her stomach grumbling as it had been doing more and more forcefully, for hours. Even Graham Wilson ate when he couldn't stand it any longer. And food was the only thing left in life from which Isabella exacted pleasure.

"Come in," she said.

Vivian pushed open the door with her shoulder, her face just a blur beyond the tray containing a small plate and a glass of milk. "Magic tuna, sweetie!" Her back was rounded from strain, her hair graying in parentheses at the front of her head. She walked to the window, smoothed Isabella's oily locks. "How about you and me go for a walk?"

"You and I," said Isabella, staring resolutely at the backyard. She prayed for the strength to resist the tuna fish. She reminded herself of the larger picture, how one sandwich would set her back days.

But oh, how she loved magic tuna. And she could no longer stand the empty, boiling hunger. She watched her mother slink noiselessly out of the room, and the moment she heard the clasp on the door engage, she flew out of her rocking chair, snatched the sandwich off the tiny cake plate, and devoured it, swallowing all thoughts of how she was, at that very moment, prolonging her suffering. The tuna was on seeded rye bread, her favorite, perfectly seasoned with mayonnaise and paprika, the celery adding a dependable crunch. She tossed her head back, closed her eyes, and chewed slowly, her taste buds deceiving her into feeling happy.

She drank the glass of milk, wiped her upper lip, and found she felt energized, in need of activity. She skated in white socks along the white floor, peered out the window at the same scene she'd been looking at her entire life: flat grass and flowers, the edge of the neighbors' deck, old Mrs. Weinstein's wheelchair folded against her garage.

Since Graham had given away his possessions to free himself from the trappings of life, Isabella decided she would do the same. She walked down the hall to her sister's bedroom and knocked. After several

84

seconds, Francesca opened the door, her head arched beneath two thickly padded headphones. The spiral cord was stretched to its limit, connecting her to the record player in the corner.

"What?" she shouted over the music.

"Take them off," Isabella mouthed, tugging on the curly cord. Francesca removed the headphones and held them at her side. Tinny music emanated from the speakers.

"I wonder if you want anything. Of mine," Isabella said.

Francesca rolled her eyes and put her headphones back on. She turned away from her sister, but did not close the door.

"Wait. Wait." Isabella climbed the stairs and followed her sister into the dark, low room. Things had changed in there. On the walls were a series of Francesca's odd finger paintings. Isabella still couldn't figure out what all the fuss was about; anyone, it seemed to her, could smear paint across a sheet of shiny paper. But could her sister write a poem? Just one! Never mind thirty-six! Never mind sustaining the voice of an authentic, internationally celebrated hero.

Another wall was smattered with charcoal sketches. A few depicted the neighbor's dog (sort of), though most were of Lisa Sinsong, recognizable immediately by her wide forehead and confused, obdurate expression. In one drawing a chess piece with a face stood beside the neighbor's dog.

Isabella pointed to it. "Weird." While clearly Francesca was becoming increasingly peculiar (who knew it was possible?), at the same time, she seemed capable of communicating something necessary, something urgent that was rattling around in her brain. Isabella recognized this ability at once and envied it. She wondered if talent and the gift for self-expression had fled her own messy mind and taken refuge in her sister's. After all, they lived in such proximity. Perhaps—she found herself staring at Francesca's head—it was less cluttered in there.

"What do you want, Bella? I'm working."

"You're working?" Isabella laughed. "On what?"

"On my work." On the bed, a large sketchpad was opened. Another picture of Lisa Sinsong.

"It's a little obsessive," said Isabella, raising her eyebrows.

"You would know."

"You could draw me instead."

"Yeah. Thanks."

"Anyhow. I came to see if you want my stuff."

"What stuff?"

"Any of it. I'm giving all of it away. I'm giving it away . . ." she had rehearsed this lie, "because I'm joining a new religion."

"What religion?"

"It's complicated. It would take too long to explain. And you're working. Suffice it to say, whatever you don't take, I'll be giving away to charity."

Francesca stared at her sister, searching for the truth. She didn't want to go to all the trouble of taking off her headphones, pausing the needle at the fourth cut of Born to Run, and following her sister down the hallway, just to be hoodwinked.

"I've already called the truck," said Isabella.

"What truck?"

"The Goodwill truck! I told you!" She padded down the three steps and out into the hallway, then gestured emphatically—a big sweeping wave of her arm—for Francesca to follow. Slowly, cautiously, Francesca traversed the hallway and stepped into the white room. There was only one thing she wanted, and she spanned the walls until she spotted it hanging from a hook on the back of the door. She pointed to the white robe, faded to a tired yellow.

"That?" said Isabella. This was going to be harder than she thought.

"You said anything."

Isabella had not expected to give away her fluffy bathrobe that always smelled so good, like fabric softener and bleach. Before she could reconsider, she popped up, rushed to the door, took down the robe from the peg, and draped it over her arm. She brought it, like a baby, to Francesca.

"Are you sure?" asked Francesca.

Isabella smiled for the first time in days. Her skin stretched in new directions. "You could wear it while you draw."

"Thanks," Francesca said. She patted Isabella's shoulder a few times and left quickly, holding the robe to her cheek. She bolted the attic door behind her.

Isabella felt a profound lack of clutter, like a cool breeze passing through the center of her body, where previously had been an obtrusion. Craving bigger change, she slipped her body between the twin bed and the wall and pushed with all her strength, until the stiff wheels of the iron frame screeched across the whitewashed floors, etching gray tracks into the middle of the room. She swung the bed around and pressed it against the other wall, suddenly remembering the tiny window at the base of the wall, just inches above the floor of the old and oddly configured house. Panting from exertion, she slapped herself in the head. "Why didn't I think of this ten years ago?" she exclaimed as she bent down and peered through the smoky window, like Alice at the threshold of the tea party. Her giant knees pressed against the pane.

Through this porthole could be seen the very inside of the house next door, the kitchen nook, where the blinds were conveniently open. The light was on over the kitchen table; newspapers were scattered. Isabella reached into her nightstand and removed the opera glasses she'd received one year for Christmas. Through the lenses, she peered at specks of dust on the drop-leaf table, studied its well-oiled surface. A butcher-block counter joined two corner walls, its surface cluttered with mail. The door to the pantry was ajar, probably because someone had been in a hurry. Or else, there was a slob on the premises.

She discovered that by moving her face all the way to the right of the window, she could see into the living room as well. She concentrated her gaze on a figure sunk into the futon couch. It was the blond, leaning back plaintively, her eyes closed, her mouth barely moving. What was she doing? Isabella struggled to release the rusted window lock, then with a grunt, lifted the window up several inches along the rusty chain. Impatiently, she swatted away cobwebs and gritty black fragments of leaves, and lifted the storm window. She heard—very soft, soft as a breeze—a soprano singing an aria in a voice strained with impossible heartache and loneliness. It brought tears to her eyes. She watched the blond neighbor, her head in her hands, her bent knees spreading wide apart, as if they could no longer keep themselves together.

She didn't even notice herself reaching for the miniature spiral notebook with its shiny green cover, nor did she remember sliding the Bic pen off her nightstand and pressing it down until the ink sprang to life. Quietly, she wrote: *Opera at 2:30 pm. Faded jeans. Blond hair with M-shaped cowlick.* As she scribbled, the Big One entered the living room and sat timidly at the other end of the couch, her big hands spread over her knees. *Footsteps big enough to shake the house,* Isabella wrote. They seemed to be discussing something very terrible, perhaps death or the loss of love after all these years, and she longed to know what it was that plagued them in the middle of the afternoon, in such a quaint, quiet house.

She jotted these questions in blue ink, invented their answers in red: The blond, a.k.a. the Little One, had loved an opera singer, Thalia, who tormented her, threw things at her, made passionate love to her, then left her for a man. Sappho, the golden retriever, was a stray who showed up one day on the doorstep. If the Big One had her way, she'd have brought home every stray in sight; she carried biscuits in her knapsack to curry their favor, preferring animals to all people. Except the blond. And who could blame her? She began to imagine the daily rituals of the lesbians next door, who had suddenly become her reason for living: *Grape-Nuts for breakfast. One reads, other brings in laundry. Hangs clothes on drying rack: jeans, sweaters, bras. Holds hips, moves her to side. Raises arms overhead, big yawn. Butt shaped like pumpkin.*

Mrs. Val Noonan was ecstatic when Isabella finally accepted her call. "Isabella! Darling!" she effused, her voice a tightrope of tension.

"I'm working on a new book."

"That's fabulous! Marvelous! I knew you'd come around. You see? Isn't it all worth it, then? This being a genius? Isn't it? When you finally sit down and let it all spill out on the page?"

So many questions, thought Isabella. Clearly they're not meant to be answered.

"Tell me what it's called."

"It's called . . ." Isabella hesitated, inventing a title. "It's called . . . *A Gift to the Universe.*"

"It is? That's fabulous! What a wonderful title! I'm so pleased for you, honey. You're such a tremendous talent. I knew you'd find your voice again. Pick up that pen. And not a minute too soon. It isn't fair, Bella darling, but if too much time passes between volumes, well, the public is very fickle. Do you understand?"

"Yes," lied Isabella, who had long ago stopped listening, distracted by the entire book unfolding in her brain. "I have to go," she said.

"Go. Go ahead. Skedaddle! Happy writing! I'll call next week."

Isabella wrote love poems to the blond in which she made observations about her sorrow. She mused how someone so beautiful could be so sad. She imagined the neighbors' morning routine (had to, since they closed the shades at night and often did not remember to open them again until early evening, when one or the other arrived home from work), describing how the blond—dressed only in a T-shirt, the hem reaching just below her underwear, tickling the tops of her thighs—delicately dipped two slices of rye bread into the toaster slots, poured steaming hot coffee into a round, white mug, then wrapped her clean hands around the bowl and sipped. Her breasts were firm. Her skin glowed like the inside of a burning candle.

Isabella seemed no longer to need sleep. Still, the thought of total sleeplessness made her nervous—as though sleep were one of the few vestiges of humanness she still possessed, and here it was, slipping away like all the others. Determined to rest, she'd switch off her bedside lamp at three or four in the morning, only to find herself wide-eyed and sharp-brained. She'd flick the light on again, retrieve her pen, masturbate once, twice, sometimes four times, continue to pour the words out on paper as if the book were already written in her head, just waiting to be captured like some witless animal. When she could not write, she reorganized her room, read Sylvia Plath, shaved her legs, curled her hair, applied her mother's makeup, removed it so she could apply it again. Sometimes, late at night, she'd run downstairs in sweatpants and a sweatshirt, barefoot, and take a few swigs of Smirnoff before heading out under the opalescent sky. She'd run her fingers across the neighbors' dusty aluminum siding, play with their driveway gravel, tickle their flowers. Sappho would bark. Mrs. Weinstein's cat flared its eyes from atop a metal trash can. Energy flushed her like fever. Even liquor was rendered impotent against her vim.

Sometimes in the afternoons, when Francesca returned from school, Isabella would knock briskly on her sister's door. She'd sit on the edge of Francesca's bed, knee shaking, and in a high-pitched voice, her eyes lit like jack o' lanterns, ramble in comma-less sentences about her book. And then this will happen, she'd say. And when that happens they'll do this, which will make everything—here she'd mushroom her arms up above her head instead of uttering the word (it seemed, to Isabella, more powerful). Francesca would tolerate these chatty intrusions, mildly interested. Most of the time she would continue to sketch, half-listening to her record player, not ungrateful for the company, and aware that her sister was somehow afflicted.

Barely breathing between paragraphs, Isabella described her book to Mrs. Val Noonan on the telephone: "The two women have a picture-perfect life: whispered affection and hours of gentle caresses, pillow-talk late at night, long walks and gourmet meals. One cooks, the other does the dishes. Everything blissful. Got it? Until one day a runaway teenage girl climbs up onto the front porch, deposits her wrinkled, brown paper bag behind the pot of geraniums, and rings the doorbell. She throws herself into the blond's arms, tells some crazy story about having been raped by someone who called himself Jesus."

"Jesus?" interrupted Mrs. Val Noonan.

"The women are devastated," Isabella continued. "They take the girl in, draw a bath for her. Later, as they watch her sleeping like an angel, clutching a teddy bear, they think despairing thoughts about humanity. Their faith is shattered. They know it wasn't really Jesus, but still."

"Yes, still."

"Who would call himself Jesus and do that to a little girl?"

"Indeed—" Mrs. Val Noonan took a long drink, scribbled something on a piece of paper.

"They give the girl her own room at the top of the stairs, storing, you know, the sewing machine, the tool chest, musical instruments, etc. etc. But the girl ends up sleeping between them in the queen size bed, reassured by the two warm bodies on either side of her, the syncopated breathing."

"So they're, are you saying they're . . ."

"What," interrupted Isabella.

"They're not lesbians?"

"Of course they're lesbians. What—am I going too fast for you?"

She described the minutiae—what sort of lamp was beside the girl's bed. What sort of cocoa she drank at night. She was not yet sure, she explained at a pace quicker than cricket's legs, whether the girl left the lumps floating around in the top of the cocoa or massacred them into submission. Also, she wasn't sure whether the blond smelled like roses or spice. And how often did the women have sex? What sort of sex did they have? Where was the girl while they did it? Who placed the gob of Herbal Essence shampoo on the girl's head when they bathed her? There was still research to do, she explained.

Mrs. Val Noonan had long since stopped scribbling, finished her drink, and poured another.

"Fall passes into winter, winter into spring," continued Isabella. "And then, tada, in April, the Big One, sporting new gardening gloves the blond gave her for Christmas, goes outside onto the porch to turn over the soil in the geranium pot. (This, I guess, is what you people call the climax.) She pulls the pot toward her and discovers, behind it, pressed against the front of the house, the brown paper bag left by the girl so many months ago. She lifts the bag, soft as tissue, and opens it slowly, expecting an old sandwich or rotten fruit. Instead she finds $20,000 in hundred dollar bills." Isabella stopped, breathless. "And that's all I know," she said.

There was silence on the line. Isabella heard ice crack under the heavy heat of scotch. "Tell me, dear," said Mrs. Val Noonan, "Where does the money come from?"

"Don't know," said Isabella cheerfully.

"I see." The sounds of ice against glass. "And what do the women do with the money?"

"I told you," snapped Isabella. "I haven't worked out all the details."

"No, no, of course not," said Mrs. Val Noonan, her voice straining with supplication. "And why would you? It's a work in progress. Why, not only that, it's the *first draft* of a work in progress."

"I have to go," said Isabella, suddenly exhausted, as though she'd been running for weeks, and only now had stopped to sit down. She found the mechanics of storytelling—plot, character development, etc.—frustrating and upsetting, preferred to focus on the passages that made her flutter inside. Descriptions of the lovely room at the top of the stairs where the runaway girl lived. Dust bunnies. Nicks in the shag carpeting. The sun pushing through the small, perfect window. Sloped ceilings, wind chimes and mobiles, faint opera rolling up through the radiator pipes. And, of course, the blond.

Chapter Nine

On Francesca's 18th birthday, Evelyn arrived at dinnertime with the archetypal yellow cake—cloudy lemon filling, grainy red roses on white frosting, Happy Birthday Francesca sprawled in lazy jelly script at a dissecting angle. Alfonse had completely forgotten. He cursed himself, but more fervently cursed Vivian, whom he felt merited a greater portion of the blame, being the mother and, thus, the one charged with keeping track of things. It was because of that damn job, pulling her in a million different directions, he muttered while ordering the pizza. He scrambled to make the house festive, unraveling streamers already marred with scotch tape and blowing up a few balloons he found on the top shelf of a kitchen cabinet, surplus frippery from Isabella's last birthday celebration.

Vivian was working as a paralegal at Kasselbaum Kasselbaum Steele, a large New Haven law firm. She worked late each evening, usually returning home around midnight, still nursing a ten-inch tall coffee from 7-Eleven, still speeding from the No-Doz or Dexatrim she'd taken at lunch time to carry her through the afternoon. Up, up, up she was, all through the long, useless hours between cogency and sleep. Bug-eyed in Alfonse's reading chair, her foot tapping restlessly, she stared at the TV lineup: the end of Late Night, Don Kirshner, sometimes a horror movie or some madcap comedy with Doris Day and Rock Hudson. Occasionally, she'd still be there when Davey & Goliath aired at 6 a.m., her face tinted a chilly, sleepless blue.

The marriage was crawling toward its demise. In a last-ditch effort, Vivian had signed them up for a Marriage Encounter weekend in the Catskills; they were scheduled to leave the next morning. But asperity settled over the hopeful weekend before it had begun. Alfonse was disgusted that Vivian had forgotten Francesca's birthday. He left a message for her at work and hurried the Valiant down to the shopping center, hoping that somewhere other than the pharmacy and the liquor store might still be open. He arrived as the office supplies store was closing up and managed to quickly select a box of charcoal pencils from the window display. Driving home with the silver foil-wrapped package beside him on the seat, a curly green ribbon taped to its center, his mood changed. He felt he'd done right by his daughter, and instead of his gift being a last-minute, scrambling purchase, he decided he'd selected it carefully, after much deliberation.

Isabella was hard at work on *A Gift to the Universe*. She'd imposed upon herself a period of confinement during which she could leave her room for only five-minute intervals. She had determined that anything she needed to accomplish outside her room could be done in five minutes or less: a shower, a snack, a quick pee, or even a bowel movement, a long swallow of vodka. At 5:47, when Alfonse left the house to purchase Francesca's gift, while Evelyn was cleaning the kitchen and Francesca was sequestered in the attic, Isabella, who had remembered her younger sister's birthday all on her own, slipped downstairs and deposited a card on the dining room table. Made from a sheet of shirt cardboard folded in half, it pictured Isabella's own attempt at artistic expression—an abstract black and white something or other that resembled the mid-section of an insect. Inside she'd written in black ink: Happy Day of Inception, and signed it, as she signed everything, "I." She returned to the sanctuary of her room.

The pizza arrived. Evelyn, Alfonse, and Francesca gathered around the small table.

"I'm starving!" Francesca declared, grabbing at a steaming slice and burning the roof of her mouth. She took a long drink of Pepsi, and sat with her mouth open, waving her hand in front of it.

Alfonse wiped his mouth with a napkin. "Well, I just don't know about tomatoes this year," he said as if they'd been immersed in this topic. "Last year we had that terrible disease, so it might be a good idea to skip a year. Give the soil a rest."

Evelyn looked up at him, the point of the pizza in her mouth, her chin close to the plate. She turned to Francesca and rolled her eyes. "Since when does soil need to rest?" she said. "I got schvarzas moving into my neighborhood." Her open mouth displayed flakes of charred crust.

"What?" Alfonse leaned over, detecting German.

"Schvarzas. Blacks," said Evelyn. "Blacks moved in right across the street. Right where I can see them, going to church on Sunday in those pastel-colored schmattas they wear with the big productions on their heads. I don't know how they all fit into one car, the women have such big rear ends." She chewed heartily with her mouth open, crumbs filling the spaces between her slack gums.

Francesca imagined her mother pulling into the driveway, removing a package from the backseat. She had no idea what was contained in the package, nor did she care. Something large and cumbersome that would require her mother to back through the door in order to get it inside. Something that could not possibly have been selected with Isabella in mind.

"And don't think I don't know what just happened to my property," continued Evelyn. She whistled like a bomb landing. "I might as well burn the house down and collect the insurance."

The telephone on the kitchen wall rang loudly. Alfonse jumped up, almost knocking his chair backward. "I know who that is . . ." he said in a singsong, then winked at Francesca. "Hello . . ." he said in the same teasing voice. His eyes looked away as he held out the receiver. "Francesca, baby, it's for you."

Francesca put down her slice of pizza and stood. She moved slowly around the perimeter of the table, took the receiver from her father. "Thanks, Papa," she said, then moved into the hallway. "Hello?" she said, half asking.

"Hi. It's me," said the grown-up voice on the other end, followed by a long exhale.

"What?"

"Don't you remember me? Lisa Sinsong. I called to wish you a Happy Birthday."

Francesca pulled the phone cord taut through the center of the small kitchen. She opened the doors to the linen closet and stepped inside, her nose inches from a stack of crisp sheets. "Thanks," she whispered.

"It is your birthday, right?"

"Yeah. How did you know?"

"I'm a genius, stupid. I remember things. How about we get together and party?"

Francesca hesitated. She spread her fingers against the clean sheets, her moist palm drawing out the sweet smell of laundry detergent. "My parents are going away tomorrow," she said before she could think better of it.

"No shit, that's perfect. I'll take the bus. Meet me at the shopping center at noon. Okay?"

Francesca nodded, her heart racing.

"OKAY?" repeated Lisa.

"Okay. See you tomorrow." Francesca moved out of the dark closet, back into the lit kitchen. Her arm lifted; her hand deposited the receiver onto the wall phone. But she was nowhere to be found.

"Was that your boyfriend?" Evelyn teased.

"It was a girl," Alfonse said quickly, looking closely at his daughter, noticing, unpleasantly and for the first time, that she was no longer 7, 8 or 9, or 10, 11, 12, even 13. That there was, in fact, nothing improper about Francesca having suitors. Still, he could not picture them. What sort of boy would she prefer? A big boy. Athletic? No. Artistic? Maybe. This seemed most likely, but even this—his tall, strong daughter next to a sensitive, long-haired boy in pale jeans and a T-shirt—seemed incongruous. Anyhow, it had been a girl's voice.

"What's his name?" Evelyn persisted.

"I don't have a boyfriend." Francesca's face reddened. She pushed some pizza crusts around on her plate, wanting the subject to change.

"Let me guess . . ." Evelyn made a humming sound, "Larry."

Francesca opened her eyes wide and jutted her chin forward, an exaggerated display of disgust. "Gram!" she cried. This wasn't the worst thing, people thinking there were boys, that boys posed some healthy, normal threat. She blushed and giggled and looked down at the table, as if it were all true: She had a boyfriend, maybe his name was Larry, but she was keeping him a big, normal secret. She could call Lisa back, say that her parents had changed their minds. Or she could just not be at the shopping center. Ridiculous: the idea that she'd leave Lisa standing there, forlorn and frightened—though there had been not the slightest hint of forlorn or frightened in Lisa's cocky tone.

How strange that only the night before, sprawled on her bed in the sleepy purple light, she had tapped out the letters of Lisa's name with her toes under the covers, as if she'd been beckoning in a secret code. Lisa rarely produced a conscious thought, though she was still the imagined audience whenever Francesca did something impressive—when she'd won the art contest, hit a home run in softball, sped her bike fearlessly down a steep hill. Sometimes, walking across the linoleum tiles in the school hallways, Francesca spelled Lisa's name absentmindedly, assigning a letter to each alternating panel of color.

"Ready, Freddie?" Evelyn called from the living room. Alfonse hopped up and turned off the lights, grinning as Evelyn entered from the kitchen threshold with the cake extended in front of her, her face tilted away from the groping flames.

"Happy Birthday . . ." she sang in brassy, Ethel Merman style. Alfonse joined in enthusiastically, singing off-key. Evelyn moved away from him, singing louder to drown him out.

Cigarette Burns, 1987

Hailed as the definitive work of the pseudo-realist[31] movement in American art, *Cigarette Burns* is arguably the most popular of deSilva's paintings. Its presence is ubiquitous on dormitory walls, postcards, café placemats, and in college classes, where it is subjected to endless deconstruction. Many feel that *Cigarette Burns* is her purest, most intellectually satisfying work. It is, interestingly, also the only remaining painting that depicts no human subject. Human life is implied, even central, but no longer on the premises. The viewer peers, like a voyeur at a crime scene, into the soft center of a bed, at the magnified fibers of a stained bedspread, dusty pastel flowers smothering its surface. At center are three large cigarette burns, grotesque and greedy as wounds, their insides black and ragged, bleeding out into brown bruises. At their borders, puffs of fiberfill escape the confines of the quilted panels. A flare of light spills across the bed, a light so hotly yellow, so shiny and slick, it reeks of Armageddon or, at the very least, Hell. Paul deVaine compared it to the aura felt by migraine sufferers just before the onset of a brutal headache.[32]

31. *Author's Note:* Paul DeVaine coined the term "pseudo-realism," defining it as a melange of reality, hyperreality, and meta-reality. See DeVaine's *Metaphor and Madness* (Chicago, ARTBooks, 1994), pp. 60–79 and *Counter Reality: the Collapse of Contemporary Sentimentalism,* in MASSART, Jan. 1995. deSilva is considered the foremother of the pseudo-realist movement. Though elements of this style predated her (Francis Bacon is said to have been an influence), Lucinda Dialo, in *Women Paint!,* claims "deSilva was the first to merge subtext, sarcasm, and reality, achieving an unprecedentedly literate product." *Women Paint!* New York: Little, Brown, 1991, pages 97–113.
32. deVaine, Paul. *Metaphor and Madness.* Chicago: ARTBooks, 1994, page 399.

Conversely, *Village Voice* art critic Michael Reilly finds *Cigarette Burns* to be a facile painting. He calls its focus myopic and its lack of human presence "narcotizing," asserting that it is precisely this drugged effect that has invited such indiscriminate acceptance: "It is the only painting of deSilva's that doesn't tell you the naked truth. For example: Two girls fucked in this bed (*What She Found*). Or: I'm your worst nightmare (*Bunyan*). Or even: 'Every-woman' is crazy (*Study of White Figure in Window*). In "Cigs" as it came to be called, she sacrifices depth for simplicity and palatability and succumbs to her own internalized homophobia. A savvy strategy, it turns out, since this remains her most popular canvas. Massachusetts has recently secured the copyright for its use in an upcoming anti-smoking campaign. What would deSilva, a pack-a-day en-thusiast, have said about that?"[33]

Conversely, Cynthia Bell, in *Lesbians in Oil,* con-ducts a thorough deconstruction of the painting. Hav-ing theorized that the setting for *Cigs* is a cheap motel, "the choice of *three* burns," she posits, "is no coincidence or simple aesthetic choice; the number three represents other, a third gender. It symbolizes deSilva's ambivalence about her gender identity."[34]

Larry Barnes, author of the *Daily News* column "Free Places to Take the Kids," became obsessed with the painting after viewing a posthumous exhibit of deSilva's work at MOMA in 1993. His outré disap-proval of her paintings led him to implore readers who were admirers of the artist to write in and tell him

33. *Village Voice*, "Big Dyke on Campus—the Whitewashing of Francesca de-Silva," Michael Reilly, 1989.
34. Cynthia Bell, *Lesbians in Oil* (Atlanta: Amazon Press, 1991), 69.

him why. "Convince me,"[35] he wrote in a special addendum to his usual column, calling it "Free Places *Not* to Take the Kids." He coined deSilva the "demented offspring of the feminist movement . . . All you have to be is angry, female, and dead, it seems, to get a show in New York these days,"[36] ranted Barnes. Interestingly, he deemed *Cigarette Burns* the only piece worth viewing in the whole collection, calling it a "meditation on one of the less discussed dangers of smoking."[37]

Lucinda Dialo writes of *Cigarette Burns,* "The painting is about sex. It is evidence of sex; it is the absence of sex and in its place the memory of sex; it is what is missing reminding us of what once was. It is emptiness and loss and desire for sex. It is a cheap bedspread. It is disappointment, thwarted desire, everything gone, all options exhausted. Like the last rest stop on a dark, monotonous highway, a fleabag motel with browned windows and a sign on the gravel lot that says 'Keep Off the Grass.'"[38]

35. *New York Daily News,* "Free Places *Not* to Take the Kids," Larry Barnes. Feb. 13, 1993. 46.
36. Ibid.
37. Ibid. *Author's Note:* deSilva's retrospective was one of the most well attended in MOMA's history. The show was mounted smack in the middle of the controversy surrounding the National Endowment for the Arts. In spite of what is widely considered to be a pervasive, deviant sexuality in deSilva's work, Jesse Helms, the father of the movement to stop funding the arts, was conspicuously uninterested. Some attributed this to deSilva's fondness for cigarettes (several of her paintings incorporate cigarettes) and Helms' ties to the tobacco industry.
38. Dialo, Lucinda. *Women Paint!* New York: Little, Brown, 1991, page 375.

Chapter Ten

Isabella stood on the wall of the bathtub peering out the window as her father loaded up the Pontiac with two suitcases and a Styrofoam cooler. She still did not believe that the car would actually leave the premises, hover over the wide street, then disappear. She ran to the edge of the landing and grabbed the banister. "Bon Vivant!" she waved to her mother.

Vivian looked puzzled. "Do you mean 'Bon voyage,' honey?"

Isabella bristled. "Of course not. I know my French. I was being wry."

"Of course you were. How silly and literal of me. 'Bon vivant!"

"Goodbye, lovebug. Take care of your sister. Keep writing!"

"I will," Bella waved again, cocked her head in a gesture which she hoped indicated appropriate sorrow.

"Ciao, Bella," Alfonse bowed in the doorway. He loved to don an accent when saying this, blow kisses, and bow like an opera singer. He was tall and tidy in his black wool overcoat, black wool scarf, and the ridiculous fisherman's hat he wore every day since he'd found it in the basement in a garbage bag full of clothes earmarked for Goodwill.

Isabella listened for the sound of the engine turning over, so quiet she almost missed it, then gravel crunching under the rubber tires. When she was certain they'd gone, she ran to her bedroom and closed the latch on the door. She pulled a shoebox from beneath her bed, upon which she'd written PROPERTY OF I. DESILVA. DO NOT DISTURB in thick, black marker. With reverence, she lifted the lid and removed the most recent issue of *Born to Die*. The six-page newsletter, on white paper, was stapled in the upper left corner, printed in blue on a mimeograph machine. *Always be grateful for the mind you have. For though it has brought you grief and torment, it also affords you the means to end your anguish,* read a bold call-out. The paper had recently been sold to a grassroots Christian organization called KIND (not an acronym), and the Letters to the Editor column reflected readers' concerns that the new editor, Joseph Paul, was trying to push them away from suicide and toward God—a far cry from the old editor's monthly homage to some great artist or thinker who had ended his or her own suffering with an exclamation point. Joseph Paul, conversely, concluded each issue with a Christian prayer and the admonition: "Praise God, since the truth of His existence will soon become more than mere speculation."

Now is a good time for a drink, thought Isabella. Her sister was off somewhere, probably dissecting a frog or poking her fingers in an anthill. Her parents: gone. How delightful it was to be truly alone. It almost made her want to live.

"Perish the thought!" she cried and headed for the liquor cabinet. She opened the two doors with great fanfare, as though behind them a ballroom awaited. "Ahhh," she sighed, deeply moved by the tall figures of glass—multishaped, variously colored—each filled to a different level. She considered lining them up across the floor, ordered according to the amount they contained, or, more interestingly, according to her opinion of them, then playing them with a spoon, like a xylophone.

She stopped and recalled her sobering purpose. How easily one became sidetracked.

Isabella took a long and mournful swallow of vodka, then lowered the heavy bottle with a thud, and stared sadly at the white wall before her. She wished she'd kissed someone. Just once. The small woman in the house next door would have been her first choice. Though she'd have settled for that policeman who picked her up one late afternoon after she'd drunkenly wandered miles from home, and dropped her off in time for dinner. The Chinese girl from the party all those years ago. Even her sister. She puckered her lips and closed her eyes, imagined a mouth against hers. Would it be warm or cold? Wet or dry? Would the skin feel like suede or denim? And how hard would she press? Where would her body grow weak, where would it ache for more?

103

She pulled out the newsletter, re-read a sidebar on composing and placing the suicide note. The note must be carefully executed, emphasized the author, and only when all else was firmly in place.

> Make sure to place it where it will be found. You can't imagine how many families find the corpse hanging or in the car or shot through the head and spend weeks not only mired in grief, but confounded as to what drove their loved one to do it. All because the culprit—the incesting stepfather, loan sharks, homosexuality—remained unknown due to poor placement of the note.
>
> Determine places frequented by your addressee. Some suggestions reported by our readers: the bathroom mirror, the telephone receiver, the refrigerator. For those of you whose families employ a maid or butler, you may choose to leave the note in their, no doubt, capable hands, but do not blind yourself to the possible pitfalls of involving a "messenger" (e.g., latent hostility or class rage, meddling, absentmindedness, to name a few possible obstacles).
>
> Never place the note on or around the toilet, on pillows (many people get into bed with the lights already out), in a car (what if they are so devastated by your expiration, they never again leave the house?) or on a piece of furniture with cushions. If you must drop it in the mail, always use certified. Return receipt, for obvious reasons, would be gratuitous."[39]

"Well," said Isabella, "No note for me. What would I write? *I am a miserable, disturbed genius with no hope? Goodbye? I'm sorry?* or *I'll miss you? Don't cry for me?* No, I cannot. I will not leave them eternally comforted by lies. Better they suffer with the truth."

She thought for another moment. *Perhaps a note that says thank you.* She pictured writing it, placing it somewhere for Vivian to discover.

39. Van, Vince. *Born to Die*, "Tiny Technicalities that Can Sabotage Your Suicide." March 1981. The author, not surprisingly, committed suicide shortly after this writing. What was surprising was his method: ingesting huge amounts of salt, inducing a sudden, violent heart attack.

Thank you for what? For the bizarre genes? Alcoholism? An obscenely high IQ? Severe emotional problems? Misanthropy? Sexual perversion? Voyeurism? An intense and persistent awkwardness around people?

Instead, she skipped this step and decided to move on to the last task: the final meditation. She sat comfortably on her bed, back to the wall, and closed her eyes, thrusting her thoughts as far back as the imagination would fling them, conjuring up early memories. There were those delightful afternoons spent on the living-room floor while her mother ironed or watched soap operas in the bedroom of the old apartment. When Francesca was still a tiny baby imprisoned in her playpen, Isabella would sit, much in the same way she was seated now, and concentrate hard until her body began to float, lifting itself into the air and hovering inches above the carpeting, steady as a humming-bird, for several seconds at a time before gently drifting back down.

Life had seemed so full of promise.

❏ ❏ ❏

Francesca untied her denim jacket from around her waist and passed her arms through the sleeves, snapped it across her chest. It was early on Saturday; the sun spread like lava over the Connecticut hills. She turned onto busy Whalley Avenue, careful to remain to the right of the white line that separated the road from the pedestrian world. At the top of the hill, the high school looked like a prison, squat and beige, surrounded by a chain link fence. Cigarette butts escaped underneath the jagged meshing.

She wanted to appear just-arrived when the bus pulled up in front of Friendly's, so she roamed the shopping center, feigning interest in the darkened windows with For Rent signs, kicking aside flattened soda cups. In the window of the stationery store was the same box of pencils her father had given her the night before. Two big-bellied salesmen in the appliance store rested their Friendly's coffee cups on top of unsold washing machines. In the window of the Puppy Center, a tiny beagle slept inches from its stool, its water dish overturned, wet and matted newspaper strips lining the bottom of its cage. Behind the shopping center, the ancient paper factory spewed clouds of smoke.

When she turned toward the bus stop, Lisa was waving. "Here I am!"

She wore a short skirt and gaudy, flesh-colored platform shoes with chunky heels. Thick straps held her small feet in place; her dark red toenails peeked between them like prisoners. Cheap plastic sunglasses made her look, at first, like a movie star, and then, as Francesca neared, like a hooker. There was nothing identifiably different, nothing Francesca could point to and say "Aha!" Yet Lisa was entirely altered, as though someone had tossed her in the air like confetti. Tough and a little trashy. She looked like one of those girls in TV movies who runs away and takes up with perverted men, then kills them.

They walked home slowly, cutting through the loading/unloading parking lot in back of the stores. Lisa's voice was throaty from cigarettes, every sentence punctuated by an expletive. She referred to her father as the pig, the prick, the pervert, and the pedophile. She pushed the hair off her face, her many silver rings flashing through her black mane like lights in darkness. "Eventually I'll leave," she said. "Get out of fucking Chinksville. Go to Cape Cod. That's where people enjoy life. The water, the restaurants. Everything you need."

"Where's that?" asked Francesca.

Lisa drew a map in the air, starting high above her head. "It's a peninsula," she explained, extending a line all the way out to form a severe point, "surrounded by the Atlantic Ocean on one side and the Cape Cod Bay on the other. The two bodies of water converge," she said slowly, and brought her hands high up over her head and then together.

Isabella reached the bottom of the stairs and stopped to steady herself, having finished nearly half the bottle of vodka. "Honey, I'm home!" she shouted, clutching her shoebox as she swung around the side of the banister, slid across the linoleum foyer and under the threshold that led into the kitchen. "Delightful!" she called in an English accent, then screamed at the sight of Francesca and Lisa leaning against the counter, staring at her.

"You scared the fucking shit out of me. Jesus," she said, and put her hand to her heart.

A strange perfumed smell hung in the air. Isabella sniffed to the left and right. "Is that marijuana?" she asked, intrigued. Francesca shook her head, then looked at Lisa. They giggled intimately.

"Lisa," Isabella snapped her fingers, running through the alphabet in search of Chinese sounding last names. "This is completely bizarre because I was just thinking of you. It's like I conjured you—"

"I don't think so," Francesca took a step into the middle of the room.

"I swear to God, just a few minutes ago. Okay, maybe an hour. But still, an hour ago! After not having thought of you for all these years." Isabella smiled, her head bobbing slowly up and down like an afterthought. "So, what have you been doing with your life?"

"Not much. You?" Lisa said dryly, searching in her bag for a cigarette.

"Not much. Except for my book."

"Yeah, Francesca told me. Congratulations," Lisa said into her pocketbook.

"What's in the box?" asked Francesca.

Isabella pulled the shoebox closer to her chest, her eyes darting nervously. "Shoes," she said. "Back to the store."

"Shoes? But are they white?" Lisa asked, then looked at Francesca and doubled over laughing.

"That's very amusing." Isabella smiled tightly, her face about to crack and spill onto the floor in a million shards. She teetered through the kitchen toward the back door.

"How are you getting to the store?" Francesca called.

Isabella stuck out her thumb, then spilled out the door, onto the driveway.

Francesca knew she should follow her sister. Just the idea of it—Isabella hitchhiking—was foreboding. But Lisa stood beside her, exhaling smoke luxuriously in all directions.

"Too bad," said Lisa. "How we both turned out."

They climbed the stairs to the chilly attic room. Francesca flipped on the electric heater with her toe. When she turned around, Lisa had lit another joint and seated herself on the bed. "I knew you'd be tall," she smiled. "Whenever I imagined you, I imagined you were tall."

"I'm not that tall," Francesca answered.

Lisa stared, noting Francesca's height, her straightness, the lack of anything decidedly female. "Do you have a boyfriend?" she asked.

"No."

"Me neither. I broke up with him after my abortion."

"You had an abortion?"

Lisa held two fingers in the air.

"Two abortions?"

"I can't use birth control because my pedophile father searches my room. I think he likes to touch my underwear. But once he found my diaphragm and threatened to send me back to China. I've never even been to China." She took a long hit, then continued talking with the smoke deep in her lungs, her voice tight, as if it were being squeezed from a tube. "Anyhow, I'm through with men. They disgust me." Lisa exhaled, stretched her legs straight out in front of her and examined them. She looked up to see if Francesca was watching. "What do you think about my mascara?" she asked. "It's blue."

"It's nice."

"I like when it gets a little wet and sort of runs under my eyes." Lisa took in too much smoke, coughed, and passed the joint to Francesca, fanning the smoke away. "Anyhow, men can't kiss for shit," she said, taking the joint again, shifting her gaze from Francesca's eyes to her mouth to her eyes again. "Remember that hut?" she smiled.

Francesca nodded, ashamed.

Lisa pressed the lit end of the joint down against a saucer they'd designated as an ashtray. She released the last streams of smoke and seemed lost in thought for a moment. Then, rather suddenly, she leaned over and kissed Francesca. It was so quick, it seemed not to have happened. Then she did it again with her mouth open. She licked the inside of Francesca's lower lip. Heat covered Francesca's thighs, spread through her body. Lisa climbed onto Francesca, mounted her, wrapped her legs around the wide hips and pressed. Hard. It felt almost too good. Everything Lisa had wanted, everything she'd always expected unfolded like a slow stain. There was no tongue thrusting, no hands crammed under the cups of her bra or inside her underpants. She would not stop now, would not think long enough to stop until she'd consumed, crumb by crumb, this body against her, so perfectly different from what she'd known, but exactly what she'd always wanted.

❑   ❑   ❑

In the garage, Isabella locked the door from the inside, and walked around to the back of the Mustang. Ceremoniously, she sat on the dirt floor and lifted the lid of the shoebox, as if inside were a restless bird. She removed the newsletter and a roll of duct tape and took a five-yard coil of vacuum hose down from a shelf overhead where she had hidden it. After fitting the lip of the hose around the mouth of the exhaust pipe and securing it with the tape, she unfurled it as she walked around the side of the car. She squeezed the hose between the window molding and the glass, climbed into the car, and closed the door. The interior was dark and smelled of leather and gasoline. Isabella lodged the hose between two spokes in the steering wheel and positioned the opening inches from her mouth.

"Please don't let me end up a vegetable," she whispered as she fitted the key into the ignition, and turned it. The radio blared loudly and the car jumped forward, then stalled. She tried again to no avail. "Shit," she slammed the steering wheel. She tried again, and again the car skipped and stalled. How could this be? Her father ran this heap of tin for hours. Was it because the tail pipe was obstructed? She knew nothing about cars and so decided to run next door and ask the Big One. She'd seen her out there working on her truck on Sundays, greasy hands, rag hanging out of her pocket. Sometimes the Big One and Alfonse would meet in between the shrubs to talk guy stuff.

But what if she asks why I need to start the car? What if she insists on coming over to have a look? She's just that type. Jesus. What a pain in the ass. Why can't I die without a big production? Is that so much to ask? She ripped the duct tape off the window, yanked the hose from the tailpipe, put everything back into the box, tucked the box behind a garbage can, and padded across the lawn determinedly. She squeezed through the hedges and stepped, reverently, onto the neighbors' lawn. Sappho sat on the stoop, his tail slapping the cement. He barked as she climbed the steps and rang the doorbell.

"Stupid mutt." Isabella patted his head. She waved pleasantly when the Big One appeared, fuzzy behind the screen door. "Hi! I was wondering if you could help me. My father asked me to start up the Mustang each day while he's gone and just run the engine for a few minutes. But every time I try, it stalls out."

"What gear is it in?" the Big One wiped her large hands on a dish-towel and glanced in the direction of the house.

Isabella shrugged. "Woops. Guess I should know that."

"Well, you need to put it in neutral."

"Neutral. Huh."

"That's the one in the center," the neighbor said, amazed at how completely useless a genius could be. "Just pull the stick shift out of first, move it around a little until it's disengaged, just sitting there in the middle." She moved her hand around in demonstration. "And don't forget to open the garage door," she called.

Isabella waved on her way back through the wall of bushes, then disappeared into the garage.

Morning light blasted through the attic windows. Francesca rubbed her eyes for several moments before her grandmother came into focus, standing in the doorway.

"Gram," she said, only then remembering the naked girl beside her.

Evelyn was smoking. "Where's your sister?" she asked.

"I don't know—"

"She's not in her room."

"She's not?" Francesca felt fuzzy, still half-stoned from the night before.

"And who is that?" Evelyn jutted her chin at the bed.

"That?"

"In the bed."

"That's my friend."

"What kind of friend. Your *boy* friend?" Evelyn slammed the door behind her and hurried down the stairs in her orthopedic shoes, hitting each step hard as a rock.

Francesca shook Lisa's shoulders. "You have to get up," she whispered. "My grandmother's here."

Lisa opened her eyes, made a visor with her hands. "Fuck me!" she slapped her head hard. She jumped off the bed, quickly dressed, and stepped into her sandals, hopping around as she struggled to get the straps over her heels. She slid her seven rings from Francesca's night table expertly into position.

"Go out the front," Francesca whispered, feeling her heart pounding in the base of her throat, making it difficult to breathe. "Oh God," she repeated, following Lisa down the stairs.

"It's okay," Lisa said at the bottom, then kissed Francesca quickly on the mouth. Already her face seemed to fade. Francesca held the door open and watched Lisa cross the grass, then stop to adjust a slippery ankle strap. Hurry, thought Francesca, glancing back toward the driveway. When she looked out again at the lawn, Lisa was gone.

Sirens neared and two police cars pulled into the driveway.

Upstairs the ashtray was full of butts and two roaches. Lisa had forgotten a watermelon lip gloss, left it standing up on the nightstand. There were three cigarette burns in the bedspread and the smell of Breck shampoo.

Neighbors recounted screaming sirens, the arrival of an ambulance and several police cars, and the disturbing early morning sight of an unconscious Isabella being pulled from the Mustang, spread on a stretcher, and carried away. The Little One stood with her arm around Evelyn who, much to everyone's shock, cursed repeatedly her own daughter for spawning such creatures. The Big One watched from inside the house. She knew Isabella's intentions and had considered checking on her in the middle of the night. But she hadn't. She didn't know why; was it disinterest? Fear of what she'd find? But Isabella had not secured the hose properly, the garage was leaky, and the car eventually ran out of gas. So she was not found dead, just semi-conscious and humiliated.

What She Found, 1983

The painting *What She Found* is concerned with Francesca's last day in New Haven, the day she fled Connecticut, stuck out her thumb on Highway 15, and set her sights on Cape Cod. The large canvas portrays an elderly woman who bears an unmistakable resemblance to Evelyn Horowitz: gray-haired, smoking, wearing rhinestone-studded reading glasses and an engagement and wedding ring, both occupying the same finger.

The bed in the background is not Francesca's: No lavender bedspread covers the two figures sheltered beneath the heavy comforter. All that is visible of their bodies are their dark heads, and only from the back, facing away and pressed deeply into the wrinkled beige pillowcases. The light is dramatic and inconsistent, cutting glaring strips through the blinds, dowsing one wide wooden beam while missing completely other spots of the room. The light doesn't make sense; one assumes it is not supposed to, further evidence that the world has been upturned. The elderly subject at the front of the canvas is bathed in a dim electric light. Her face is large and grossly detailed. With abject horror, she stares at the viewer, demanding our sympathy. On the floor beside the sleeping figures are two white bras, hurriedly strewn, along with a sweatshirt and a white blouse.

What She Found is intriguing on many levels. It is the first canvas to tell the story of budding lesbianism. In addition, while it impels the viewer to feel offense at the central subject's ugly prejudice and self-righteousness, it also invites us to sympathize with her situation.

Lucinda Dialo writes extensively about this painting in *Messenger of Conflict: Homophobia and the Lesbian Artist:* "*What She Found* portrays the artist's split sympathies. If we knew nothing about deSilva (and I suggest we know far too much), we would not be able to glean from this painting where her sympathies lie. Is she in collusion with the disgusted subject—the poor, elderly woman who walked in on such a shocking and illicit scene? Or does the artist favor the two girls, innocently asleep in the bed, unaware that their secret has been discovered, and their lives changed forever?

"deSilva's decision not to assert her own bias here is fascinating. The subject of the painting is the horrified onlooker; but is she the protagonist? What about the two young girls in the background, washed in the chaos of natural light, sleeping close and protected only by the dark comforter? They are pure in their nakedness, desire, clinging to one another and hiding from the hostile world. The work betrays the artist's ambivalence about homosexuality, her struggle to understand the connection between love and disapproval, and, one could argue, her fierce disappointment in the family unit.[40]

40. Dialo, Lucinda. *Messenger of Conflict: Homophobia and the Lesbian Artist.* Manly Beach, Australia: Art Down Under, 1994, pages 96–102. Dialo received the Australian Out-Rage award for this book, given annually to "A woman who introduces an important, controversial female figure to the Australian reader."

Suburbia Dissected

Cape Cod, 1981-1988

Chapter Eleven

Francesca hitchhiked for two days, through crowded Connecticut towns, past the sharp metal skyline of Providence, Rhode Island. Everything appeared deadly familiar: stores, fast-food restaurants, ranch houses, strip malls, as if she were going nowhere or worse, there were nowhere to go. When finally the Sagamore Bridge rose like a giant arched creature from the shivery sea, she sat forward and held her breath. At last, something different. From that point on, the world seemed to have transformed. Quaint clam stands and clapboard houses crowded the narrow strip of land that separated the ocean from the bay. Sand tiptoed onto the highway, pitting the black pavement with tawny dust and bits of shell.

The driver, a curly-headed hippie gone AWOL from a small, liberal arts college in Vermont, was headed to Provincetown to wash pots for a living. She'd considered staying on for the ride, but he was irritating with his drawn-out, nasal accent and milk crate full of Grateful Dead bootleg tapes. She feared he was getting the wrong idea about her and, anyhow, she was hungry. The pizzeria across the road provided an excellent point of departure.

She thanked him, patted his dashboard, and ran recklessly across the highway, suddenly famished—she hadn't eaten since she and Lisa finished off the leftover birthday pizza. The aroma of tangy sauce and baked garlic blew hot through the exhaust fan of the small storefront, overriding the fumes of passing cars and the rich salt air.

"Two cheese slices and a Coke, please," she told the person behind the counter. She pressed her stomach to the glass counter to silence the audible gurgling. Heat rattled through the radiators. The person was either male or female, Francesca knew that much, and seemed medicated or half-asleep, maneuvering through a thick, heavy fog.

Ravenous now, she tried not to glare spitefully as he/she slowly separated the slices and guided them into the oven. 'Give me the fucking pizza,' she wanted to scream. She drummed her fingers on the countertop and searched for clues: short, cropped hair and a chiseled face; a small body like the tidy engine of an appliance; small, comma-shaped ears slapped onto the sides of the head. All indicated female.

"I don't need them hot," she said.

"It only takes a minute." The voice, too, was female.

Finally, the employee transferred the steaming pieces onto a cardboard plate sheathed in thin paper. The cheese was running off the sides and the thick lip of crust at the top had burst large craters, the hollow edges blackened and thin. Francesca held up her money. The aroma was painful now; her stomach seemed to simmer with a boiling liquid. The person carefully counted out two dollars in change. The slices were beginning to cool, the paper beneath them darkening with oil. 'Please, please, please,' she silently pleaded.

At last, the employee handed over the plate, then filled a waxy cup with a combination of cola syrup and soda water that spat from an old-fashioned machine.

"Thanks, Ma'am," said Francesca, snatching the food and soda, peeking upward for a reaction. There was none. Like a hungry dog, she ran to the front of the empty restaurant. She finished the first piece in five bites—crust and all. Never before had she eaten pizza crust. She always left it, dejected, on the side of the plate for her grandmother to conquer when everything else had been consumed. Grandma. She would never see her again.

The employee had tired of her reading material. She walked to the front of the store and peered out the glass door, watching someone walk a dog across the street.

Francesca cleared her throat, mustering courage. "Do you know of a place to stay?" she asked.

"What kind of place?"

"A cheap place."

"Not if you need running water and a toilet."

It took Francesca a moment to measure the value of these extra perks: running water. A toilet. She supposed she didn't. At this point—the sky beginning to darken, her feet tender from walking the paved highway—she'd sleep in the back of a car if she could find one with the doors unlocked. "I don't care," she shrugged.

The employee ripped down an index card that was tacked to a small bulletin board at the front of the restaurant. "This is my boyfriend's place. It's a dump." She dropped the card onto the table and returned to her position in front of the window. "There's a pay phone right there," she said. "I think he's home if you want to call him."

Francesca examined the card: One room cabin. No runing water. $30 a month. 487-0983. "Runing" was underlined several times. Francesca spread her money out on the Formica top of the booth and counted what was left: $54 dollars, most of it in ones and fives, and 23 cents. It was all she'd saved from her weekends spent helping Alfonse with his landscaping jobs. She stepped outside and dialed the number.

"Hello." It was more of a bark.

"I'm calling about the cabin."

"The cabin?" He moved away from the phone and succumbed to a coughing fit, then returned. "It has no running water. Only a spigot in back."

"I saw that on the sign," said Francesca.

"And no toilet."

"Yeah, I know."

"What do you want it for?"

"To live in."

"By yourself? With no water?"

"Yes."

"I want $30 a month."

"I know."

"Cash only."

"Okay."

The man hesitated, trying to think of a few more disincentives. "I could meet you there tomorrow, I guess." His voice was hoarse, seemed to force itself up from the deep.

The door to the restaurant swung open and the employee stepped outside.

"Would it be possible to move in tonight?" Francesca asked, tears forcing their way up.

"Give me the goddamn phone," the employee said, reaching her large hand over Francesca's shoulder. "Get off your lazy ass and meet her there, you moron." She returned the receiver to Francesca and stormed inside, down the length of the restaurant and behind the counter.

Sherry, as the employee was called, described how to get to the cabin. To facilitate the effort, she loaned Francesca a rusted bicycle kept in a shed out back. Francesca thanked her profusely, comforted by the kindness that hid in the most unconventional places. She rode quickly the half a mile or so that separated the pizza place from the small cabin, and leaned the bike against the front. The building was run-down and small, covered in cheap asbestos tiles.

The landlord arrived promptly. He was short, homely, with dark, thin hair, a heavy five o'clock shadow, and broad shoulders. He climbed out of his truck and walked across some sunken train tracks, then pointed to the ground. He followed the tracks with his finger as they dissolved into a distant curve. "These here are functioning train tracks. You can expect a train to come ripping through here four times a day." He looked her over uncertainly.

Francesca took the money out of her pocket and placed it on the palm of his hand.

"I told you there's no running water. Just a spigot." He fiddled with the rusty padlock. "That means no toilet." He turned and looked at her, then pushed open the heavy door and handed her the key. "I want the rent on the first of each month. You can bring it to Sherry."

Francesca stepped into the dark room. The mustiness was so thick, it made her eyes water. The room was dark but for the large, paned windows that let in the weak evening light. A dry sink was surrounded by cabinets, a hot plate, a mini-refrigerator; several cubbies were built into the wall. There was a bunk bed, and a wood stove occupied the center of the room.

"Spigot and outhouse are in the back," he said. "I'll get the outhouse cleaned for you tomorrow." The smell of liquor wafted between them, even as he moved a wad of peppermint gum from one jaw across his tongue to the other. "Lights work," he tugged on a string, illuminating a bare bulb in the center of the ceiling.

"Thanks," she said.

After he'd left, Francesca rushed outside to scavenge for firewood before night settled. Behind the cabin a small field was surrounded by woods. She piled sticks on her right arm, straining her fist around a bundle of kindling, then returned to the cabin and dumped her bounty in the center of the floor. She removed her shoes, tucked them neatly under the bottom bunk, and bolted the door.

It was quiet. The whisper of Route 6 traffic blended with the grass sashaying in the ocean wind. She sat on the thin mattress. "I must learn every sound," she said calmly, "so nothing will startle me." She remained still for quite a long time, listening for the nearing of large black birds, vehicles, the creaking of the cabin's foundation. Semi-darkness made the windows fade and the room grow chilly. For the first time since leaving New Haven, she was frightened. She remembered her grandmother scowling. Lisa standing on the lawn—a slim, dark-headed form against the dawn. Everything moved in her memory but Lisa herself—clouds overhead, ambulances approaching, Francesca's own heart and blood. Neighbors cluttered the driveway to investigate. For one moment Lisa stood certain as a stain, her head turned, looking at something off to the right. Then she was gone.

She could run out and use the pay phone by the pizzeria. Call Lisa and tell her to come quick. They could be together. Away from Mr. Sinsong. *You'll never believe where I am*, she'd say. *I'm here. In Cape Cod.* Or was it *on* Cape Cod?

And then darkness descended thoroughly. She unpacked her knapsack and covered the large panes of glass—several of them cracked—with her clothes, tucking sweatshirts and jeans into the crevices between the window frames and the walls. Better not to know what's out there. The train passed later in the evening, making the walls shudder and the floor vibrate: The whole structure seemed on the verge of collapse, more frail even than the hovel she'd constructed so many years ago. Still, it was hers; she'd gotten away. She unraveled her sleeping bag on the top mattress, then persisted gallantly in trying to light the wood stove, relying on Sam Gribley's advice: (1) Roll the paper into logs. (2) Straddle them with kindling in the shape of a teepee. (3) Add logs, the smallest ones first. (4) When the flames are as tall as your finger, blow gently.

Fortunately, there was a pile of old newspapers, yellowed and crisp, from 1978, beside the stove. She lit the paper logs in several spots and puffed hopefully until a small, red ember swelled. Patiently, Francesca listened for the popping sounds of burning wood, but heard only a dry hiss, like someone was trapped in there. Spooky. Worse, it meant that the wood was rotted and wet. That there would be no fire.

She slept on the top bunk, in all of the clothes she hadn't used to cover the windows—two sweatshirts and an extra pair of jeans. At 4:30 a.m. a freight train seemed to be gunning directly through the room—rattling cans, tossing the legs of the iron bed. When she opened her eyes, her first thought was that she was home, amid an earthquake or explosion. She sat straight up and looked around at the unfamiliar room. Then she remembered.

Sherry told her about a nearby flea market, the major source of industry in the milder months of the off-season. Sherry's old friend, Gus, ran a booth called Antique Alley, and she offered to put in a good word for Francesca. He was always looking for some kid to help him peddle his secondhand merchandise—bottles, lamps, broken musical instruments.

"You got any experience in retail, kid?" he asked her, lighting up an Old Gold, throwing the paper match on the ground. He wore crazy pants made of patchwork like you'd find on a quilt on some grandmother's bed and a New York Yankees hat that said Redsocks Suck on the back.

"I'm very adaptable," said Francesca. Truer words had never been spoken.

He hired Francesca to work alongside him for the first two weekends so she could learn the ropes. "It just needs strings," he would tell the customer, or "You just have to oil it," and he'd demonstrate the stickiness of the keys. He paid her fifty dollars a weekend to work all day Saturday and Sunday.

It turned out she possessed a knack for convincing people to buy things they didn't need: little glass sun-catchers, mobiles, dusty antique bottles in unusual colors. She couldn't squeeze a twenty from a millionaire, Gus teased, but she could get a quarter out of almost anyone. Even Jack, the sneaker guy across the way, visited every afternoon to listen to Francesca pitch something frivolous (an embroidered napkin for his wife, a synthetic scarf that said "Made in Portugal" on the label, a candle in the shape of a frog with the words "Prince Charming" across its waxen sweatshirt), and he always walked away with something.

It wasn't long before Gus left her to run the table alone, freeing him up to work another flea market further inland. For Francesca, New Haven took on the shape of a morning dream, reduced, finally, to flat pages shaved from a picture book. Each day it became easier to stay away. She passed the pay phone on her street and sometimes thought of calling Lisa, but she could no longer imagine what she'd say. She wondered whether Evelyn, having had some time to think things through, might be sorry and, upon hearing Francesca's voice, beg her to return. But she didn't want to return. She was solitary now; it suited her. At night she ate hot dogs, beans, and Snickers bars, cooked dinner on the small hotplate, read comic books as it grew dark outside. Sometimes she'd crack the door to the bar refrigerator, lie on the top bunk, and admire her home in the dense yellow light of the utility bulb. "Mine," she'd whisper, unafraid.

Her flea market days began at 5 a.m. and often lasted until 8:00 at night. Still, she needed no alarm clock. The freight train woke her each morning, just as her landlord had promised, and she hurried around to the back of the cabin, held a milk container under the spigot, reveling in the sound of water pummeling the soft, pliant sides. She washed up, brushed her teeth, and gathered wood to heat the small room upon her return in the evening. Then she dressed for the day and rode her bike to the flea market. All of this, strange as it may seem, made her happy.

❏ ❏ ❏

A chilly, overcast Saturday in October. The sky was thick with flattened clouds, and the market was empty. It was the end of the tourist season and all the merchandise was stiff with salt. Vendors wore windbreakers and denim jackets, hovered over steaming paper cups of coffee. No matter how many watery cups of Snak-Shak-Wendy's coffee Francesca consumed, her eyelids fell heavy as wet towels. She considered closing up early, covering the goods with the large, blue tarp, and asking Jack, the sneaker guy, to keep an eye on things until Gus showed up.

She was, in fact, looking across the aisle at Jack, weighing her options, when a red Porsche parked behind the booth in front of a "No Parking" sign. The fender was marred by a large, rusting dent, and the windshield was dusted with sand. Out of the car stepped a woman in a great hurry, sharp and unnatural against the slow humidity of the day. She arrived at Francesca's table, pressed her hip to the ribbed metal casing, clamped her thin waist with her manicured hand, and removed her dark sunglasses which she clipped to the pointed opening of her blouse. She had ripe tomato-colored hair and skin covered in freckles that were, in turn, covered in powder. "This is exactly what I'm looking for!" She wrapped her right hand around the head of a smooth blue bird, then tapped the glass with her fingernail. Under the table her two long, arched feet pressed into steep shoes, their heels secured by a precarious strap. The short hem of her dress brushed against the table's edge.

She sat the plump bird in her palm. "Heavy," she said approvingly, dipping her hand up and down to demonstrate.

Vanilla perfume drifted across the fold-out table. Francesca took a step closer, detected lipstick, thick black mascara over brick red lashes, intricate, freckled ears.

"How much?" The woman held out the bird.

Francesca shrugged. "Two bucks."

"How about one?" She stared, unflinching, into Francesca's eyes.

The book lady on the other side of the aisle was watching. Jack peered over the lip of his coffee cup.

Francesca shrugged. "Yeah, alright."

The woman's long fingers opened her small black bag and disappeared inside. She gathered, along with bits of tobacco from the deep corners, a pile of sticky change which she spread on her palm, moving the pieces about until she'd amassed ten dimes. She scratched them up with long nails, arched her wrist, and let the coins fall onto Francesca's palm.

"I'm Lucky," she said.

"I'm not."

"No, I mean I'm Lucky. That's my name."

"I was making a joke." Francesca crossed her legs at the ankles and removed her worn pack of Marlboros from the center pocket of her overalls. She stuck one in her mouth and ran her finger along the rough metal wheel of her Bic. Then she leaned in like a cowboy and squinted against the groping flame. She looked up and grinned.

"Good one. First time I ever heard that." Lucky rolled her eyes. "I've seen you around here. What's your name?"

"Francesca."

"Very nice name," Lucky nodded, impressed. "Very sophisticated. Have you ever been to the Provincetown hills?"

Francesca shook her head. "I've never even been to Provincetown."

"Never been to Provincetown? How old are you?"

Francesca shrugged and played with the heavy pile of quarters in her pocket.

"You don't know how old you are?" Lucky leaned over, showing Francesca the muscles in her neck, one slate blue vein that ran just under the skin, a hint of cleavage. "Hello?" Lucky waved back and forth.

"I'm an orphan from Appalachia and no one ever told me when I was born."

Lucky squinted her eyes. "An orphan?"

Francesca nodded sadly.

"You don't sound like you're from Appalachia."

"I haven't lived there in a long time."

"And now you live here." Lucky put one hand on her hip. "At the flea market."

Francesca was learning she had no gift for flirtatious banter. "I have a cabin."

"You live alone in a cabin?"

It made her feel powerful to give away so little about herself. She looked up at Jack across the way. He watched, solemnly, as did the other vendors on all sides. "I don't think you're very popular here," said Francesca.

"They don't like their own mothers. Could I have a bag or something to wrap this in?" She held up the bird.

Francesca found a sheet of newspaper under the table. She placed the bird down on its side on top of several sheets of newspaper and rolled the paper tight around it, then tucked in the ends carefully and taped them together. She found a piece of pink ribbon that happened to be hanging around and made a bow at the center.

"That's sweet," said Lucky. She put on her sunglasses and peered dangerously over the tops. "Want to come over for dinner?"

"Why?"

"I'm making steak," Lucky replied flatly. "Yes or no?" Again, she put her hand on her hip; the other was extended holding the bird. "Come on. It'll be fun. I'll bet you haven't had a good steak in a while."

Francesca wasn't sure she'd ever had a good steak. There was the rib-eye special at Bonanza. She thought it was tasty, tender, but Evelyn insisted it was nothing more than a pile of Steak-umms pounded into pressboard. "I can't leave 'til at least 4," she said.

"I have errands to run. I'll come back for you." Lucky turned and walked away, providing a view of her smooth, practiced hips shifting from side to side inside her tight skirt.

For the rest of the afternoon, Francesca waited impatiently for the day to end. A man asked about a violin Gus was selling for forty bucks. She knew right off that he wasn't going to buy it. She could always tell from the body language. When they kept a few inches between themselves and the table, they were browsing. Someone who wanted to buy, who had the cash to buy then and there, either would give everything equal consideration or walk, determinedly, to one item and stay there. This guy was wasting her time.

But Francesca wanted someone to waste her time. Anything to

pass the last two hours until the woman with the bird returned. She explained patiently to the man about the minor repairs that were necessary to make the violin play—bridge work and new strings, rosin for the bow—these were Gus's stock answers, though he knew nothing about violins. After a while, the man thanked her and walked away. She settled in for a smoke.

"Jack," she called. "You got the time?"

Jack crossed the aisle. "2:40 or so," he said. She offered him her pack of cigarettes.

"You shouldn't be smoking those things." He took one, leaned in for a light.

They stood a few moments, smoking. Much as the vendors scolded her for smoking, saying they never would have started if they'd known what people know today, they trusted her more now that she participated in the favorite pastime at the flea market. They'd been wary of her at first: half-girl, half-boy, dirty and parentless, showing up from nowhere, so recalcitrant she seemed to be either a snob or an idiot. They thought she was a dyke from Provincetown, but when they learned she'd never even been into Provincetown, had never ventured beyond Wellfleet, they forgave her for looking like a queer.

"You know that woman?" asked Jack.

"Which woman?"

"You know." He waved his hands around his head, indicating hair.

"I don't know her. She just showed up."

"I know her. Everybody knows her. You know why we know her?"

Francesca shook her head.

"Because she's got a reputation. She tell you she's married?"

Francesca shook her head.

"Yep," he said. "Married. I don't know what you know or don't know or what all kinds of folks you cavort with, but that one's not good people." He stopped, as though he'd finished, took a long drag of his cigarette. "She buy anything?"

"A bluebird."

"She might be married, but she's one of them lesbians."

Francesca shrugged. "That doesn't mean she's not a nice person."

127

"Yeah, well, she ain't. I'm not saying they're all bad people or nothing like that. I got no prejudice. I'm just telling you what I heard."

Francesca stuck her thumb in the air. "Okay, Jack. Thanks for telling me."

"I'm just telling you. "

"I appreciate it. Thanks."

"So you have the facts. You have to be careful."

"I know. I will."

"A young girl like yourself." Jack spanned the table. "Sell anything else?"

"Just the bird."

He nodded. "I hate when it rains," he said. "I just feel crappy." He turned and walked away, waving from behind. He stopped a few feet in front of his table to examine his wares from the customer's perspective, adjusted a few boxes, shifted the pairs of sneakers around, then stepped behind the table and waved once more. She waved back. Probably, she thought, I should be afraid. Most people in my position would be. But I have nothing, just like Janis Joplin sang, so I have nothing left to lose. Even if the woman murders me, who cares? Who would notice? Jack. Maybe Wendy. Sherry's boyfriend might come looking for me if he doesn't get his rent. My parents would never even hear about it. And even if they did, they'd probably be relieved. And Lisa has forgotten all about me.

Lucky drove like a 16-year-old, with the top down and heat blasting. She downshifted into third and the old engine seemed to beg for a tune-up, sucking in its sides as they climbed into the hills. When she wasn't shifting gears or fussing with the radio, her fingers wandered all over the floor searching for a wayward lipstick.

They whined up a steep hill and approached the house. "Lynn Cooke lives there." Lucky pointed. "You know, Lynn Cooke—" She broke into song: "'And there . . . that's where I wanna be. Where the lights come up, the day tastes sweet. The big brass band sweeps you off your feet . . .' She's very famous. She does some work at the local theatre in town. And over there . . ." Again she pointed, this time behind her. "That guy's gardens are famous, too. All over the world. Very famous. I don't think he lifts a finger to tend them because he's never here. But, there you go. That's how the rich are. They pay people to do the work and they get all the credit."

"Aren't you rich?" Francesca asked.

"Me? Not exactly, babaloo." She squeezed Francesca's knee. "I'm doing the opposite of slumming. Whatever that is." Lucky pulled up to the house and pressed a button that sent the garage door swinging open. She pulled the car in, pressed the button again, and Francesca stared as the door made its way back down, grinding and clamoring into place.

Unopened bags of fertilizer and peat moss were neatly shelved along the sides of the garage. There was no smell of oil like back home. No grit on the floor. The walls were painted a smooth, industrial gray and on them hung gleaming, unrusted yard tools.

"This is the cleanest garage I've ever seen," said Francesca.

"Thanks."

"It wasn't necessarily a compliment."

Lucky turned and looked at Francesca. "You're a smart-ass," said Lucky. "I like that in a girl." She opened the side door to the house, then stood back, taking a deep whiff as Francesca passed through the narrow space. "Straight ahead," said Lucky.

Francesca walked through the foyer. She turned back to watch Lucky drop her keys on a dark farm bench, then kick off one shoe with the other and use her naked foot, toes thick with Misty Mocha enamel, to slide the remaining shoe to the ground. "Let's sit in the kitchen," she said. Francesca nodded and followed Lucky down a long hallway, then sat on a stool abutting the counter.

"Is this a mansion?" she asked.

"Yeah, I guess so." She put a finger in the air. "Actually, technically, I don't think it is, because I think to have a mansion you have to have a certain number of acres? Maybe? I really don't know. But Edgar—" Quietly, she pressed along the cool marble floor, each footstep leaving a temporary, steamy smudge. "That's my husband—" She turned and looked firmly at Francesca. "He calls it 'the mansion.' But he's a big show-off."

Francesca couldn't tell whether that was said affectionately or not. "Does he live here?"

Lucky opened her eyes wide, shocked. "No! My God! He hates it here. I hope you don't mind," Lucky pulled a box of ziti down from the cabinet. "But we're going to have pasta."

"I don't like steak anyhow," said Francesca. "Other than hot dogs, I'm pretty much a vegetarian. Can I smoke in here?"

Lucky removed an ashtray from under the sink. "Everybody likes steak," she said. "You're just being a good sport." She pulled a jar of Ragú down from the second shelf of the cabinet. Francesca could see the cabinet was empty, but for one box of cereal and three cans of clam chowder. "Edgar's a pretty well-known artist," she said. "Those are all his." She nodded at the kitchen walls. The titles were painted in black in the bottom corner of each canvas.

Francesca hadn't even noticed the strange paintings, though suddenly they seemed to be everywhere. In the kitchen alone, there were four: *Long and Narrow* occupied a wall between the broom closet and the refrigerator, *Squat and Wide* hung over the oven, and two small paintings—*Orange on Yellow, Yellow on Orange*—were asymmetrically arranged over the kitchen sink. In the living room, explained Lucky, was Edgar's most famous painting. Soon it would hang in the Provincetown Museum of Art. She put down the box of ziti and the unopened sauce and motioned for Francesca to follow. They passed under a threshold, across white carpeting to a bar with black leather sides fastened by furniture tacks. "How about a scotch, mon amour?" Lucky flicked a switch and a series of track lights flooded a large, abstract painting depicting a series of lines, one after another, like an illustrated echo or the rings made by tossing a rock into still water. A pale blue light washed the canvas clean.

Lucky cranked the heat higher, then ran her hands up and down her naked arms. She stood close to Francesca. "I hope you don't mind a little heat. I like to keep it tropical, so I can wear as little clothing as possible and still break a sweat." She poked Francesca's ribs and chuckled at her own joke, then sighed and crossed the room. She poured two scotches and carried them to the coffee table. "Here's your drink," she said.

Francesca stared at the painting.

"He's got a whole studio in the basement," Lucky continued. "Paint, canvases, easels. I'm surprised he doesn't keep a live model chained down there." She flopped down on the plush, blue divan, and held Francesca's scotch in the air. "Plant your caboose right here," she said.

Francesca turned and saw Lucky reclining on the divan, her hand balancing the drink inches above the floor, eyelids heavy with lust.

"Guarantee this is the best scotch you'll ever have," Lucky said, placing Francesca's glass on the coffee table.

Francesca took the glass of scotch and sat on the couch, far away from Lucky. She sipped the hot liquid, continuing to stare at the painting. "It's awful," she said, thinking both of the scotch and the painting.

Lucky shrugged. "Human beings will get used to anything." She sucked on an ice cube and faced the painting. "It's called *Woman Fed Up with Marriage Fades.*"

"Sounds like a newspaper headline."

"Ha, ha!" Lucky stuck her tongue out quickly. "Well, that's about as sentimental as the old goat gets. Can you tell it's me?"

Francesca looked hard and long. The lines were red and curvy. Was that meant to convey Lucky? "Not really," she said.

"Good. Because that girl has no tits. And I have huge tits. Huge stand-up tits." She pointed with her drink first to her tits, then to the painting. "It's in there, though. The person. He says she's faded because she's already left. I'll tell you, I haven't looked at the damn thing in—" she thought hard, "I don't know if I've ever looked at it." There was silence while both of them stared at the painting.

"I don't think he's a very good artist," Francesca said boldly.

"Bingo!" Lucky shot her finger in the air. She brought her long feet up onto the coffee table and rotated them at the ankles, then put her hand over Francesca's. She separated each finger, stroked it top to bottom, dipping into the thin skin that connected them. "You have hands like a boy," she said. She placed Francesca's hand on her thigh, high up, where it was taut and warm. Francesca closed her eyes. "A

131

sweet, sweet boy," said Lucky, leaning over and covering Francesca's mouth with her own, a giant open cave. Francesca tasted lipstick, scotch, cigarettes. Long, cool fingers climbed under her shirt. Lucky's tongue, cold from ice cubes, widened the gap between her gums and the inside of her lip.

Francesca loved Lisa. But as Lucky unbuttoned her shirt, took one olive pit nipple in her mouth, and sucked, hard, working the other one with her fingers, Lisa was as faded as a morning dream by afternoon. Lucky unbuttoned Francesca's Levis, followed her fingers with her tongue like a feather down the front of Francesca's body. "Lower," Francesca moaned, trying not to squirm, trying not to do anything that would stop Lucky from continuing. Her jeans, peeled off, were tossed away. The snaps hit the coffee table, making a sharp sound. Lucky hung one leg over each of her shoulders.

"Please," Francesca moaned, raising her hips.

"Please what, baby?"

"Pretty please?" asked Francesca

"What do you want me to do?" Lucky asked, her voice throaty and bossy.

"Lick me," said Francesca.

"But I am licking you," Lucky demonstrated the gentle, feathery touch along the outside.

"Inside."

"Inside? Like this?" She pressed her tongue inside.

Still, this wasn't quite it, wasn't quite where Francesca needed her. "Not there."

"No?" asked Lucky inching up.

"No," Francesca breathed, her stomach butting into the air as Lucky neared the center, so slow, slow as honey, working all around until finally the warm, soft tongue barely touched the slippery bead, where all of Francesca's longing had converged. Lucky covered it with her mouth, blowing gently all around, making it swell larger and larger. Every flick of the tongue made Francesca want more, more than was possible, more than existed.

She loved Lisa. Still, she pressed against Lucky's open mouth, spread her legs as wide as she could. "Oh God," she cried out, coming hard. She threw her head against the arm of the couch, her hips in the air. Her toes pressed the other end of the couch so hard she might have separated the blue divan. And it was over. She guided Lucky's head away, could stand no pressure. Lucky lay across Francesca's naked chest. A fine moisture covered them like a blanket.

Woman Reclining on a Blue Couch, 1984

In a 1983 lecture at Yale University, preeminent feminist scholar Lucinda Dialo lamented the lack of a female erotic aesthetic: "What art in the Eurocentric tradition provides," Dialo told a standing-room-only crowd of 250 students and art historians, "is an exhaustive record of the male subconscious, much of which, consistent with biological research, is sexual in nature. Any attempt by female artists to represent their own sexuality is necessarily influenced by this paradigm: The woman artist's eroticism either varies from that of the male; mirrors it; opposes it; or—God help her—intentionally ignores it. But always her work is measured against it.

"In an unsexist, unbiased world, how would the woman artist depict eroticism? Answering this question is tantamount to measuring the beauty of a rose, unswayed by the cultural baggage piled onto each petal, the metaphors injected into each thorn. In our culture, we know, as if by osmosis, the meaning of the rose—whether this meaning exists in poetry, song, art, or even life. Each genus has a different meaning. A rose is not a rose is not a rose—not really. Which is perhaps why Stein's saying is so widely quoted: It promises simplicity where none exists."[41]

In 1986, Dialo stumbled upon *Woman Reclining on a Blue Couch* while reviewing a scantly funded, short-lived show at the Lower East Side gallery Shame the Peacock. The painting hung between

41. "Toward a Female Erotic," Lucinda Dialo, Yale University, May 1983.

135

What She Found and *Barbecue* (destroyed in the 1989 blaze). *Woman Reclining on a Blue Couch* moved Dialo so profoundly, she wrote to deSilva. An excerpt of the letter is reprinted here:

"When I gazed upon [*Woman Reclining on a Blue Couch*] I felt momentarily devastated, as though I'd finally witnessed what I could never actually envision but believed in nonetheless—rather the way religious men [sic] must contemplate the face of God. As you probably know, for years I've been bemoaning the lack, and even the impossibility, of a women's erotic aesthetic, one that would reach beyond the labiatic stamens of O'Keefe and the simultaneously self-deprecating/self-aggrandizing self portraits of Kahlo (not that I in any way disparage the genius of these artists). But gazing at your painting, I felt for the first time I was witnessing, even immersed in, an expression of unapologetic, unabashed, entirely female desire . . . What a welcome shift from depictions of banana penises and eroticized Christs."[42]

Woman Reclining on a Blue Couch depicts a voluptuous, naked woman sprawled on a blue divan. The voluminous cushions mirror the Olympian curves of her body. She lies on her back, her right hand dangling, nearly grazing the floor. Her long,

42. This letter, along with missives from Yoko Ono, Phillip Hamil, Elton John, and an endless roster of admirers and colleagues, is part of a forthcoming, as-yet untitled collection of deSilva's correspondence. The volume contains letters written between 1984 and 1989.

manicured fingers (the polish on the index and middle nails is noticeably chipped) straddle the bowl of a wineglass, tilting the thick red libation dangerously toward the mahogany floor. The tension of this image disrupts an otherwise peaceful setting. It reminds us of the changing world outside the painting and creates in the viewer the sense that s/he is invading a private moment.

The painting is ardently sensuous; one can almost hear opera drifting in from an alcove, where an open window forces silky curtains to submit to the summer breeze. It is late afternoon. Outside, the sun is white and crisp; but the room where the subject rests is sleepy, as though she's just been made love to moments ago or has just awoken after a night of sexual pleasure. The rich, butterscotch tint to her flesh is in vibrant contrast to the royal blue couch. She is clearly the object of desire: The artist wants (and has likely had) what she paints. She gives us the luxuriously padded female with plump red lips, thick hair, and a body tender with life, post-coitally spread. One sharp and phallic spear of light invades through a cracked shutter, dissecting the subject's belly and concluding at the edge of her orange pubic hair.

Not surprisingly, *Woman Reclining on a Blue Couch* has been largely ignored by male critics. Michael Wright dismisses the painting as "thoroughly unerotic . . . unless one is titillated by alcoholism and pedophilia . . ."[43] Larry Barnes, not surprisingly, found this painting particularly objectionable, dubbing it

43. Wright, Michael. *Art That Heals.* Minneapolis: night-night press, 1991, page 112.

"Grotesque Expressionism."[44] It is hard to know which aspect of the painting men find so abhorrent: (1) the realistic portrayal of the female body; (2) lesbianism; or (3) the presumed context in which lesbianism prevails—i.e., an erotically charged atmosphere with no man on the premises.

"Why all the controversy?" asks Dialo. "What is so upsetting about a nude woman in her thirties with pear-shaped breasts, folded belly, double chin, chipped fingernail polish, and red pubic hair? Perhaps, it is because this is a *contemporary* woman, not a rotund, period-appropriate Rubens or a deconstructed Dora Maar. This woman has shuddered her way through a lifetime of orgasms."[45]

Cynthia Bell takes Dialo's argument one step further, claiming the eroticism in the painting is not simply female, nor even lesbian, but specifically rooted in the butch/femme lesbian tradition—"One of the oldest and most thoroughly despised couplings in recorded history . . . No matter how earnestly, even desperately, the art world wants to embrace deSilva, she will never be one of them. In any other context, she would have repelled them—had they seen her on the street, they might have called out an insult, or if they were more genteel in their disgust, whispered 'freak' or 'muff-diver' to a companion. Certainly, *Woman Reclining on a Blue Couch* would pose a threat to their family values. deSilva is concerned with the *queer* experience of sex—woman to woman sex. This painting, more than any of her

44. Barnes, Larry. "Free Places *Not* to take the Kids," *New York Daily News,* February 13, 1993.
45. Dialo, Lucinda. *Women Paint!* New York: Little, Brown, 1991, page 149.

others, is a flagrant portrayal of lesbian desire. Scholars try to make it float in the mainstream, but it sinks like a stone."[46]

Anna Leighton, in a Marlboro College paper on deSilva's work, compares deSilva's portrayal of her subject to the relationship between Michelangelo and David: ". . . Just as Michelangelo seemed to tap with the chisel ever so gently in order to free his beloved from the tomb of stone, so deSilva caresses Lala's pelvis with a finger of light that spills in through a cracked shutter."[47]

Perhaps the only indisputable observation made about *Woman Reclining on a Blue Couch* can be attributed to Phillip Hamil. In his essay "Live Fast, Die Young, Watch the Vultures Feed," Hamil stated: "Never has there been more concrete proof [*Woman Reclining on a Blue Couch*] that rumor and speculation about an artist's personal life pervert our understanding of the work."[48]

46. Bell, Cynthia. *Lesbians in Oil.* Atlanta: Amazon Press, 1995, pages 229–230.
47. Leighton, Anna. "Lala: Pseudo-Realism and Homosexual Symbolism in the Work of Francesca deSilva," 1996. Paper on file in Marlboro College Library.
48. Hamil, Phillip. "Live Fast, Die Young, Watch the Vultures Feed." *Vanity Fair,* April 1993, page 112.

Chapter Twelve

Francesca stood in the threshold, heels hanging halfway out into the cool morning, and Lucky exacted a melancholy kiss. "Thanks, honey. That was great," she whispered, grazing Francesca's ear and making her wet all over again. To make matters worse, the autumn seemed, in one sweaty night, to have shifted into winter. Francesca's stomach rumbled, loud as a can with a bullet inside. Several times Lucky had offered to drive her home, though never without making mention that she had to be in New York in less than five hours. Otherwise, she said, there'd be a big breakfast in bed.

Francesca sensed she'd just become privy to an element of life she'd never considered before. She wanted to get away as quickly as possible. The hot taste of sex clung to her mouth. She could still hear the tremble of the earth—Lucky coming that second time, while Francesca held her down, every last tremor clamoring for the surface. She'd been indoctrinated all right, into something deeper and uglier and more perfect than she'd ever contemplated. And now, walking alone in the stiff early morning, she knew there were ways a person could be satisfied that had nothing to do with love.

Her only regret was that she hadn't seen the basement. Particularly now that a picture of Lucky—naked, round, fleshy, glowing from inside with lust—was painted in her brain. If she'd awoken a few hours earlier and sneaked down there, she might have dislodged the painting from storage and impressed Lucky with her prodigal talents. Instead, having never spent the night in such a comfortable bed (the closest was Evelyn's, coated in satin sheets), she'd slumbered until Lucky had woken her at 8:30.

"You live in a cabin all alone?" Lucky had replied in the 3 a.m. darkness of the seaside bedroom, against the heavy breathing of waves hitting the shore. "Isn't there someone you want to live with?"

"You?"

"Me?" Lucky laughed. When she realized Francesca was completely earnest, she laughed again, harder this time, the laughter winding down like the end of a record, until it finally, thankfully, stopped. "Sorry." She patted Francesca's knee. "I'm married, honey. And even if I weren't married, I'm not a rough-it kind of girl. I'd go out of my mind." She pressed her hand to her chest and shivered, as if it were already happening. "Isn't there someone else?" Lucky asked.

"Actually, there is someone."

"Well, where are they?"

"Back home."

"Oh. That's too bad." Lucky reached across Francesca's body. "May I?" she lifted Francesca's pack of cigarettes.

Francesca nodded. "This person is the chess champion of the entire state."

"What state is that?"

"Connecticut." Francesca ran her finger along the wheel of her blue Bic and lit Lucky's cigarette. What did it matter? Nothing made an impression on Lucky. She'd seen it all.

Over the next few weeks Francesca sent cards to Lucky thanking her for something unspecified. She confided in Snak-Shak Wendy the details of her adventure; Wendy confided back that while she appreciated Francesca's well-placed trust, there were no secrets to be had at the flea market: Everyone knew she'd left with the rich chick. And no one was scratching his head trying to put together a blow-by-blow of what had happened next.

"Do you mean she used me for sex?"

Wendy hugged her little friend maternally and teased, "No flies on you. Anyhow," she added, "it shouldn't come as a surprise, you gorgeous androgyne."

"A what? What am I?"

"Androgyne, lovey. Half-boy, half-girl. Or half-girl, half-boy. In your case, it's pretty much divided down the line. Women go for it. They're gonna be pulling each other's hair and scratching each other's eyes to have you as their plaything. You'll see."

141

All day Francesca repeated the word to herself: androgyne. It reminded her of android, and thus seemed fitting since she'd always felt she'd been erroneously deposited from some isolated sphere of the universe. Surprisingly, it didn't hurt much, the idea that she'd been used for her body. In fact, it seemed fitting since her mind, almost without exception, couldn't be detained. She looked forward to the possibility that others might try and use her this way as well. She'd fared just fine in the bargain: three orgasms and lessons in cunnilingus that, she hoped, would be stored in the body, like riding a bike.

What she wanted from Lucky, even more than another go at her fleshy form and salty, insistent lips, was the opportunity to transfer from brain to canvas the deep, bluish vision of her body against the flash orange of her hair, the long, alternately flaccid/firm breasts (salmon-colored nipples) and the slim legs that extended forever, spotted by freckles the color of pale lips. So, she'd been used by a married woman. Tossed out in the morning like hired help. Still, she'd do it again in a second, without hesitation, if only for another chance to stare at Lucky's naked body, to memorize its peculiarities, the softly chiseled spaces that separated the ribs, the ditches between the collarbones, dark shadows behind the ankles, red coils of pubic hair.

❑   ❑   ❑

The flea market ended in late November. To get through the long winter, Francesca secured snow-shoveling jobs with several neighbors. As Christmas neared, she sank under the weight of the dark days, lying on the top bunk and pining over the strange gifts that would surely be sent from Alfonse's distant Italian relatives—unnecessary things like Italian books on tomatoes, pressed butterfly wings in onion skin pages, socks knit from Shetland wool—always arriving in a big carton with Italian airmail stickers plastered across the top. There would be eggnog on New Year's (though never with rum because of Isabella). On Hanukkah, Evelyn would make brisket and latkes. They'd watch Tom Jones' Christmas special or Julie Andrews'—whoever had a show that year. Evelyn would gasp: "Isn't he handsome!" and "Look at the figure on her. Gorgeous!"

Evelyn had instilled in Francesca an antipathy for gaudy Christmas decorations. Still, she was comforted to see that here, where the ocean surrounded the world like quicksand, people succumbed to the season's spell. She was further relieved when the snow finally came, even as it silenced what had all summer been a bustling, often vociferous world. She headed out on her bicycle, shovel tucked into the space between her backpack and her body. First, she dug the pizza restaurant out from under the heavy, wet snow, had a cigarette on the stoop, her pants growing heavy with the cold melt, and watched trees struggle against the wind. Her face stung. Nor were her gloves made for true cold; she'd chosen them because they had no fingers, thus permitting her to smoke. She headed down the block to a white Cape owned by Charlotte Wallace, a gray-haired lady who lived alone. The driveway was gravel, which made for more difficult shoveling, but Mrs. Wallace had agreed to pay a substantial $30 each time Francesca shoveled; spent correctly and with enough snow, this would last through the season.

Mrs. Wallace opened the door. She wore a light blue robe, pulled tight around her body, the pale color reflecting the silver tones in her hair. Her pewter colored glasses were attached by a silver chain, parked low on her nose. "Hi, dear," she said. "Come inside and I'll make you a cocoa."

A trellis with thick brown vines strangled the siding; the brick steps, protected from snow by an overhang, were stained greenish from a light coating of moss. Francesca thought it was the most beautiful little house she'd ever seen. She kicked her feet together to loosen the snow, tapped each foot against a step, slapped her hands against her bulky jacket and shook the snow from her cap, until Mrs. Wallace said, rather impatiently, "Oh, just come in already or we'll let all the heat out."

Francesca stepped inside. Sunlight bore through the clean, wide windows, warming her face and hands, making her shiver. A wood stove in the center of the room ran so hot, the air above trembled. "This is a lovely house," she said, reaching for a new refinement in her choice of adjectives.

Mrs. Wallace smiled. She put on a pot of water and busied herself at the counter, removing a container of cocoa from a cabinet, then filling a pitcher with milk, selecting a blue mug, taking out a teaspoon. She seemed not to want to talk, so Francesca gazed from object to object—the shiny silver stove, the fresh white paint, the wood trim and oiled cabinets. Two paintings hung on one wall, both small, both depicting the same lady in the same pose; yet they were inexplicably different. She squinted for a closer look, then walked to them.

"Do you like those?" asked Mrs. Wallace.

"They're the same, aren't they? Oh, wait. No, they're different. And they're the same."

"That's exactly right. You can see their difference?"

"No." She looked more closely. In one painting, the subject's head tilted to the right and the background was darker. "This one is sadder," she said.

"That one is expressionistic," Charlotte corrected. "The other is realistic. Which is a fancy way of saying what you just said." She smiled.

"Are you an artist?" Francesca asked.

"Me? Heavens, no. I just run a small gallery."

"What a coincidence. I'm a painter!" She pointed to herself and laughed. Confidence rushed through her body. Fate, at long last, was cooperating. How else to explain it? She was here, just shoveling the walk, minding her own business; the woman invited her inside for cocoa—what were the odds of that? And then, she just happened to own an art gallery!

"Where have you exhibited?" asked Charlotte.

Francesca turned. "Exhibited? Oh, I'm only in high school. Well, I was in high school. But I attended a special school for the gifted. Only seven students from the entire district were chosen to go."

"How exceptional!" Charlotte said. "Well, the Cape is filled with painters. You're in good company." The kettle began to whistle, then scream. Mrs. Wallace turned off the flame. She prepared the cocoa, put the mug on the tray with the pitcher of milk, the spoon, and a napkin, and carried the tray to the table. Ceremoniously, she placed the cup in front of Francesca. "This cocoa is imported from Holland. I have it sent all the way from Zabar's."

Francesca presumed Zabar's was an African country, though how the cocoa arrived in Africa by way of Holland was puzzling. "It's delicious. Thanks," she said. It tasted like all the other cocoa she'd had in her life; whipped cream would have made it festive, but undressed, it was hot and sweet.

By the time Francesca had finished shoveling Charlotte Wallace's driveway, sweat was trickling inside her heavy jacket and down the sides of her head. She'd taken her cap off early on, stuffed it in her pocket, seeking out the cold air on her sweaty head. She needed soap and steam. Until two weeks before, she'd have biked over to the YMCA where a young, attractive woman always let her in, even provided one of the towels reserved for the members. But in the off-season, a new woman, who was immune to Francesca's charms, worked the desk, and she required proof of membership. These days Francesca resorted to the cold spigot behind her cabin, a bar of Ivory soap, and a large towel to warm her the moment she was clean enough—i.e., armpits, genitals, face, ears—to turn off the water and run inside.

Spongy palettes of snow continued to fall from the sky, thickening the beachside air, hitting the pavement like dollops. She considered asking Charlotte Wallace whether she might borrow the shower in her guest bathroom. But she couldn't bear the idea of asking for something so essential, something that people were supposed to just have.

What happened next did not spring into her head fully formed, the way, say, a painting might. It gained momentum gradually, compelling her to push harder on the pedals of her bicycle, and harder still, until she found herself climbing the steep hill that led to Lucky Perkins' seaside mansion. The structure was as ugly and ostentatious as ever (some might say it looked nearly identical to the other homes in the neighborhood; Francesca would have disagreed).

She rested her bike against the garage, broke a trail through the fresh snow up to the porch, and rapped on the solid oak door.

As she expected, no one answered. She spanned the house for an entrance, examining windows, the back door, even the dryer vent. An unfastened hatchway looked promising. She pried apart the two frozen doors, only to find herself in a sub-basement. She could smell the turpentine of the husband's studio, but there was no entry into the house. Once again, she followed around the exterior of the house, sliding her fingertips along the smooth siding. She checked underneath a pot of expired geraniums—her mother always kept a key under a planter of dead chrysanthemums on the porch—but there was nothing. She lifted, with some effort, a series of slate slabs forming a wall by the sprinkler. On the back porch, she tipped back the lid of an old tin milk-box with her boot. Finally! In the bottom of the box sat one key, the hole in its center filled with ice. She grabbed at it with frozen fingers until it came loose, then made her way around the side of the house where she attempted to force it into the notch on the side door. It didn't fit.

On her way back to the milk box, she spotted a red door at the bottom of a small, dark stairway, covered in cobwebs and fastened with a rusted padlock. Carefully, Francesca descended the icy steps into the small cave at the bottom and slipped the key into the lock. Reluctantly the arc loosened and she pushed open the door. Inside was a tiny room with a twin bed and a painted dresser. A baby's room perhaps, or servants' quarters. This room led to a long hallway, carpeted in soft blue. The house was musty and dark, but the moment she flicked a switch along the wall, the corridor lit up like a Broadway stage. Track lights made yellow pools across the floor, spilling light into rooms in both directions. She crossed a large vestibule and found herself in the kitchen, though it seemed impossible that she'd have gotten here from there, almost as though she'd traveled a secret passage.

The pantry was cool and empty but for several six-packs of beer, a bag of onions, a box of Oreo cookies, and some soup. Inside the refrigerator was an unopened jar of fancy mustard, milk, peanut butter, and a Tupperware filled with rotted crudités. A magnet held a list of reminders against the refrigerator door:

(1) water houseplants (3, including the cactus)
(2) dust
(3) turn on the alarm when you go out (obviously unheeded)

(4) switcharoo the lights to fake out intruders.

(5) Miss me. (A little smiley face and a line of X's followed.)

"Yuck," said Francesca.

On the magnet was printed The Wallace Gallery, followed by an address. It took her a moment to recognize Charlotte's name. She made her way into the living room where the thermostat was located. She turned the heat high, as Lucky had done, then stepped back and stared at Edgar's painting. Was there genius in that? she wondered. In the choice of colors or the images evoked? She saw none of it. *Perhaps*, she thought, *I wouldn't know genius if it stabbed me in the eyeballs.*

Francesca climbed the stairs, past the bedroom where she'd spent one night less than two months before, then kicked open the door to the bathroom. The room was large and clean. A terrycloth robe hung on the back of the door—green, but not unlike Isabella's. She turned on the hot water, and climbed into the clean stall, held her face under the needling stream. She soaped every inch of her cold skin, scrubbed her head, her ears, and the back of her neck; lifted her leg and let the water squirm deep inside of her, then bent over and did the same. Until she was certain every area of her body had been flushed.

By the time she shut the water, the room was opaque with steam. Heat honeyed through the pipes. She wiped clear a spot of the mirror and splashed after-shave onto her face and neck, then opened a bottle of perfume and smelled Lucky. She wore the robe downstairs and made a cup of coffee, then perched in front of the bay window just in time to watch mothers gather at the bus stop to retrieve their children. Clustered like birds around breadcrumbs, they shifted in one large unit toward the paused bus. From a distance they were perfect— protective palms pressed to their sons' backs or caught in the clinging static of their daughters' hair. She imagined the even weight of their hands, their afternoon smell—cigarettes, coffee, faded perfume. Though she knew that up close, none of it really existed.

Snow accumulated quickly. By late afternoon a power line was sprawled across the road. The lights went out; the television was useless. Wind forced the screen door to open and slam shut against the side of the house. Francesca sat at the breakfast bar, eating a plate of Oreos. Through the kitchen window she studied the darkened sky; an eerie brightness passed behind it, swift clouds the color of baby aspirin.

She pushed away the plate of cookies and felt sick. As though she'd been punched in the gut. What was she doing here, wearing the bathrobe of a man whose wife she'd fucked? Where were her parents? Why didn't it frighten her to be here, illegally? She could be arrested, wind up in jail. She might never see anyone again. Would she miss anyone? She thought of Lisa. And Evelyn. She missed them a little, if she allowed herself. They had loved her in their stingy, unreliable way.

Francesca knew she never wanted to return to New Haven. She couldn't stay here, of course, in Lucky's mansion, but she could remain on the Cape forever, work for Gus, finagle free pizza from Sherry, free burgers and coffee from Snak-Shak Wendy, eventually venture into Provincetown and find other girls like her. Still—she glanced at the wall phone—it would be nice to talk to someone who knew her. Someone who loved her, no matter how ineffably. The wall phone could give her a swig of humanity. She could hear her grandmother's voice, learn she was forgiven. Evelyn might beg her to return. Her parents surely would. Their indifference would have fermented into contrition and guilt. "Thank God you're all right," they would say.

But what if no one cared much to hear from her? What if they'd hardly noticed her absence, except to be relieved? What if Evelyn hadn't forgiven her? What if Evelyn hated Francesca so much for what she was, she could never love her again?

Still, she had to talk to someone. She grabbed the receiver of the wall phone and dialed Lisa Sinsong's number. She remembered every digit.

"Hello," barked Mr. Sinsong.

"Is Lisa there?"

"Lisa gone."

"Gone?" Francesca repeated. "Well . . . when is she coming back?"

"She not coming back," he said and hung up the phone.

Francesca walked numbly, determinedly, toward the basement as if she'd been there many times before.

"Lisa gone," she said aloud.

The door was covered in plastic and taped closed to keep out the cold air. She yanked at a loose end and tore off a Texas-shaped piece of paint along with the tape, then lit a candle that sat on the telephone table and used it to guide her way down into the decisive darkness. Immediately, her eyes watered from turpentine and mold. She stepped onto the cool floor and held the candle out, spilling a spooky warm light across the cement. Three votive candles sat on a small table; she lit them as well.

At the center of the low room two wooden easels faced the same point. Stretched canvases lined the wall like record albums, forming a ledge beneath a series of cubbies that were built into the walls and stuffed with hundreds of paints. On an old, rickety table, the tops of brushes peeked over the lips of mason jars, grouped by size, thickness, material. Rectangular cans of turpentine formed a pyramid in the corner; before them was a laundry basket filled with rags. Francesca felt she'd stumbled into a Tolkienesque paradise, a subworld stocked with the supplies to her soul. Here, in a rich lady's basement, where she ought not to be, was everything she needed. She stroked a virgin tube of white, then pushed her finger down hard and dented the metal. The canvases were rough and scratchy as the shell of her snorkel jacket. She lifted one and placed it on the easel before her, then lit a cigarette and stepped back to examine it. The blanched color reminded her of Isabella. She remembered her sister dressed as Anne Frank, walking around the house with a yellow star sewn into her clothes, speaking in a German accent. What a weirdo, Francesca laughed. Why would anyone adulate a girl who spent her life in an attic, then died of typhoid and lice? Where was the glamour in that—in premature death and posthumous appreciation, public scrutiny of your diary? She would never understand Isabella. And it could not simply be genius that separated them: her own mediocrity, Isabella's superiority. How then to explain Lisa's preference for her, when Lisa, Francesca knew instinctually, was the more intelligent of the two? She wondered whether her sister was even alive, but she had the sense it would take a nuclear explosion or a car falling from a skyscraper directly onto her head to decimate Isabella. There was something iron cast about her, something impermeable. Still, it was suddenly apparent to Francesca how isolated she was: No Evelyn, no Lisa, no mother or father. No crazy sister—irritating, but at least there. No one loved her anymore and in turn she felt no love swishing about in her heart. She wished she had a dog. Or even a turtle. Something she could look at in the evenings. Something she could touch.

There was, she decided, something very wrong with Isabella. Something that made it impossible to know her. As if there were, at her very core, something that interfered.

Francesca looked down at herself and wondered if she, too, were like this, if she were impossible to know. But Lisa had known her. At least for a moment. There had been love between them; not like with Lucky. She and Lisa had touched with slow, frightened fingers. Nervous fingers, the way people touch when they have something to lose. Then again, it might have just been first-time jitters; there was that possibility, too.

The blank canvas made her lonely. She stepped away from it, toward the cubbies, and pulled out, at random, unopened tubes (ignoring the wrinkled, half-used ones)—browns, oranges, greens, yellows—and squeezed a bit of black onto one of Edgar's pallets, over a pliant swell of dry paint. She placed a large dollop of white beside it, closed her eyes, and conjured Lucky's full breasts, the generous slope of her hips. She lifted her brush to the canvas.

"Lisa gone," she said again, mocking Mr. Sinsong's accent, still holding the brush midair, frozen like a photograph. The tiny window at the top of the room reminded her of the attic—the severity, the drama of the light. The basement was the polar opposite. No wonder she felt comfortable. Once again, she'd found isolation. She remembered the light of her attic room in the hot, white morning, saw Lisa's arched feet dipped in dewy grass. Lisa's face came to her—the wide skull, the pearly skin.

And she began to paint.

By the time Francesca realized she had to pee, the power had been restored—nearly every light in the house was on. The lawn lamp blared against the bright day. She cooked an entire box of pasta, ate several chocolate bars she found in a drawer, obviously Halloween surplus, made a pot of coffee, smoked a cigarette, and returned to the basement.

The Lisa Trilogy (Lisa Gone, Genius, Virgin), 1982

In her review of deSilva's 1993 retrospective at the Whitney Museum, *New Yorker* critic Clara Feinstein offers little praise of the thirteen extant paintings. She does, however, recognize the historical importance of the exhibit, providing as it does an opportunity for the public to witness a celebrated artist's humble beginnings: "Though in five, maybe ten years' time, Francesca deSilva will amount to no more than a colorful sidebar to 20th-century American art (except, of course, in feminist annals, where she will no doubt be exalted as a martyr, to the exclusion of other, more deserving artists), one hopes that this retrospective serves a higher purpose. Perhaps it will act as an agent of inspiration to young, unrecognized artists, a call for them to step up to the plate and pursue the enigmatic itch, so often the first stirring of creative talent. Perhaps these thirteen studies in mediocrity might infuriate these youngsters and impel them to ask themselves: *If that Francesca deSilva person can do it, why can't I?*"[49]

49. Feinstein, Clara. "Much Ado About Mediocrity—the Whitney's Retrospective of Francesca deSilva." *The New Yorker.* Feinstein, who graduated from the Rhode Island School of Design in 1977 and briefly pursued a career as a collage artist, frequently bemoans the plethora of unrecognized female artists. What is interesting is that deSilva, whose rags to riches story contained all the elements Feinstein relished, irritated her so. Even more puzzling is that after deSilva's death in 1989, Feinstein warmed toward the artist. In a 1993 New Yorker article, she wrote, "deSilva brought art to the proletariat because she was one of the people and, like most of the people, was concerned only with herself. The popularity of her small-town vision, combined with the public's prurient curiosity about the colorful antics of her personal life, fueled an anomalous success. deSilva demonstrates self-involvement serving community. Her own myopia penetrated the public's apathy by

Lisa Gone, deSilva's first work, is an unfettered portrait. Sloppy, harried, and teeming with emotion, it presages deSilva's dominant theme, her signature metatext: the exploration of the artist in relation to the subject. In *Lisa Gone,* as in later works such as *Woman with Stool, Woman Reclining on a Blue Couch,* and *What She Found,* the artist struggles with her relationship to the subject at the same time as she grapples with the actual, physical execution of the painting. Dialo describes the simultaneous coexistence of life and art as "electricity. One feels the painting inside the body, as if enduring a mild, yet pervasive, shock."[50]

The subject is positioned slightly left of center (very possibly a miscalculation on deSilva's part, one that ultimately, like most of her technical errors, managed to enhance the work's perspicacious intensity). The face is serious and aloof, looking beyond the artist at some pale-colored object in the distance, the glare of which is reflected in the subject's dark irises. Behind Lisa, a long wooden table reveals one place setting, already sullied—lamb chops? Ketchup?—and left for her to clear. The fork, carelessly abandoned, dissects the plate at four o'clock. Were it not for the overall content of *The Lisa Trilogy,* the table setting might convey solitude; at worst, loneliness. But in the context of its companion pieces, *Lisa Gone* can only be interpreted to depict servitude, even abuse.

converting their concerns, i.e., themselves and their social reality, into art."

Note: A fable in the lesbian underground tells of a party held to raise funds for a statue of Ana Mendieta to be erected on the block where she "fell" to her death. Feinstein is said to have dogged deSilva all evening, finally making a grand scene when the artist definitively rebuffed her.

50. Dialo, Lucinda. *Women Paint!* New York: Little, Brown, 1991, page 26.

Dialo says of *Lisa Gone*, "It is a challenging work to interpret. The title tells a story beyond that depicted by the artist. What we see before us—a girl, a place setting for one, a dismal expression, and a desolate backdrop—indicates isolation. A large, existential isolation. *Lisa Gone* from life? From society? From herself? Perhaps the artist is trying to bring her to safety, or less altruistically, to keep Lisa for herself."[51]

The second installment in the *Trilogy, Genius,* jumps light years ahead of *Lisa Gone* in execution, both conceptually and technically. A nightmarish portrait, it is said by many to have unmasked deSilva's own genius. It depicts a tiny Lisa squatting on a huge chessboard. The chessboard is paved, the tar uneven and pockmarked by swells, resembling in texture a poorly maintained parking lot.[52]

"This work is terrifying," writes Michael Wright. "The child is confined to one small square; she squats and contracts her prepubescent body. She struggles to remain unnoticed, innocent, small enough to contain all that she struggles to protect. Her life has been sacrificed to the fulfillment of her parents' narcissism. Thus the chessboard, once a haven, becomes an asphalt jungle where the young Lisa is stalked, where she crouches in fear from the invasive father."[53]

And finally, *Virgin,* the third installment, inspired the controversy and opposition that would dog deSilva's career for the eight years following her opening exhibit

---

51. Ibid.
52. Perhaps the site of the Wellfleet Flea Market, where deSilva worked upon arriving on Cape Cod.
53. Wright, Michael. *Art That Heals.* Minneapolis: night-night Press, 1991, page 135.

(and would no doubt have persisted had the artist survived). Only days before deSilva's first show was to open at the Wallace Gallery in Provincetown, a group of "local" protesters from CAWD (Christ in All We Do) publicly, vehemently objected to *Virgin* on the grounds that it juxtaposed two discordant themes: incest and the Bible. The "grassroots"[54] organization called the painting, in which a mandorla[55] hovers over the head of a girl about to be sexually abused, pornographic. CAWD, supported by two conservative Republicans campaigning for reelection, publicly accused deSilva of being anti-Christian and, as such, a threat to the sanctity of the family.[56]

Thankfully scholars and critics interpreted the painting differently, emphasizing its haunting colors, the darkness of the figure, and the images of anguish and fear. The painting captures a young girl cupping her naked breasts in her hands while a stalking figure, portrayed only as a trousered leg thick as a redwood tree, lurks behind her. A halo hovers inches above the subject's head. She glares at the viewer (or the artist) as though we (or the artist) are, at least in part, to blame for what is happening. Writes Charlotte Wallace (deSilva's manager and owner of the Wallace

54. CAWD was actually a satellite of Christian Component, the largest coalition of religio-political lobbyists in the United States. For an in-depth analysis of CAWD's fervent and baffling objections to deSilva's work, see: Tagson, Susan. *Religion As Illness*. New York, Martin Street Press: 1989.

55. A halo used in ancient religious paintings, usually in connection with saints or the Virgin Mary.

56. The irony here is that deSilva knew next to nothing about Christianity. Half-Jewish, half-Italian, she had a secular upbringing. She'd been raised without any religious beliefs, had experienced God in only the most superficial manner—e.g., tripping on the sidewalk and being told by her mother that God was punishing her for some childish transgression. There was no basis for the sort of nihilistic rebellion of which she was accused.

Gallery) in an editorial to the *New York Times,* "Rather than calling a depiction of the impending molestation of a teenage girl 'pornographic,' CAWD ought to consult God about why, for heaven's sake, they experience this image in such a way."[57] And Paul DeVaine asserts that deSilva's invocation of the mandorla, rather than being an antireligious or intentionally controversial gesture, was, conversely, "hopeful and sentimental, a naive attempt to elevate the subject from her wretched life."[58]

Of course, it would be disingenuous to pretend that there is ambiguity as to the identity of *Virgin's* subject.[59] The title of the Trilogy, combined with what we know of deSilva's obsession with her young love, makes such speculation spurious. Nearly as fascinating as the paintings themselves is the artist's mature grasp—at the tender age of 18—on the specific nature of her subject's suffering. Lisa's cynical countenance indicates a preparedness, even an acceptance of her fate. And because the perpetrator is approaching from behind, we know this particular incidence of molestation has not yet occurred. Thus, deSilva tells us, if we cared enough, we could stop it.

"But we never lose sight," writes Lucinda Dialo in *Caleidoscope,* "and this is the genius of the work, that this is just a painting. One cannot stop the horror

57. Wallace, Charlotte. Editorial. *New York Times,* New York City, 1985.
58. DeVaine, Paul. *The Accidental Rebel: Controversy in the Work of Francesca deSilva.* New York: Little, Brown, 1996, page 56.
59. In response to Christian opposition to the painting, demonstrations were held in New York City by an organization called the Pacific Islanders Coalition (PID). The group claimed that CAWD's objections to the painting had less to do with incest than abject horror at an implied connection between the Virgin Mary and a Chinese-American girl.

from happening in a painting. deSilva puts it in front of us, but we cannot prevent that which the painting warns us about, the crime that has surely happened by now. She relieves us of the burden of intervention, massages our collective conscience, and this abdication of responsibility permits us to consider whether, given the opportunity, we would intervene. And deSilva believes, as Lisa knows, that we would not."[60]

60. Dialo, Lucinda. "Counterstrokes of Violence: How Society Informs Women's Art." *Caleidoscope, A Journal of Feminist Art,* Winter, 1995.

Chapter Thirteen

Francesca peeled the magnet from the refrigerator door and watched the list it held in place float and drift underneath the appliance and out of sight. She held her four canvases, two under each arm, and headed out into the bright day. The air seemed impossibly clean. No dust, no turpentine. The descent onto Commercial Street deposited her in the east end. From there, it was easy to find the gallery; its chimney spat smoke into the cold air. The other buildings were inert, hibernating through the long season.

Mrs. Wallace was seated in an office at the back of the room, talking on the telephone. Francesca put her paintings carefully on the damp ground, pulled open the heavy door, her pulse quickening, and, grabbing her canvases, stepped inside. Her sneakers hiccuped against the polished wood floor.

A series of uniform paintings hung on the white walls of the spacious room. A large card posted at the beginning boasted "Jack Wagner, long-time Truro resident" in careful calligraphy. The first canvas, centered on its own wall, was titled *Triple Sail on a Foggy Day*. Francesca stared at the gruesome expressions on three fishermen—wet hair stuck to their gray skin, rain needling their faces as they struggled to gain control of the bloated sail. She continued through the room, skimming the twenty canvases. They were all concerned with the sea: men, boats, various afflictions of natural violence. They reminded Francesca of the covers of saltwater taffy boxes sold in souvenir shops along Route 6.

She walked slowly toward the office, clutching her paintings, trying to silence her rubber soles against the polished floor. This had been a bad idea, she decided, the result of too much loneliness, a swollen head, too many toxic chemicals, too much fantasy. Just as she put her paintings down outside the office, hard little wheels backed up over the warped, wooden floor. Mrs. Wallace hung up the phone and turned to her. "Are those original paintings?" she asked.

Francesca turned. "Yes," she said.

"I'm Charlotte Wallace. Curator. And you are?"

"Hi, Mrs. Wallace. Remember me?" Francesca put the paintings down in case Charlotte wanted to shake.

"I'm sorry—" Charlotte stared at Francesca, but there was no connection to be made between the girl who had shoveled her walk and the one standing before her.

"I'm Francesca DeSilva. I shovel your path." Francesca gestured, pretending to have-at a stubborn pile of snow.

"Oh my goodness! I didn't recognize you without all your gear!" She glanced out the window, expecting snow.

Francesca gestured. "I brought my paintings. But then I realized I'd made a mistake."

"Oh." Charlotte looked disappointed. "You mean because of Jack?" She nodded at the walls. "Don't pay him any attention. He's my ex-husband's lover and, as part of my divorce agreement, I have to give Jack his own little show every year. Frankly, it's becoming a nuisance. It gives people the wrong impression. That's why I stick him in December, when no one is likely to come around." She glanced at the canvases. "As long as you're here, give us a look."

Francesca followed Charlotte through the gallery and into the office. Charlotte clicked on a gooseneck lamp and lifted *Woman Reclining on a Blue Couch* onto an easel. She rubbed her hands together. "Hmm . . ." She narrowed her eyes. "Now who is this? This person looks familiar."

Francesca shrugged.

"Did you use a model?" asked Charlotte.

"Nope."

"A photograph?"

Francesca pointed to her head.

"I see," Charlotte said, impressed but not convinced. "Okay, what's next?" She laid *Woman Reclining on a Blue Couch* carefully upon her desk, lifting Virgin into its place. She took a step back and watched the new painting for several moments, as if it might run away. "And what do you call this happy picture?"

"Virgin."

"She's very thin."

"She is very thin," Francesca agreed.

"And that's a halo?"

"A mandorla," said Francesca. "It's religious imagery from—"

"Yes, I know what it is," Charlotte interrupted. "Is this person from your imagination as well?"

"From memory."

Charlotte nodded, grateful for information that seemed authentic. She looked into Francesca's hopeful brown eyes. She folded her arms across her chest and peered over the top of her silver bifocals. "Where have you studied?"

"Studied?" Francesca laughed. "Nowhere. I've been painting in a basement."

"DeSilva," Charlotte said, thoughtfully. "Is that Spanish or Italian?"

"Italian."

"De Silva or Da Silva?"

"De."

"Big D or little D?"

Francesca had to think for a moment; the questions were coming so fast. "Um . . . little D," she lied.

"De Silva. Italian with a little D," Charlotte smiled, as if this had been the correct answer. "Very nice. Very painterly." She turned back to the painting. "I'll tell you right now. You need to paint somewhere with light."

"I like painting in the dark. All of these," she indicated *The Lisa Trilogy,* "were painted by candlelight."

"During the blackout," said Charlotte. She turned to regard them once again. "That's what it is. That's the sadness."

"No," corrected Francesca. She pointed to her head. "The sadness is in here."

The opening was scheduled for September 17, 1983. Weeks of controversy preceded the event. Somehow the preparations had been infiltrated (Charlotte suspected the UPS man). A letter appeared in the *Cape Cod Times* signed by several leaders of an influential right-wing organization who deemed the paintings "obscene and pornographic." The letter accused "this deSilva person" of deliberately comingling patently incompatible themes—namely religion and sex. Ironically, all this hullabaloo proved pornographic itself: By 8:50 p.m. the gallery was thronged with people. Journalists, art enthusiasts, and dealers from as far away as New York, most of whom would have otherwise known and cared nothing about the exhibit, butted shoulders to gaze at the rough-hewn pictures.

A large banner was posted across the front of the gallery: *Suburbia Dissected—New Work by Francesca deSilva.* The whitewashed brick walls were polished, and an antique Ben Franklin stove burned aromatic piñon wood, shipped from Arizona for the occasion. The door was left open, inviting the clinging mosquitoes of the season and the cool fall to mingle with the perfumed guests and the piquant scent of fire.

Francesca sat in her cabin on the bottom bunk, staring at herself in the cracked mirror on the wall. She felt nothing like a woman and not nearly so much like a man as she'd hoped to in her rented tuxedo. Instead, she seemed to be lingering in between, and this depressed her. And the idea that she would feel depressed on the most important night of her life depressed her further. Of course this would not work. She would be humiliated. People would scoff at her paintings. She'd receive horrible reviews. She never should have left New Haven. Should have gone to work for Alfonse or, instead of making art herself—how presumptuous!— secured a job in an art supplies shop. Something in keeping with her limitations.

She entered the crowd at 9:30, seeing only the blurred periphery of her paintings on the white walls and Charlotte in front of her.

"Finally!" Charlotte grabbed her arm. "You can't be late for your own opening!" She straightened Francesca's bowtie. "Forget it. It doesn't matter. Here you are and you look darling. And you are going to be extremely famous."

Each painting was allotted several yards of wall space. This was Charlotte's two-fold strategy: it invited slow, thoughtful consideration of each painting, creating a purposeful, serious atmosphere; at the same time, it helped the nine canvases appear to fill the room. Francesca's bio was posted at the start of the exhibit, carefully worded by Charlotte to indicate rebellion and reticence, rather than inexperience and a paucity of training.

Charlotte waved over a lesbian couple in tortoiseshell glasses. One wore a dark red cashmere sweater with black pants; the other, a navy-blue wool cardigan and bone-colored corduroys.

"Francesca," she said, "This is Avery Patton and Diane Berman. Ladies, Francesca deSilva. Avery and Diane are hoping to buy *Birds, Everywhere*."[61]

Francesca nodded and tried to smile. A guy in a suit grabbed her elbow.

"I'm in love with you," he whispered, too close to her ear.

"Excuse me?" Francesca leaned in politely.

"Yes," said the man. "I am hopelessly, disturbingly, pathetically in love with you. And you're a lesbian, aren't you?"

"Phillip! Leave her alone." Charlotte slapped the man playfully. "Don't answer that," she whispered to Francesca.

The man laughed much harder and longer than was warranted. He handed Francesca his card. "Phil Hamil." He extended his hand. "Don't listen to her. I'm your friend." He bowed elaborately. "I want to be your slave."

"Phillip, how much champagne have you had?" asked Charlotte.

"Thanks a lot, Charlotte. She'll never marry me if she thinks I'm a sot." He looked hard at Francesca and grinned. "You wouldn't, right? Marry me."

---

61. The sale of this painting to Berman and Patton, well-known New York collectors, disintegrated. *Birds, Everywhere,* never sold, was destroyed in the fire. The spooky work depicted a nuclear family lunching on fried chicken, seated, one beside another, on the sole picnic bench in a serene, manicured suburban park. On all sides are gray water and a heavy pink sky. Perched in the treetops and covering the surface of a large gray rock, unseen by all but one daughter who gazes fearfully at the trees as she bites down on a chicken leg, are throngs of crows. For discussions of this work, consult Paul DeVaine (*Metaphors and Madness.* Chicago: ARTBooks, 1994) or Cynthia Bell (*Lesbians in Oil* (Atlanta: Amazon Press, 1991).

"Marry you?" Francesca wrinkled up her face. "Are you blind?"

"I'd say so," offered a woman with a smoky voice.

Phillip Hamil patted Francesca's back and laughed. "I'm teasing. Of course I'm teasing. Why would you want to marry a schlub like me?"

"It's true, Phillip," the smoky woman said. "She's more of a man than you'll ever be."

Phillip doubled over, laughing. Charlotte returned to Diane and Avery, but they had disappeared. Only slightly discouraged, she flitted off to attend to other guests. Phillip curled his right hand around Francesca's elbow; his left held a glass of champagne. The gold liquid matched his class ring, the jaundiced whites of his eyes, the yellow fading of his hair.

Francesca felt as if she were viewing everything through cheap sunglasses, the kind scratched from bouncing around in a pocket, against keys and a lighter. She stared up at *The Lisa Trilogy*, the three portraits of her beloved, posted on naked walls, and felt she'd done something unforgivable and obscene, dragging Lisa into the middle of this carnivorous world, splaying her for cheap entertainment. Glasses clinked; perfume made the air itch. The world was lit up and ugly. And the paintings, by association, seemed specious.

Sherry from the pizzeria arrived with a friend of hers, another female who looked nothing like a woman. They stood apart from the rest of the people, drinking club soda and staring at the walls, as if Francesca's paintings were dangerous animals at a zoo. Francesca waved heartily, comforted by their earthy, familiar presence, but just as she was about to penetrate the crowd to get to the other side of the room, someone tapped her on the shoulder. She turned to the right, flashing past several gawking faces, then stopped abruptly. Lucky Perkins stood before her, dressed in a wine-colored dress, décolletage down to her ribs. The dark color of the fabric against her fair skin made her seem dusted in flour. She waved slowly, one finger at a time. "You look like you just got hit by a stray bullet," she said, popping a grape into her mouth.

"How are you?" Francesca extended her hand, growing dizzy.

Lucky leaned in intimately and whispered, "Don't pretend I'm not your worst nightmare." She made a quick, scary face.

"It's nothing personal," said Francesca.

Charlotte hurried over, practically knocking over an elderly couple in her zeal, and placed a hand firmly on Francesca's elbow. "Oh!" she called. "I forgot to tell you! Lucky has offered to entertain us. Francesca, you never told me you knew Lucky. And that she'd played the Opry."

"The what?" Francesca asked.

Charlotte touched Francesca's arm with two fingers and placed her lips less than an inch from Francesca's ear. "Don't worry about her," she whispered, "That bitch. I took care of it. Let her make an ass out of herself if it makes her happy. You're the main attraction." She patted Lucky's shoulder and walked off, into the crowd.

"I didn't know you sang," Francesca said casually.

"Yeah." Lucky pushed some unruly red hair off her face. "I'm trying to get back into it. I figured this is a good place to get my toes wet. I mean, you've been painting for like a week. And this gallery—if you want to call it that—" She looked around disparagingly. "This is half a step up from a church fair." She rolled her eyes and flicked Francesca's collar. "You look fancy."

"Thanks."

"Anyhow. I wish you'd told me you were a squatter. You ate all my candy bars."

Francesca cleared her throat. "It just happened. I was cold."

"Poor baby. And did I do something to make you think I was a whore?"

"A whore?"

"Thank God you're a shitty painter or everyone would be able to recognize me all fat and splayed out like a prostitute. Why isn't the Chinese girl naked?"

Francesca shook her head. "I don't know. That's not how I remember her."

"So she wasn't a whore?" Lucky shook her head slowly, incredulous. "You're lucky Edgar isn't here. He'd recognize the couch. At least you got the couch right."

"It's impressionistic. It's not supposed to be a portrait."

"Sure, sure. That's what he always says."

"If anyone should feel like a whore, it's—"

"Oh please. Don't even try it."

"I like your dress," said Francesca.

Lucky spread her arms so Francesca could get a better look. "Anyhow," she ran her fingers up and down her arms, "I'm not going to press charges."

"Charges?"

"That's right, baby. That's what happens when you break into a mansion and live there. The police put little handcuffs on you and take you off to jail." Lucky rolled her eyes, half amused. "What balls! Just be grateful you have a shrewd agent. She's saving your skinny tomboy ass."

Charlotte struggled to mount a small, wooden chair. The silver discs sewn into the fabric of her dress glistened under the track lights, refracting rainbows on the ceiling. Balancing precariously, she tapped a spoon on a plastic champagne flute, but no one paid any attention. She enlisted Phil Hamil's assistance. He whistled like a hunter retrieving hounds. "Everyone," he bellowed. "Feast your eyes on this elegant lady."

Lucky smiled. "Well, this is my cue," she said. "Lovely to see you again." She kissed Francesca's cheek and walked determinedly through the center of the room toward Charlotte's office. Charlotte leaned on Phillip Hamil's shoulder as she addressed the crowd. "Well, this has been a thrilling evening so far, hasn't it?" She smiled intimately. There was uncertain applause. Charlotte cleared her throat and peered down at an index card positioned away from her face. She read over the tops of her glasses: "Lucky Perkins is a local artist and musician. She performed her hit song, 'I Ain't Cheap,' at the Grand Ole Opry in 1974 and was a featured act at the Fat Cigar in Las Vegas for six years before relocating, with her husband, to the East Coast. In 1978, Johnny Cash declared her a rising star, and *Country Club* magazine said 'Perkins sounds like Patsy Kline with an ellipsis at the end of every line.' (Charlotte looked up, a bit confused; there were good-natured smiles throughout the audience.) "Tonight, not only are we appreciating the exemplary talents of a young, local painter . . ." (Exuberant applause.) "But we are about to be treated to Ms. Perkins' first performance in . . ." Charlotte looked up. "It says here, five years? Could that be?"

Lucky smiled coyly and waved from the office threshold.

"Looks like we're the *lucky* ones! Ladies and gents, please welcome Lucky Perkins!" Charlotte hopped down from the chair with Phillip's assistance and the audience applauded wildly, convinced now that they recalled that name . . . Lucky Perkins. Lucky emerged, dwarfed by the large guitar strapped around her back. She kissed Charlotte and maneuvered awkwardly through the crowd, trying not to whack anyone with the neck of her instrument, looking like a drag queen in too-high heels. People backed away, allowing her an important semi-circle at the front of the room, positioned right before *Woman Reclining on a Blue Couch*.

"First, congratulations to Francesca." Lucky extended her hand, inviting applause. She spoke at once, silencing the clapping. "Well, here's a little tune. Maybe a few of you remember it." She took a long sip of champagne, then returned her plastic flute to the stool in front of her and perused, one last time, the lyrics to her song, typed out on a small piece of notebook paper. She swung her guitar around to the front and began to tap her foot, peering off through the crowd at a fixed point in the distance, jutting her chin forward and yanking it back in time with the rhythm, and singing in a strange, unidentifiable accent that Francesca had never heard trace of, all of it quite incongruous with the Porsche and the sophisticated gown.

Charlotte arrived beside Francesca. "What she thinks she has to gain from this little stunt I'll never know."

"Revenge," Francesca shrugged; it was all she could think of.

And Lucky sang:

> *You think because you're tall and dark*
> *And just a little handsome*
> *That you can hold me like a prisoner of love—*
> *Never paying any ransom.*
> *You set me up just to put me down*
> *Flaunt your wares at every bar in town*

But I'm no toy you can take to sleep
Baby, I ain't cheap.

Lucky grinned at the audience, reliving the glory.

I ain't cheap and you best remember
If you're looking for easy tender
Go and find yourself a girl in some red-dirt town
Who don't mind being treated like a hand-me-down
If you want someone to herd like you was Ms. Bo Peep
Find yourself a sheep 'cause baby I ain't cheap.

And on it went. Francesca felt sick. The paintings had nothing to do with any of this; they seemed suddenly ridiculous, tainted by pretentious strangers who knew nothing about her. She stepped out into the cool, moist evening, undid her bowtie, and inhaled the sea air in needy gasps, unable to get it far enough into her body. *How ridiculous,* she thought, *renting this tuxedo. Who am I kidding?* She kicked at beach sand and cigarette butts along the curb.

The gallery door opened and a young woman stepped out. Shaped round and plush, with verve in her black eyes, she pushed her dark hair off her face and extended her hand. "Hi."

"Hello," Francesca said quietly.

"I'm Shanta Wall."

Francesca shook the woman's hand, then looked away and lit a cigarette, wishing only to be left alone with her disappointment and angst.

"So, I really love your paintings."

"Thanks."

"No, I'm sure everyone says that—"

"Not really," said Francesca. "A lot of people hate them."

"Exactly," Shanta replied. "That's how you know you're really good. If you weren't, why would anyone care?"

Francesca laughed uncertainly.

"Unfortunately, I have ulterior motives." She held out a folded-up piece of paper. "In case you're ever in Boston. Or not. I'd travel."

Shanta grinned and shifted her weight from foot to foot. She was Indian, apparent now from her smooth features, her eyes, the thickness of her obsidian hair. She's beautiful, thought Francesca. And she followed me out here because she wants me. Because I painted those nine pictures. Even though I'm exactly the same fucked-up person I've always been, suddenly women like this want me.

The door to the gallery opened and Charlotte leaned out. "Hello? What are you doing out here?" Charlotte looked at Shanta, then back at Francesca.

"I'll be right in."

"Wasn't that something?" Charlotte shrugged and rolled her eyes, looking like a child who'd had too much sugar. "Not as bad as I'd feared."

"Yeah."

"Francesca, there are a lot of important people here waiting to speak with you."

Francesca held up her cigarette. "A few minutes, please," she said.

Reluctantly, Charlotte left them alone, closing the door, muting the crowd behind her.

"I hate important people."

"I'm not important at all," Shanta answered.

Francesca laughed. "I'll bet someone thinks you're important.

Shanta shrugged. "Anyhow, it's your party. Why stay if you're not having a good time?"

It took little to convince Francesca to bring her bike around from behind the gallery. Shanta climbed onto the back of the banana seat and held on. They drifted between cars parked on both sides of the narrow road until they had reached the quiet highway. Francesca pumped up hills with boundless energy, sped down the other side. The wind wrapped itself around them and, at the same time, kept them warm in a way that only humid sea air can. They took a long route to Shanta's condominium, along the old and barren Route 6, stopping in the middle of the road to kiss, then share a cigarette. Once again, Francesca felt her life change. She laughed at how crazy it was. First she'd been Francesca number one: hiding in the hut, dirty and reticent and awkward. Then Lisa kissed her and she became Francesca number two: awake, but lost. Now, she was Francesca number three: the artist. Freedom filled her body. She chucked her cigarette far out into the tall reeds and continued pedaling down the empty road.

Chapter Fourteen

In the small house on Longwood Terrace where she'd resided since 1946, Evelyn Horowitz began to forget where things were. Things that had always been in the same place. The broom, for instance. Forks. She put away the milk in the cabinets with the canned goods, left the curling iron on for hours at a time while she went to the Stop'n Shop, arriving at the store only to discover she could not remember why she'd come. She stood in the parking lot, wearing her housecoat and slippers, metal clips ensconced in her dirty, cement-colored hair, trying to remember whether she'd walked or driven, what she'd meant to purchase, how to get back.

Her driving, too, had become erratic. The Chevy, its engine parched from lack of oil, retched along the middle of busy Whalley Avenue. Evelyn moved her foot from gas to brake, sometimes unable to remember which was which, speeding up when she meant to slow down and vice versa.

Alfonse had broached the subject as though crossing a minefield, touting the merits of the bus, boasting how he'd been a cabbie for a time and wouldn't mind honing the old skills. Never mentioned were phrases like "license revoked" or "hazard on the road," or anything minimally inflammatory. Still, she'd pitched a fit, backed him across the carpeted living room, speckling his face in angry spit.

May 10, 1983 was a warm day. Moved by the bright blue sky and gentle spring breeze, Evelyn felt a nostalgic urge to drive to Edgewood Park and feed the ducks. She dialed the DeSilva house, then ran the tap to rinse off some dishes, always preferring to multi-task while talking on the telephone. "Put Franny on," she said to Vivian.

"What?"

"I said put Franny on," Evelyn repeated, irritated, slamming dishes around inside the ceramic sink.

"Ma," Vivian put her hand on her heart and capped her pen. "Francesca is gone."

"Who is this?"

"Ma, you called me," said Vivian.

"Wha—?" Evelyn held the receiver away to inspect it, then banged it against the long arm of the faucet and listened again. She hung up, put on her fake beaver coat, slipped her tired, sculpted feet into bedroom scuffs, and stepped outside. At the end of her street she turned left, edged nervously along the sidewalk of the main road, having forgotten why she'd left home. A young couple passed, holding hands, swinging briefcases.

"What's the date?" she demanded.

They looked at her, then at each other.

"The date. What's the date?"

"May 10?" the man asked the woman. The woman nodded.

It was Francesca's birthday! Of course! That's what she was doing. She checked for her purse but found she'd forgotten it. No problem: Mort had known her for years. He'd let her purchase on credit. Still, she chastised herself for neglecting to order the cake ahead of time, as she used to in the old days, before age corroded her excellent memory.

She walked with greater confidence now, repeatedly whispering the word "bakery" to herself as she made a left at the bottom of the hill. She glanced up at the house where her friend Sylvia had lived before she'd gone to Florida, lost her husband, returned to New Haven, and died in the Home. Everything right on schedule. She shook her head and turned right at the main road, crossed a block, then noticed a family in front of Burger King, eating hamburgers on the hood of a car. She shook her head. "No class," she muttered, then stepped inside the air-conditioned bakery. The bells on the door rang.

"Hi ya!" she shouted and waved in an exuberant gesture.

"Afternoon, Mrs. Horowitz," said the baker's son.

"What about it?" she asked.

The boy looked at her, confused.

"You said 'afternoon,' so I said 'what about it?'" She paused, then

172

made a silly face, pointed her finger at him, and laughed. "Gotcha."

He forced a laugh. "Yes, you did."

"I forgot to order in advance," she announced. She looked at the glass case. The cakes were so fancy. So many colors and shapes. Purple flowers, green vines. She pointed to a caramel-colored square cake with white and yellow roses on top. "That's nice," she said. "That's a German chocolate cake." He removed it from the case, brought it up onto the counter, inches from her nose. She could smell the sweetness of coconut and butter. "What kind of name is that?" she asked.

"Pardon?" He leaned in closer.

"German? What's German about it? That's a stupid thing to call it. Where's Mort?" She peered into the kitchen.

Another customer entered the shop. He looked at Evelyn, then at the cake.

"What's in it?" she asked, shifting her shoulder in front of the cake so the new customer couldn't see it.

"It's a coconut-chocolate instead of plain chocolate frosting, very creamy, with a caramel filling and chocolate fudge cake."

"Whew! Busy," said Evelyn.

"It's our most popular cake," added the son, glancing at the new customer.

"Call it something else and I'll buy it." She paused a moment, then winked. "I'm pulling your leg," she said. "I want it personalized. For my granddaughter."

The son slid the cake off the counter and onto a wood slab behind him. He removed the icer from underneath the shelf, selected a dark, red cream from the refrigerator. "And what'll it say, Mrs. Horowitz?" he asked.

"How do you know my name?"

The son pointed to himself and tried to look harmless. "I'm Ira. Don't you remember? I went to school with—" he stopped.

"You own this place now?" she asked, glancing up at the fluorescent lights aiming for the center of her eyes. She turned to look at the other customer—a stranger. More and more, people were strangers. When had so many people arrived in her city? Her face tightened with panic and she began to sweat.

"I'm Mort's son," he said gently.

"Oh, of course you are." Evelyn waved good-naturedly. "Anyone can tell that. Christ."

"Is the cake for Isabella?" he asked.

"Isabella? What are you, crazy? Franny. For my Franny."

Ira looked toward the kitchen, where his father was sliding a tray of challah breads into the oven. "I'll be right with you," he raised his index finger and nodded at the other customer.

"Take your time," the man nodded knowingly.

"You look familiar," Evelyn said to the stranger.

"I'm Don Stein. I sold you homeowner's insurance."

Aha, a German. But she could no longer remember why this mattered. *Homeowner's insurance? What the hell is that?* I need to be insured against owning a home? She wrinkled her brow, thinking it was a crazy world, and found a dusty tissue at the bottom of her coat pocket. She dabbed at her forehead, then found some Juicy Fruit gum, folded a stick onto her tongue even though it irritated her dental work. She begrudgingly held out the pack to the German.

"You want?" she asked.

He shook his head and smiled. *Good.* She put it away, feeling around in there, finding hair clips, a receipt, some pennies.

Ira returned. He used a rubber spatula to transfer the red cream into an icing bag, then turned the cake on the wooden board and wrote *Francesca*.

"Has Francesca come home?" he asked casually.

"What?" Evelyn divided her cautious gaze between the boy and the German. "How much is this gonna set me back?" She felt at her sides for her pocketbook. "Where's my bag?" Her heart began to pound. She glared at the German.

"Perhaps you left it at home, Mrs. Horowitz," Ira said carefully.

She hated this more than anything, the way the young, whose charge it was to be insolent and crass, were always so damn polite now that she was old. "Someone took my f-ing bag." She began to rub her head, leaving red marks where her fingers disrupted the loose skin.

"Try not to worry, Mrs. Horowitz. I'll bet it's at home. You can pay us another time."

Evelyn stared at the son. "You think I left it home?"

Ira flipped around, slid the boxed cake onto the counter. "Here we go," he said.

She pointed her finger. "You're a good boy." She took the cake from the counter and held it carefully by a delicate knot tied at the center of the butterscotch box.

"Tell Francesca Happy Birthday," said Ira.

Evelyn stopped in the doorway, disoriented. She noticed the cake—somehow it had gotten there—and stumbled out into the day. She walked toward the parking lot, feeling her pockets for the keys and looking for the Chevy. Mort emerged from the back door then, looking like a doctor in his white coat. For a quick moment, she feared he was coming to take her away. He clapped his floury hands on his linen apron.

"Mrs. H.," he said. "How's my favorite customer?"

"You big flirt," said Evelyn.

"I only flirt with my most beautiful customers. The rest come in and I hide in the kitchen—"

"Oh, get out of here—" Evelyn blushed, waved her free hand.

Mort opened the car door. "Let's go find that pocketbook."

"It's probably right where I left it," said Evelyn, making a face, disgusted with herself.

Mort bent over and extended his hand in a grand gesture of chivalry. Evelyn eased herself into the car. He closed the door gently and hopped around to the other side.

Such a young man. So good looking. She wished she could remember his name. He turned the air conditioning on full blast, and backed out of the gravel lot, took the side streets up through the small neighborhood. Evelyn looked at him. She could not remember who he was or where they were going. Behind him, through the window, she saw the familiar matchbox houses, the gardens of daffodils, geraniums, little aprons of grass. How comforted she was by her neighborhood. Even if she could not remember where she was coming from or where she was going, she always knew these plain little streets.

Though Mort offered to help her up the stairs, Evelyn was adamant she could do it herself. Still he waited in the car. She tried to hurry but her knees were unsteady and it was tricky, balancing the cake and concentrating as she raised each foot up to the next step. She dragged her hand along the rusted banister. When finally she got to the top, she was relieved to see she'd left the door unlocked. Her pocketbook was right there on the sofa. She picked it up and walked back to the door, held it in the air. Mort waved, tooted his horn, then backed out. She watched him go, trying to remember who he was and what he was doing in her driveway. She looked at the cake in her hand and thought she might sit down and have a slice along with a cold glass of milk.

Chapter Fifteen

By 1987, Francesca had achieved notoriety as a young painter of prodigious talent. Paul DeVaine, in *art,* called her "the first female painter to make gender irrelevant,"[62] though many others objected to this classification. Lucinda Dialo wrote, in a letter to the editor, "In fact, deSilva's concerns are not with making gender irrelevant—quite the opposite. Never has a painter turned such a fierce and unsparing eye upon the female gender."[63]

And Cynthia Bell added, in a letter published in the same issue of the magazine, "DeSilva is less concerned with the *experience* of women; rather, like so many celebrated male artists throughout history, she was driven by desire for women and all the conflicting feelings unearthed by that desire—repulsion, disgust, fascination, worship, and so forth. Once again, Paul DeVaine, surprising no one, sidesteps the unique source of tension in deSilva's work: her reluctance to view the world through the only lens she possesses—that of a lesbian. In her ambivalence about the female gender, she is far more connected to her male peers than her female predecessors; however, because she remains branded a "female painter," she bears sad little connection to any of them (except perhaps her friend and compatriot, Jean Michel Basquiat)."[64]

In 1987 alone, Francesca's work exhibited in seven national shows and two international ones. Most notably, she'd been special guest (read: sole United States citizen) at the lauded Women's Work exhibition at the National Museum in Canada; several of her paintings hung in a

62. DeVaine, Paul. "Spare, Bold, Defiant—The Gender-Neutral Paintings of Francesca deSilva." *art,* October, 1987.
63. Letters to the Editor, *art,* December 1987.
64. Ibid.

show titled "The Women" at the Museum of Modern Art in New York City and were also included in the New Women Artists Celebration in Berlin.

What's more, she had attracted a fanatically devoted following of college students—*deSilvans*—who traversed the country to see her paintings "live," convening in parking lots to exchange photographs of her work, tidbits about her career, and gossip. They distributed buttons, T-shirts, and bumper stickers on which were printed "deSilva: The Art Your Government Warned You About." Such devotion to a visual artist was unprecedented, earning Francesca deSilva the honor of being the first painter—finally, not just the first "female" painter—to bridge the gap between art and pop culture.[66] She was a frequent speaker at universities and colleges and, in an effort to "keep things fresh," taught introductory summer sessions at the Fine Arts Work Center in Provincetown, Mass.

Even so, Francesca's lack of education and her taciturn, often defiant manner brought out the worst in many of those who were in a position to boost her career, namely critics and scholars. Her paintings frequently inspired skepticism and elitist criticism, much of which seemed designed to scare the young artist away from the canvas. She was accused of relying upon the occurrence of "accident" to give her paintings "meaning,"[67] an insult, deSilva noted in her 1989 interview with Michael Reilly of the *Village Voice*, also leveled at Jackson Pollock after he'd ingeniously dripped paint on a giant canvas instead of relying on the paintbrush. deSilva paraphrased Pollock's response to the peevish reporter's accusation: "Echoing the great Jackson Pollock's response to that question," she said, "I do not *use* the accident . . . I deny the accident."[68]

Underestimating her prodigy's stubborn preference for privacy and squalor, Charlotte Wallace had the barn behind her house remodeled. She installed a sleeping loft, indoor plumbing, and a catalytic wood

66. Warhol, it must be remembered, was not a painter.
67. Grosjean, Jean. "Francesca deSilva: An American Painter in the Dark". BRUSHSTROKES, Canada, Montreal, 1988.
68. Reilly, Michael. "Conversation with Francesca deSilva—Painter, Agitator, Reluctant Rebel." *Village Voice*, 1989.

stove; had two cords of kiln-dried logs piled tidily behind the structure, all to persuade Francesca to abandon her unsavory cabin (a place Charlotte considered unworthy of Francesca's art supplies, never mind her person) and take up residence somewhere suitable to an artist of acclaim, which, Charlotte often repeated, Francesca was.

But Francesca insisted on living and working in the 12' x 16' cabin. The cabin was her home, the site where her real life had begun. What Francesca could not say was that there, in the dark privacy, amid scampering mice and spiders that dangled boldly from the ceiling, she closed the door and remembered herself. There, she was unalterable, certain she existed apart from the art world and the female fans, the intrusive memories of her crazy sister, her perennial sadness about Lisa, the rejection she'd suffered at the hands of her family. In the cabin, the unloved, barely tolerated, unexceptional child reappeared, the child whose greatest achievement was her ability to build a hut. Though the public possessed some fleeting curiosity about her, wanting to pry her apart as if she were a preserved frog on a slim glass slide, Francesca knew not to become attached to this. People, she had learned long ago, were fickle and cruel.

So, though the painting was good and though she felt, when she was painting, that she had been born for a good reason, not just to flail about for fifty, sixty—*please, let it be no more*—years in torment, things hadn't changed so much. She still wanted to stay where she couldn't be found, and sometimes she remained inside the small, dark room for days at a time—painting or sleeping or staring at some fixed point on the wall. In the cabin she did not have to pretend at schooling or privilege or knowledge of the great movements in art history. She could lounge on the bottom bunk smoking cigarettes, feeling grungy and empty inside. In the cabin when she turned out the lights, she was herself again—the shell of a human being, all the image and fantasy and notoriety swallowed by ordinary darkness.

Her opening at the Wallace Gallery had pulled in over $20,000, leaving her enough to live on for at least a year. Plus, paintings continued to sell, fetching at least $15,000 each; they did not sell quickly, but when they did, enthusiasts were willing to pay top dollar. Thus, there was no more shoveling snow or selling knick-knacks for Francesca.

Still, she missed her old life—the insecurity and endless solitude; the long, unrelegated nights. Occasionally she broke through her embarrassment at her good fortune and stopped by the flea market where she met with a flurry of slapping hugs and stories about the old days, tales for the benefit of newcomers: "You should have seen her when she walked in here . . ." and "You'd never have known she was a genius by looking at that one." Good-hearted, well-intentioned insults that scratched like the thorns on branches—not too deeply, just enough to make her rub her arms and be glad when it was over.

Except for the occasional suit she had to wear when attending dreaded dinners with collectors or curators, Francesca's life as a painter fitted her brilliantly. Rarely were there even small moments—cleaning brushes, brushing her teeth, sweeping the floor of the cabin—when she was without gratitude for the favorable shift in her fortune. Her years in New Haven seemed farther and farther away, the house on Riverview Street demure as a tiny island from which she'd floated in a small boat. She noted with bittersweet relief that each day she thought less of Lisa. Lisa's intense face or small hands or some tough, flippant comment she'd made, the quickening of her breath during sex, her rings moving in the night like lightning bugs as she lit up a joint—these things appeared only two or three times a week instead of hourly. Now, when she encountered some interesting sight or overheard a tidbit of unsettling conversation, she kept it entirely to herself rather than filing it away or jotting it down to share with Lisa at some later date. She no longer inhaled deeply each time she passed the scent store on Commercial Street, searching out the aroma of lavender oil that reminded her of love. When she painted and the painting was good, the ideas leapt from inside her fully formed, larvae transformed into butterflies, anxious to be freed from the soft cage of her brain.

She began to recall quieter aspects of her childhood, details more curious than unpleasant. She remembered her odd habit of getting lost in the supermarket, her strategy of gazing straight ahead at the forest of ladies' hands rather than up at faces where she might have efficiently distinguished her mother's dark hair and narrow features. While wandering the aisles of the store, she was driven more by curiosity than panic, trying to recall the specifics of her mother's fingers. Halfheartedly, she'd conjure the small diamond engagement ring and slim gold band, the raisin enamel that coated Vivian's trimmed fingernails.

She'd wind up at the front desk, sucking a lollipop or nibbling on a cookie while some awkward man tried to describe her over the intercom: *We have a lost little girl named Francesca. She's eight years old with brown hair. If this is your little child, please come to Customer Service.* In the time between the announcement and her mother's arrival, she'd rough out her new life in an orphanage—a dank, puddly basement where hundreds of ugly children spoke with British accents. At least she would have company.

Or she'd imagine that her mother had run off and she'd been sent to live with Evelyn. Or she was adopted by the awkward man at the grocery store and his blond wife. (She knew nothing about the man's wife, but always imagined everyone's wife to be blond. Nice mothers, too: blond. Unlike her own. The wives of Francesca's imagination were fair and pleasant, like kind, aging princesses from fairy tales.) If there were to be siblings in her new home, they would be male and athletic. (No geniuses.) Together, they'd play tetherball after dinner, pounding the yellow ball until its cord strangled a shady oak in the backyard. Or ride bicycles in the turnaround at the end of the road. If she fell down and scraped her skin, there would be Mercurochrome and a Band-Aid.

Then, just as she'd begun to chisel from her imagination the specifics of her new life, her mother would arrive in the little Customer Service control tower, breathless, exuding sweet concern and thanking the man for his trouble. On the way home, they'd stop at Dairy Queen, even if it were nearly dinner time, where Francesca would be offered a soft serve in lieu of an apology.

Francesca continued to see Shanta Wall during the year that followed her opening, though she never considered the relationship to be anything more than a protracted summer fling. She steadfastly restricted their time together to two or three nights a week and, further, only nights when she felt like fucking and sleeping instead of painting. Mornings after staying at Shanta's luxury condo she'd take a hot shower that would have to last until her next visit (unless she used Charlotte's facilities in the meantime), and bicycle home through the silent streets, the smell of oil paint on her skin mingling with the aroma of early morning coffee brewing in the Provincetown restaurants and the sweet fat frying inside Portuguese bakeries.

Shanta was so beautiful and she smelled of all sorts of interesting, expensive scents. Her wardrobe was filled with tight-fitting garments that seemed to have been tailored for her fleshy, ample form. But it was painting, not sex, that Francesca craved.[69] And all the painting she did, combined with the large continent of her heart occupied by Lisa, did not leave much left over. Thus, anytime they discussed the possibility of Francesca abandoning the cabin (her landlord had increased the rent to $65 a month, well aware of the change in Francesca's circumstances) and living at Shanta's condo, Francesca felt as if someone were tightening a clamp around her chest. The sensation began as a tight little cough, almost like the onset of a flu, and ended with Francesca, inarticulate and angry, gasping for air on the balcony, dragging on a cigarette.

Shanta had never been permitted to visit the cabin and this, more than any other of Francesca's rules and peculiarities designed to maintain a stiff distance between them, she found offensive. Francesca knew it was perfectly reasonable for Shanta to wish to visit the cabin—*at least once!* They were lovers, after all, and Shanta wanted to see where it all happened. Finally, Francesca agreed to a visit. They scheduled it on the evening of an obligatory extravaganza; this way, Francesca figured, there would be a time limit. Shanta would pick up Francesca at the cabin,

---

69. In 1990, after founding San Francisco's pro-sex publication *LICK,* Wall wrote an article about her summer romp with deSilva called "The Stone Goddess of Truth." She later self-published a slim account of their affair (à la Peggy Caserta's lewd tell-all volume about Janis Joplin, *Going Down with Janis*) titled *Suburbia Upended,* under her own imprint, boundandgagged books, San Francisco. Here, she asserted that Francesca deSilva used her painting as a means of avoiding intimacy and that the artist was, unadmittedly, a stone butch—i.e., one who provides sexual pleasure but does not want to be touched.
Author's Note: Other evidence controverts this.

as usual, but this time, instead of waiting in the car, she'd come in.

"But you can not," Francesca insisted, pointing her finger, "comment on the paintings. In fact, I want you to act like you don't even see them."

Shanta agreed. "Sure, sure. Of course, baby," she said, immediately dismissing all instructions. How would it be possible to enter such a tiny room, filled to the brim with paintings completed by the most brilliant artist she'd ever known, and not take a peek?

Francesca hung her tuxedo on the metal bedpost, filled the espresso maker, and lit the stove. She left a cigarette burning in the ashtray while she brushed her teeth, spit out her toothpaste, and inspected her face in the cheap mirror that hung from a nail. Her hair was unruly, if reasonably clean. But no matter how mightily she scrubbed her fingers, they were stained grayish red, paint stuck like street tar under her nails. Oh well.

She unwrapped the tux from its stiff, plastic bag, slid the pants on, chose a clean running bra and undershirt, dusted off the starched shirt and buttoned it carefully up the front. She clipped on the bow tie and fussed with her cummerbund, pulling on the jacket just as Shanta's Saab came to a stop alongside the cabin. Shanta yanked up on the emergency brake. Keys jangled. Doc Martens thumped over the train tracks, along the gritty, pebbly ground toward the door. "Hello?" she called.

"Come in," said Francesca stepping back to the edge of the room, pressing her hot mug of coffee to her chin.

Quietly, reverently, Shanta entered the dark cabin. She wore low-slung jeans and a tight gold top. Her dark, short hair glistened in the late afternoon light. Her lips were coated in thick blackberry gloss.

"Is that what you're wearing?" Francesca asked, gesturing.

Shanta shook her head. "I have three dresses in the car. I want to see which one you like best."

"Oh, good. God. I thought I put this stupid thing on for nothing." Francesca sat on one of two plastic lawn chairs while Shanta brought in the three gowns, wrapped in plastic, and laid them on the top bunk. Shanta walked slowly, deferentially, around the small room, taking in each darkened beam, the stack of cigarette packs on the windowsill, tubes of paint abandoned to a pile in the corner, the collection of over-turned coffee cups drying out beside the sink. Obediently, she did not glance at the walls—which were empty—nor at the three easels set apart from one another, all holding canvases that were turned to face the wall. There was nothing for her to see. Nothing at all. Any remaining canvases loitering about the small room had been covered with sheets and clothing, creating an odd air of insanity, as if Francesca were not a painter at all, but just a lunatic who collected blank surfaces and pretended they were art.

"I like it," Shanta said, nodding repeatedly, smiling.

"Like what?" Francesca glanced around. *Had she forgotten to cover something?*

"The cabin. All it needs is a lava light." Her teeth glowed coconut against her brown skin.

Francesca pulled a cord and illuminated a bulb that hung from the ceiling. "Sorry. I like to paint in the dark."

"You're kind of a hippie," said Shanta.

Francesca shrugged. "That's my aesthetic—"

"Is that what you call it—an aesthetic?" Shanta teased.

Francesca lit a cigarette. *That word,* she thought, *I hate that word.* "Are you saying I have no aesthetic?" she asked, her voice tight. She took a long drag of her cigarette. She remembered—still—how her mother had scoffed at her for possessing such a refined thing as an aesthetic, as though Francesca couldn't possibly desire something described by more than two syllables: Hut. Ball. Ice cream. Bed-spread. Record.

Shanta slid onto the bottom of the bunk bed, wriggled back against the wall. "So, you know what I want, don't you? Right here in your cabin." She unbuttoned the fly of her jeans, one heavy button at a time, blinking as if startled each time a chunky knob popped free.

"I asked you a question," said Francesca.

"What was it?" She slid her jeans down the length of her legs and onto the floor.

"I asked if you think I have no taste."

"You have very nice taste," said Shanta, her eyelids sinking lower.

"And I think you taste very nice, too." She removed her designer brand underwear and spread her legs wide.

"I don't think we have time."

"Oh yeah, this'll go fast. Trust me." Shanta pressed her feet up against the underside of the top mattress, flexing the muscles in her calves.

Francesca took off her jacket slowly, rolled up her sleeves, and placed her cigarette on the lip of the ashtray. She took a step closer and stared down. Shanta's naked cunt was splayed there, glistening. It looked dangerous. As if to kneel down and put her face there, to bury her face there as she had done so many times before, might cost her something precious. Her dignity, or her freedom, something too big to risk. It was the wrong context and in this context it seemed perverse—standing above and peering down like a clinician. She stepped closer and inhaled the first whiff of sex hitting the damp air. She shook her head. "I can't."

"You're kidding, right?"

"I'm all dressed. Let's do it afterward."

"Afterward?" Shanta sat up. "What do you mean, afterward?"

"After the thing. When we get back to your place."

"I want it here. In *your* place. I want you to fuck me here. Like a big butch."

Francesca stepped back in horror. She put her hands in the air. "Whoa. What did you just say?"

"I said I want you to—"

"Tell me . . ." interrupted Francesca, "Tell me that you didn't just call me a big butch."

Shanta hesitated. "Okay. I didn't."

"Did you?"

"Did I or not? What do you want me to say?" Shanta stood up and bent over, searching for her underwear.

"I want you to say you didn't."

"Okay. I didn't."

"Good. Because that does nothing for me. Let's get that perfectly clear. Just because I'm wearing a tuxedo. Just because you see me as, I don't know, kind of masculine or something. That doesn't mean I want to be a guy."

"First of all," Shanta said, searching frantically for her underwear, "being a butch is not the same thing as being a guy. If you knew anything at all about lesbianism, you'd know that." Her voice quivered. She pulled on her panties and turned her attention to the dresses, separating a wine-colored gown from the others.

"So now you're saying I don't know about lesbianism."

"You're not listening to what I'm saying. But then, you never do."

"First, you tell me I have no taste. Now you're saying I'm too stupid to know the difference between being butch and being a man." Francesca lifted her cigarette from the ashtray and took a long drag. She stood with her back to the wall, one hand rammed in her pocket.

"I thought you'd like being called a butch. I thought you were going for that." Shanta removed the dress from its hanger. She turned her body away from Francesca and stepped carefully into the gown. "So, sue me," she muttered, suddenly, ineffably tired. Tired of being so careful all the time.

"I'm not trying to *be* anything. I'm just dressed up. I'm just being myself."

"Got it. It won't happen again."

"I don't want to be *butch*. I don't feel *butch*. I mean, are *you* trying to be something?" Francesca waved her hands around, as if searching for something in the dark.

Shanta had never heard Francesca talk this much, flail about hopelessly for so many words. Her paintings were as deep as the ocean at its most aqueous, but, sadly, there had been no gift for language bestowed in equal measure. She refrained from expressing her frustration, stopped herself from likening, aloud, this conversation to discussing complex and intellectually demanding issues with a toddler. Whatever Francesca's deep thoughts, Shanta decided, they were better left unmolested, reserved for her paintings.

The darkness settled slowly, turning the interior of the cabin, lit by one bulb, to a soft gold. Shanta removed stockings from her knapsack, tossed a small, black beaded handbag onto the bed, then rolled the stockings up over her muscular legs, all in perfect silence. She stood up.

"Ta da," she said with no enthusiasm. She opened her arms.

"You look great."

"Good. Because I feel like shit. Let's go." She wanted to crawl into the dusty cubby beneath the bunk bed.

"Your skin . . ." Francesca stepped forward and wrapped one large hand around each of Shanta's hips, "is so beautiful. It reminds me of wine."

"Whatever," Shanta said, pretending.

Francesca held Shanta's chin and kissed her on the mouth, long and slow, a gentle kiss full of the affection she felt in that moment. And she felt, in that moment, great affection. It was a relief. If only she could tether this feeling to the inside of her. If only she could force her feelings for the good-natured and lovely Shanta into the cordoned-off section of her heart. But that was Lisa's kingdom. Perhaps love can feel like this, she thought. Perhaps this is love. You have nice sex. Someone's face is pleasant to look at, like a beautiful color. They say interesting things about half the time. You have a warm feeling. A protective feeling. *Perhaps I am too fussy.*

Outside, she held the car door open as Shanta gathered the bottom of her gown and wrapped it around her body, sliding effortlessly into the driver's seat.

Francesca wished she could be the one doing the driving— opening the passenger's door for Shanta, walking around the front of the expensive car and assuming the position of control, blanketing the leather-coated stick shift in her palm. Instead, she climbed in on the passenger's side, pushed in the cigarette lighter, and rolled down the window.

"You smoke too much," Shanta said.

"I hate these dinner things."

"Do you even know what this is for?"

"Some award." She shrugged.

"Do you know *who* it's for?" Shanta asked, her voice tightening.

Francesca shrugged. "Me?"

"No, it's for *both* of us. We're *both* receiving an award from the community."

"What community?"

"Jesus Christ, Francesca. The gay and lesbian community. You *are* a member of that community, you know. Whether you like it or not."

Francesca stared at Shanta. "I know that."

Shanta had known for weeks about a bitter debate surrounding their selection for the award. She'd chosen to protect Francesca from the petty infighting, knowing how her lover dreaded these affairs, wanting to do nothing to aggravate her discomfort. But now, after what had just happened in the cabin, she felt vindictive. Had she not looked fabulous in her gown and known there would be gobs of fascinating people at this event, she might be in a puddle on the floor right now, inconsolable. Every time she convinced herself that Francesca was good for her, something reminded her it was a lie. Still, Francesca, whether she admitted it or not, was so deliciously, beautifully butch, so enigmatic, so tortured, so damaged and reticent and impossible to know; and Shanta was helpless to do anything but wait until the day when Francesca hurt her for good.

"I wasn't going to tell you about this—" She shifted deftly into fourth gear and opened the sunroof as they cruised onto the highway, passing signs for the beaches, leaf-smothered entrances to hiking paths, two men and their dog. (Shanta beeped and waved; they returned the gesture, peering after the car.)

"What."

"There was a lot of controversy. About us."

"Us? Why?"

"Someone spread a rumor that you . . ." Shanta smiled. "You're really going to hate this—"

"What."

"That you weren't born a woman."

"What do you mean? What else would I be?"

She shrugged. "I don't know . . . A transsexual?"

Francesca felt sick. Her head seemed pulled taut as a rubber band. She didn't mind being a tomboy. She knew she was a tomboy. A little on the masculine side. Maybe she was even butch, though she hated that word and all it connoted. But now people were questioning the authenticity of her gender?

"What ever happened to just liking women?" she asked.

"Don't let it get to you, baby. The whole transgender thing is a fad. I assured them I had firsthand evidence to the contrary," she winked. "And it all would have blown over the way these ridiculous controversies do . . . if this vocal contingent of gay men hadn't opposed being represented by a transgendered lesbian. Which of course you're not. I told them that. But gay men are weird about butches. Not that you're butch. Then these New York lesbians got involved."

"New York?" Francesca started to sweat. "Why are people from New York involved?"

"Tourism and politics. Provincetown's national pasttime. The New York Chapter of The Lesbian Avengers joined with SALSA, this Latina group, also from New York, to protest the historical underrepresentation of people of color among awards recipients."

"I don't understand why New Yorkers are involved. Can we turn on the A/C?"

Shanta pressed a button that closed all the windows simultaneously. The air conditioner exhaled, and that, combined with the jerking motion of the car—Shanta was not a gifted driver—made Francesca sick to her stomach.

"Do you have any pot?" she asked. "I need to calm down."

It just so happened that Shanta, who maintained a daily habit, had tucked a joint into the smooth, satin pocket of her beaded purse. Francesca unsnapped the little black bag, found the joint, stroked the pouch's bumpy exterior before closing the clasp with a pop. She pushed in the lighter and sat farther back into the leather seat. "I don't understand why people from New York have to get involved in something like this. I mean, they can come and all, but why do they have to make such a big deal?"

"New Yorkers like to have a say in everything. They're like God." Shanta took a long hit off the joint. "Good idea, baby," she said, indicating the joint. "I thought we'd go out on the deck and smoke it later. But there will be plenty of weed there." She was enjoying herself, having leveled the playing field. Now, at least, she wasn't the only one feeling lousy. "Of course," she continued, the pot making her more garrulous. "I don't count as a person of color because I come from money. Apparently, if you're 'of color' and you're 'of money', one cancels out the other."

"I'm not 'of money.'"

"But we're *both* getting the award. So we're *both* under scrutiny." Shanta wanted to slap her. The whole timid, self-absorption thing made it impossible even to have a decent fight. The minute she raised her voice, she felt shrewish, as if she were berating a retarded child. "Anyhow," she said, "you're problematic for other reasons. Some other NY group, with the acronym JALOPY—"

"JALOPY?" Francesca laughed. She was high, thank goodness; her mood was greatly improved. "Let me guess: they're upset because I don't drive. They're opposed to nondriving lesbians who look like men."

Shanta ignored Francesca, not amused, focused on deconstructing the acronym, one letter at a time, as she pulled into the parking lot of the restaurant where the dinner was taking place. They waited behind two other cars for valet parking. "I think it's . . ." She spoke slowly, "*Jews . . . and Lesbians . . . of Pride*—Yes! Something like that."

"What's their fucking problem?"

"They object to your internalized anti-Semitism."

"What internalized anti-Semitism?"

"Well, you are rather quiet about the whole thing." Shanta pulled up alongside a young boy wearing eyeshadow and a light green suit. She handed him the keys and winked at him. "You look fabulous, sugar."

"And so do you, honey." He batted his lashes.

For a moment, Francesca did not know who she was, where she'd come from. Was she Jewish? Had she forgotten that she was Jewish? Why had she never thought of this? She shook her head and giggled as a tall—very, very tall—couple of middle-aged men in taffeta crossed before them. Shanta introduced them as Joan and Bette. Shanta knew everyone at the event, it seemed. The greetings rolled in, one after another, while Francesca stood smiling—a reluctant icon of her community—which seemed to be all that was required of her.

Bunyan, 1988

Abandoned when deSilva left Cape Cod to return to New Haven on March 9, 1987, the gargantuan *Bunyan* is a wry parody on the paternalistic folktale of the same name. Like *Reality Has Intruded Here, Bunyan* was executed upon a door appropriated from a demolished house down the street from Charlotte Wallace's home.[70] But unlike *Reality Has Intruded Here,* which lures the viewer closer, *Bunyan* demands that the viewer step all the way to the back of the museum to survey the 10' x 4' work in its entirety. In its simplest incarnation, *Bunyan* is a portrait of the behemoth American folk hero; upon closer inspection, and in conjunction with the endless deconstruction to which it has been subjected, *Bunyan* is a complex self-portrait, a cultural, personal, and political parody in which the artist hyperbolizes her gender rebellion, transforming herself into an "American ultra-butch,"[71] a deviant icon, blatantly embodying classic, stereotypical male attributes: size, strength, masculinity.

Writes Phillip Hamil in the 1990 essay "Deconstructing deSilva," "[In *Bunyan*] . . . deSilva's suit of armor is in-deconstructible . . . no matter from what angle she is attacked—e.g., her choice of the megamale, hyper-American folk hero as an alter ego—she

70. Both *Bunyan* and *Reality Has Intruded Here* were created on materials rescued from the excavated property of an elderly woman, Mrs. May, of whom deSilva was very fond. Like Evelyn Horowitz, Mrs. May had a talent for mahjong and cards; but unlike Evelyn, Mrs. May was a lesbian. After the woman's death, her property and the 150-year-old house where she'd lived since childhood, were leveled and developed for condominiums.
71. Bell, Cynthia. *The Butch Is Back.* Santa Cruz: Labrys Press, 1995.

subverts our need to censure and destroy. She invites our castigation, assures us she can take it, that she is tougher than any man."[72] Hamil goes on to liken public resistance to *Bunyan* to the myopia that greeted Van Gogh, Beckett, and James Joyce before their work was, finally, sanctified.

Bunyan, as deSilva portrays him/her, is tall and broad, with huge feet firmly planted in creased black boots, the toes encrusted with hardened, red mud. One shoe is unlaced, lending an unexpected humanity to the work, a feeling of daft imperfection, even slovenliness—characteristics not usually attributed to the legendary logger, the tireless worker, fantasy of the American Dream. Woolen pants cover Bunyan's sturdy legs, held in place by matching red suspenders. He/she wears a faded black Henley underneath a red and black checked flannel hunting jacket. His/her hands are giant, dirty, with thick, yellowed nails. One elbow is bent, the forearm resting upon a huge ax, its metal gleaming, even in the smoky afternoon light of the Pacific Northwest. The other hand rests modestly at his/her side, sporting a gold wedding band. The name of Bunyan's beloved blue ox, *Babe,* is printed in dark blue clouds across the hazy sky, though the animal itself is nowhere depicted.[73]

72. "Deconstructing deSilva." *Illustrated Gent,* January 1990, page 52.
73. deSilva's use of language-as-image was unprecedented in her work and thought to have been a tribute to Jean-Michel Basquiat. The word BABE here acts as metatext, commenting on the sexist paradigm responsible for creating the legend of Paul Bunyan and embellishing it with all the attributes coveted by the hearty American male, including access to the nubile female, or "babe." "What is the word babe in modern American culture?," asks Dialo in *Artful Deviation: An Examination of Gender Treachery in Woolf's Orlando and deSilva's Bunyan.* "An epithet. A term of endearment. A woman's name.

And then, lo and behold, resting upon the Leviathan shoulders of this American icon of masculinity, is the faintly bearded face of Francesca deSilva. "One is simply in shock," writes Clara Feinstein in her review of the deSilva Retrospective at the Whitney, "rather like a surprise encounter with a charging bull . . . The viewer is forced to stand with his [sic] head snapped back, gaping at this monstrosity that stretches nearly as high as the ceiling . . . [its] crude face mocks you for paying it any attention—which, of course, it does not deserve. It is less a painting than an assault."[74]

Lucinda Dialo asserts that one must consult the legend in order to effectively examine Bunyan. In *Artful Deviation: An Examination of Gender Treachery in Woolf's Orlando and deSilva's Bunyan,* she writes, "The original legend of *Paul Bunyan* is as perverse as any painting Francesca deSilva could have created. American as indigestion, it oozes excess, consumerism, machismo, and homoeroticism. Some renditions claim the giant's head 'penetrated the sky.' That he 'dismembered redwood trees and used the needles of their branches to comb his meticulous moustache.' Others report he was—only!—the size of three-story buildings, 'towering over, but walking humbly amongst regular folk.' And while Bunyan's wife is mentioned on rare occasion—she is referred

A cheap cologne. It is a female-identified word, implies a familiarity, or, conversely, perhaps conjointly, devaluation. deSilva's choice to omit the blue ox as an image, but to instead paint its name, draws our attention away from the friendly figure of the story, into semantics, and the folktale's more disquieting themes."

74. Clara Feinstein. "Much Ado About Mediocrity—The Whitney's Retrospective of Francesca deSilva." *The New Yorker.*

to only as Mrs. Bunyan—we are told nothing about her but that she was handsome and large. One hopes very large."[75]

This casual disinterest in females on the part of a huge, handsome, and by all accounts kempt man has not escaped postmodernists, who speculate endlessly about Paul Bunyan's sexual orientation. Such speculation, is, of course, "supported" by selected passages from the multitudinous tellings of the legend. R. Randy Dorff, Ph.D., Transgendered Activist, Queer Theorist, and Chair of the Gay, Lesbian, Bisexual and Transgendered Department of Queer Cultural Studies at Harvard University claims that Babe, Bunyan's "faithful, huge [i.e., well-hung] blue ox is a metaphorical surrogate for Bunyan's gay lover."[76] He also raises the question of a "genital vacuum" in the painting, resulting in the absence of "identification of or commitment to a specific gender. The absence of a defined link between the female head and the well-endowed masculine body points out a conflict within the artist."[77] He disputes the classification of Bunyan as hypo-realism (or pseudo-realism, as it would later be called) and, instead, calls it "metanarcissistic self-portraiture . . . In other words, wish fulfillment—the painter portraying her

75. Dialo, Lucinda. *Artful Deviation: An Examination of Gender Treachery in Woolf's Orlando and deSilva's Bunyan*. New Haven: Yale University Press 1995, page 346.
76. Dorff, R. Randy. "The Queering of Machismo in the Eurocentric Folk Legend." *A Multi-Cultural Reader*. Harvard University, April 12, 1994. Note: The ox, which popularly conjures a huge creature of boundless strength, actually refers to any of several members of the bull family (e.g., yak, buffalo, bison, gaur) and is most accurately defined as "a castrated, domesticated bull, used as a draft animal." [Webster's New World Dictionary; Third College Edition.]
77. Ibid.

self as she would like to be seen, hyperbolizing her desire, emphasizing her wish to embody the ultimate specimen of the dominant gender—a male, macho giant. Bunyan," writes Dorff, "attacks at the most primal level; it depicts the male's worst nightmare: a giant dyke with an ax."[78]

78. Ibid.

Chapter Sixteen

To celebrate Isabella's 25th birthday, Vivian invited an array of her own acquaintances for a barbecue. Only an hour or so before the guests were due to arrive, Isabella lay with legs spread beneath the faucet of the bathtub; thousands, even millions of fingers tapped her clitoris until she shook and clenched the porcelain edges, gritting her teeth, fierce in her determination to rid herself forever of desire. How much longer could she go unintroduced to oral pleasure, without words whispered close to the earlobes, fingers pressing the knobs of her spine? She was too old to be sexless and knew she could not—would not!—live much longer. Hence, there was no point in saving herself. And though she sensed there were problems next door, she was not confident that LeeAnn Frank's (i.e., the Little One) fan of blond hair would soon be spread across her yellowed pillowcase.

Six years had passed since her suicide attempt. The details were vague: an uncooperative Mustang, her sister and the Chinese girl getting it on in the attic. She'd woken in a hospital room, an oxygen mask over her face, her head throbbing so hard it seemed someone was inside, hitting her skull with a hammer. The first sight upon opening her eyes had been Vivian blowing long gray streams of smoke out the tiny crack of an open window. She'd never felt so sick, so horrible, so repentant. She'd promised her parents: never again. No more suicide attempts. They were relieved, if not wholly convinced.

Isabella moved into the attic, where she hoped to be afforded maximum privacy with which to focus on her novel. Really, really focus, she told Mrs. Val Noonan. Still, she maintained an arsenal of pills and vodka just in case. It wasn't long before she'd abandoned *A Gift to the Universe* and begun a volume of sestinas in the voice of Sylvia Plath. But this proved more difficult than it had initially seemed. Over and over Isabella struggled to use the word "oven" in six stanzas without resorting to mentions of cooking or the holocaust.

"Perhaps you are focusing too much on the suicide. Are you aware that she went to Smith?" Mrs. Val Noonan had suggested, always trying to work her alma mater into any conversation. Once again, Isabella had tried to articulate the importance of suicide, how it was to her what, say, Vermont was to Frost, Maude Gonne to Yeats, the Self to May Sarton.

Vivian let Isabella borrow a light-green, ultrasuede dress to wear to the party. Its deep plunge highlighted Isabella's ample cleavage. Vivian herself donned a bright orange dress with white sandals, a bold choice that drew out her bain-de-soleil tan. Her veined hands ended in slick painted nails, manicured smooth, curved at the edges, the coffee-colored shells long enough to conjure femininity, short enough to assert competence.

The guests arrived in groups. Alfonse manned the grill, pressing down on the burgers so he could watch the fat hit the hot coals, while Vivian adjusted napkins and checked to see that the citronella candles were working. Isabella stood alone against the house, sworn to remain sober. Must not embarrass Mom, she repeated like a mantra.

And then, emerging from around the side of the house, sulking behind his parents, appeared Aaron Newman. Like an angel. He was the stepson of Joycie Newman, a partner at Kasselbaum Kasselbaum Steele, the New Haven law firm where Vivian worked as a paralegal. Vivian worshipped Joycie the way girls adore, say, Julie Andrews, always describing her as "a beautiful, brilliant black lady." Each time she said it, she wondered whether Joycie would take offense at her including the word "black" in her description, or whether it would be more insulting if she omitted it. Joycie's four books on women's prisons, all autographed, dominated the shelves in the DeSilva living room, their stark white covers having long ago usurped the volumes on raising a gifted child.

Isabella watched as Aaron Newman skulked behind his stepmother and father, practically yawning from boredom. He was blond and thin, not quite a boy, nor a girl. Something much more interesting. She knew she could push him around if it came to that, imagined that having him on top of her would be like a fine quilt, his weight evenly distributed, covering her limbs. His lithe body and smooth fingers made her nipples hard.

She shifted her feet and leaned her body against the house, tucked two fingers under a rotting shingle, and swallowed hard. "God," she whispered.

"Say hello to Joycie, Terence, and Aaron," Vivian demanded cheerfully.

Isabella forced a smile and glanced down nervously, suddenly worried that something was wrong with her dress—her breasts were exposed or she'd spilled something on the front.

Alfonse came over and shook everyone's hand. His apron, on which was printed "Life is too short to drink cheap wine," was already splattered with grease. Vivian pointed at the stains disapprovingly, and said "Oh, Al! I can't take you anywhere," then shook her head at Joycie. All the adults but Alfonse scattered; still Aaron remained. He stood near Isabella and faced front.

"Nice dress," he smiled.

"Thanks. Is that your mother?" Isabella asked.

"That's not really possible," said Aaron.

"Oh," Isabella nodded. "Because she's black?"

"No. Because she's only 35. She'd had to have had me when she was, uh . . ."

Isabella knew the answer; still she waited. He was supposed to be some sort of whiz kid, according to Vivian.

"Thirteen," he said finally. "Don't think so," he flashed a sarcastic smile, then bent over and took a beer from the cooler.

"I like her tights," Isabella said.

"Yeah," he surveyed his stepmother. "She loves purple."

Isabella watched as he twisted the cap. She heard the crack of gas. The cold steam curled above the brown lip of the bottle. Aaron threw his head back and took a long drink, his Adam's apple bobbing up and down like something stuck in his throat. She listened for the sound of the beer maneuvering around this huge, centrally located obtrusion, but there was no evidence of a struggle. God, she thought, I would kill for one sip. She praised herself for having had the foresight to wedge a bottle of Smirnoff's between the oil burner and the basement wall. And then, too, there was the emergency stash in the attic.

"You look beautiful, baby," Alfonse touched her back on his way to the grill, nodded at Aaron, scrutinizing his tennis shoes and slack, faded jeans.

Isabella felt delicate and feminine. Like a piece of glass on a windowsill refracting the late afternoon light. Like Natalie Wood in *West Side Story*. She wished she could speak in a breathy voice, laugh up and down the scale, cover her mouth shyly with two fingers. Vivien Leigh in *Gone with the Wind*. Catherine in the presence of Heathcliff. Anna Karenina. Madame Bovary. Did a woman ever run out of inimitable role models?

She took a step closer to Aaron, inhaled his smell—sweat, lemony deodorant, beer. She watched the top of the large Styrofoam cooler lifted each time a misted brown bottle of German beer was removed, then passed among uninterested fingers.

"Wanna go for a walk?" Aaron asked.

Just then the lesbians emerged from the hedges. The Little One carried a gift-wrapped book. "Hello, Bella," she said, smiling at Aaron.

"Thanks so much," Isabella took the package. "This is Aaron," she motioned to her left and tucked the book under her arm. "Aaron, these are the neighbors."

Vivian arrived with a plate of hot dogs and hamburgers on bright white buns, half the burgers blanketed in orange slices of cheese. "Isabella," she said in a high pitch, "Go show Aaron the house. Leave the neighbors alone." She held the plate out to the lesbians. The Little One took a hot dog; the Big One waved the plate away. "Thanks. I don't eat meat," she said.

Isabella wanted to tell the neighbors how she'd tried to write a book about them. But there was Aaron. Waiting. She looked at his shoes, his bare feet inside sneakers. The neighbors, after all, lived right next door. She might never see Aaron again.

"See you," she said to the neighbors, certain the Little One had flinched with jealousy.

She had not yet said hello to Mrs. Val Noonan, who was standing at the Weber beside Alfonse. The agent's legs were crossed at the ankles, her head was bent; she giggled and pulled at a corner of molten cheese with bitten-down nails. Alfonse patted her shoulder, gestured and laughed.

"I have some vodka in the basement," Isabella said.

Aaron followed her around the side of the house. She felt him look at her body as she quietly pulled back the screen door. They slipped in, walked slowly, uncertainly, down the basement steps. It was cool and dark. A pile of dirty laundry lay on the cement floor. Isabella kicked it aside. She located the bottle but could not dislodge it from behind the oil burner. Aaron happily took over, rocking the neck of the bottle several times until it finally came free. He handed it over proudly. Men loved that sort of thing, she knew: stepping in and doing things women couldn't finish. She licked her lips, turned the cap, and heard the tear of paper. She spun the plastic cap until it toppled off and onto the floor. Like a stripper's last article of clothing, Isabella thought, raising the bottle and taking a hefty swallow.

Aaron removed a small package and a tiny spoon from his front pocket.

"Cute," said Isabella, pointing to the spoon. She took another drink, wiped her hot, numb mouth with the back of her hand, and hoped he would not ask for the bottle. He did eventually, though he barely put his lips to it, handed it back, then bent over and dipped the tiny silver spoon into a pile of powder. Carefully he lifted the spoon, positioned it at the base of his nostril, and inhaled hard. Like he had a bad cold.

He offered Isabella the spoon.

"What happens?" she asked, turning over some of the powder with the tiny utensil.

"You'll feel really awake," he said.

"I'm always really awake."

Aaron shrugged and took the spoon from her, dug another mound, and sucked it into his nostril. His eyes glittered. He ran his finger along the hard wall of his gums. Isabella took another swig of vodka, exchanged the spoon for the bottle, and sucked in the powder. Her brain was suddenly flooded with sunlight.

Too quickly they finished the cocaine, depleted the vodka. Aaron stuck out his finger and put it under Isabella's top lip, pressed her tingling gums. He pulled her body close to his, pressed against her, and covered her mouth with his own. He was so eager, so fast, and the world seemed numb and far away. Still she liked the smell of him, the softness of his lips against her unfeeling skin. She was wet between her legs. He undressed her, undressed himself. She lay back on the daybed and thought that finally she was doing something women were expected to do. Finally she was not in a white room or an attic. She was not at a party full of strangers. Finally, ow (he apologized), she was staring up into a face that gave her pleasure.

Chapter Seventeen

Francesca sat in the pizzeria chatting with Sherry, describing the previous evening's excesses: plates of neatly cut lines of cocaine passed around the table, boys fucking in the coat room, Shanta taking so many quaaludes, Francesca had had no choice but to send her home with some sturdy, very willing Butch ("with a capital B," Francesca said, realizing in the moment, that Sherry also fit that description) who actually knew how to drive a car. "I gotta learn to drive," she said ruefully.

Sherry nodded in agreement.

Just then, Charlotte Wallace pulled back the restaurant door and stepped inside, flustered and excited. Sherry took one look at her, exhaled a long, disgusted sigh, and escaped to the back of the room. Charlotte opened her eyes wide. "What," she said to Francesca. "What did I do?"

Francesca shrugged, feeling her worlds collide.

"You know," Charlotte said, scooting into the booth and facing Francesca, "I don't care what sort of upbringing a person has had or not had, there is no excuse for rudeness. Why can't she just let bygones be bygones?"

Francesca shrugged. "Charlotte, please. I don't want to get involved."

"I know. I'm sorry. But, if it hadn't been for me, they would have shut this place down. Does she realize that?"

"I said," she tightened her jaw and spoke through gritted teeth, "I don't want to be involved."

Charlotte waved her hand in the air and zipped her lip. She closed her eyes a moment, trying to forget the whole thing. What did it matter what some white trash pizza restaurant proprietor who looked like a

202

car mechanic thought about her? Perhaps, in a perfect world, they would be friends. They were neighbors, after all. Who wouldn't want to be friends with her neighbor? What kind of nut case didn't at least try to be friends with her neighbor?

"The fact is," Charlotte said calmly, "there were rats in the dumpster. And something had to be done." She shrugged. "She needs to just get over it."

"What's that?" asked Francesca, pointing to an envelope in Charlotte's hand. "Mail for me?"

"I saw you in the window," said Charlotte. "It's from New Haven."

Francesca snatched the envelope and examined the postmark. She tore it open and read the contents aloud. It was from someone named Suzy Bishop, a young art collector who, judging from her poor syntax and punctuation non grata, spoke English as a third or fourth language, at best. It was composed on an old electric typewriter, not even the likes of a Selectric, and (with some difficulty) expressed the collector's desire "to see the paintings of the artist and I am considering to buy one about chinese girl."

"Look how well she spells," Francesca pointed, subjecting the letter to rare scrutiny. The New Haven postmark intrigued her, and Sunday's *Register* had featured Francesca in its article about up-and-coming artists in the Northeast. She brought the envelope back to the cabin, placed it on the wire spool table in the center of the room, and turned it over to examine the postmark, then again to look at the printed address: Francesca DeSilva. With a capital D. What if someone from her past had found her? What if they'd been looking—all this time? Perhaps her photograph had been on milk cartons all these years, hanging on bulletin boards at bakeries, hair salons, grocery stores. *Have you seen this girl? Last seen May 11, 1981. Naked. In bed with another girl.*

She stared at the canvases lining the walls of her cabin, the table scarred with lumps of paint, strewn rags, all of it, to her, as beautiful as the stains on her fingertips, the greasy taste of oil paint when she accidentally put a finger in her mouth while she was working, maybe to move something from behind a tooth. And all of it, suddenly, ephemeral. The life she'd been enjoying as she'd never enjoyed life before, might be taken from her in one small gesture. The arrival of her mother might accomplish it; or she might be brought down by a shadowy figure from her past—someone determined to expose her for what she was: a witless, defenseless excuse for a human being, posturing as someone extraordinary.

❑ ❑ ❑

Though Francesca had never discussed her past with Charlotte, it hadn't been terribly difficult for Charlotte to put together a rudimentary outline based on spartan facts: Obviously, there had been an unhappy childhood; a Chinese girl of misguided importance. Something with the sister, some sort of rivalry, the intense sort that makes the loser, in this case Francesca, retreat to the corner like a wounded animal. Enough neglect or bad will to seed the damage more deeply, to send Francesca spinning through life wrestling the core belief that she deserved nothing more than a moldy shed by the train tracks. It broke Charlotte's heart. Charlotte had no children of her own, but if she were to have one, Francesca would be the daughter she'd construct for herself—brilliant, subtly beautiful, kinder than she wanted anyone to know, and desperately in need of love, so desperately in need, Charlotte had decided, that Francesca could tolerate love only when she didn't see it coming, when it wormed its way into her world undetected, like a fragrance slips in from outdoors and sweetens the air. Anyhow, Charlotte told herself, Francesca's reticence only contributed to her mystique and, thus, her marketability. Her paintings oozed with all she would not say.

While Shanta was lovely and darling (a little like a zaftig, Indian Julie Christie, Charlotte would say when describing her), any layman could tell Francesca was not in love. Still, Shanta's adoration seemed to make Francesca happy, and Charlotte very much wanted Francesca to be happy. And there was an unuttered benefit to the prosaic nature of the relationship between Francesca and Shanta: it allowed Francesca to keep painting.

Charlotte had a hunch about Suzy Bishop. The uncooperative collector could manage lunch only on May 10, Francesca's birthday, so Charlotte apologized to Francesca but went ahead and scheduled the appointment. Francesca assured her it was fine, a good thing in a way since it would distract her from that perennial marker, one she usually defended against by disappearing into the darkness of back-to-back movies or long, shin-splitting walks on the beach.

In preparation for Suzy Bishop's visit, Charlotte had the driveway swept, the hedges trimmed, the rugs cleaned. She arranged a catered lunch, filled the dining room with fresh freesia. At 11:45 Francesca watched from behind the wisteria patch—according to Charlotte, the oldest on the Cape, limbs thick as squid strangling a 30-foot-wide lattice wall against the potting shed—as a small red VW Rabbit appeared at the bottom of the drive. Slowly the car crept up the driveway and stopped beside the entrance to the flagstone patio. Charlotte hopped like a bunny to the driver's side, looking as if she were going to curtsy as the door opened and Lisa Sinsong, a.k.a. Suzy Bishop, stepped out. She shook Charlotte's hand, dropped a cigarette onto the pavement, and squished it with the pointed sole of a leather boot.

Charlotte spied Francesca hidden in the woody climbers. "There she is!" she cried. "Francesca!"

Lisa didn't wait for Francesca to step forward. Instead, she strolled over, cocky and self-assured. "Hey," she said, her voice deeper than it had been the last time. With some difficulty she freed a small box from the snug front pocket of her jeans. "Happy Birthday. Sorry I missed the last seven." She looked strung out and pale, as if she desperately needed to eat something green.

"Francesca, this is Suzy Bishop," Charlotte ran up from behind.

"I know who it is."

"You do?" Charlotte turned full throttle and set a wary glare upon Lisa's face. "Who is it, then?" she asked.

"This is Lisa Sinsong. Lisa, this is Charlotte."

"Lisa," Charlotte barely uttered the name, trying to identify its importance. She stared at the drawn features. "Lisa. You mean Lisa Gone?"

"Yeah. Right," said Francesca.

Charlotte was rapt. How amazing to meet the subject of

Francesca's art, after having only known the art. And how plain this girl was. How very . . . *Chinese*. Small, thin, serious-looking. Her arms like noodles at her sides. Her pale neck. (Body thin as a chopstick. Eyes black as soy sauce.) More than ever, she was convinced of Francesca's gift. It was incredible, the intensity of emotion Francesca had injected into such a plain face. An unadorned face. Once again, she was awed by the incredible power of art. She remembered a quotation she'd read recently, the words of H.L. Mencken: "Nothing can come out of an artist that is not in the man." The intensity, then, thought Charlotte, lies not in the subject, but in Francesca. Francesca had aggrandized this plain girl, breathed life into her tired face, enriched her pallor, added dimension to her limp form. Because she was in love. And it was this love, this deep and irrepressible love, into which Francesca had first dipped with her brush. And her beloved, this very plain Chinese girl, had gone to the trouble of creating an alter ego and tracking Francesca down, probably to avoid being rebuffed. How this girl must love Francesca, then! Charlotte wanted to rejoice! How suited to someone of Francesca's genius to possess such a love, to tend to it so carefully, to guard it so jealously (she'd hid Lisa's little present away in her pants pocket, not wanting to subject it to the ordinary light of day). Charlotte could have grabbed Lisa Sinsong and kissed her in that moment, or forced the two of them together in an embrace.

Instead, she invited Lisa into the house for lunch, guiding her into the dining room where high sun poured through the picture window. A vase stuffed with freesia sat at the center of the table, the yellow flowers straining forward with the weight of their task.

"Freesia," Lisa smiled, pointing.

"Do you like freesia?" Charlotte squeezed her elbow. "It is my very favorite flower." She spoke in sparing phrases of broken English, the way people do when they are trying to capture the syntax of someone who speaks a foreign language. But Lisa spoke English as well as either of them; it was only her face that made her seem, to Charlotte, a foreigner.

Francesca was distracted by a clash in color between Charlotte's crimson velvet dress, forming a shelf at her ample bosom and falling steadily like curtains, and Lisa's apple red sweater. She was highly sensitive to light and accustomed to dark, sedate hues; the contrast caused her to squint when shifting her gaze from one to the other. Her eyes felt scarred by the high sun drilling through slats of the blinds. She drank some wine, trying to relax, trying to slow down her thoughts.

Lisa finished her first glass of Chardonnay and cleared her throat. "Charlotte," she said sweetly, "were you aware that Francesca once built a hut?"

"What?" Charlotte faced Francesca, eyes wide. "You didn't build that place, did you?"

"What place?"

"You know." She made a face, as if something sticky were crawling on her leg. "Where you work . . ." Charlotte leaned forward.

"I don't live in a hut. I live in a cabin," Francesca said.

"Well, I don't know," said Charlotte, abashed. "What's the difference, really?"

"Oh, this was amazing," Lisa chattered on. "It was more like a little—" she turned to Francesca and smiled.

"It was made of sticks and mud," Francesca interrupted.

"Yeah, but that doesn't do it justice." said Lisa.

Charlotte pointed her fork at Francesca as if to say, You devil. "Tell me about Francesca as a child," she addressed Lisa exclusively. "I know so little about her."

"I like it that way," said Francesca.

"No, she doesn't," Lisa said, ignoring her. "She's dying for someone to take an interest in her. No one paid attention to her. They were all too busy waiting on her sister. They missed Francesca entirely," Lisa looked at Charlotte, gesturing with her hand to Francesca behind her, as if she were the prize behind door number three. "There she was, right in front of them."

"That's a tragedy," Charlotte said.

"It all worked out in the end." Francesca lit a cigarette. She might have been annoyed by the exchange, the two women chatting as if she were a character in some novel they'd finished months ago. But she was happy. Happy, happy, happy. And, too, a little bit drunk. She never drank. In fact, it occurred to her now, the last time she'd tasted anything alcoholic had been the night Lucky had seduced her on the blue divan. *At least,* she thought, *I got a painting out of that. Actually,* her thoughts continued on, *I got a studio out of that, too. In a sense, I owe it all to Lucky Perkins. That cunt.*

She refilled her glass, trying to go with the strange turn of events, to relish, simply, Lisa's reentry in her life. But happiness made her nervous. It promised too much and contrasted starkly with the monotony of life: sleep, paint, eat, smoke. Occasionally, fuck. All of it ordered, all of it designed to keep at bay anything that might make her afraid. She preferred her world unmoved: nothing ventured, nothing gained. Yearning was untidy. It was like leaking, leaving behind a trail of things you need but could not manage to hold onto.

"Actually," Lisa turned to face her, "Francesca's sister called me one night. Drunk. It was her birthday and she'd just had intercourse for the first time."

"That's not funny," said Francesca. "Don't joke about that."

"I'm not joking. She looked up my number." She turned to Charlotte and addressed her, though the story was clearly meant for Francesca's benefit. "'Do you remember me?' she asked, 'I am Isabella DeSilva.'

"'Francesca's sister!' I said, which was the last thing crazy Isabella wanted to be remembered for." Lisa took a long slug of wine. "Then she told me this very involved story about some friend of her mother's who had this son who looked like an angel—literally, she kept saying. *He was literally an angel.* She was sort of amusing. But you could feel that things were not right. Here." She pointed to her head, then took a drink. "Anywho."

"Anyhow," corrected Francesca, moving Lisa's wine glass away. "I'm glad she's alive. Of course I knew she was. I could feel it. We are sisters, after all. Whatever the hell that means." Francesca examined Lisa's tidy profile, wanted to kiss a straight line from her cowlick at the very center of her hairline, down to the dimple in her chin. "So what happened with this guy?" she asked.

"Well . . ." Lisa looked at Charlotte and managed a sly, charming smile. "He had drugs, I guess. A tiny little spoon, was how she described it."

Francesca looked at Charlotte. "That's cocaine, Charlotte. You use a little spoon."

"You think I don't know that? I work in the art world!" said Charlotte, rapt by the story, wanting to know how it all turned out.

"And I guess they went down to the basement—"

"The basement!" interrupted Francesca.

"Yes, and Isabella was wearing some fancy dress of your mother's and she had a bottle of vodka stashed down there."

"She loves vodka," they both told Charlotte at the same time.

"And, of course, he had sex with her. And then, I guess, she realized she'd been used and she tried to kill herself." Lisa reached for the glass but Francesca had the base of her large hand wrapped firmly around its stem; she held Lisa's eyes steady.

"She didn't do it obviously," said Lisa.

"Did this really happen?" Francesca asked.

"Would I drive all the way here, track you down—which was not easy to do and would have been impossible to accomplish had I not seen the article about you in the *Register*—"

"Oh!" Charlotte smiled, pleased at the reach of the publicity.

"—just to make up this story?" Lisa tugged on the stem of her glass, pulling it free. She emptied it, then slapped it down onto the table. "Excellent."

"So, Isabella didn't die?" Francesca asked quickly, knowing she hadn't, feeling obligated to ask.

"I would have told you that. I would have begun the story by telling you that. Or not. Actually, I wouldn't have told the story. I mean, I would have found some more tactful way of telling you. I am capable of tact, you know." Lisa smoothed her napkin on her lap. "She just wanted the boy's attention."

Lisa asked Charlotte whether she was permitted to smoke. Francesca located a lovely marble ashtray in the kitchen, placed it beside Lisa's small, left hand, and watched as Lisa's fingers unraveled the plastic cord on a pack of Camels, rumpled the cellophane coating into a ball, and tucked it, discreetly, beneath the lip of her plate. Then she neatly unfolded the foil corner of the pack. *Camels,* thought Francesca. *Not Marlboros or Winstons or Newports. Not Gitanes like Shanta.* She didn't roll her own like the Chinese girl Francesca had picked up in a bar one night just because she reminded her—ever so slightly—of Lisa. Camels. It was too perfect. How she loved the expression on Lisa's inebriated face—a perfect balance of goodness, mirth, and a manageable sadness. She loved Lisa's sadness—that it was there and that it was manageable. Tears started inside her. She leaned in and lit Lisa's cigarette, watched her pale skin glow against the match flame. Then she lit a Marlboro for herself.

"Lisa is the chess champion of the world." Francesca said.

"Really?" asked Charlotte.

"No." Lisa began to shake her head, hard, one side to the other, exhaling a long, much-needed first drag. "No, no, no, no, no. Christ, Francesca." She turned to Charlotte. "A) I *was, was* the chess champion. I am no longer. B) It was of the U.S. girls division, not the world. And C) I was about three."

"She was at least ten," Francesca said.

"Isn't that lovely how you brag about each other. If only we all had someone to brag about us. Then we'd never have to sing our own praises," said Charlotte, feeling sorry for herself.

"Charlotte owns this beautiful gallery on Commercial Street. Let's take Lisa there, Charlotte, and show her the gallery—" offered Francesca.

"I wasn't trying to solicit that," Charlotte winked at Lisa. "Though it was my gallery where Francesca had her very first show."

"I'd love to do that. Tomorrow. But right now, I'd like to take a nap." Lisa forced a yawn. "I'm whupped."

"Where are you staying, dear?" asked Charlotte.

"Yeah. Where are you staying?" asked Francesca.

Lisa shrugged. "Wherever," she said, having known from the moment she'd thrown her small suitcase into the trunk of the car that she'd stay wherever Francesca would have her.

Francesca waited outside while Lisa said her good-byes to Charlotte. She removed her shoes and rubbed her toes on the cool, thick blanket of grass. She pointed in the direction they were to go, following behind Lisa, studying, Lisa knew, her walk, her movements, the shimmying of her hips. Everything seemed slowed almost to a halt. They were both drunk, groggy from the afternoon sun, the food, desire.

"So, do you still play chess?" Francesca called from behind.

"Nope."

"How come?"

"It's a long story," Lisa sighed, exhausted, as if she'd been trying to tell it over the course of her entire life and had been interrupted each time. "Is this where you live?" she asked, pushing on the door.

Francesca nodded, pulling out a set of keys. "All my work's in there. So I keep it locked."

"You live alone?"

"Of course, alone." Francesca fitted the key into the padlock and pushed open the door.

Everything seemed turned up to full volume: the air was crisp, the sun too bright, the ocean rough; even the birds seemed to be shouting. Lisa felt desire, like an itch, as she crossed in front of Francesca. She stood inches from her; heat and longing filled the space between them.

"I've lived here since I left New Haven," said Francesca. "Seven years ago. You knew I'd left New Haven, right?"

Lisa nodded. "I feel bad."

"Don't feel bad," Francesca said, glad that Lisa felt bad. "Did you wonder where I was?"

"Yeah. Of course."

"Did you worry about me? Did you wonder if I'd been picked up by some serial killer, raped and murdered?"

"Sure, I did. But you know, I was all fucked up."

"Really? What happened?" Francesca stepped behind Lisa and put her flat hands on Lisa's stomach. She slid her fingers underneath Lisa's sweater and sighed at the feel of soft, familiar skin, the shape of Lisa's ribs.

211

"Francesca," Lisa said, "Please don't hate me."

Francesca swallowed. "Okay." She moved her hands up onto Lisa's breasts, then leaned forward and kissed Lisa's long neck, salty tasting and damp. She stroked the length of it with her tongue, and whispered into Lisa's ear: "I used to think of you every time something happened to me. If I got stung by a bee, I'd think of you. If I ate a hot dog and it tasted good—or bad—I'd think of you."

Lisa turned, waiting for Francesca to kiss her full on the mouth, wanting to be filled with her tongue.

"Did your father tell you I called?" Francesca asked.

Lisa shook her head, lying.

"He never told you?"

She shook her head again, her eyes closed.

"He said you were gone."

"I was gone. But now I'm back," Lisa said. "Don't you want to kiss me? I thought that would be the first thing you'd do."

"I was expecting Suzy Bishop."

Lisa smiled, pleased with herself. "Suzy Bishop. That was fucking brilliant. Right?"

"Yeah. But I knew."

"You did not."

Francesca nodded, turning away from Lisa, her face cracking into a sly smile. "I did," she whispered. "Not consciously. But somewhere in here," she pointed to a place between her heart and her stomach, "I knew." Slowly she pressed her mouth to Lisa with lips ajar, as if this modicum of restraint would preserve her. But Lisa leaned in and with one heavy breath, parted Francesca's lips.

There in the cabin, where Francesca felt more like a man than a woman, more like an artist than a man, she kissed Lisa in the intimate cool of autumn, surrounded by her paintings and the late afternoon light. She felt herself float out of her body, out of the world. Her existence became only this: kissing Lisa. Hard. Then harder still, mouth straining open, tongue venturing as far as it would go. She tasted the inside of Lisa, licked the still familiar wide lips, the square teeth. Instead of the lavender oil Lisa wore in her dreams, the faint odor of smoke and onions lingered on her fingers and lips.

212

Francesca's body flooded with desire. With longing, and sadness and, no matter how she tried to deny it, tidal waves of genuine, never-to-be-duplicated love.

Study of White Figure in Window, 1988

One cannot discuss *Study of White Figure in Window* without first addressing the more complex issue: How much does knowledge of an artist's personal life skew our interpretation of her work? Would this painting hold even a fraction of the interest it has generated if we knew nothing of deSilva's tormented relationship with her sister, her struggles with depression and a less than nurturing childhood spent largely in an attic room, the fact that the painting was hidden beneath her bed, that deSilva returned to New Haven shortly after its completion and there died in a strange fire, the cause of which has never been determined?

deSilva completed *Study of White Figure in Window* during her final months in Truro. Upon finishing the work, she hid it under her bed where it gathered dust; the corners of the stretcher became reinforced by cobwebs. The wood grew slack from swelling and shrinking with the changing seasons. It was not until after Francesca's death in 1989 that Charlotte Wallace happened upon the canvas. Ever since its discovery, the quiet, arguably unremarkable painting has been the subject of relentless probing and analysis.

In his essay, "Live Fast, Die Young, Watch the Vultures Feed," Phillip Hamil expresses his deep dismay about the "junk addiction"[79] he claims has afflicted both the academy and the public. "I'd like

---

79. Hamil's term has been popularized, its meaning expanded to describe an insatiable appetite for voyeuristic prattle.

to think this lowly preoccupation is a misguided quest for truth. But I am convinced it lays bare a more insidious problem: a culturally sanctioned lack of curiosity that impels us to simplify works of art never intended to be simple. Art is not a code meant to be deciphered, as in 'this object correlates with this object in the artist's childhood,' and so forth.

What would be the point of art if all it required for its appreciation were a catalog of illicit facts? Imagine if, upon visiting a museum, we were handed such a pamphlet, detailing not where the artist trained and with whom, his influences and colleagues, the various evolutions of his work, but instead with whom he slept, whether or not he cheated on his wife and molested his children, his various mental maladies, concluding, perhaps, with some chatty anecdote about the time he slept it off on the village green, or a neighbor's account of how his father beat him nightly with a two-by-four."[80]

At first glance, *Study of White Figure in Window* is almost commonplace in its subject: A ghostly, faceless woman is huddled beside a tiny attic window. Her rounded shoulders abut the sloped wall behind her. She is faded and blurred as cotton washed a hundred times, and stares wistfully out the window and down at something unseen but clearly important. Covering her form, bumpy as a rock buried in riverside soil, a thick white robe gathers in folds. The belt is unknotted, hangs down with defeat; its edges graze the dirty wooden floor. Rainy light, the color of

---

80. Hamil, Phillip. "Live Fast, Die Young, Watch the Vultures Feed." *Vanity Fair,* April 1993, page 112. Author's note: Some might say that Hamil's prophecy has been realized.

watered-down wine, shades her face, shrouds uncertain cheekbones and a blunted chin. A wilted wasp nest of hair balances precariously and heavily on her head, as if it were something she could not shake (representing, perhaps, the constraints of femininity). The strands are faded, the ends ragged as tinsel. She is enervated, resigned; she no longer resists or pursues anything. She appears atrophied, frozen in the same position for an eternity.

It has been speculated that the subject is a prisoner, a madwoman in the attic, someone's crazy aunt, even Charlotte Perkins Gilman (an author both Isabella and Francesca admired). Whoever she is, she seems suspended between life and death, her eyelids barely open, her mouth parted just enough to permit entry to only the slimmest sheathes of air.

This quietly devastating work asks many questions and answers none. The prevailing interpretation is that *Study of White Figure in Window* is a portrait of deSilva's estranged sister, Isabella: The white bathrobe, the positioning of the subject voyeuristically peering out the window, the despondent posture all support this theory. Still the same details could as easily position *Study of White Figure in Window* as a self-portrait. Lucinda Dialo writes extensively about *Study of White Figure in Window* in *Women Paint!:*

"The artist's treatment of her gentle painting is tremendously significant. deSilva banished the painting to a dark and dusty fate. This act serves as a metaphor upon a metaphor. The exile of the painting furthers its meaning: that of a woman locked away because she is inferior, a woman who cannot confront the harsh censure and ostracism of an insensitive society. The painting, analogously, reveals too much about its artist, makes her vulnerable and, it might be said, occasions its banishment to a space under the bed where it can be both protected from public scrutiny and prevented from bringing shame upon its creator.

"The feminist content of *Study of White Figure in Window* cannot be overstated. The subject is not Isabella or Charlotte Perkins Gilman or Jane Eyre, nor is it Francesca deSilva herself: it is Everywoman. Everywoman who could not assimilate, could not marry and push the stroller down the cheery street, who prefers a life of isolation to the untenable pain of exposure. deSilva hid the painting away to protect herself, sensing, and with eerie accuracy, that the public would not appreciate a simple, sad portrait of a woman."[81]

Hamil's rant against junk addiction notwithstanding, it is difficult, if not impossible, to turn a blind eye toward the odd parallels between the subject of *Study of White Figure in Window* and each of the D/deSilva sisters.

Psychiatrists May Jones and Ann Particip claim, even insist that *Study of White Figure in Window* gives credence to their hypothesis of the "inexplicable connectedness among siblings. Evident in this painting," the scientists posit, "is the seamless merging of personae. The figure, dressed in the white robe and peering out the window—much as Isabella might have done in Francesca's memory—is situated

---

81. Dialo Lucinda. *Women Paint!* New York: Little, Brown, 1991, page 162.

in the attic, Francesca's childhood room. Even more uncanny is that during the time deSilva worked on *Study of White Figure in Window,* her family of origin, with whom she'd had no contact for eight years, was in upheaval: Isabella was institutionalized, Alfonse and Vivian separated for a time, and Evelyn was suffering the onset of a devastating illness. How do we explain this synchronicity in the face of prolonged separation and emotional distance, if not through a genetic connectedness, one impervious to external circumstances?"[82]

82. Jones, May and Particip, Ann. *Creativity in Female Siblings—The Case for Eugenics.* Chicago: Mind and Matter, 1994, page 211.

Chapter Eighteen

"This is one of those things someone should have taught you a long time ago," Lisa said, pulling her car up alongside the pay phone and climbing out. "Scoot over."

Francesca shook her head.

"Francesca, come on. You need to be able to drive. What, are you going to ride a bicycle to your show in New Haven?"

"I'm not going to go to my show in New Haven." She crossed her arms.

"It's very easy." Lisa tapped on the window and motioned, once again, for Francesca to shift over into the driver's seat. She opened the door and took from Francesca the two large coffees, assumed custody of the grease-stained bag of oversized blueberry muffins. "Move over," she said, calmly.

Francesca obeyed, then sat stiff in the driver's seat, waiting for further instruction. She put her hands on the wheel and felt the old car rattle under her fingers. "Don't make me do this," she said.

"You love when I make you do things."

"Yeah. Not this."

"Move the seat back. Go on." Lisa bent over and pulled back on the lever attached to the driver's seat; gently she pushed the seat backward. "Ready?" she asked. Without waiting for Francesca's reply, she shifted the car into drive. Slowly, it began to drift. "Just steer, and when you're ready to go faster, step on the gas. Gently."

"Do you know how many women have tried to get me to drive?" asked Francesca.

Lisa shook her head. "How many?"

"At least three. My grandmother. Charlotte. This friend of mine. And you. Four. And you're the only one who has succeeded."

Francesca grabbed the wheel and let the car putter along the side street, eventually accelerating to 30 mph, hugging the side of the road, panicked each time a car neared on the opposite side of the street.

"How's it feel?"

"I hate it," said Francesca. "It feels unnatural."

"Of course it does. It takes time."

Francesca shook her head, disbelieving.

"Pull onto Route 6. Go on," Lisa said.

Francesca clutched the wheel with both hands as she sped up and pulled onto the highway. For a quick moment she removed her right hand from the wheel to adjust the rearview mirror, which she checked repeatedly as she crawled along in the right lane.

"You have to go faster," said Lisa. "The speed limit is 45. You need to go at least 35." She put her hand on Francesca's knee, for comfort.

Francesca reached 35, then 42 before pulling off at the first rest area and parking—roughly—beneath the spattered shade of a pine tree. "Man," she sighed and pushed in the cigarette lighter.

"It doesn't work," Lisa said, finding an old book of matches on the floor. "I hate this car."

"I'll get you a new one."

"I hate my life," Lisa said. "Would you get me a new one?" She removed a bent joint from her shirt pocket.

"You should play chess again," Francesca said. "Maybe by denying yourself chess, you are sabotaging your happiness."

"That's very American," Lisa said, "But not at all Chinese. We don't worry about happiness."

"But you are American."

Lisa shrugged. "In this way, I am Chinese."

"So you're never going to play again?"

"I play. I teach these old guys where my father goes during the day. I play with them. I just don't want to compete."

"Since when?"

Lisa hesitated. "I don't want to tell you this. I've never told anyone this."

"Tell me."

She took a long hit of the joint, exhaled, then waited for the pot to alter her mood. Even a little. "I haven't wanted to play since I lost to this kid a few years ago."

"What kid?"

"This faggot kid in this gymnasium in Bridgeport. The game was on the twelfth floor in this decrepit factory building with only one malfunctioning elevator that stopped just a few feet above the floor, so you had to hop down. There were huge dusty windows all the way across the length of the gym, flooding the room in this steely, depressing city light. I told myself I was doing it for the money—there was a $3,000 prize—but it was more complicated than that. I needed to win. My ego needed a win.

"My father came and sat a few feet away and nodded his head every time I did something right—there weren't too many instances of that. The rest of the time, he stared straight ahead. At nothing. Other than our being the only Chinese people there, you'd never guess we were related. Finally, I followed his gaze to see what the fuck he was looking at—" Here she traced the air with her finger, remembering. "All the way across the gymnasium. There was a sign that said: *Return Basketballs to the Closet.* That's what he stared at. A fucking sign."

"He's a prick. He's always been a prick."

"Yeah. Right." She took several hits of the joint, licked her forefinger and tidied up the rolling job. "So, I never think about my mother," Lisa exhaled. "I don't let myself think about her. Because what's the point? But all of a sudden, in the middle of this high-stakes chess game, I could think of nothing else. And I started to cry. And I wanted to throw myself through the windows and over the side of the building. Like my mother. You want some more?" she asked, offering it to Francesca for the first time.

Francesca shook her head. "You know," she said, "just because I live in that shack doesn't mean I have to stay there. Charlotte built a beautiful cottage behind her house and she's always after me to move in there." This was as close as Francesca could come to what she wanted to say.

"That's a nice offer." Lisa put her hand on Francesca's.

"You could move in there by yourself, I'll bet." This was a rare moment between them—no sex, no sarcasm. Genuine, almost innocent acknowledgement of love. Lisa nodded, as if watching it unfurl.

"That looks pretty," she said. "But I'm not gay. I could never live a gay lifestyle. And look at you. You are so gay." She laughed a sharp—and once again sarcastic—laugh.

Francesca looked down at herself, as if Lisa had given her an instruction. She wore worn carpenter's pants and clogs. What was so gay about clogs? "I'm wearing clogs," she said. "Don't you ever wear clogs?"

"I don't happen to like clogs."

"But they're not gay. Lots of people who wear clogs aren't gay."

"It's just what you are," said Lisa. "It's the way you carry yourself, and the look on your face—silent and separate from the regular world. And your giant hands. And your paintings. They're so gigantic and audacious. Straight women don't paint like that. You're going to be so famous." Lisa stubbed out the joint, licked her thumb and forefinger, and squeezed the tip of the roach, then dropped it into a film canister she kept in her pocket. "Drive."

"You drive."

Lisa shook her head. "We can sit a few more minutes while you tell me about your girlfriend."

"No."

"Is she pretty?"

"Yes."

"Is she smart?"

"Yes."

"Do you love her?"

"No. She's just someone to be with. You can't be alone all the time."

Lisa nodded. This was a good answer. Of course Francesca couldn't spend her entire life alone. In a way, the knowledge that Francesca was cared for by others was a relief. Lisa knew she couldn't stay; she recognized her limitations. She had to get back to her father. With each day she was away, there would be more anger to deflect, more humiliation, more tasks he'd have saved up for her return: dirty laundry, plates and bowls with lichens of food along the edges, ashtrays to empty. He would grill her as he always did when she stayed away overnight, and she would lie. Chess tournament, she would tell him (she'd already rehearsed it, practiced sternly sticking to her story in spite of his leery expression). But just the idea of it exhausted her.

They switched seats. Lisa turned the key in the ignition, but the car wouldn't start.

"Oh God. What did I do?" Francesca asked.

"You didn't do anything. I'm surprised this piece of shit even got me this far. It should have died a long time ago. I don't think I've changed the oil in about ten years."

"You haven't been driving for ten years," said Francesca, climbing out of the car and sticking out her thumb. Lisa lit a cigarette and waited in the driver's seat. She was worried this would delay her departure and relieved, too, knowing she'd have at least another night with Francesca, maybe several. The longer she stayed away from Mr. Sinsong, the less real he became. Whatever dreariness awaited her couldn't multiply infinitely; after a while, they'd have to plateau. He'd have to tire of hating her and be glad she'd returned. Perhaps if she stayed away longer, he'd appreciate that she'd come back. And if not, she could always run out again, hop a train out of New Haven, back to Francesca. Maybe she'd do that anyhow. She sighed, crossed her foot over her knee, pulling at some loose white threads hanging from the hem of her jeans, and glanced at Francesca through the cloudy windshield, certain that she was the most beautiful creature walking the planet.

The mechanic confirmed what Lisa had said. It was a miracle, he told them, the car had run this long. He said it wasn't worth fixing, and anyhow, he wouldn't even have a chance to look at it until the end of the week.

"But I can't wait that long," Lisa said. She turned to Francesca. "My father's going to kill me."

"Your father's going to kill you?" Francesca repeated, certain that Lisa, in her infinite intelligence, would hear how ridiculous the statement sounded. But Lisa only nodded.

"I have to take him to the club. He plays poker on Thursday night."

"So he'll take a bus," Francesca said.

Lisa shook her head. "I have to get back there."

Francesca felt like she'd bitten into some intoxicating confection that she could not stop eating. She ate and ate of it, long past the point of sickness, caring about nothing except making it last as long as it could. Even after all these years, Lisa still stirred a longing that was pure and lethal. *Longing for what?* Francesca didn't even know. She still imagined they would get away—but from what? They would go somewhere—but where? Someplace different, where their circumstances would be erased and they could grow up again, into the people they might have become, had they been able to evolve, un-hampered. She looked at Lisa now, Lisa gone, at her pale skin and tinged eyeballs, her thin, abandoned body. She did not feel lust. She wanted to protect Lisa. The idea of bad things happening to Lisa— as surely they had—was too much to bear. She would kill—even then, in that moment—anyone who harmed her Lisa. She would kill Mr. Sinsong with her big, paint-stained hands. Look, she wanted to say, holding her wide palms in the air, look what I'd do for you.

The mechanic assured Francesca that the engine would have seized up whether or not she'd driven it. Probably, Lisa teased, Francesca had driven too slowly, and the car became confused and disoriented and, finally, convinced all hope was lost, just died.

"It's true that some of these old cars like having one driver," said the mechanic, unwittingly worsening Francesca's guilt. As far as driving it back to Connecticut, he said it was not an option. Besides the fact that the engine appeared to have seized, the tires were all bald, the radiator was leaking, and the exhaust system was entirely rusted out, barely attached to the bottom of the car. He suggested public trans-portation or a rental.

"I can't afford a rental," Lisa whispered. "I'll take a bus."

Though Francesca did not want Lisa to leave—ever—she knew she could not keep her there. Thus, that night, after Lisa had gone to sleep, she wrapped *The Trilogy*, with which she'd been unable to part in spite of popular demand and Charlotte's urging, as if Francesca had known this day might come, in brown paper and let it lean against the wall of the cabin. She sat in a lawn chair and smoked nearly a pack of cigarettes, her throat rough as cut metal by the time morning softened the sky. When Lisa woke, the coffee was made. Francesca used the pay phone to call and book Lisa a seat on a small plane leaving the Provincetown airport. She presented the paintings, explaining that if Charlotte were at all savvy in these matters, they'd be worth great money someday soon. In the meantime, she insisted on giving Lisa two thousand dollars to buy a used car. "I'd give you more, but I don't have a lot of cash," she said, counting out the bills, placing them, one at a time, onto Lisa's outstretched hand.

❑ ❑ ❑

The early morning mist muddled the roads, thick as cotton, thinning out across the runway—really just a lea with tall stripped reeds and dusty desert shrubs. Francesca handed the paintings to the pilot, then stood with her hands in her pockets while he helped Lisa climb up into the cacophonous vehicle. It would be good, Francesca thought, to run over, climb up into the cab, and plant one more kiss on her sweet morning mouth, savor the taste of separation. Instead, she removed the small box Lisa had given her for her birthday and tore off the red and yellow paper, which she stuffed into her pocket. Inside, seated on a pillow of cotton was a bottle cap, immediately familiar, still encrusted with dirt from the floor of her hut. It was from Mello Yello, rusted and dented, as the best bottle caps always are, and Francesca held it in her hand, as if it were the only evidence she'd ever seen of her life before this one.

She cried quietly as the plane punctured the stiff, egg-white sky. The deafening clamor faded to that of a tractor, then a departing motorcycle, shrinking, finally, to the white noise of a vacuum cleaner operated in an apartment down the hall. Francesca did not stop listening until it had gone completely.

Then, a hole of sunlight appeared as if through a pinprick, throwing a wet, white light on her sleepy face that made her yawn and yawn and yawn, as if only now, after a very long stupor, she were waking up.

Chapter Nineteen

With Lisa gone—again—Francesca escaped to her work. Half relieved to return to her familiar reclusion, she succumbed to what now seemed to be her bittersweet fate: to love only Lisa, to be loved only by Lisa, to never lose Lisa nor have her entirely. It was a confounding and not wholly satisfying outcome, but things might have turned out worse. Lisa might never have loved her at all. Lisa might never have returned. Instead, she might have birthed a pile of babies, married a beast (because surely, any man Lisa chose would be a beast), never come to visit. Or she might have gone off a building like her mother. And wouldn't that have made all sorts of wicked sense—suicide— after a life spent poor and unfulfilled, caring for a tyrannical father. Never hearing a kind word. Never hearing "thank you."

At least they'd had five days together during which Francesca had unearthed the truth, finally, after all these years: Lisa did love her. But Lisa was even more terrified of love than Francesca was. Neither could tolerate the nitty-gritty of love, the day in and day out, the talking it over and making it up. They were not constructed in this way, with strength enough to risk suffering so grand a loss. Things between them must never get ordinary or the love they relied upon to sustain some faith in existence, a dream of how perfect their lives would be if they could just spend them together, might prove deluded and naïve. And if this were to happen, life, overall, would be too cruel to endure. Paradoxically, the one thing that could bring them happiness was off limits; it must remain untested.

❏ ❏ ❏

Francesca had finally obtained her driver's license, though she still preferred her bicycle in all but the most inclement conditions. Occasionally she drove the Rabbit, now repaired, into town, and descended the stairs to a seedy lesbian bar that was sprawled across the basement of a seaside memorabilia mall. The pool table stretched out like a giant bed and women huddled in darkened corners, sipping gold drinks, smoking cigarettes, and examining each other's bodies unabashedly. The femmes came in—all sleek and showered, emanating perfume as they pranced around the perimeter of the smoky room to grant anyone watching a good look. The butches glanced up surreptitiously, pretending not to care. It reminded Francesca of a movie about lesbians, the sort where the butches are all suited up and the femmes wear panty hose over thick, working ankles.

Francesca, being sort of famous and famously aloof, held a certain allure. She knew this about herself. The less she heeded her effect on women, the more evident it became. Particularly in relation to the feminine ones, with bobbed hair and dark lipstick, smooth, tanned legs and full breasts. They watched her from far away, walked past her as they made their way to the bar, sending a breeze across her body. They loved about her the very things she'd once despised and disguised in herself: her tallness; the contradiction of her full breasts, rock hard thighs, sculpted arms, and the slight curve of her waist (all of it obscured beneath thick clothing); the smell of musky perfume in her uncombed hair; the salt of sweat on her lips; her large, turpentine-stained, desire-soaked fingers. Always, she felt their eyes on her as she skimmed the perimeter of the pool table, chalking her cue, resting her burning cigarette on the lip of a black, plastic ashtray.

One cold, November night, several weeks after Lisa had gone, Francesca rode home from a small bayside apartment where she'd spent the evening with Tanya, a local painter of bright, cottony waterscapes that hung in several Commercial Street galleries. She was still covered in paint from the previous day's work on *Study of a White Figure in Window* and wished, as she turned onto Route 6 and headed away from Provincetown, that she'd used Tanya's shower. But these encounters were so fraught with contradiction—freedom and limitation, passion and awkward mechanics, intimacy and utter isolation—that often, when their purpose had been served, Francesca could ask nothing, not even the time, but would crawl from the apartment (or condominium or hotel room) to disappear.

She considered stopping by Charlotte's to clean up, but decided this would require her to explain why she was frazzled and riding her bicycle in the dark. Instead, she decided to endure the outdoor spigot behind her cabin.

She reached her cabin and leaned her bike against the front wall, then walked around the perimeter, feeling something disagreeable, some pointless, unpleasant sensation—restlessness? Guilt? Worry? Perhaps, she thought, it is because I slept with someone other than Lisa. Tanya had been the first woman she'd picked up since Lisa's departure. Had she been unfaithful? She turned on the water and poured mineral spirits over her fingers, rubbed her hands together, then yanked a rag down from a nail tacked to the outside wall and began to scrub the skin hard. She usually tolerated, even enjoyed the paint stains on her hands, quiet reminders of why she was alive, but now she went at them with determination. Paper cuts and scratches stung on every digit; her eyes filled with tears. It took nearly ten minutes for the last markings of red to fade, for the color of her skin to return, and even then there were faint patches of gray clinging to the gullies of her knuckles.

She dried her hands on her pant legs, then stared at her skin, reddened and chapped, but clean for the first time in months, naked against the cool air. She missed Lisa terribly, violently. It seemed wrong for them to be separated by several hours of highway miles. Especially now that Francesca could drive.

She stepped into the dark street. The sky was tipped forward, the earth warped like an old floor. She moved along the silent street toward the neon light of Sherry's pizzeria, now closed for the night. Through the glass she saw a silhouette of Sherry sweeping the linoleum floor. The pay phone, her destination, looked deserted, as if someone had failed to show up for an appointment: The door was open, the light above glowed a blankety blue, and the receiver waited on the cradle. Francesca was about to step inside the acrylic walls of the booth when a man appeared.

"Sir," he said in a British accent. "I'm expecting a call. Will you be brief?"

She stared at him. "I don't know."

"If you wouldn't mind, Sir. It should only be a few minutes."

"First of all, I would mind. Second, I'm not a sir." She thrust her chest forward.

"So sorry. Pardon me. Ma'am. If you wouldn't mind . . . there's another pay phone just a few blocks away."

"Yeah," she said, stepping inside, "But I want to use *this* pay phone."

"I'll give you five dollars—" He began to fish for his wallet. "—if you'd walk to the next one."

She shook her head.

"Ten dollars," he said, now producing the wallet. "Please."

She poked her head out from the booth and asked quietly, "How long have you been waiting for this call?"

"All my life."

"Then it shouldn't be a problem to wait a little longer." She felt high on cruelty, huge, imperious.

"Please. Could you just go down the street?"

"Nope," said Francesca.

"If you would just come back in five minutes . . ." he pleaded.

Perhaps she could call someone other than Lisa—maybe her grandmother. She lifted the receiver, enjoying its smooth plastic weight. She stroked the shiny metal buttons, pushed her finger in and out of the change slot, stalling. She could hear the man breathing—short, shallow breaths. His foot fluttered nervously.

She might call her grandmother. She'd often fantasized about this call. How Evelyn would sob and beg forgiveness for being so cruel, then assure Francesca that she loved her as much as ever and would continue to love her, that her love was undiminished, no matter how Francesca lived her life, regardless of how many naked girls there had been in her bed (though still, after all these years, there had only been Lisa naked in her bed). But she was less given to fantasy now, more seasoned, aware that life rarely sewed its seams tight, and that once ruptured, things were never as good as new. Anyhow, the possibility of Evelyn's rejection after all these years was enough to keep her away forever.

The man knocked on the door.

"Look," said Francesca. "I have a right to use this phone. This phone is located here, outside a place I frequent." She pointed to the pizzeria. "I am a resident of this neighborhood. I live just a block away. I use this phone all the time."

"I understand. I don't want to anger you." He put his hand to his stomach and she could see his anxiety. So she agreed to walk around the block for a few minutes while the man attended to his business.

"I'll be back in ten minutes," she stated, tapping her finger against her naked wrist.

On a Wednesday evening, Lisa told her father she had to pick up some groceries. She drove her car—a Ford Pinto, purchased with Francesca's money—downtown and parked in the lot beside the train station, climbed over a shallow stone wall, ducked under some barbed wire, and skimmed the tracks. They abutted the river, and all around them the ground was soft and pungent as rusty water. Thick, polluted liquid turned her brown shoes black, splashed up and spotted her socks with grime. She pulled the gun from her pocket and let it dangle between her fingers, feeling so much better now that life had paused, that she was no longer living, but instead wading through the canal between existence and death. She was walking in her mother's footsteps, though instead of riding an elevator to the top of a Manhattan building, she was passing through the squalor of this little city she hated and loved and hated and loved, equipped to end her life at any moment. At any point she could make it all stop. What liberation—to be alive absolutely out of choice and know that just when she'd had enough, she could lift the needle off the record.

She believed, as those who are about to take their own lives usually do, that there was nothing for her to live for: no family, no children, no career. She thought of Francesca, of walking along the beach in Provincetown carrying coffees, the boisterous wind making conversation impossible, so that all they could do was feel the shore pull between them. Their hands brushed each other, their hips bumped; they stopped to kiss and taste the salt of the ocean, mysteriously, on each other's lips. Lisa felt bad about Francesca, but not bad enough to reconsider her decision. Anyhow, what hope was there for them? What could Lisa do? Leave her father and move to Provincetown? Become a lesbian? It was ridiculous even to contemplate.

She turned the gun over in her hand, stroking the molded butt, so easy to squeeze. She cocked the gun and brought its cold nose close to her face, pressed the long metal arm to her skin. She felt no fear. Then she pointed it to her heart—still nothing. Then she pressed it to the side of her head. Finally, a trace of fear, her heart pattering quick as rain. She slid it gently, like a friend, into the center of her open mouth until she felt her gag reflex, and let it rest upon her tongue. Then she pulled the trigger. After a quick blast, everything was still. A freight train neared, smearing the scene like it was made of oil paint, turning everything a soft, mutable gray.

❑   ❑   ❑

"I'm looking for Lisa." Francesca told Mr. Sinsong. Finally the man with the strange attachment to the phone booth had gone. Francesca could see him in the distance, his resigned figure shifting into the spillover of a street lamp. He seemed to still be alone, and Francesca pitied him. Probably the call he expected had never come.

"Who is this?" asked Mr. Sinsong.

"This is Francesca deSilva."

"The one who paints?" he asked.

"Yes. Right."

"There is bad news," said Mr. Sinsong. "Very bad news."

"What kind of bad news?" She felt her heart escaping.

"Bad news about Lisa."

"Where is she?" Francesca felt the front pockets of her shirt for her cigarettes; there were only two left in the pack. She pulled one out with her lips, then felt for matches in her back pockets.

"Lisa not here."

"O-kay," Francesca said caustically, trying to mitigate her impatience and disgust. "Just tell me where I can find her."

"You can't find her," said Mr. Sinsong, hesitating, rummaging for a soft touch. "Nowhere to find her."

"Look," said Francesca. "I'm sure there's *somewhere* to find her. If you don't want to tell me where that is, okay then. That's that. But don't pretend she's disappeared into the atmosphere."

"No, no, you not listening," he cleared his throat. "Lisa died."

"*What?*"

"She died!"

"She *died?*"

"She died. She died."

Francesca's mouth grew tacky, tasted like dirt. "I'm sorry," she spoke quietly. "You said . . ."

"She died," Mr. Sinsong repeated, louder. "You want paintings, I can tell you where to go."

"I don't understand. Was it a car accident?"

"No," said Mr. Sinsong. "Accident with gun."

"She was murdered?"

"Yes."

"You're saying Lisa was murdered?"

"No, not murdered. Shot. She had accident with gun."

Everything started to spin all around her, and Francesca seemed to be the only stationary object in the purling universe.

"You're saying she had an accident. With a gun." She hesitated, suddenly understanding. "Are you saying she shot herself?"

There was a brief silence. She leaned her back against the wall of the booth and felt a thin sweat break out all over her skin. "I can't believe this," she whispered. She wanted, ridiculous as it was, to talk things over with Mr. Sinsong, to acknowledge how shocking it was that their Lisa would take her own life, and with a gun no less.

"You want paintings back?" snapped Mr. Sinsong.

"No. Thank you." Slowly she replaced the receiver and opened the doors, stepped out into the soft darkness. She thought about going inside to talk with Sherry, but the lights in the pizzeria had been turned down low. As Francesca walked along the silent street toward her cabin, she felt she had been hurled, hard, back into her original, unabridged life—the unprettied version. Everything since leaving

233

New Haven had been one of those contrite dream sequences television writers concoct to bide time until they can come up with a viable story line. Instantly, as if it had been a dog sleeping in the corner, her real life woke up. Her instinct had been correct all along: Lisa had needed to be saved.

Now she would never have to worry about whether she *could* make Lisa happy, whether she *could* be someone's mate, live as a normal person, have normal person needs. Lisa had made her own decision, a decision Francesca hated even while she understood it. Life, she concurred, was a terrible, crushing thing. But couldn't Lisa have given Francesca the opportunity to make it better? Had Lisa always planned to die like her mother—in one final, willful gesture after a life of submission?

Then and there, Francesca decided there would be no other loves. Ever. This would be her homage to Lisa.

She dreamt daily of New Haven. Sometimes the dreams were terrible— e.g., she was trying to tell her mother that her grandmother had stopped breathing but her mother wouldn't stop talking about inane, unimportant matters. Or: A violent killer was stalking the family, running about with a steak knife through the darkened halls of 312 Riverview Street while she painted, rather dispassionately, on the garage door. She heard screams as her family was attacked, and finally ran into the house to call 911, but upon reaching the operator, found she'd been struck dumb. She ran through the halls and discovered the entire family huddled on the bathroom floor, bloodied from stab wounds. "Save us," whispered her mother, the only survivor.

She stacked the winter's supply of wood, shifting it from where it had been dumped, just a few yards from the train tracks, to a pile behind the cabin. She sat on the edge of her bed smoking, staring at the canvases before her, *Bunyan* and *Study of White Figure in the Window*, both incomplete. She watched time move—the afternoon light dimming into the faded yellow of evening, the blueberry shade of dusk, midnight's

234

smoky navy. She awaited the gradual invasion of light as the next day moved in.

She left the cabin only when she ran out of cigarettes, had to use the outhouse or restock the woodpile, or needed food. No one knew the reason for this self-imposed isolation. Francesca had peddled the usual story: hard at work, can't be interrupted, antisocial artist type, and so forth. But the sudden cessation of her once-weekly trips to the art supplies store downtown had alarmed the proprietor, who loved Francesca's work as well as her loyal patronage. He had called Charlotte to express his concern, Charlotte had spoken to Sherry, Sherry had contacted Shanta, and Shanta had left a message on Sherry's machine that said, rather curtly, "I have no idea where she is or what she's been doing. And I don't care. Sorry. Ciao."

Occasionally Francesca stepped out into the cold air and climbed into the passenger's side of Lisa's car to smoke, worrying a tear in the upholstery, digging her finger deep into a break in the foam. Sometimes she flipped through the softened papers in Lisa's glove compartment and touched old cigarette butts marked by pink lipstick. She thought she smelled Lisa inside the vehicle, which made her feel that in some small way, Lisa was alive. If a person's smell still existed in the air, they had not been eradicated. A smell, after all, resulted from chemistry, from the confluence of things alive. It was all that was left of Lisa— the dirty black interior, the ashtray stuffed with butts, bird droppings turning yellow and black on the windshield. Francesca sat in the car and cried in her small, understated way. She no longer felt entirely alive.

Then, late one afternoon, she awoke from a long nap to the first dusting of snow. She stretched her body so tall that her feet hung over the edge of the top bunk. Her eyes spanned the circumference of the room, as if seeing its contents for the first time. There were clothes piled on a chair in the corner. The stove was ticking rapidly, sending waves of heat in all directions. Her paintings waited like patient lovers, untouched for weeks. The cabin was oddly clean, the floors swept, the dishes put away, ashtrays emptied. Obviously, amid her stupor of grief and isolation, she'd managed to tidy up, though she remembered none of it. The only thing she recalled was endless, pervasive sadness and the interior of Lisa's car.

Francesca sat up and pressed down on her stomach, trying to quell a sick feeling of hunger. She spotted a Snickers bar in a basket, on top of the chest where she kept her clothes, and hopped down from the bed, tore off the wrapper, and began to eat. Within moments, she was chewing with abandon, making espresso on the stove, rigging up her favorite Laura Nyro song, "Brown Earth," on the cassette player. Then, as she waited for the coffee to spit and cough and threaten to pour in a frenzy over the sides of the espresso maker, she found Lisa's bottle cap on the counter top and put it in her pocket. She turned to face a blank canvas stretched and stacked against the wall. At once, without permitting a reprisal of despair and inertia, she lifted the canvas up onto an easel. She opened a window and stoked the fire, shed her heaviest layer of clothing, stripping down from three sweatshirts to two, and lit up a smoke.

Outside, snow had sprinkled the tracks, salted the dying grass that surrounded the cabin. Lisa's Volkswagen was parked alongside the wall of the cabin; the Styrofoam smiley face rammed onto the antenna bounced about in the winter wind. Francesca brought her bicycle inside the cabin and laid it against the wall, then crossed the room and lifted a brush from its resting spot on the palette. Worms of paints had dried on the metal plate. She squeezed out a fresh bit of blue, mixed black and white to create a snowy gray, added a tawny shade for depth, and began to paint a portrait of the pay phone. Who knew more about the secrets and suffering of man than a pay phone? Who encountered more strangers in crisis; people in love; panicked children needing a ride home? News of lovers' suicides? What object ran smack into the human condition with such frequency? And what was the ratio, wondered Francesca, of plain calls—"I'm sorry I'm late. I'm stopping at 7-Eleven. Do we need milk?"—to—"I still love you, even if you are fucking her."

What was the percentage of good to bad, tragedy to glory, pedestrian to momentous? As she painted the soft shades of the body, she felt Lisa. Not in the cabin, not in her fingers, not even in her heart: in the colors and shape of the pay phone. Lisa seemed to be the paint Francesca used, into which she dipped her lean brush, messing with it, busting open its sleek shape, spreading it across the canvas, thinning it, turning it into something else. Lisa was spilled like blood onto the painting, staining Francesca's fingertips, sticking to strands of her hair.

She lightened the black coal of the road that flew past the pay phone, softening its shade until the tar resembled ashes from a cigarette, creamy and smooth. It was nighttime; this she communicated by a violet sky, a creamsicle moon, the lit sign reading PHONE, and its Bell Atlantic branding below, all glowing the soft blue shade of deep water. She prodded the pay phone to life, capturing its particulars: the rounded wear of its push buttons, the scratches on the change slot. And then, after she'd detailed her subject and its surroundings, but before she added the human figure seated curbside, she painted in white graffiti on the gray asphalt, I LOVE YOU TOO MUCH.

Chapter Twenty

November 30 was the first bitter cold day in 1988. Evelyn, having once again eluded her nurse, Crystal (a.k.a. Pistol), stood outside the Stop 'n Shop in her housecoat and slippers, metal clips dangling from a wasp nest of hair, her naked ankles blue and chapped from the cold. She conversed animatedly with other shoppers—though they pretended not to notice—and clutched a bag of unpurchased groceries (Pop-Tarts, orange juice, peanut butter). She'd just finished releasing onto the pavement a hot stream of urine that, having missed her red orthopedic shoes, followed two nuns and their carriage through the lot. No one looked as Evelyn straightened herself, adjusted her moist underwear, and pulled it from where it had gathered in her crack. Nor did anyone seem to notice the ambulance drifting quietly through the parking lot with its lights spinning. Shoppers fitted keys into car doors and transferred bags from metal mesh carts into neatly packed trunks. No one noticed the moment when Evelyn's life began to wind down like the end of a carnival ride, the music distorting, the horses rising and dipping in slow-motion yawns.

The double doors at the back of the white vehicle opened out and Evelyn stared as the paramedics hopped heroically from either side of the van. Like the opening to a TV show, she thought.

Vivian and Alfonse pulled up alongside the ambulance in Vivian's car, their emergency lights flashing. Vivian wished she'd eaten breakfast. Her mouth tasted like the inside of a dark, sealed box. But there had been no time for food. The last forty-five minutes had been devoted to string-pulling and brown-nosing, doing anything she could, with the help of Joycie Newman, to get her senile mother admitted to the Jewish Home. Kasselbaum Senior had thrown his weight around, and, ta-da, Evelyn rose like curdled milk to the top of the list.

Alfonse hopped out of the car, ran to Evelyn's side. "Mama," he took her thin arm. Evelyn glared at him, her eyes watery and red. "Here," she said, and handed him the bag of groceries. They watched the EMTs readying the back of the van. Vivian stepped out of the car, shivering, arms wrapped around herself. She seemed wispy in her light blue sweatsuit and brand new running shoes. Her hair was held off her shiny face by a matching blue headband.

"Who is that?" Evelyn barked.

"Mama, you know who that is." Alfonse sniffled and wiped his nose on his sleeve. He placed the bag of groceries on the pavement.

Evelyn allowed herself to be led up the two steep metal steps into the ambulance, then seated on the hard gray bench. Finally, someone was helping her. Alfonse sat on one side of Evelyn; the female EMT sat on the other. Evelyn was relieved to be in the middle of two able-bodied people. "Dopey," she said to no one in particular, sighing deeply, then looked at her daughter propped on the edge of the opposite bench. Vivian's eyes were tearing, either from the cold or sadness; who could tell?

"What's the matter with her?" Evelyn snapped.

"I think it was the largesse of her gestures that made them call," Vivian ignored her mother, spoke directly to the EMT. "Thankfully, the manager knew her." She'd always wondered what it would feel like to speak of her senile mother while she was in the room. Like so many other events in her life, it was, in the end, anticlimactic.

Evelyn's glasses had fallen from her face when she'd bent over in the parking lot. They hung idly from a chain and rested over a stain on her navy blue polo shirt. She turned to the sturdy woman next to her. "This is asinine," she said. "I know exactly where I am. I'm at the Stop and Shop. It's Passover and I'm going to make matzo ball soup. Ask him," she indicated Alfonse. "He loves my matzo balls."

The vehicle began to move. Evelyn knew what was happening, even from inside the thickness of the bubble. She had named it the bubble, a plastic film formed between her and the world. Occasionally it seemed even to separate her from herself. At first, it had frightened her, but she'd grown used to its way of making things unreal, and, thus, less upsetting. Everything was far away and foggy, but some part of her understood that she'd just stepped into the final phase of her life. It was a strange and welcome sensation. "Whew," she sighed. She was so very tired. And she hated that horrible Pistol. White people, she'd decided, are lousy nurses. They were innately less kind.

Anyhow, thought Evelyn, twenty-nine years alone is enough. She'd had enough regret and heartburn and root canal. At first her friends had been a comfort. But now they were dead, one by one, without explanation, as if abducted. No one even bothered to call anymore to deliver the news. Unless she heard otherwise, she just assumed they'd all passed away: Sylvia, Gert, Molly, all her favorite ladies. And now, riding in the bumpy rear of the ambulance, she remembered Yitzchak's heart attack, how she'd screamed at the driver to go faster, be careful, faster, be careful, knowing that she was contradicting herself, unable to stop.

"Twenty-nine years." She sighed and turned toward the window.

Vivian looked at the EMT. "She's thinking of my father. He died twenty-nine years ago, almost to the day."

"Poor Mama," Alfonse patted her knee.

Evelyn could remember, though not so well anymore, when her life hadn't included these people. "That's right," she said, pointing at Vivian. "You weren't even born."

"That's not true," Vivian smiled at the EMT, then faced the window, her expression turning to stone.

Evelyn watched New Haven snap past the small windows at the rear of the ambulance. She knew what happened to ladies like her, old ladies still subject to an occasional fit of youth, the urge for a tantrum or to dance across a long room barefoot, toenails painted bright red, perfume on the pulses. She'd volunteered at the Jewish Home, brought cards and chocolates, watched adults invert into helpless, frustrated babies. As the age between her and the patients grew less distinct, she came to fear the Home, its waxed floors and fingers of dust on the molding. It appeared in her dreams amid other incongruous locales: The nurse's desk waited at the end of a long corridor in Sheridan High School; an orderly pushed a cart stuffed with dirty linens into the deepest part of her own basement. Eventually, she'd stopped volunteering on the floor and requested a job in the gift shop.

"And you'll have a TV, a beautiful view of the Sound, and a lovely roommate. What's her name, Viv?" Alfonse asked cheerfully.

"What?"

"The roommate. Mama's roommate. That nice lady."

"Mrs. Knoblovsky," said Vivian.

"That's right," he snapped his fingers. "Mrs. Knob—"

"Mrs. wha—?" She glared at Alfonse, as if it were his fault. "What is that, Polish? I thought this place was for Jews."

"Not everyone in the hospital is Jewish, Ma," said Vivian.

"Why not? It's a Jewish hospital," Evelyn replied.

"Well, she may very well be Jewish. Some Polish people are Jewish," said Alfonse.

"That's ridiculous." But Evelyn could not remember what they were discussing. "You remind me of my granddaughter," she said to the woman next to her. She patted the woman's hand, then wrapped her bent, veiny knuckles around it. There they remained. Vivian and Alfonse looked at the woman and they, too, recognized a similarity to Francesca—the Francesca of yore, the one they remembered, not the one they had seen in a newspaper photograph. Each of them realized— separately, always separately—that they knew nothing of Francesca today except the few facts they'd read, that she was alive and even thriving and seemed to suffer no ill effects from their deficient parenting. Vivian liked to think she'd done a pretty good job after all, and had in some way set the stage for Francesca's success.

The ambulance arrived at the gate of the Jewish Home and idled behind several wide American cars, all awaiting entry.

"See that?" Alfonse patted Evelyn's knee. "For security."

"Forget about what's outside. I'm worried about what's inside," Evelyn scowled, her heart pounding wildly. Like being awake for major surgery, she thought. Locally anesthetized, seeing them cut you open and manipulate your innards. Not that she'd ever had major surgery, but she'd heard enough about it from the ladies to know.

"They'd better be Jews," she said. "And I don't just mean the doctors."

"I'm sure some of the nurses are, too," said Alfonse reassuringly.

"That's asinine," Evelyn waved him away. He's so stupid, she thought. He's always been stupid. She turned and peered through the meshed windows of the ambulance at the cinder-colored building. Poor Sylvia, she thought. Now she understood how terrifying it must have been for her best friend, newly widowed, still stiff with tan and salt from the Florida sun, to be captured at the airport and dumped here. No wonder she'd died the next day.

Reality Has Intruded Here

New Haven, 1989

Reality Has Intruded Here, 1989

Ten feet tall, suspended from a thick wooden beam, *Reality Has Intruded Here* is a huge, throbbing work, set apart from the other paintings in the FdS museum, lit from behind by a spotlight. The trees, drawn by dark ropes of paint, suggest a deep, dead winter: the red, thick sky recalls tensely knit hats and down jackets, scarves wrapped again and again against the white cold.

deSilva created the huge and beguiling *Reality Has Intruded Here* after several weeks of isolation. It is an odd, anomalous work, particularly as it launched her final year of painting, during which some of her greatest pseudo-realistic pieces were completed (*Woman with Stool* and *Bunyan* are other extant works from this period).

Upon a door confiscated from the remains of a neighborhood Cape that she watched being torn down, deSilva tossed and splattered bright, thick colors. Lines, dots, splashes fill the door in an assault, even a war against what lies inside, namely privacy. In the lower right quadrant of the door is a bullet hole, a central detail that is, ironically, missed by many who view the painting (and, it would seem, fail to read their brochures). The hole appears to be simply a surface defect, perhaps the result of water damage or a neighborhood bully's BB gun. Only she who succumbs to curiosity by pressing her eyeball to the hole in the door is treated to the truth of the painting, i.e., what deSilva needed to say. At this point, the painting takes on the properties of sculpture. Beyond the bullet hole, visible only when the eye is flush to the aperture—a disconcerting sensation in itself—a small shoebox contains a diorama, such as a child might make in grade school.

Inside the shoebox appears a kitchen similar to Evelyn Horowitz's: a small table covered by a checked cloth, four metal chairs with vinyl covered seats, and a Tupperware of baked goods set out on a placemat. An old woman—created from a skeleton of pipe cleaners—is seated at the table alone, drinking coffee. Puffs of frantic gray hair rise in a cloud around her head. This world, unlike the cold, violent one around it, is calm and small, if strained with expectation. The woman's bent posture and cramped quarters seem to be trapped in time, as though she'd given up on anyone ever visiting, awaiting only the incontrovertible arrival of death.

Lucinda Dialo noted, "This is a painting that must be confronted; even the title is aggressive. deSilva wants the viewer to step up and assume the role of the intruder; as in *Virgin* and *What She Found,* she has us experience the scene from both sides. In *Reality Has Intruded Here,* we are peering salaciously through an old woman's peephole. What we see inside is so ordinary and private—the inevitable indignities of old age—that, in hindsight, our curiosity feels that much more prurient, as if, having peeked, we have violated a basic tenet of respectability."[83]

Reality Has Intruded Here seems to blatantly, even desperately, defy description at the same time that it makes an "accurate interpretation" (were such

83. Dialo, Lucinda. "Counterstrokes of Violence: How Society Informs Women's Art." *Caleidoscope, A Journal of Feminist Art,* 1994.

a thing to exist) impossible. The painting refuses to provide a definitive narrator or an inhabitable point of view. "The truth is, this is not simply an abstract painting," asserts Dialo. "The title prevents it from being such. If we are to be true to the artist's intentions, we must ask ourselves, what reality has intruded? We are the reality. We are intruding upon the small life behind the opaque door. We may not have made the hole; but we peer inside it. And to what end? So that we may know everything. So that we may steal from this poor old woman her solitude, her self, and finally, her home. This work is concerned with existential crisis, the moment in time when one recognizes that not only hasn't she fought to relieve the despair of those around her, but she has become a proponent—no matter how reluctant—of that anguish. She has ceased to be an agent of change and become, instead, a part of the problem."[84]

84. Dialo, Lucinda. *Message of Conflict: Homophobia and the Lesbian Artist.* San Francisco: Labrys Press, 1995, pages 72–87.

Chapter Twenty-One

It was the hub of night, the richest, thickest hours. Francesca's favorite time to work. Charlotte rapped on the cabin door.

"Your mother called," she said. "At 3 a.m." She shrugged. "She claimed it's urgent. She wants you to call back right away."

"How did she find me?" Francesca put down her paintbrush, thick with gray oil. Her body froze, as if after all this time on the lam, she'd been discovered.

"She saw the article in the paper and tracked us down. She said she's been meaning to call anyway. But now this . . . whatever this is."

Francesca shrugged and reached for her cigarettes. Without another word, she adopted a nonchalant gait and headed toward the door. She had a feeling something like this would happen, what with the publicity in *The New Haven Register*. She was asking for trouble by agreeing to do the New Haven show, inviting, if indirectly, the reentry of her family into her life.

"I'll wait here," Charlotte said, yawning. She ducked her head and sat on the bottom bunk, checking for cobwebs overhead.

Francesca entered the booth of the pay phone. She wiped her forehead on the sleeve of her jacket. The panels were open, the bottom buttons of her shirt were unfastened, and she pressed her naked stomach to the metal phonebook shelf. She still remembered the number.

"Hello?" It was Vivian.

"It's Francesca."

"Francesca! Oh, goodness. Honey, thank you for calling back."

"Charlotte said it was an emergency."

"Well . . . your grandmother. I'm afraid your grandmother—"

"Yes," Francesca interrupted. She'd known in some way.

"I hope you'll come to the funeral," said Vivian. "Though, of course I understand if you can't be there."

"I'll come."

"You will?" Vivian choked up quickly and Francesca could hear it in her voice. "Oh, your grandmother would have been so happy. She felt so terrible about everything."

"Really?"

"We all do. That doesn't even describe it: terrible. Heartbroken. It was a real tragedy. But your father and I, we're so happy you've done so well."

"What about Isabella?"

"Bella? She'll be beside herself when she hears you're coming home."

"So she's alive?"

"Oh, heavens, yes! She's just, well, you know your sister. She's prone to big gestures. Wait 'til I tell your father. He's over at the Home collecting Grandma's things. You might want some of them. I know she'd love you to have them. Maybe some of her jewelry." Here, Vivian thought of the girl in the picture, aware of the absurdity of that suggestion. The girl in the picture would never wear the thick gold brooches shaped in roses or the charm bracelet with little ballerinas and pianos dangling from its links. A good thing anyhow, since she was hoping to keep them for herself.

"I should pack," said Francesca.

"Okay. Take your time. The funeral isn't until Monday. Grandma only passed away an hour or so ago, but it's the Jewish Sabbath so we have an extra day." She sighed. When Francesca hung up the phone. She felt glad her sister was alive. The others left her empty as an echo.

Charlotte was waiting in the cabin, still on the bottom bunk, though she was leaning against the back wall, falling asleep. There was one candle glowing on the table, its flame jostled by the wind that followed Francesca into the room.

"My grandmother died. So I have to go home." Francesca lit a cigarette, then stood in the center of the room, turned in all directions to survey her work. Without saying a word, she took *Pay Phone* from where it was stacked against the wall and leaned it against the front door. Charlotte watched in silence; she could think of nothing to say, nothing wise, nothing comforting, nothing that she felt certain wouldn't turn Francesca irascible and distant. For there was surely something volatile in the air.

"Is it safe to drive this time of night?" she finally asked.

Francesca grabbed *Birds, Everywhere* and leaned it against *Pay Phone.* "This is the safest time to travel. No passengers on the road."

"You can't possibly mean to take those paintings with you. I have a truck hired to bring them to the exhibit."

"I'll be right in the neighborhood. I'll drop them off. Introduce myself."

"I don't think that's a very good—"

"I'll call you when I get to New Haven," said Francesca.

Charlotte stood up. She nodded her head for a long time, silencing one admonition after another. "You know," she said, "You don't need those people. If you want to see them, I understand completely. But you don't need them. You are a much better, stronger person than any of them could ever hope to be."

Francesca thought of a crow, cawing.

Charlotte walked to the door, then stopped. "Are you going to get *The Trilogy?* I assume you'll be seeing Lisa. I'm sure we could make room for those three works in the show."

"I haven't talked to her. So I'm not sure."

"But you wouldn't go to New Haven without seeing her."

"Of course not."

Charlotte hesitated. Something was wrong. But she felt Francesca holding her off. She'd never known Francesca's family as a direct influence, had no idea what sort of effect to dodge. Plus, the hour was too late for quick thinking; she was half asleep. "Send Lisa my love," she said.

"Will do. Bye, Charlotte."

After Charlotte had gone, Francesca took her paintings, one by one, and stacked them in the car. She removed some from their stretchers, rolled them into cylinders, and laid them across the floor of the passenger's seat. She knew it was strange, irrational, but she could not stop the sudden compulsion to show her work to her family. A voice reminded her about the upcoming show in New Haven, but even this was not soon enough. Or it did not matter. Perhaps she just needed her work with her on such a daunting mission. She packed approximately nineteen paintings, closed the door to the woodstove, tugged on the cord to shut out the light in the center of the room, and stepped outside of the cabin, leaving the door ajar, as if all that had happened inside there were no longer of consequence.

It wasn't as though Francesca had never indulged fantasies of reuniting with her grandmother; she had, though with decreased frequency as the years piled up. Most recently, she imagined parking the VW in Evelyn's squat driveway, running up the front stairs (dragging her hand along the rusted banister), arriving at the top, ringing the bell, rubbing black and orange chips from the creases in her palm while she waited to surprise Evelyn. Unbridled joy and relief on her grandmother's face; that was the main thing. The familiar odor of dark chocolate peppermints, Tone soap, cigarettes; the afternoon sun sneaking through the dusty living room shutters.

Too late, apparently. There would be no visit, no tearful reunion. No shouting "Gram!" No driving Evelyn to Rose D'Antone for a hair setting or to buy the new Tom Jones record (which Francesca had heard and, in spite of herself, rather enjoyed). And even if Evelyn weren't dead, WHICH SHE WAS, nothing goes that way. Nothing does. Things that are so thoroughly fucked up don't just get fixed. There was comfort there, in the bleak reality, where all was familiar and finite, leaving no room for romantic regret.

Of course she would go to the funeral. She'd always planned to return to New Haven at some point, and this was an appropriate occasion. Now that it had happened, she had no choice but to go. She was being lured by something that had already been set in motion, and all that she could do now was to follow its course. At least she had her paintings with her: armor.

She'd packed an overnight bag—toothbrush, sketchpad, Vonnegut novel, one change of clothes, a suit for the funeral, a few paints and brushes, and a blank canvas. The radio was playing "Burning Down the House" as she drove into the thinning darkness. Perfect middle-of-the-night music. She wondered whether any remains of the hut might still be standing alongside the narrow river where she'd long ago whiled away so much time. Perhaps just the foundation, which had been the most sturdily constructed.

She stopped at Cumberland Farms and bought two packs of Marlboros, hopping back into the car just in time to hear the rest of the song. It reminded her of Lisa, as did nearly everything. It had been on the jukebox one night while they shot drunken pool in a lesbian bar. Francesca had cornered Lisa against the wall, unbuttoned her jeans, and made her come quietly in the half darkness, in hazy view of the other women who pretended not to see. Thinking of it now, she felt a tightening inside her and this seemed wrong—lusting after a dead person. Everything she felt for Lisa now seemed wrong—perverse and inappropriate. How could she remain in love with a dead person? How could she stop loving a dead person?

Just over the Connecticut border she stopped at McDonalds and bought a coffee before taking her place in the restroom queue, which was surprisingly long for such an early hour. Each time she looked up, a pair of eyes seemed stuck to her like burrs. In Provincetown, she'd been spared such barefaced hostility. But here, people savored their disgust. Their eyes loitered on her body, all the way up, all the way down. Suddenly she hated her black jeans, her long, hard legs, all sinew and strength, the way her hands hung at her sides like an ape. She slurped coffee, peered down at the steam escaping through the sipping hole, avoiding her own face in the bathroom mirror as she leaned against the door, trying not to despair at the sight of her chiseled skull, her square jaw. (All she lacked was a beard.) Her hair was thick, haphazard, unkempt. But what bothered people most, she knew, was the heavy leather jacket, smattered with paint, a nascent pack of Marlboros peeking out from the side pocket. It made her a defiant, dissonant note in the world's symphony. Even worse, it suggested arrogance, pleasure taken in her perverse existence.

A woman in line glared at her. "This is the ladies' room," she snarled. She led her twin boys into one stall, then pressed her head to the door. "Tyrone, put down the lid when you're finished," she ordered through the crack. "Zip up. Both of you." She listened for flushing, then moved the boys to the row of sinks and supervised wash-up. Francesca spread the lapels of her jacket and thrust out her round breasts. She stared hard as the woman passed by, but there was no response, not so much as a glance of concession.

When finally she secured a stall, Francesca sat on the toilet, propped her elbows on her naked thighs, rested her head in her hands. Exhaustion came fast. She listened to the sounds peculiar to public bathrooms—the anonymous rush, then trickle of urine; a round of flushing toilets; accidental flatulence. People knocked on her stall; she ignored them. Finally, she pulled on her jeans and stepped out under the jitter of fluorescent lights, passed again through the gauntlet of stares. At the mirror ladies were busy holding their hands under the automatic taps and pounding up on the soap dispensers, examining their tired faces in the bad lighting, frowning, trying to fix what they saw with lipstick and rouge. She envied them the solace of the ladies room. She'd never known, nor would she, the ease of exchanging sweet, uncharged smiles with other women, the slowing of breath that occurs away from the assessing stares of men. Nor would she ever experience the solidarity they felt in scrutinizing her, despising her. Evelyn, she knew, was one of them.

Chapter Twenty-Two

Isabella wore a swimsuit under her clothes. It was her latest innovation, to emphasize her shrinking form, the slow dissipation being the result of a diet Vivian had insisted upon after Isabella gained 26 pounds in the mental hospital. She sat in the living room now, on the day after Evelyn Horowitz's death, awaiting the arrival of her long-disappeared sister. She tried to think of her grandmother, to feel anything at all about poor, dead Evelyn. But ever since she'd received word of her sister's imminent return, she'd been distracted. Never mind the fact that the seam of the bathing suit pulled at the tender flesh inside her thighs. She crossed her legs, uncrossed them, recrossed them with the other leg on top.

"I know," she said, surprised when the words escaped the barrier of her lips, "I'll make a cup of tea." A cup of tea, thought Isabella, was a good, slimming thing, with the added benefit of calming her nerves or at least helping her appear to be someone who possessed calm nerves. She walked into the kitchen and put a pot of water on the stove. Slowly, ceremoniously, she removed the flat red box of teabags from the cabinet, pulled one out by its string, and placed it in a mug. Each movement she performed carefully, self-consciously, as though her sister was already home. Watching.

In the hospital, with no vodka to slow down her thinking, Isabella had learned to soothe herself by enumerating metaphors: the crack of ice cubes under heat (mania) versus the slow bleeding of brown tea into hot water (depression). The patter of boiling water on the pillow of tea (mania) versus the immeasurable slowness of heat (depression). Less coherent analogies followed: the hyperproductive, prodigious fertility of tropical fauna (mania) versus the cold, still bottom of the sea (depression). Cities were mania; farmlands, depression. Paris was mania; New Hampshire, depression. The jungle, mania; the tight claustrophobic woods of New England, depression. Cars, food, music. All of it could be mania, all of it depression. Occasionally, one could be trapped inside both moods at the same time. This was the worst of all feelings. A fast slowing down. A slow speeding up. A car accident in slow motion; a coma full of busy, sexy adventure dreams while people stood over you, talking, weeping, holding flowers, invading your pleasure.

She was, she decided, looking forward to seeing her sister. She'd never really disliked Francesca. It was more of an overcrowding problem: There hadn't been room in the house for both of them. There were only two bedrooms, after all, and they were a physically substantial family—every one of them but Vivian clearing five-seven, every one of them but Vivian sporting broad shoulders and wide hips. In fact, Isabella thought, she'd even missed Francesca from time to time. After all, she'd been the one to learn of Francesca's existence from a newspaper article, to cut out her picture and track down Lisa Sinsong (that bitch), to make sure Francesca was alright.

She was glad to have a sister. Someone with whom she imagined playing charades and eating pizza, running about the neighborhood in the wee hours and setting the dogs on edge. Though she wished Francesca had grown up as expected, into a simple, ugly girl with scant personality, employed by a factory or a bar, flipping burgers or pumping gas, and living in New Hampshire in a trailer. Perhaps coming home to visit occasionally, very occasionally, accompanied by a mangy mutt whose presence drove Vivian so crazy, she couldn't wait for Francesca to leave.

But friendship seemed unlikely now that her sister was a cult figure while Isabella was a melted candle, a smoked cigarette, the ashy remains of a wet, fireplace log. The antithesis of the child prodigy, having nothing to look forward to but appointments with her psychiatrist, advancements in pharmacology, and the hope that, if she did not kill herself, she might lose her mind once and for all, rather than simply misplacing it over and over again and finding, upon its return, that it offered less promise and more grief.

These were her thoughts at the moment she heard the crunching of gravel under tires.

She ran to the picture window, pressed her palms to the glass, leaving sticky childish prints behind, and watched as a small, red VW Rabbit came to a stop at the bottom of the driveway.

"Mom! Come quick," she screamed, then ran upstairs and hid in the attic.

Francesca parked in the bottom of the driveway. Everything around her appeared set to a different scale: The house was a bleary shade of tan, standing squat, situated too close to the neighbors. The lawn was brown, hungry from winter's pillage. It occurred to her, for the first time, as she pulled up on the brake and unfolded from the car, that her family was rather poor. She'd always known they weren't rich, but in comparison to what she'd seen on the Cape, the house, the neighborhood, and all that surrounded it looked shabby and neglected.

She took a deep breath and tossed her cigarette into the shrubby hedge. She bent over and touched her toes, then slowly erected herself. Mindfully, she folded her leather jacket and placed it neatly on the driver's seat. Time slowed way down. She rolled out every moment that remained between standing outside in the driveway (here, she lit a cigarette, took a long, vital drag) and entering the house she'd fled so desperately. Then the back door swung open.

"Francesca! Honey! You're here!"

Vivian shook with sobs. Her hands flailed ahead of her as if they were lost in mist, trying to pull Francesca all the way from the car. "I can't believe it's you!"

"It's me." Francesca forced a smile, though she felt her face freeze into a look of fear, almost as if she were about to cry. She wished she could turn around, get back in the car, and be on I-95. She stepped onto the stoop and put one arm around her mother's slim waist. In her other hand, she held her knapsack.

"Oh my God." Vivian pushed Francesca away to look at her. "Bella, come here. Come see your sister."

Isabella stampeded down the stairs as if she'd only this moment learned of Francesca's arrival. When she reached the first floor foyer, she stopped, inhaled loud and long, then continued to move slowly through the kitchen. She saw her sister through the threshold, leaning over, embracing Vivian, and decided she looked rather like a colt—a slim, young colt (*mania?*) as opposed to a grown, shod horse (*depression?*). She was even manlier in person than she'd appeared in the newspaper photograph. Isabella struggled to think of something normal to say, something to distract herself from the raging, inappropriate impulses that beckoned. She felt the urge to whisper to Francesca: "Quick! Run! And don't look back or you'll turn into a pillar of salt!" Or to push Francesca out the door, down the two squat steps, then bolt the door behind her.

"Look. Look who it is," Vivian cried.

"Oh my God," said Isabella. "It's Francesca!" She waved frantically, then stopped and let her arms drift apart until between them was just enough space to accommodate a small hug, one reserved, perhaps, for a toddler or a ball. Francesca squeezed herself in between Isabella's hands and awkwardly the sisters embraced under the teary gaze of their beleaguered mother.

Vivian woke Alfonse from his nap, and he came down the stairs slowly, like an old man, his back bent at the top so that his shoulders curled forward. He'd gone gray, and the lines in his face were etched deep. His hair was messed from sleeping, squished on the left side so that it stood inches above his scalp. Francesca thought he looked almost mentally arrested, a small boy in an old man's body.

"Oh my goodness," he said, his pace quickening when he got a look at Francesca in the living room. "You're really here." He began crying, as if someone had pulled a switch.

Francesca gave in to it now. Something about her father made it all inescapable—the familiarity, the promise of family, of love, of all that she'd forced from her thoughts. Weepy Alfonse, his emotions always so ready, made it impossible for her to remain stalwart.

They sat in the living room. Vivian watched Francesca as if she were the newest panda bear in the Washington zoo. She was grateful to Francesca for coming home; it would be such a relief to not have her daughter's absence remarked upon all through the funeral and the shiva afterward. Still, Vivian could not completely eradicate the anger she felt at Francesca's complete abdication of her responsibility as a daughter. Sure, she herself had failed in many ways, most strikingly in her ability to divide her attentions between a demanding genius and a quiet girl who had seemed so ordinary and self-sufficient.

On the other hand, she knew, as did Alfonse, about the morning Evelyn had walked in on Francesca and the Chinese girl, and this, Vivian told herself—and Alfonse told himself as well—was the real reason Francesca had fled. She'd always seemed a strange child, what with her penchant for things wild and natural, her lack of interest in anything feminine (I want a *purple* room!), her finger painting. And on the day when Evelyn related the story, through a filter of disgust and rage, Vivian and Alfonse could no longer hide from themselves what Francesca was. This, they decided then, was why she'd gone, so she could live among other people like her. Evelyn had been happy to accept this explanation, since it took the onus off of her and made Francesca's disappearance inevitable.

❑   ❑   ❑

Alfonse piled spaghetti, three meatballs, and a heaping tablespoon of freshly grated Reggiano Parmesan onto a plate.

"That Joycie. What a mensch," said Vivian, referring to Joycie Newman, who had dropped the food off in Tupperwares that afternoon.

Alfonse held the plate out to Francesca. "Our guest of honor," he said.

Isabella put one hand in the air. "Ask her if she eats meat," she demanded.

"Oh—" Abashedly, he retracted the plate.

"I do eat meat. Thank you." Francesca took it from him.

Alfonse glared at Isabella.

"What," Isabella said firmly. "A lot of lesbians don't eat meat."

He ladled a large heap of pasta and sauce onto another plate and held it out to Isabella.

"What? I can't eat that!" She blocked it with outstretched hands. "Didn't she bring any salad?"

"Joycie brought spaghetti. That's how it is. People bring the food and we eat it. It's not a time to be difficult," said Vivian.

"I'll just have an apple," said Isabella.

"Viv, tell her to eat the spaghetti." Alfonse spoke quietly.

"It's okay," said Vivian. "Just don't eat too much."

Isabella looked at the plate, panicked, as if upon it sat an unpredictable wild animal she didn't want to rouse. She swallowed hard and shook her head. "Just sauce," she said, handing the plate back to Alfonse. "Please."

"What do you mean, just sauce?"

"It's fine, Alfonse," said Vivian. She turned to Isabella. "I know for a fact that Joycie uses very little oil in the sauce. And lean meat. You know Joycie—she's always on a diet." She patted Isabella's hand.

"That's ridiculous. She's too skinny as it is," said Alfonse, disgusted.

"It's the white flour. It metabolizes into sugar and forms a layer of flab right here." Isabella patted her belly.

Alfonse pushed the spaghetti back into the saucepan, mixing it in with the mound of clean noodles, staining everything a weak orange. He slapped the pot down and presented Isabella with her abridged plate, now smattered with sauce and pimply bumps of meat. "Happy?" he said, his voice tight.

Gingerly, Isabella moved two laggard strands of spaghetti to the side, then took the plate from her father. Sauce is depression; spaghetti, mania. She should have chosen spaghetti, some meatballs, a big glass of Coke. Tears filled her eyes, silent and unstoppable, clouding her vision. She felt around her plate for her spoon, trying to focus on the sad puddle of sauce before her, struggling not to resent her sister's monopoly on approval. She shook her head, grimacing. She was trying so hard. Oh, how she was trying. She reassured herself that although Francesca was visiting, and so was being fussed over and lavished with gobs of attention, her parents were and always would be hers. Utterly. Exclusively. This fact, while unspoken and, of course, unspeakable, was still a fact. Already they were so ill at ease with each other, her mother and her fly-by-night sister, that it was only a matter of time until they ran fresh out of patience, or whatever resource they were rapidly depleting. There was nothing to draw them together except perhaps the tiniest physical resemblance—the posture, the leanness, the sharp features. And the big hands. Vivian had smaller hands but they were big for her size, for her carriage—long fingered and thick palmed. Francesca's were just plain big. Anyhow, this was a superficial likeness, so subtle as to go unnoticed, and Isabella knew that very soon they would revert to a state of mutual loathing. How sad. Sad, sad, sad. It was all she could do not to "tsk tsk" aloud. She wished everyone well, somewhere deep down and hard to get a hold of. Like a tiny gold ring at the bottom of the ocean. "All done!" She placed her tablespoon diagonally across her plate, took the saltshaker from the middle of the table, and dumped a long spray over the stain of sauce that remained. She sprung to her feet.

"Good for you." Vivian said.

"Good? Why are you telling her that's good?" asked Alfonse, his voice cracking.

"That's why she's so slim."

"Yes, *she* is. Thank you," said Isabella. "If you'll excuse *her* . . ." She walked into the living room and flung herself on the couch.

"Tell her to get back in here," Alfonse demanded.

"You should have seen your sister," Vivian told Francesca. She puffed out her cheeks and hung her hands at her side.

"I saw that, Mom," called Isabella.

"No, you didn't," Vivian replied smartly, as if this were a game.

"Viv, tell her to come back in here."

Why, Francesca wondered, had Lisa ended her life when lives like these continued on and on with no apparent purpose?

Isabella's needs were tapping, tapping, demanding attention. She'd tried to allow the focus to stagnate on her sister. But Francesca didn't need their attention; that was obvious. And oh, how Isabella did. She needed it more with each passing moment. She appeared in the doorway. "Here I am." She sat down at the table and, to please Alfonse, took her napkin and smoothed it over her lap. "I'll have some spaghetti, Papa."

"No point now. We're nearly finished."

"But I'm hungry."

He took her plate, rather roughly, and spooned a small amount of pasta, maybe a quarter cup, over the heap of salt, then used the ladle to cover it with sauce. But as soon as Isabella had taken the plate from him, she knew she couldn't eat. Quickly, she searched for a distraction.

"My new book is going very well," she said. "It's a memoir."

"We know," Alfonse said.

"How do you know?"

"You told us." He picked up his fork.

"When?"

"I don't know. Recently."

Isabella thought hard. "Oh. I guess I've been so busy working on it, I forgot." She paused, heard only the sounds of silverware tapping dishes. "Uh oh. Did I give away the ending?"

"I'm sure you didn't," said Vivian.

"Good, because it's the best part. The ending. But they say you're never supposed to tell. Because once you tell, once you say the story out loud, which, of course, is so much easier than writing the whole thing down, page after page after page—then you needn't write it."

"Oh, go ahead," Francesca pushed her plate away, relieved to have her sister back in the room. Isabella, at least, had vim. Inside that pale, frayed exterior, one could feel the life trying to get out. "Tell us, Bella."

"Alright. If Francesca wants to hear it. Since she's the guest of honor." She leaned closer to her sister until their faces were inches apart, and spoke intimately, in a low, spooky voice. "It's all about the mental ward. And the narrator—is . . ." she whispered, "a pedophile."

"Jesus Christ." Alfonse dropped his fork, put his hand to his heart. "Vivian!"

Vivian turned to Isabella. "Either you sit down and act like a regular person, or you can stay in the other room."

"I'm telling Francesca." She cupped Francesca's ear but spoke loudly enough that the others would hear. "He managed to work a deal with the prosecutor where he's in the loony bin to beat a jail rap," she whispered. "This actually happened."

"Isabella, stop fibbing," said Vivian.

"Why does she always want to write about perverts?" asked Alfonse.

"First of all, I never write about perverts." She wasn't sure whether this was true. "Second, it's a classic theme, Papa. The antiprotagonist.

The main character who does horrible things and yet we are made to identify with him. Dostoyevsky did it. Nabokov did it." Finally, thought Isabella, the spotlight was rightfully hers. "Even Shakespeare was obsessed with it."

"Nabokov always wrote about pedophiles," offered Francesca.

"Well, he was a very strange fellow. He had that thing about butterflies," Alfonse added, trying to participate.

"Papa, I doubt you've ever read Nabokov," said Isabella.

"I've read plenty. I've certainly read Italo Calvino. He's a very fine writer. And he writes about beauty and his country and love, of course."

"But Nabokov turned the whole genre upside down. No one since Chaucer had written such defiantly literary dirty books! Unless you consider Henry Miller literary." Isabella shuddered with distaste.

"Could we please talk about something else?" Alfonse dropped his silverware and let his chin hover inches from his plate. He looked at Vivian, then Isabella. "There must be other things to discuss. I haven't seen Francesca in seven years."

"Eight," added Isabella.

"Why is it always lunatics and suicide and holocaust victims and pedophiles? What about something nice? Love, maybe?" He looked at Isabella. "Why don't you write about love?"

Isabella shrugged. "Because I don't know about love," she said in a flat voice.

"That's not true, Bella," said Vivian. "Now just stop it."

Isabella looked at her mother, thinking about her words: "That's not true." *Were they correct? Was it not true? Was she just being melodramatic?*

"I don't mean parental love," she clarified. "I know about parental love."

"Just let the rest of us eat," said Vivian.

Francesca felt impotent, and this feeling was unpleasant and familiar. She wanted to intervene, to defend her sister, at least to prod Isabella into defending herself. *Tell them to shut the fuck up,* she wanted to say. *Tell them you're 28 years old.* Instead, she did nothing. She began to imagine the drive back to Cape Cod, stopping at Wendy's for a

262

chicken sandwich (instead of McDonalds), returning to her cabin and unloading all the paintings from the car, unadulterated, having never subjected them to the scrutiny of these fatuous people.

Isabella began to cry quietly. She wiped tears with her sleeve and sniffled, then pulled her chair back from the table, preparing to stand. "Papa? Do you want me at the table?" she looked at him.

"Of course he does," said Vivian. "We all do."

"Does Francesca want me?" asked Isabella.

"I really do," said Francesca.

And so, Isabella sat quietly, close to her sister, feeling, for the first time in her life, that she had a sister. Francesca patted Isabella's knee, then left her large hand there, heavy and reassuring.

That night Alfonse slept fitfully, dreaming of Vivian and his daughters sitting on the neighbor's porch. In the dream, they were all lesbians. From next door he smelled Evelyn's cooking instead of old Mrs. Weinstein's garbage rotting in the garage. He seemed to be going blind. He tried to look at his younger daughter and the lesbian neighbor, but he could not see them anymore.

He awoke in the middle of the night, his throat dry and filled with the taste of copper and garlic. The clock said 3:12. He walked down the dark hallway, the floorboards creaking beneath his bare feet, and stood at the kitchen sink, drinking glass after glass of tepid, sulfur-stained water, gazing out at the silent yard. How, he wondered, could he have tolerated so many years of not knowing whether his youngest daughter was even alive? How had it happened that he and Vivian had returned from a marriage encounter weekend to find one daughter nearly dead, the other gone? The song they'd chosen, for every couple had been required to choose a song, was "For All We Know." The title took on an unpleasant, ironic sting: It seemed they didn't know much. He'd driven around the neighborhood, stopped by the school, talked with some teachers. He'd even called Mr. Sinsong, who claimed not to remember ever visiting 312 Riverview Street and had suggested, accusingly, that perhaps Alfonse had the wrong Chinese family.

By the time he and Vivian had extracted details from Evelyn—how she'd found Lisa in Francesca's bed, the clothes on the floor—days had passed. "That one from Chapel Street," Evelyn kept saying, as if Lisa's neighborhood and all it symbolized were to blame.

At the police station, the detective had explained there was nothing to be done about an 18-year-old who chooses to leave home. Unless they suspected foul play. Did they feel she'd been abducted? the policeman had asked. Vivian nodded with certitude, but Alfonse said nothing. He'd wanted to suspect wrongdoing, something to make fade the glaring, throbbing truth that there was nothing criminal about her disappearance: no one had abducted her, forced her to leave; in fact, she'd fled her miserable life. He thought of Francesca's face—lined now with age and sadness. But youthful. It was the face of an honest life. He thought of her deep voice, the way she sat, shoulders straight, head slightly forward, and wondered what sort of thoughts occupied her mind. He wanted to believe she'd escaped unscathed. But he knew that was a lie. Anyone with eyes could see that hers were sad as a war-torn country.

In a sense, they'd forgotten her. The panic had faded to pain, first acute, then unremarkable. In the same way the acuity of any loss lessens, things filling up its gaping hole, the absence of Francesca came to be routine. She was a name rarely mentioned—the daughter they'd once had, the one they'd lost. People in the town stopped including Francesca's name in the general inquiries. Of course, some years later, when it became clear that Isabella would never fulfill her promise, when Evelyn's mind hit the dirt like compost, people no longer inquired, just smiled and said hello. That was the sort of town it was—everyone knew but pretended to know nothing. He supposed all towns were like that, and it seemed sad to him, how little comfort people spared for each other, how separate and safe from each other's tragedies they all chose to remain.

Chapter Twenty-Three

The basement, disguised as a guest room, more closely resembled a friendly prison cell, with hard linoleum tile and plastic paneled walls, one secret window tucked just beneath the ceiling, its pane cracked and cloudy from cobwebs. The air was heavy and mildewed. The seat of a metal folding chair was tucked under the surface of a bridge table, and in the far corner of the room Francesca's old record player balanced precariously on a column of albums, her headphones poised on top. A sheath of moonlight managed entry as she lay on the daybed, her body covered in brick-red wool blankets, topped off by the lavender bedspread of her childhood. She should have stayed in a hotel; she knew this as she dipped her feet under the cold sheets and felt the springs give under her weight. But there was something here that she needed. She felt herself easing into the heaviness of the house, like stepping into a pair of old slippers that are soft and unstable. She chose the basement over her mother's office, the room that had once been Isabella's bedroom. (She had categorically declined her sister's offer to share the attic room.) The basement had the fewest memories, afforded the greatest privacy. And it was tomblike, somewhere safe and dark to which she could retreat.

She dreamt of Lisa—discombobulated, incomprehensible dreams—images violent as the ocean during a storm: pieces of Lisa's face, Lisa's fragmented fingers, Lisa's black shoes stepping in and out of the rusty tracks, moving across the dusty floor of her cabin. Wasn't it strange, Francesca wondered upon waking, that Lisa had gone to the train tracks to die? Or was it pure coincidence? By even thinking it, was Francesca trying to bolster her own significance in Lisa's life?

It wasn't uncommon for her to dream of Lisa; Lisa nearly always stood about in Francesca's dreams, even the innocuous, everyday anxiety ones where she tried desperately, in vain, to buy socks or cigarettes. Always Lisa lurked—picking up cigs at the liquor store, driving past in the VW—the embodiment of everything Francesca longed for and lost. But to dream of her in this house, while she lay swaddled in the dreaded bedspread, a few feet away from her Beatles collection, across from the oil burner (making a strange knocking, as if a pebble were bouncing against its steel sides), amplified the loss of Lisa, banged on the bruise in her heart.

She reminded herself that she hadn't stepped back in time. She was Francesca deSilva with a lower case "d," just as she'd been yesterday, still a renowned artist who had long ago fled this suffocating structure and its damaged inhabitants. Still . . . she seemed to have invited all of it inside her again, allowed it to penetrate a cavity that had heretofore been sealed off.

She sat up and lit a cigarette, suddenly overcome with the desire to hear music on her old phonograph, a side of some album absurdly time-worn and dated. She crossed the cold, lacquered floor and lifted her record player—it was surprisingly light and cheaply constructed— into the center of the room and rested it on an unfolded bridge chair. She plugged in the appliance, chose *Sergeant Pepper's Lonely Hearts Club Band* (worse still: "She's Leaving Home"), and laid the needle gently down, then inserted the headphones jack and reclined on the daybed, her back to the wall, her large feet protruding in front of her.

For a moment, she was soothed, distracted, even transported to the attic room, the early evening hours before dinner when she'd be blissfully alone with music amid the slow capping off of light; before she'd have to join the others for a strained, brief meeting at the dinner table. They weren't all terrible memories. Life had, ultimately, turned in her favor. Art had wrought new possibilities. Lisa had loved her, briefly.

But then, as if she'd been struck from behind, a steep blow to the head by the point of a rock or the edge of a brick—she remembered, afresh, that Lisa was dead. That she'd failed to pick up on the clues that were surely being dropped like a thin trail of breadcrumbs behind Lisa's feet. That she'd failed Lisa in every respect, and this failure on her part seemed inherent, even destined. Growing up in this colorless, ailing house had made certain that she would never be attuned to the finer dips and curves of life. Nor the joys. Though she experienced little skits of pleasure, life was, had always been, an ongoing, concerted effort to keep pain at bay, to get through this day and onto the next. And all of this mitigating had caused her to miss Lisa's agony altogether; she was too consumed by her own. Now she would spend the rest of her life knowing she hadn't helped the person who mattered most to her in the world.

So much for feeling better.

Upstairs, she brushed her teeth, moving about quietly so as not to rouse her parents, whose company in that moment was as welcome as pins lodged under her fingernails. One more inane conversation in which they'd all behave as if things, having gone a wee bit awry, were now happily repaired, and Francesca felt she might come unhinged, kidnap her sad sack of a sister and return to the beach, never to see or speak with her parents again.

She put on the same clothes she'd worn yesterday, then stepped outside into the cool morning air. It was Sunday; the museum was closed, so there was nothing to do about the paintings. At least, Francesca decided, she'd busy herself by taking a drive; maybe she'd find the housing project where Lisa had lived or drive through downtown New Haven and visit the laundromat where she'd waited, in vain, for Lisa to run away with her so many years ago, when she still swelled with innocence and bravado enough to try and save her.

For a moment Francesca mistook for a raccoon or possum or some other suburban pest the body of her sister, seated inches from the car door on the paved ground, wearing a bulky white sweatshirt and corduroys. Isabella's eyes were closed, her palms pressed flat onto the cold, wet grass.

"Isabella?"

Isabella opened her eyes.

"Were you sleeping?"

"Maybe. I think I couldn't sleep so I came out here." She looked up toward her room, remembering.

"Have you been here all night?"

Isabella shrugged. "I think so. I think I have. I was so upset after dinner. So I came out here, hoping LeeAnn would step outside. She often does and we have a nice chat, and then I feel better."

"Who's LeeAnn?"

Isabella jutted her chin toward the neighbor's house. "You'd remember her if you saw her, I'll bet. She's blond."

"But aren't you cold?"

Isabella shook her head. "I never get *too* cold. A person can learn to tolerate extremes in temperature. For example, when it's really hot outside I hardly sweat. My body simply adjusts. Sometimes I've stayed out all night during snowstorms, though often I take breaks in the garage so I don't get wet. Because once you get wet, a formidable chill is unavoidable."

"But why not read or watch TV if you can't sleep?"

Isabella's face tensed. She looked away from Francesca and focused on the side of the neighbor's house. "I prefer the outdoors. It soothes me."

"I understand that." Francesca squatted down beside her sister. "I often stay up all night working and take breaks outside. Sometimes I just stroll along the road outside my cabin or I ride my bike or I just sit in my car and smoke." She patted the passenger's side of the VW.

"Maybe we get it from Papa. He loves the outdoors."

"Maybe." Francesca groaned and stood up. "Well, if Mom and Papa ask where I am, say that I went to do some errands. Could you scoot over so I can back out?"

Isabella looked up at the car, unconvinced that her location precluded this. "Can I come? Please? I won't even speak. I'll just sit quietly and watch things out the window."

"Alright," Francesca said. "But let me get some of these paintings out of the car so there's room."

"What paintings? " Isabella stood and peered into the car. Sure enough, piled willy-nilly on the floor of the passenger's side, the back seat, tucked into all the floor spaces, even resting up top on the rear ledge, were paintings—many, many paintings—some taken off their stretchers and rolled into loose cylinders, fastened with shoelaces, others stacked flat and tight. "Tell me those are not *your* paintings."

"Of course they are. What other paintings would I be driving around with?"

Isabella punched Francesca's arm playfully. "You're fucking kidding me, right? Your paintings are in that little hunk of tin? What are you, nuts?"

"I didn't want to leave them on the Cape."

"That's crazy, man. What about those? You took them off the frames?"

Francesca shrugged. "I couldn't fit them in the car on their stretchers."

"No," Isabella shook her head. "That doesn't make sense."

"Help me bring them inside."

"You wanted to show Mom." Isabella pointed at Francesca, grinning. Something about this idea thrilled her, that her sister, like her, could be driven by some pathological need to impress their mother.

"Are you coming or not? Because if you're not coming, I'll just leave them there."

"Of course I'm coming. Duh." Quickly, Isabella covered her mouth. "Mom hates when I use that word."

"Yeah, well, it doesn't bother me. You can say 'Duh' every five seconds for all I care." Francesca opened the passenger's door and pulled out several of the paintings. There were twelve rolled and tucked into the front floor space on the passenger's side.

"Can I help?" Isabella asked, rubbing her hands together.

Francesca handed her sister the cylinders, one by one, passing them carefully, as if they were babies. "Just put them in the garage."

"The garage?" cried Isabella. "What are you, crazy? That garage is about to fall down all over itself. We can't put them in there. Imagine if it collapsed while we were at the funeral and all of your paintings were destroyed?"

"I don't want to imagine that," Francesca said.

"We'll put them in the house. In the basement with you. Or in the attic if you want. It's very dry up there." Isabella coughed to emphasize her point. Francesca continued to pile paintings on Bella's outstretched arms. "I don't understand this at all," Isabella said, pulling away to indicate she had enough to carry. "What if you'd crashed and your car had exploded?"

"Then I'd be dead."

"What about posterity?"

"I don't think about posterity, Isabella." Francesca shook her head. Her sister was so strange, but compelling. There was something about her mind that Francesca wanted to understand, to follow, and her responses to things couldn't be called emotional or intellectual, but were something else—instinctual. You could feel the intelligence ricochet off her like electricity. But it seemed to have no reason for being and nothing to do.

They brought the first batch of paintings down into the basement and deposited them on the card table. Isabella sat on the daybed, winded from the effort and enthusiasm. She rubbed the gritty bedspread with her hands. "You hated this bedspread," she said.

"I know."

"Do you think Mom put it here on purpose?"

"No," Francesca said. "Do you?"

"It wouldn't be unheard of. She does that sort of thing—tiny, passive-aggressive gestures. But I don't know why she'd do it to you. What does she have to be angry with you about? Except that you left the family and never called to say you were okay."

"No one ever tried to find me," Francesca said, lighting a cigarette. She leaned against the wall and stared at her sister.

"Yes, they did. They tried to find you."

"How do you know?"

"Duh . . ." Isabella covered her mouth, then remembered she didn't have to. "I remember them talking to the police." Isabella stared at the paneled wall, wincing with shame. "But I was in the hospital. So they were distracted."

"What the hell happened anyway?"

"I tried to kill myself. Didn't Lisa tell you?"

"Lisa?" Francesca asked, startled at the sound of Lisa's name uttered by someone else, uttered anywhere other than inside her brain. "Yes, she did. But I thought it was something more recent."

"Oh. Right. There was that time, too." Isabella stared at a crack in the paneling. She pushed her index finger into the slat where the plastic had separated and tried to widen it. "I have an allergy to life," she said sadly. "I tracked her down, you know. When I heard you were alive. I called every Sinsong until I found her, then told her what I'd read in the paper. And she said she'd get in touch with you. Did she? Did she get in touch with you?"

Francesca nodded.

"Could I have a cigarette?" Isabella asked, thinking her sister looked cool.

Francesca held out the pack. Gingerly, Isabella took one and leaned in for a light. She sucked on the cigarette, smoke puffing out like stuffing from all directions. "Is this where you slept?" she made a sympathetic face. "It reminds me of a prison."

"Yeah. Me too. The whole house reminds me of a prison."

"Want to come sit next to me?" Isabella patted the bed.

Francesca moved slowly across the room, then sat on the daybed beside her sister.

"How is Lisa Sinsong?" Isabella asked.

"Why do you say it like that? Her whole name?"

Isabella turned toward her sister, panicked, as if she'd been accused of something diabolical. "I don't know," she stammered. "I guess ... I think ... I like the way it sounds. I think that's the only reason. And then, too, I guess I've always been interested in Mrs. Sinsong—whose first name I do not know—because of how she died, jumping off the building and all, in the middle of New York City." Isabella paused. "Hey," she said, "Why don't we go visit Lisa? See? No last name that time. I can learn."

"Because she's dead," Francesca answered flatly, staring down at the notches of her knee, visible even through her heavy jeans.

"What?"

"She killed herself a few months ago."

Isabella stared straight ahead while the words sunk in. Silently she rifled through a series of responses, all of them inappropriate, then sat for a moment until she could think of something reasonable to ask, something a normal person would want to know. "Did you see her before she died?"

271

"She'd just visited. A few weeks before."

"Was she depressed?"

Francesca looked long at her sister, trying to remember. "I guess so. She wasn't very happy. But then—"

"Who is?" interrupted Isabella. "Certainly not Lisa. Not you. Not me."

Francesca shrugged. "I didn't take it that seriously. I knew she was still living with her father. I knew she was still scared of her father. But I thought maybe she'd move to the Cape and we'd live together. So, no, I didn't see it coming. I didn't realize she was particularly depressed. I missed it entirely. I missed it totally."

"No, that's not it," Isabella said. "You can't draw that conclusion." Isabella spoke surely, sounding for the first time like an older sister, "Some people just don't enjoy life. In the same way that some people might not be interested in children or work or love. Some people just aren't that enamored of life. It seems counter to our purpose as human beings, I know, because that's what we're here to do: live. So, it's depressing for those people."

"Are you like that?" asked Francesca.

"Yup." Isabella stubbed out the cigarette, thinking of poor, little Lisa, so many years ago, of her own sick fascination . . . Oddly, there was a strong current of life running through Isabella, almost a violence, something unstoppable, and it seemed she couldn't end her life even as she tried. It was the opposite of Lisa, whose commitment to her own existence was tenuous at best.

"Was it a building?" asked Bella. "Did she jump off a building?"

"No," Francesca said. "She shot herself in the head."

"She put a gun to her head?"

Francesca nodded.

"Wow," Isabella said, newly impressed, her mind spinning with weird emotions—envy, admiration for Lisa's chutzpah, newfound courage to take matters into her own hands. "Where'd she get a gun?"

Francesca shrugged and patted her sister's knee. "That's enough," she said. She gestured for Isabella to follow her up the stairs. As they passed through the kitchen, they heard Vivian and Alfonse stirring on the second floor.

272

"Tonight," said Isabella, "this place will be crawling with little old Jewish ladies."

❏   ❏   ❏

Francesca popped the trunk and began unloading the remaining paintings. The door to the house next door opened and LeeAnn Frank stepped outside, her hands wrapped around a tall, oblong mug of coffee. Steam drifted up and into her face. Francesca noticed her at once—she was rather beautiful—and watched as LeeAnn kicked the welcome mat free from the ice that had soldered it to the porch. She wore gray sweatpants, a large, navy sweatshirt with YALE in block white letters. Her graying hair was pulled straight back into a shiny, unwashed pony tail.

"LeeAnn," called Isabella, her voice pitched loud and desperate.

The neighbor looked up and waved.

"LeeAnn, come meet my sister," said Isabella.

LeeAnn leaned her broom against the front of the house and patted some loose strands on the sides of her ponytail. She walked, barefoot, along the frozen ground and squeezed in between the hedges until she stood, shivering slightly and hopping from foot to foot. "Nice to meet you. I remember when you were a little girl."

"You do?" Francesca asked, extending her hand. "How could that be?"

"Francesca," Isabella offered her assistance. "LeeAnn has lived in that house for—how long has it been LeeAnn?"

"Twenty years."

"LeeAnn has lived in that house for 20 years. And she's a piano teacher."

"What's that have to do with it, Bella?" asked Francesca, fumbling for her cigarettes and, finally, finding them.

"Just that she's an artist, too," Bella offered, tentatively.

LeeAnn began to shiver.

"Are you coming over today?" asked Isabella. "We're sitting shiva for grandma."

"Yes, I know."

"Grandma liked LeeAnn," Isabella told Francesca. "We all do. She's been our neighbor for a long time. I miss Sappho, too," Isabella said, getting wound up, beginning to ramble. She felt little shocks of impulse working their way to the surface.

"Who was Sappho?" asked Francesca.

"Our dog."

Francesca nodded, putting the pieces together—a blurry picture of a big woman working on her car. A yapping dog. "Was it a beagle?"

"No . . . duh. Golden retriever," blurted Isabella.

"Ah," Francesca nodded her head. She opened her mouth, searching for something else to ask the blond neighbor, but it was too late. The back door opened and Vivian appeared in her bright blue terry robe.

"Good morning," she called over a yawn. "Oh. Good morning, LeeAnn. Isabella, are you bothering LeeAnn?"

"No, she's not, Vivian. We were just chatting."

"I introduced her to Francesca, Mom."

"Oh, that's nice. LeeAnn, are those bare feet I see?"

"Yes," LeeAnn hopped back and forth faster, self-conscious now under Vivian's watchfulness. She excused herself and slipped back through the hedges, turning once more as she opened the front door to the yellow house for a glance at Francesca, rewarded by the sight of Francesca doing the same.

The sisters emptied the car of the remaining paintings, making several trips more through the kitchen and into the basement. Francesca hoped, over and over again, that Vivian would ask what it was they were carrying with such care, but she never did. Rather, Vivian, preoccupied by recent events—her mother's death, her daughter's return—put on a pot of coffee and sat at the kitchen table, smoking and staring off at the cold, frozen yard.

This is How She Looked in the Morning, 1989

In a 1990 article in *Genetics: The Journal of Science and Humanity,* entitled "The Inexplicable Painting: The Phenomenon of Sororal Symbiosis as the Basis for Stylistic Inconsistencies in the Final Work of Francesca deSilva," Psychiatrists May Jones and Ann Particip advance their theory of "metaphysical attachment"[85] between the d(D)eSilva sisters. The authors challenge the authenticity of the painting *This is How She Looked in the Morning,* considered to be deSilva's final work, found in the garage the morning after the fire. They question whether the painting might have been the work of Isabella DeSilva. The majority of scholars, however, dismiss this hypothesis as absurd and, further, insulting to the artist's legacy.

The oils still wet when it was discovered, *This is How She Looked in the Morning* is an intimate portrait of the DeSilvas' next door neighbor, LeeAnn Frank. Though all scholars agree that this painting is contradistinct from deSilva's known body of work, the majority assert that the painting bears certain, definitive marks of the artist. Most fundamentally, the size, four feet by three feet, is consistent with deSilva's work, though *This is How She Looked in the Morning* was painted on a scrap of wood taken from a pile at the back of the garage; thus the size might have simply been the result of a lucky find. Other

85. The authors define this as "a merging of personae unmitigated by physical distance." Jones, May and Particip, Ann. "The Inexplicable Painting: the Phenomemon of Sororal Symbiosis as the Basis for Stylistic Inconsistencies in the Final Work of Francesca deSilva." *Genetics: The Journal of Science and Humanity,* Vancouver, BC, Canada, 1990.

imprints: the subject of the painting is, as always, female; there is the almost obligatory window; and, too, a seamless intimacy exists between subject and artist.

No one argues that *This is How She Looked in the Morning* isn't a sharp departure from the decadent and lustful environ of *Woman Reclining on a Blue Couch* or the tension of *What She Found,* or the alienation and social commentary of *The Lisa Trilogy.* The mood is wholesome, unbesmirched. White sun bathes the subject clean; the window is dusted in a fine powder; and while the subject is clad in only a white v-neck T-shirt, she seems to have inspired in the painter a chaste admiration, resulting in a portrait that transcends carnality.

Half-reclining, the subject rests on her soft, naked hip, her weight supported by an outstretched arm at the end of which her strong hand spreads like a crest. Each digit is long, separated, concluding in a clear, pearly fingernail. Her face is generic, as if it is not quite recalled, and she is naked but for her shirt, her legs curled beneath her. The strong line of her quadriceps is painstakingly depicted. A glimpse of her feet is provided, it seems by accident, the toe-nails painted a radiant orange. Cynthia Bell notes that this tiny detail rescues the painting from "utter innocuousness. It is a mark of lust, an embellishment that depraves the subject just enough to make her compelling."[86]

While the torment that marks deSilva's body of work is conspicuously absent from *This is How She*

86. Bell, Cynthia. "Dyke Envy: The Latest Heterosexual Pasttime." *Culture Shock,* New York City, 1994.

Looked in the Morning, deconstructionists seem allergic to the notion that the artist might have felt, albeit briefly, lighthearted and hopeful, not to mention altered by her unusual circumstances. Lucinda Dialo exhorts, in an editorial in ArtNews, "It's absurd [for Jones and Particip] to attribute the final work of one of our greatest painters to her mentally ill older sister, who, as far we know, had never so much as dabbled in the visual arts! It infuriates me, frankly, that scholars have given this cockamamie theory consideration enough to bother debating its merits. What psychologists fail to recognize, and what psychologists have never understood about art, it seems, is that art is mystery. It descends from somewhere uncharted and it surprises even its creator. Thus tenderness can emerge from a hardened soul, happiness from a wretch. And there is no psychological basis for this anomaly; its only reason is art."[87]

Argues Bell, "The temptation to attribute this painting to Isabella DeSilva is the result of rampant cultural homophobia. The artistic and psychological community can't accept that this relationally impaired artist might have experienced, however fleetingly, a higher love, one that transcended the insufficient and superficial liaisons attributed to lesbians and homosexuals. Hasn't history shown that mature love alters one's view of the world? The need to eliminate the possibility that love softened deSilva's vision is the need to deny the viability of lesbianism."[88]

Though one can easily find the mark of deSilva's

---

87. Dialo, Lucinda. Editorial: "The Psychologization of Art." *ArtNews,* Summer 1995.
88. Bell, Cynthia. "Dyke Envy: The Latest Heterosexual Pasttime." *Culture Shock,* New York City, 1994.

artistry in *This is How She Looked in the Morning* Jones and Particip do raise intriguing questions. They point out, for example, that the painting is haphazardly executed, as though the artist were rushing[89] (perhaps, the psychologists suggest, Isabella was hurrying to finish the painting before her younger sister returned from the neighbor's house and caught her mucking with the art supplies). Why, they ask, would Francesca deSilva paint a nude portrait of the next-door neighbor, whom she hardly knew? Further, when did she have the opportunity to view LeeAnn Frank in the morning? Naked!

Any of these irregularities can be reasonably dismissed—and have. Only one small detail of physical evidence is difficult to discount: A small spiral pad was found near the painting, atop Alfonse's old lawnmower. On the first page of this tiny tablet is scrawled the title of the painting. It is impossible to dismiss that Isabella, known to do her writing on these miniature pads and perpetually obsessed with the beautiful neighbor, is a plausible source of this artifact. Experts who have analyzed the piece of paper report it could have been the work of either sister, so alike was their handwriting.

One final note: While only a naif could characterize the life of Francesca deSilva as happy, or find in this

89. *Village Voice* writer Reilly, raises an outré, tongue-in-cheek, and yet compelling possibility (see "We Like Our Lesbians Angry, Please . . ." *Village Voice,* 1992). Why would deSilva be rushing, he muses, if she did not know the house would be burned down? Isn't it possible that she escaped the charring inferno and is living (à la Jim Morrison and Elvis) in Buenos Aires, painting wall size canvases for cheap hotels?

Author's note: It is not impossible. While it appears that deSilva's remains were crushed under the weight of the fallen house, and while evidence confirms an extant fourth corpse, it cannot be definitively proven that the corpse was, indeed, Francesca deSilva's.

story a cheerful ending, it is, perhaps, small comfort to consider that on the night of the fire, the members of the DeSilva family seemed, for the first time, at peace with one another. It is therefore odd that the academy persists in its cynicism, its need to steal from deSilva's legacy a ray of hope, and in so doing to rob the public of the heartening notion that exceptional talent and inspiration can thrive even after an artist's torment and suffering have abated.

Chapter Twenty-Four

The funeral was brief, held under gray skies with ashy clouds blowing past. The coffin was propped on three green canvas strips that were attached to a metal structure, the entire contraption floating over a cavernous, symmetrical hole. The family stood bunched together like shrubs, several feet from the hole, on the blanket of synthetic grass the funeral home had unfurled. Alfonse turned away to stop himself from imagining, in gory detail, poor Evelyn crashing into the deep cavern and spilling forth from her tidy coffin. He hated funerals. And the idea that his mother-in-law, who had always seemed so sensible, would choose burial instead of cremation confounded him. Vivian had explained—repeatedly—that Jewish people did not believe in cremation. Still, the dirt thrown on top, the bugs, all of it, seemed horribly slow and torturous. *Perhaps,* he thought, *it is because I am a gardener. Because I know the unceasing activity below the ground, how the roots from nearby trees strangle everything in sight.*

"Mama would have liked how nice everything looks," he whispered to Vivian, trying to chase away his misery.

"I wish it didn't remind me of a putting green," Vivian wrapped her gloved hand around his bare one for a moment, then took it away.

Birds cawed, landed atop nearby monuments, flapping their wings and spanning the crowd with paranoid button eyes. The rabbi seemed to be rushing, as though he were late for an appointment across town. He recited Evelyn's good deeds like a grocery list: dance lessons at the synagogue; raised money for Hadassah; volunteered at the Jewish Home; took care of her ailing husband, may he rest in peace. Everyone breathed formless puffs of steam, rubbed their hands together and pattered their feet in place on the frozen ground.

After the service, Vivian lit a cigarette. The rabbi helped her into the Nissan. Alfonse adroitly occupied the driver's seat. He felt like a man. The daughters he had sired were in the backseat. Even if they weren't fair and bewitching as every man hopes his daughters will be, still, there they were, pressed against opposite windows. And though Evelyn was dead, though he and Vivian were not happy and hadn't been for as long as he could remember, though Isabella was crazy, and though he hadn't yet managed to engage in conversation of any import with his estranged daughter, still he felt almost giddy, as if it were a Thursday night in June fifteen years ago, the air cool, the sky light, and they were on their way to Evelyn's for brisket.

He waved with masculine efficacy to the funeral director, proceeded through the cemetery, and led the procession out onto the street.

"Brr . . ." Vivian rubbed her upper arms. "Is there a window open?"

"Yes," Isabella muttered, "But if I close it, we'll all die of smoke inhalation." Her mood was fouled by the amount of attention paid her sister at the funeral. Particularly by Joycie Newman, usually Isabella's biggest fan, who had virtually ignored her, the whole time fawning over Francesca. One flick of the wrist, a disingenuous wave before the service began, was all Joycie had spared for Isabella; she'd been too busy flirting with her sister. And, of course, Isabella had hoped to see Aaron, just so she could muster all her willpower and snub him. He was engaged to be married, she'd heard, and she wanted to smile and congratulate him, as if no news had ever mattered less.

"How come Aaron wasn't there?" she inquired calmly.

"Who's Aaron?" asked Francesca.

Vivian sprinted to a new subject: "Did everyone see the obituary?" She removed a small square of paper from her wallet and unfolded it carefully. Isabella ardently reached out her hand, but Vivian handed it to Francesca. "Francesca, honey, read it out loud, would you?" she said.

"Isabella, you read it," said Francesca.

"Yes, thank you." Isabella took the piece of paper, pleased that her sister had happened upon the correct solution. She cleared her throat: "Evelyn Rose Horowitz, 76, beloved wife of Yitzchak Horowitz (deceased). Mother of Vivian Horowitz DeSilva, New Haven. We will miss her spicy conversations and peppered opinions.

Send contributions to United Alzheimer's Foundation or the Jewish Home for the Aged."

"What's wrong with it?" Vivian wrinkled up her face.

"Nothing!" Alfonse patted the carpeted hump between them.

"Francesca?" she flapped down the sun visor and studied her younger daughter in the compact mirror.

Isabella folded the obituary and handed it over the top of the seat to her mother. "I know what's wrong with it," she said cryptically.

"There is nothing wrong with it," said Alfonse.

"What's with peppered and spicy in the same paragraph?" Isabella asked.

"I like that," he stated passionately. "It made me think of Grandma's cooking."

"Exactly!" Vivian pointed her finger emphatically at his cheek, then pushed in the cigarette lighter and searched for a Merit Ultra Light 100, her new brand.

"Since when did Grandma cook anything peppered and spicy? Fatty and overdone would be more like it. We'll miss her fatty conversations and overdone opinions." Isabella grinned at her sister, pleased with her own wit.

But Francesca paid no attention. She was preoccupied with when to leave and how to minimize the moment's significance. How to get the paintings back into the car without causing a stir, without igniting sudden interest (though there was little chance of that; why, she allowed herself to wonder, had she brought all the fucking paintings in the first place?); and how to turn the paintings over to the curator while engaging in as little chit chat as possible. Plus, there was *Bunyan* to finish and *Reality Has Intruded Here.*

"Tomorrow, I have to go home," she said.

"Tomorrow?" Isabella cried. "But why?"

Vivian turned back and smiled, her head cocked to the side. "We understand, honey," she said. "Your sister has a very busy life."

Now Francesca wanted only to arrive at the house, unfold into the cold air, steal a few moments of solitude. Just five minutes without a tactless, unanswerable question (Where did you learn to paint like that? Do you know how much your grandmother loved you? Judy

Garland used to dress like a man, too, and she was considered very modern, very stylish). Five minutes without someone braying about her surprise existence. They all stared at her as if she were a statue come to life. And then there were the thoughts of Lisa. Deep in her body, something throbbed each time she thought of Lisa, a little piece of death she carried with her, the suggestion that her own demise might not be so far off in the future. Though Francesca did not believe in life after death, the possibility that she and Lisa might meet again—as vaporous souls, trees, minerals, whatever—brought her comfort.

She half wished she could bring Isabella with her, set her up in the cottage behind Charlotte's house. Perhaps she'd be preventing a second suicide.

Vivian watched as Francesca stepped behind the house to smoke a cigarette.

Alfonse was silent. He pulled the keys from the ignition and lifted his left hand from the steering wheel, shifted it toward the door handle, everything slow like syrup.

"I feel like she just got here," he said as he unfolded from the car.

"She did," replied Isabella. "And now she's leaving."

"She'll be back," said Vivian.

"Duh! No, she won't," Isabella cried out.

"Isabella, what did I tell you about that word?"

"Sorry."

"That can't be true! Why is that?" asked Alfonse, at once devastated.

"Look at us! Then look at her!" Isabella said. She climbed out of the car and stormed into the house. "Would you come back if you were her?"

"Are we so terrible?" Alfonse looked down at his inexpensive overcoat, his black Oxfords. He knew there was truth in what Isabella said but couldn't bear the idea of it, that there was something inherently flawed—even bizarre—in him, and that Francesca had seen it—maybe not then, when she'd run away, but now, having returned as an adult. Hadn't he intended better things for himself? A better marriage?

283

Happier children? More fulfilling work? How had he allowed himself to become so misguided and disconsolate? When had all notions of improving slid into the mist?

❑   ❑   ❑

Against the kitchen wall, a giant hefty bag was filled with paper plates and plastic utensils. Ashtrays had been emptied; vast quantities of liquor, purchased for the week-long observance, were hidden up high so as not to tempt Isabella and risk another embarrassing episode. The kitchen counters were laden with tinfoil-covered Pyrex dishes, warm and heavy with kugels, brisket, pickled tongue.

When will these Jews catch up with the times? thought Vivian, surveying the mess. *Maybe if they ate some fruit and vegetables instead of so much beef and fat, they wouldn't all die of heart attacks,* as her father had and, most likely, her mother as well. Thank goodness the neighbor had brought something healthy—though a little too unusual for a Jewish Shiva, Vivian thought—some sort of Moroccan salad made of wheat and tomatoes and parsley.

Finally, Vivian sent off the last of the mahjong ladies, submitting to their thick, lipstick kisses. The neighbor left, too.

She brought the trash outside and glanced back at her house from the vantage point of the freestanding garage. At last, her home seemed blissfully motionless. The yellow lamps in the living room were lit. Everything looked warm and normal. She returned to the kitchen and glanced around approvingly. Joycie Newman was rinsing the last of the dishes.

"I don't know what I would have done without you, Joycie," she pretended to rest her head on Joycie's shoulder. "I would have been cleaning for days."

"Oy vay," said Joycie, feeling Jewish. She finished rinsing the dishes, turned off the faucet, and entered the living room, drying her hands on a dishtowel. She pulled a fold-up chair over to the couch and sat down near Francesca. Their knees bumped. "Thank God they're all gone," she said, exempting herself. "Is it strange to be back here?"

Francesca shrugged. "Yeah, sure."

"It's so provincial, isn't it? So small-town," Joycie rolled her eyes. "I often wish I'd left New Haven for a bigger city. New York, say, or Chicago."

"Well, compared to Provincetown, this might as well be New York or Chicago."

Joycie laughed and squeezed Francesca's knee.

Francesca glanced at Joycie's manicured hand resting on her knee. It remained there for several moments until Francesca feigned an itch and uncrossed her legs, then shifted her body out of Joycie's reach.

She remembered her brief conversation with LeeAnn Frank outside, over a cigarette. LeeAnn rolled her own cigarettes, carried a blue plastic pouch stuffed with moist gold tobacco. She'd made a cigarette for Francesca just like that, standing there, fingers frozen, had licked it from both sides into a perfect cylinder.

Alfonse retrieved Joycie's snazzy nubuck coat from the front hall closet. He helped her on with it, patted the puffy shoulders. "Warm," he said cheerfully. She promised to return first thing the following morning.

Vivian closed the door behind Joycie and mock-barricaded it with her body. Half drunk, she weaved through the living room and collapsed into the armchair. She extended her legs and clutched a heavy, glass ashtray with her stockinged toes, dragged it in this manner along the surface of the coffee table until it was close enough that she could reach it with her fingers. "This was your grandmother's ashtray," she nodded sadly at the ugly piece, as if it were Evelyn herself flattened on the table. "She loved this ashtray. And she loved you, Francesca. Remember that."

"What about me?" asked Isabella.

"Of course she loved you. But everything isn't about you, Bella." Vivian lit a cigarette, exhaled luxuriously, and tossed her head back, molded her neck into the soft back of the chair, and stared at the water-stained ceiling.

The headlights on Joycie's Lexus smoothed across the living room wall. Vivian sat up and looked first at Alfonse, then Francesca, then Isabella. "I don't think Grandma would mind if I said . . ." she hesitated, "that I feel happy. Because everyone is here." Her face twisted up with an expression that made everyone uncomfortable—it was so anguished and involuntary—and her eyes filled with shiny tears. "You know," she said, "I think your grandmother only pretended to hate me."

"Of course she did," Alfonse put his hands on her shoulders from behind.

"Maybe that's what she did with me too," said Isabella.

"I'm sure it is!" Alfonse exclaimed. "Your grandmother was a funny lady. She didn't like to show her feelings. Like your mother. And your sister." He groaned and stretched his body as high as he could manage, striving to tap the light fixture as he did each night on his way upstairs—a quick way to chase the kinks from his back. He was pleased with himself for his astute observation, particularly where Francesca was concerned. "I'm going to tinker with that furnace a while. See if I can get it to stop making that sound," he said with authority.

"What sound?" asked Isabella.

"That terrible, high-pitched sound." Vivian made a face, as if she were being subjected to it at that very moment.

"What high-pitched sound?" Isabella persisted.

"I heard something," offered Francesca. "But it was more of a knocking. Then again, I sleep next to a train track, so . . ." She shrugged.

"A train track?" Alfonse asked. "Where is it?"

"Right outside my cabin. Ten yards away," Francesca boasted.

"Oh boy," he sighed. "She's had a wild life, your sister." He looked at Isabella and raised his eyebrows. Then he left the room. The door to the basement squeaked open. This, too, he wanted to fix, the squeak, but it would have to wait. He took his old metal toolbox down from a shelf he'd built into the back of the stairs, and descended into the basement.

Vivian stood up, suddenly exuberant. "I'm going to make cookies! Who wants to help me make cookies?"

Isabella raised her hand.

"Francesca?" Vivian asked. "How 'bout making some cookies with your old Mom?"

"I'd love to," said Francesca, picking out the green M&Ms from a mixed assortment and dropping them one at a time into her mouth.

"But I'm going to visit the neighbor. She's going to play the piano for me. She plays Chopin, and I love Chopin." She shrugged casually, slid her pack of cigarettes into her jacket pocket, and kissed Vivian, then Isabella on the cheek. Vivian wondered whether she'd even recognize Chopin. Could she discern him from Bach or Beethoven, or even Liberace for that matter?

"I hope she's not going to cook for you," said Isabella. "She's a terrible cook. I should know. She's cooked for me."

"Don't fib, Bella," Vivian scolded briskly, trying not to get upset. She wanted Francesca to stay home. *She should stay home. She should be with her family.* But she restrained herself. She would do nothing to upset the fragile ambiance of family that had settled over the house.

Francesca hurried to the door. "Save some cookies for me," she called behind her and was gone, through the darkened bushes.

"I've never heard her play Chopin," Isabella whispered. "I think it's a ruse."

Vivian moved to the living room window and watched Francesca cross the lawn into darkness, then re-emerge under the lamp of the neighbor's porch. There was something about her youngest daughter. It had always been there. She'd just never considered that it might be an asset. She couldn't put her finger on its exact nature, only that it was quiet and appealing. Life would be different now, she thought. No more weekly visits to the Jewish Home. No more having to remind her mother who she was, tolerate Evelyn's caustic complaints and abuse. An era ended. She was so tired, as if she'd taken a pill.

The door to LeeAnn's house opened and Francesca vanished inside. Now Vivian could see only slices of warm light escaping around the drawn shades. She returned to the kitchen and washed her hands, put an orange apron on over her funeral clothes. She tugged at the torn black rag safety-pinned to her collar. She liked wearing it; it made her feel she was sad.

"How come I don't get to wear one of those?" asked Isabella, opening the bag of chocolate chips.

"Only the children of the deceased." Vivian climbed onto a chair to pull a mixing bowl down from the top shelf. She held the cabinet door to steady herself.

"Careful," Isabella winced, imagining Vivian falling and breaking her hip or worse . . . Her grandmother had made death suddenly frightening. No longer some abstract concept, an easy escape. She was still certain she wanted it for herself, but she knew she didn't want it for her mother. Ever.

Alfonse gave up on the oil burner, and Vivian said she'd call "the guy" in the morning. Alfonse wanted to be "the guy," but he was exhausted. He climbed the stairs and splayed out on the bed, then let out a deep, reassured sigh.

Isabella inhaled the warm, sweet smell of melting chocolate. Even though the light in the neighbor's house had gone out, she didn't care. She kissed her mother goodnight. "Love you, Mommy," she said.

"Love you, pumpkin," said Vivian, her mouth sweet from batter she'd licked off the rubber spatula. The cookies were cooling on the hot stovetop. She left a light on in the kitchen and scribbled on the back of a condolence card: Francesca—Eat these. Mom, with a messy row of x's and o's, then followed Isabella up the stairs.

❏   ❏   ❏

Hours later, Francesca left the house next door and stepped into the garage, desperate to paint though it was freezing outside. The power in the garage was out and had been for weeks, so Francesca plugged an electric heater into a thick, yellow utility cord she ran through the backdoor and into the living room. She wore gloves with no fingertips and wrapped her face many times in a bright red scarf the neighbor had given her.

When she became too tired to continue working—it had been a long two days!—she entered the kitchen. Immediately, she was soothed by the smell of chocolate chip cookies. She read her mother's note several times and took it, along with several cookies, downstairs. There, she sprawled out on the daybed and smoked a final cigarette, exhausted from death and sex and art. The furnace made a new grinding sound that drowned out any others. It concerned her, but she was so tired. She smelled something burning while she dreamt of Lisa's sleeping face, but it mixed with other odors: LeeAnn and cigarettes and the rough, clinging musk of paint and turpentine. Her brain was littered with thoughts that hadn't existed yesterday. She was happy about LeeAnn. Sad about Lisa. Happy her parents were still together. Sad her grandmother was dead. Happy her sister was still alive; sad they would never be friends. Happy she had a life to return to. And sad.

Hilary Sloin is a novelist, short fiction writer, essayist, and playwright. Her work has been published in many small journals and anthologies including *Parting Gifts, character i, Notes, Phoebe,* and *Lesbian Love Stories I and II. Art On Fire* has been an almost-winner many times: It was a finalist for the Heekin Foundation Award, the Mid-list Press Competition, the Dana Awards, and The Story Oaks Prize. It received a grant from the Massachusetts Cultural Council, and was mistakenly awarded the non-fiction prize in the Amherst Book and Plow Competition. She has been a resident at the Cottages at Hedgebrook and the Dorset Colony House, and during the '80s and '90s her plays were produced in major cities across the country. She lives in the hills of Western Massachusetts with Pluto, her tiny Jack Russell Terrier, and has a side business acquiring, restoring, and selling antiques.

Acknowledgments

Art on Fire, which for years was known by the toothy title *The Unfinished Life of Francesca deSilva,* took a long time to write and an even longer time to find a publishing home. Along the way so many people read and critiqued my various versions of the manuscript, kindly pointing up the places where I had swerved into a cement pole, that I cannot possibly name everyone here—much as I'd like to. I know and remember enough to thank the Cottages at Hedgebrook and the Dorset Colony House for giving me space and time to write and for helping me develop the discipline and work ethic required to complete a long project. The immortal Val Clark was the biggest champion I have ever had. For years, novelist and poet supreme Susan Stinson and Bywater author Sally Bellerose were astute and patient readers, excellent friends and fellow mischief-makers. We worked hard and played hard and this book would not have come to completion without them. Meryl Cohn and Mary Beth Caschetta propped me up when I had pretty much thrown in the towel. My cousin, Harry Gold, a staunch critic who, I am sad to say, is no longer with us on the planet, loved this book and told me he was certain I had "it"—words every writer longs to hear from a discerning source. Meredith Rose provided hours of intelligent and challenging conversation about the writing life and whether it was, in the end, worth the trouble (the jury is still out). Barb Hadden strutted into my world one day and, with her paint-smattered clothes and killer smile, seemed to be the materialization of my adored character. This was scary and fascinating and made me open the pages once again to see if I could do anything more to help the manuscript see the light of day. Finally, I feel I have been rewarded for something good I did along the way by the arrival of Revan Schendler's friendship. Her brilliance and generosity astonish me and I find she is often all the audience I need.

I'd like to thank Bywater Books for publishing *Art on Fire* and taking a chance on material that was a little out of the mainstream—even the lesbian mainstream.

I only wish my mother were still here to see me finally get published. She couldn't believe there would be a cover and everything!

THE GIRLS CLUB

Sally Bellerose

"In her debut novel, Bellerose deftly tells the story of Cora Rose, Marie, and Renee LaBarre, a trio of working-class sisters in small-town Massachusetts who are best friends, mortal enemies, and forever loyal to each other. . . . A fast-paced, well-written tale with characters who will linger in the reader's memory long after the final page is turned." —*Publishers Weekly*

"Bellerose moves these wonderous creations of hers through the ordinary pitfalls of life, showcasing their heartbreaks, their triumphs, and their shame with equal assurance. *The Girls Club* is an incredible book—not just for girls, but for everyone." — *Out in Print*

"Winner of the **Bywater Prize for Fiction,** this first novel provides an intense study of human frailty and hope; sure to appeal to readers who enjoy literate coming-of-age and coming-out fiction." —*Library Journal*

"Bellerose's warm novel embraces the concept of sisterhood with propulsive gusto" —*Book Marks*

Print ISBN 978-1-932859-78-2
Ebook ISBN 978-1-61294-020-5

Available at your local bookstore
or call 734-662-8815
or order online at www.bywaterbooks.com

Bywater Books

RED AUDREY AND THE ROPING

Jill Malone

Winner of the Bywater Prize for Fiction

"A wonderfully impressive writing debut."
—Sarah Waters

Fight or flight? Jane Elliott has tried both. Surfing, letting the waves take her. Teaching Latin, clutching at its rules to feel safe. Safe from a lover, safe from her friends, safe from her mother's death—and her guilt. And now she lies in a hospital bed, alone.

Set against the landscapes and seascapes of Hawaii, this is a story of one woman's courage and her struggle to find a balance between what she desires and what she deserves. Gripping and emotional, *Red Audrey and the Roping* is also a remarkable literary achievement. The breathtaking prose evokes setting, characters, and relationships with equal grace. Splintered fragments of narrative come together to form a seamless suspenseful story that flows effortlessly to its dramatic conclusion.

Print ISBN 978-1-932859-54-6
Ebook ISBN 978-1-61294-002-1

Bywater Books

A FIELD GUIDE TO DECEPTION

Jill Malone

Winner of the Lambda Literary Award

"*A Field Guide to Deception* is beautiful, essential reading."
—*Out in Print*

"Malone is back with another story that takes us deeper into the shadowy depths of the mind and heart with every twist of its plot . . . keeping the reader rapt all the way to the unforeseeable conclusion." —*Jane and Jane Magazine*

The day the kid fell in the river—that was the moment for Claire and Liv. The first inkling of a possibility of something to pull them together.

But sometimes the possibility of love is too much to bear. As opportunities slowly unfurl like the petals of a flower, Claire and Liv negotiate love's challenges as well as its rewards. And on one terrible winter night, they confront the true cost of loving.

Print ISBN 978-1-932859-70-6
Ebook ISBN 978-1-61294-003-8

Bywater Books

VERGE

Z Egloff

Winner of the Bywater Prize for Fiction

"*Verge has heart and wit and intelligence.*"
—Emma Donoghue, author of *Room*

"*Verge is powerful, quirky, and fresh.*"
—Alison Bechdel, author of *Fun Home*

Claire has three goals: to stay sober, to stay away from sex, and to get into film school. A drunken affair with her professor's wife means she might just have blown all three at once. Stuck without the camera she needs to complete her course work, she turns to Sister Hilary at the community center for help. Sister Hilary has a camera to lend, but the price is recruiting Claire as a reluctant volunteer. The only trouble is, Claire's more attracted to Sister Hilary than to helping out. Claire ought to know there's no future with a nun, but can't this two-timing, twelve-stepping, twenty-something film freak get a chance at happiness?

ISBN 978-1-932859-68-3

Bywater Books

SHAKEN AND STIRRED

Joan Opyr

"What a great read! Character, story, dialogue—it's a trifecta of a page turner." —Kate Clinton, author of *I Told You So*

"Opyr is a master of mixing light and dark—of telling a story about family dysfunction, alcoholic rage, and life without a lover with laugh-out loud panache." —*Book Marks*

"It's a wonderful novel" —*Out in Print*

Poppy Koslowski is trying to recover from a hysterectomy, but her family has other ideas. She's the one with the responsibility to pull the plug on her alcoholic grandfather in North Carolina. So she's dragged back across the country from her re-built life into the bosom of a family who barely notice the old man's imminent death.

Plunged into a crazy kaleidoscope of consulting doctors, catching fire with an old flame, and negotiating lunch venues with her mother and grandmother, Poppy still manages to fall in love. Because nothing in the Koslowski family is ever straightforward. Not even dying.

Print ISBN 978-1-932859-79-9
Ebook ISNBN 978-1-61294-018-2

Available at your local bookstore
or call 734-662-8815
or order online at www.bywaterbooks.com

Bywater Books represents the coming of age of lesbian fiction. We're committed to bringing the best of contemporary lesbian writing to a discerning readership. Our editorial team is dedicated to finding and developing outstanding voices who deliver stories you won't want to put down. That's why we sponsor the annual Bywater Prize for Fiction. We love good books, just like you do.

For more information about Bywater Books and the annual Bywater Prize for Fiction, please visit our website.

www.bywaterbooks.com